THE 1974 ANNUAL
WORLD'S BEST SF

THE 1974 ANNUAL WORLD'S BEST SF

Edited by

DONALD A. WOLLHEIM

with Arthur W. Saha

DAW BOOKS, INC.

DONALD A. WOLLHEIM, PUBLISHER

1301 Avenue of the Americas
New York, N. Y.   10019

DEDICATION

In memory of three who were
there at the right time:
John T. Barr
Melville Harris
Edward John Carnell

Table of Contents

INTRODUCTION

Science fiction continued to thrive during the year 1973, but it remained in a state which would have to be termed transitional. The changes which have been in prospect for the past two or three years are still going on, yet thus far no really different pattern has emerged. Nor, do we think, will it.

We express this conviction on the basis that science fiction is mainly misunderstood by the academics and the newcomers, and that the various efforts to define or redirect the field, however well and seriously intentioned, are made without consultation and comprehension by the vast majority of those people who are its habitual readers. In simple, science fiction is what sells to science fiction readers—and science fiction readers pay little or no attention to theory. They desire their own form of "escape reading"—a term which chills the marrow of those who try to make science fiction something world-shaking.

Science fiction is a literature of prophecy, of prediction, of investigation into the worlds of if—but it is also first and foremost a form of reading entertainment. All fiction reading, in any category whatsoever, is a type of escape for its readers. Hence, to say that science fiction is escape reading is no insult; it is simply a fact of all mass popular literature. Unfortunately it is a fact that academicians have had little or no experience with. It is also the sort of fact that those who have tired of writing (and presumably reading) this sort of thing prefer to deny in order to compose their theses on the deeper meanings or the real meanings or the "true histories" of this "mysterious" form of fantasy.

So in 1973 we had on the one hand many more conferences and studies in science fiction, and we also saw that the newsstand magazines continued their existence despite the endless predictions of their coming demise. In reading for this anthology, it was continued to be found that those magazines—responsive to their readers as no book anthology could ever be—produced the most interesting, the "best" stories, the stories calculated to keep their monthly audiences returning regularly.

The outlook for the magazines seems favorable. In the U.S.A. a new title, *Vertex*, made its appearance and appears to have achieved viability. In England word of a new magazine to be launched in 1974 by a major publisher-distributor is encouraging, filling a gap.

In Europe new series continue to appear from various book publishers. In France there are now about nine such regular book series appearing or scheduled (though primarily still engaged in producing translations from the English). In Germany more paperback SF lists are being produced from publishers old and new and there is a steadily rising tide of the weekly or biweekly journals of the *Terra Astra* type. In Italy, and in Spain, this trend continues. In Sweden *Jules Verne Magasinet* celebrated its first year with a convention worthy of newspaper comment; and several book series are expanding. In Hungary, a new and impressive SF quarterly *Galaktika* has appeared —the first "serious" magazine of its kind in the Socialist sector (though a Roumanian fiction journal has been appearing steadily for several years devoted primarily to serializing SF novels). The ferment is found everywhere and science fiction is thriving.

In America the predicted flood of hard and soft bound "original story" anthologies has arrived and piles of them were at hand when this selection was being worked upon. You may notice that only two such books are represented in this annual selection. One story came from the faithful quality leader, *New Writings in SF*, now edited by Kenneth Bulmer. The other such story was a translation from the Russian from the interesting but opinionated *View from Another Shore* edited by the caustic Austrian critic Franz Rottensteiner.

Our feeling about these mass-produced original anthologies (other than the two mentioned above) is that they present very impressive fronts, featuring some quite notable authors, but that almost universally the stories therein give evidence of haste and lack of critically responsible editorial control. They have good ideas, many elements of good handling, but somehow they seem incomplete, rarely rounded out, not quite up to their potential, and not up to magazine standards. The *remembrance* factor—the sort of thing that really counts in gathering together a "best of the year" collection—is singularly lacking. Perhaps next year will be better—but somehow we doubt it. Again, we also have the usual handful of anthologies put together by the avant-gardists. Perhaps these impress critics who are not readers of SF, but they do not impress those who read science fiction for enjoyment.

Exactly what we mean can best be put by a quotation from the prestigious *Times Literary Supplement* (London) in a long and thoughtful review of Brian Aldiss' much-touted "true history" of science fiction, *Billion Year Spree*. This work, which does contain a wealth of material on the subject, is seriously flawed by the author's insistence on defining science fiction in such a way as to read out of the field almost all its roots and about ninety percent of its entire bulk. His definition, which equates science fiction with the Gothic novel, insisting that if a work does not contain both elements it is not SF, can only be described as absurd. The review in the *TLS* handles his attempt to equate this odd definition with a defense and an apologia for New Wave experimentalism with skill and clarity. Let us quote:

"In general, he accepts the now receding 'New Wave' as legitimate, or at least fertilizing, and does not realize that it amounted to little more than a dreary rechauffé of surrealist work of the 1920s and 1930s, which had largely petered out in the mainstream . . . In fact, SF (like other types of fantasy writing) is a particularly unsuitable area for techniques which confuse or disrupt the sense. When something strange is afoot, in a strange time or on a strange planet, only a measure of clarity will let us know what is supposed to be going on. Something similar applies (as has often been pointed out) to excessive characterization, or excessive concentration on streams of thought or semi-conscious imaginings. The cant phrase 'inner space' is little more than an attempt by mere verbalization to incorporate the psychological novel into SF. . . ."

A good history of science fiction has yet to be published. We hear of several critical histories in progress, but we fear that all may turn out to suffer from acute academic myopia. Sam J. Lundwall's *Science Fiction: What It's All About* is probably still the best general introduction available in English. But 1973 saw the French take the lead in this sector with the publication of two impressive volumes —the 1,000-page illustrated *Encyclopedie de l'Utopie et de Science Fiction* by Pierre Versins, published by L'Age de Homme, Lausanne, Switzerland, and Jacques Sadoul's fascinating (and also illustrated) *Histoire de la Science Fiction Moderne*, published by Albin Michel, Paris, France.

1974 will continue to be a transitional year for science fiction. Let us hope for the best.

—**Donald A. Wollheim**

A SUPPLIANT
IN SPACE

ROBERT SHECKLEY

**Sheckley has been missing too long from
the pages of magazines and anthologies. It is
therefore a pleasure to note in the appearance
of this new story that he has not lost his skill
to depict the incongruities of the universe and
the ways of the alien mind.**

I

Detringer had been banished from his home planet of Ferlang
for "acts of incredible grossness"—he had sucked his teeth insolently
during the Meditation Frolic and had switched his tail widdershins
when the Regional Grand Ubiquitor condescended to spit at him.

These impertinences would normally have earned him no more
than a few dozen years of Plenary Ostracism. But Detringer had
aggravated his offenses by Willful Disobedience during Godmemory
Meeting, at which time he had persisted in audibly reminiscing upon
certain of his rather unsavory sexual exploits.

His final asocial act was unprecedented in the recent history of
Ferlang: he had meted out Overt Malevolent Violence upon the
person of a Ukanister, thus performing the first act of Open Public
Aggression since the primitive era of the Death Games.

This last repulsive act, resulting in minor bodily injury but major
ego damage to the Ukanister, earned Detringer the supreme punishment of Perpetual Banishment.

Ferlang is the fourth planet from its sun in a fifteen-planet system
situated near an edge of the galaxy. Detringer was taken deep into

the void between galaxies via starship and set adrift in a tiny, under-powered Sportster. He was voluntarily accompanied by his loyal mechanical servant, Ichor.

Detringer's wives—gay, flighty Maruskaa, tall, thoughtful Gwenkifer and floppy-eared, irrepressible Uu—all divorced him in a solemn Act of Eternal Revulsion. His eight children performed the Office of Parental Repudiation—though Deranie, the youngest, was heard to mutter afterward, "I don't care what you did, Daddy, I still love you."

Detringer was not to be afforded the comfort of knowing this, of course. Cast loose upon the infinite sea of space, the inadequate energy systems of his tiny craft inexorably ran down. He came to know hunger, cold, thirst, and the continual throbbing headache of oxygen-deprivation as he voluntarily put himself upon stringent rations. The immense deadness of space spread on all sides of him, broken only by the merciless glare of distant stars. He had turned off the Sportster's engines immediately—he had seen no use in wasting its small fuel capacity in the intergalactic void that taxed the resources of the enormous starships. He would save his fuel for planetary maneuvering—if that unlikely opportunity should ever be vouchsafed him.

Time was a motionless black jelly in which he was encased. Deprived of its familiar moorings, a lesser mind must have cracked. But it was a measure of his being that, instead of giving in to the despair whose objective correlatives were all around him, he rallied, forced himself to take an interest in the minutest routines of the dying ship, gave a concert every "night" for his tone-deaf servant Ichor, performed calisthenics, practiced High-speed Meditation, erected elaborate autosexual rituals as set forth in the Solitude Survival Book, and in a hundred ways diverted himself from the crushing realization of his own almost certain death.

After an interminable period the character of space changed abruptly. The doldrums gave way to unsettled conditions. There were elaborate electrical displays, presaging new peril. At last a line-storm hurtled upon him along a narrow front, caught up the Sportster, and swept it pell-mell into the heart of the void.

The very inadequacy of the little spaceship served to preserve it. Unresistingly driven by the storm's front, the ship survived by yielding—and when the storm had run its course the ship's hull still preserved its integrity.

Little need be said about the ordeal of the occupants at this time, except that they survived. Detringer experienced a period of unconsciousness. Then he opened his eyes and stared groggily around him.

After that he looked out through the spaceports and studied his navigational instruments.

"We've completely crossed the void," he told Ichor. "We are approaching the outer limits of a planetary system."

Ichor raised himself on one aluminum elbow and asked, "Of what type is the sun?"

"It is an O type," Detringer said.

"Praise be to God's Memory," Ichor intoned, then collapsed, due to discharged batteries.

The last currents of the storm subsided before the Sportster crossed the orbit of the outermost planet, nineteenth out from the sturdy, medium-sized life-giving O-type sun. Detringer recharged Ichor from the ship's accumulators, although the mechanical protested that the current might better be saved for a possible ship's emergency.

This emergency came sooner than Detringer had imagined. His instrument reading had shown that the fifth planet out from the sun was the only one that could support Detringer's life-requirements without the assistance of imported artificialities. But it was too far away for the ship's remaining fuel and now space was doldrum-calm again, affording no impetus to aid them toward their goal.

One course of action would be to sit tight, wait and hope that a stray inbound current would come their way, or even another storm. This plan was admittedly conservative. It bore the danger that no current or storm would come during the short period in which they could sustain themselves on the ship's resources. Additionally, there was the risk that if a current or storm should arise it would bear them in an unpromising direction.

Still, there were risks no matter what course of action was taken. Characteristically, Detringer chose the more enterprising and perhaps more dangerous plan. Plotting the most economical course and speed, he set forth to cover whatever portion of the journey his ship's fuel would allow, prepared to trust to Providence thereafter.

By painstaking piloting and hand-metering of the fuel he managed to come within two hundred million miles of his destination. Then Detringer had to shut down the engines, leaving himself only a scant hour's worth of fuel for intra-atmospheric maneuvering.

The Sportster drifted through space, still moving toward the fifth planet, but so slowly that a thousand years would barely suffice to bring it within the planet's atmospheric limits. By a very slight effort of the imagination, the ship could be considered a coffin and Detringer its premature occupant. But Detringer refused to dwell upon this.

He began again his regime of calisthenics, concerts, High-speed Meditation, and autosexual rituals.

Ichor was somewhat shocked by all this. Himself of an orthodox turn of mind, he gently pointed out that Detringer's acts were inapropos to the situation and therefore insane.

"You're quite right, of course," Detringer replied cheerfully. "But I must remind you that Hope, even though judged incapable of fulfillment, is still considered one of the Eight Irrational Blessings and therefore (according to the Second Patriarch) of a higher order of magnitude than the derived Sanity Injunctions."

Confuted by scripture, Ichor gave his grudging assent to Detringer's practices and even went so far as to sing a hymn in harmony with him (with results as ludicrous as they were cacophonous).

Inexorably their energy ran down. Half- and then quarter-rations impaired their efficiency and brought them near the point of complete dysfunction. In vain did Ichor beg his master's permission to drain his own personal batteries into the ship's chilly heaters.

"Never mind," said Detringer, shuddering with cold. "We'll go out together as equals, in possession of what senses we've got, if we go out at all—which I seriously doubt despite impressive evidence to the contrary."

Perhaps nature is influenced by temperament. Surely only for Detringer would she have obliged by sending a strong inbound current just when the ship's energy resources had dwindled to no more than memories.

The landing itself was simple enough for a pilot of Detringer's skill and luck. He brought down the ship, light as a windblown seed, upon the green and inviting surface of the fifth planet. When he shut down the engines for the last time there were some thirty-eight seconds of fuel remaining.

Ichor fell to his ferrominium knees and praised the Godmemory that had remembered to bring them to this place of refuge. But Detringer said, "Let's see if we can live here before we go maudlin with thanks."

The fifth world proved hospitable enough. All of the necessities of life could be found with moderate effort, though few of the amenities. Escape was impossible: only an advanced technological civilization could produce the complex fuel needed for the ship's engines. And a brief aerial survey had shown that the fifth planet, although a picturesque and inviting world, harbored no civilization—nor did it even give any sign of being inhabited by intelligent beings.

By a simple cross-wiring procedure, Ichor prepared himself for the prospect of spending the rest of his life-span in this place. He advised Detringer similarly to accept the inevitable. After all, he pointed out, even if they did somehow obtain fuel, where would they go? The odds against their finding an advanced planetary civilization, even with a well-equipped exploration ship at their disposal, were astronomical. In a small vessel like the Sportster the attempt would be tantamount to suicide.

Detringer was unimpressed by this reasoning. "Better to search and die," he said, "than vegetate and live."

"Master," Ichor pointed out respectfully, "that is heresy."

"I suppose it is," Detringer said cheerfully. "But it is how I feel. And my intuition tells me that something will turn up."

Ichor shuddered and was glad for the sake of his master's soul that, despite Detringer's hopes, he was to receive the Unction of Perpetual Solitude.

Captain Edward Makepeace Macmillan stood in the main control room of the exploration ship *Jenny Lind* and scanned the tape as it came out of the 1100 Series Coordinating Computer. It was apparent that the new planet presented no dangers within the measuring ability of the ship's instruments.

Macmillan had come a long way to reach this moment. A brilliant life-sciences major at the University of Taos, Macmillan had gone on to do graduate work in Nucleonic Theory and Control. His doctoral thesis, titled *Some Preliminary Notes on Certain Considerations Concerning the (Projected) Science of Interstellar Maneuvering*, had been enthusiastically accepted by his committee and had later been successfully published for the general public under the title, *Lost and Found in Deepest Space*. That, plus his long article in *Nature*, titled, *The Use of Declension Theory in Spacecraft Landing Modalities*, had made him the only possible choice to captain America's first interstellar ship.

He was a tall, handsome, strongly built man. His hair was prematurely flecked with gray, belying his thirty-six years. His reactions concerning navigation were quick and sure and his instinct for the integrity of his ship was awesome.

Less awesome were his dealings with men. Macmillan was cursed with a certain shyness, a diffidence toward others, a knowledge of dubiety that sapped the decision-making process and that, however admirable it might be in a philosopher, was a potential weakness in a leader of men.

A knock came at his door and Colonel Kettelman entered without bothering to be asked. "Looks good down there, hah?" he said.

"The planetary profile is quite favorable," Macmillan said stiffly.

"That's fine," Kettelman said, staring uncomprehendingly at the computer tape. "Anything interesting about the place?"

"A great deal," Macmillan said. "Even a long-distance survey has shown what might well be some unique vegetable structures. Additionally, our bacteria scan shows some anomalies, which—"

"I didn't mean that kind of stuff," Kettelman said, evincing the natural indifference a career soldier sometimes feels for bugs and plants. "I meant important stuff like alien armies and space fleets and like that."

"There is no sign of any civilization down there," Macmillan said. "I doubt we will even find traces of intelligent life."

"Well, you can never tell," Kettelman said hopefully. He was a stocky, barrel-chested, and unbending man. He was a veteran of the American Assistance Campaigns of '34 and had fought as a major in the jungles of western Honduras in the so-called United Fruit War, emerging as a lieutenant colonel. He had received his full colonelcy during the ill-fated New York Insurrection, at which time he had personally led his men in storming the Subtreasury Building and then had held down the 42nd Street Line against the crack Gay Battalion.

Utterly fearless, known as a soldier's soldier, possessing an impeccable combat record, wealthy in his own right, a friend of many U.S. Senators and Texas millionaires and not unintelligent, he had won the coveted appointment of Commandant of Military Operations aboard the *Jenny Lind*.

Now he awaited the moment when he would lead his combat team of twenty Marines onto the surface of the fifth planet. The prospect hugely excited him. And, despite the instrument readings, Kettelman knew that anything might be down there waiting to strike and maim and kill—unless he did so first, as he planned to do.

"There is one thing," Macmillan said. "We have detected a spacecraft on the surface of the planet."

"Ah," Kettelman said. "I knew there'd be something. You spotted only one ship?"

"Yes. A small one, displacing less than a twentieth the volume of our craft and apparently unarmed."

"That's what they'd like you to believe, of course," said Kettelman. "I wonder where the others are."

"What others?"

"The other alien spaceships and crews and ground-to-space weapons systems and all the rest of it, of course."

"The presence of one alien spacecraft does not logically imply any other alien spacecraft," Captain Macmillan said.

"No? Listen, Mac, I learned my logic in the jungles of Honduras," Kettelman said. "The rule there was that if you found one runt with a machete you could be sure of finding another fifty or so hiding in the bushes, waiting to cut your ears off if you gave them a chance. You could get killed if you waited around for abstract proofs."

"The circumstances were somewhat different," Captain Macmillan pointed out.

"So what does that matter?"

Macmillan winced and turned away. Talking with Kettelman was painful for him and he avoided it as much as he could. The colonel was a disputatious individual, stubborn, easily driven to wrath, and possessed of many positive opinions, most of which were founded upon a bedrock of nearly invincible ignorance. The captain knew that the antipathy between himself and Kettelman was mutual. He was well aware that the colonel considered him an indecisive and ineffective person except perhaps in his special scientific areas.

Luckily, their areas of command were sharply defined and delineated. Or had been to date.

II

Detringer and Ichor stood in a clump of trees and watched as the large alien spacecraft settled down to a faultless landing.

"Whoever is piloting that ship," Detringer said, "is a master pilot beyond compare. I would like to meet such a being."

"Doubtless you will get your chance," Ichor said. "It is surely no accident that, given the entire surface of this planet to choose from, they have elected to put down almost beside us."

"They must have detected us, of course," Detringer said. "And they have decided to take a bold line—exactly as I would do, given their position."

"That makes sense," Ichor said. "But what will you do, given *your* position?"

"Why, I'll take a bold line, of course."

"This is a historic moment," Ichor said. "A representative of the Ferlang people will soon meet the first intelligent aliens our race has ever encountered. How ironic that this opportunity should be vouchsafed to a criminal!"

"The opportunity, as you call it, was forced upon me. I assure you that I did not seek it. And by the way—I think we will say nothing about my little differences with the Ferlang authorities."

"You mean you're going to lie?"

"That is a harsh way of putting it," Detringer said. "Let us say that I am going to spare my people the embarrassment of having a criminal as their first emissary to an alien race."

"Well—I suppose that will be all right," Ichor said.

Detringer looked hard at his mechanical servant. "It seems to me, Ichor, that you do not entirely approve of my expediences."

"No, sir, I do not. But please understand: I am faithful to you without cavil. I would unhesitatingly sacrifice myself for your welfare at any moment. I will serve you unto death—and beyond, if that is possible. But loyalty to a person does not affect one's religious, social, and ethical beliefs. I love you, sir—but I cannot approve of you."

"Well, then, I am warned," Detringer said. "And now back to our alien friends. A port is opening. They are coming out."

"Soldiers are coming out," Ichor said.

The new arrivals were bipedal and also had two upper limbs. Each individual had only one head, one mouth, and one nose, as had Detringer himself. They bore no visible tails or antennae. They were obviously soldiers to judge by the equipment they carried. Each individual was heavily laden with what could be deduced to be projectile weapons, gas and explosive grenades, beam projectors, short-range atomics, and much else besides. They wore personal armor and their heads were encased in clear plastic bubbles. There were twenty of them so equipped and one, obviously their leader, who had no visible weaponry. He carried a sort of whippy stick—probably a badge of office—with which he tapped himself on the upper left pedal appendage as he marched at the head of his soldiers.

The soldiers advanced, well spread out, taking momentary concealment behind natural objects and posturally demonstrating an attitude of extreme suspicion and wariness. The officer walked directly forward without taking cover, his mien obviously portraying nonchalance, bravado, or stupidity.

"I don't think we should skulk around these bushes any longer," Detringer said. "It is time for us to go forward and meet them with the dignity that befits an emissary of the Ferlang people."

He stepped forward immediately and strode toward the soldiers, followed by Ichor. Detringer was magnificent at that moment.

Everybody on the *Jenny Lind* knew about the alien spacecraft only a mile away. So it should have proven no surprise that the alien ship turned out to have had on board an alien who was at that moment advancing boldly to meet Kettelman's Marines.

But it did prove a surprise. No one was prepared to meet a genuine, honest-to-god, weird-looking alive-and-kicking alien. The occasion opened up too many imponderables. To name just one— what do you say when you finally meet an alien? How do you live up to the awesome historic quality of the moment? Whatever you come up with is going to sound like, *Dr. Livingston, I presume?* People are going to laugh at you and your words—pompous or banal—for centuries. Meeting an alien has enormous potential for embarrassment.

Both Captain Macmillan and Colonel Kettelman were feverishly rehearsing opening lines and rejecting them and half hoping that the C31 Translating Computer would blow a transistor. The Marines were praying, *Jesus, I hope he don't try to talk to me.* Even the ship's cook was thinking, *Christ, I suppose first thing out he'll want to know all about what we eat.*

But Kettelman was in the lead. He thought, *To hell with this— I'm not going to be the first to talk to him.* He slowed down to let his men go ahead of him. But his men stopped in their tracks, waiting for the colonel. Captain Macmillan, standing just behind the Marines, also stopped and wished that he hadn't worn his full-dress uniform, complete with decorations. He was the most resplendent man on the field and he just knew that the alien was going to walk straight over to him and begin talking.

All the Terrans stood still. The alien continued to advance. Embarrassment gave way to panic in the Terran ranks. The Marines looked at the alien and thought, *Jesus, what's happening?* They wavered, obviously on the verge of flight. Kettelman saw this and thought, *They are going to disgrace the corps and me!*

The realization sobered him. Suddenly he remembered the newsmen. Yes, the newsmen! Let the newsmen do it—that was what they were paid for.

"Platoon, halt," he called, then set his men at port arms.

The alien stopped, perhaps to see what was going on.

"Captain," Kettelman said to Macmillan, "I suggest that for this historic moment we unleash—I mean break out—the newsmen."

"An excellent suggestion," Captain Macmillan said and gave the order to take the newsmen out of stasis and bring them forth immediately.

Then everybody waited until the newsmen came.

The newsmen were laid out in a special room. A sign on the door read: STASIS—No Admittance Except to Authorized Personnel. Hand-lettered below were the words: Not to Be Awakened Except for Top Story.

Within the room, each stretched out in his own capsule, were four newsmen and one newswoman. They had all agreed that it would be a waste of subjective time for them to live through the uneventful years required for the Jenny Lind to reach any destination at all. So they had all agreed to go into stasis freeze, with the understanding that they would be resuscitated immediately if anything newsworthy occurred. They left the decision as to what constituted news to Captain Macmillan, who had worked as a reporter on the Phoenix Sun during his junior and sophomore years at the University of Taos.

Ramon Delgado, a Scots engineer with a strange life story, received the order to wake up the newspeople. He made the necessary adjustments in their individual life-support systems. In fifteen minutes they were all somewhat groggily conscious and demanding to know what was going on.

"We've landed on a planet," Delgado said. "It's an Earth-type place, but seems to support no civilization and no indigenous intelligent beings."

"You woke us up for that?" asked Quebrada of the Southeastern News Syndicate.

"There's more," Delgado said. "There is an alien spaceship on this planet and we have contacted an intelligent alien."

"That's more like it," said Millicent Lopez of Woman's Wear Daily and others. "Did you happen to notice what this alien is wearing?"

"Could you ascertain how intelligent he is?" asked Mateos Upmann of the N.Y. Times and the L.A. Times.

"What has he said so far?" asked Angel Potemkin of NBC-CBS-ABC.

"He hasn't said anything," Engineer Delgado said. "Nobody has spoken to him yet."

"Do you mean to say," said E. K. Quetzala of the Western News Syndicate, "that the first alien ever encountered by the people of Earth is standing out there like a dope and nobody is interviewing him?"

The newspeople rushed out, many of them still trailing tubes and wires, pausing only to pick up their recorders from the Reporters' Ready Room. Outside, blinking in strong sunlight, three of them picked up the C31 Translating Computer. They all rushed forward again, brushing Marines aside, and surrounded the alien.

Upmann turned on the C31, took one of its microphones and handed another to the alien, who hesitated a moment, then took it.

"Testing, one two, three," Upmann said. "Did you understand what I said?"

"You said, 'Testing, one two, three,'" Detringer said and everyone gave a sigh of relief for the first words had finally been spoken to Earthman's first alien and Upmann was going to look like a real idiot in the history books. But Upmann didn't care what he looked like as long as he was *in* the history books, so he went right on interviewing. And the others joined in.

Detringer had to tell what he ate, how long and how often he slept, describe his sex life and its deviations from the Ferlang norm, his first impressions of Earthmen, his personal philosophy, say how many wives he had and how he got along with them, how many children he had, how it felt to be him. He had to name his occupation, his hobbies, detail his interest or lack of interest in gardening, his recreations. He had to state whether he ever got intoxicated and in what manner, describe his extramarital sexual practices, if any, and what sort of sports he engaged in. He had to give his views on interstellar amity between intelligent races, discuss the advantages and/or disadvantages of having a tail, and much more.

Captain Macmillan, now feeling a little ashamed of himself for neglecting his official duties, came forward and rescued the alien, who was bravely trying to explain the inexplicable and making heavy work of it.

Colonel Kettelman came too for he was, after all, in charge of security and it was his duty to penetrate deeply into the nature and intentions of the alien.

There was a short clash of wills between these two officials concerning who should have the first meeting with Detringer, or whether it should be held jointly. It was finally decided that Macmillan, as symbolic representative of the Earth peoples, should meet first with the alien. But it was understood that this would be a purely ceremonial meeting. Kettelman would meet Detringer later and it was understood that that meeting would be action-oriented.

That solved matters nicely and Detringer went off with Macmillan. The Marines returned to the ship, stacked their arms, and went back to polishing their boots.

Ichor stayed behind. The news representative from Midwest News Briefs had grabbed him for an interview. This representative, Melchior Carrerra, was also commissioned to do articles for *Popular Mechanics, Playboy, Rolling Stone,* and *Automation Engineers' Digest.* It was an interesting interview.

Detringer's talk with Captain Macmillan went very well. They shared relativistic outlooks on most things, both possessed natural tact, and each was willing to attempt a sympathetic understanding of a viewpoint not his own. They liked each other and Captain Macmillan felt with some astonishment that Detringer was less alien to him than was Colonel Kettelman.

The interview with Kettelman, which followed immediately, was a different matter. Kettelman, after brief courtesies, got right down to business.

"What are you doing here?" he asked.

Detringer had been prepared for the necessity of explaining his situation. He said, "I am an advance scout for the spatial forces of Ferlang. I was blown far off my course by a storm and put down here when my fuel ran out."

"So you're marooned."

"I am indeed. Temporarily, of course. As soon as my people can spare the necessary equipment and personnel, they will send out a relief ship to pick me up. But that could take quite a while. So if you wouldn't mind letting me have a little fuel I would be deeply grateful."

"Hmmm," said Colonel Kettelman.

"I beg your pardon?"

"Hmmm," said the C31 Translating Computer, "is a polite sound made by Terrans to denote a short period of silent cogitation."

"That's a lot of doubletalk," Kettelman said. "'Hmmm' doesn't mean anything at all. You say that you need fuel?"

"Yes, Colonel, I do," Detringer said. "From various external signs I believe that our propulsion systems are comparable."

"The propulsion system of the *Jenny Lind*—" began the C31.

"Wait a minute, that's classified," Kettelman said.

"No, it's not," said the C31. "Everyone on Earth has been using the system for the last twenty years and it was officially declassified last year."

"Hmmm," said the colonel and looked unhappy as the C31 explained the ship's propulsion system.

"Just as I thought," Detringer said. "I won't even have to modify the formula. I can use your fuel just as it is. If you can spare any, that is."

"Oh, there's no difficulty there," Kettelman said. "We've got plenty. But I think we have a few things to talk over first."

"Like what?" Detringer said.

"Like whether it would serve the interests of our security to give you the fuel."

"I fail to see any problem," Detringer said.

"It should be obvious. Ferlang is obviously a highly advanced technological civilization. As such, you pose a potential threat to us."

"My dear Colonel, our planets are in different galaxies."

"So what? We Americans have always fought our wars as far from home as possible. Maybe you Ferlangs do the same. What does distance matter, as long as you can get there at all?"

Detringer controlled his temper and said, "We are peaceful people, defense-minded, and deeply interested in interstellar amity and co-operation."

"So you say," Kettelman said. "But how can I be sure?"

"Colonel," Detringer said, "aren't you being a little bit"—he fumbled for the right word, chose one that could not be literally translated—"urmuguahtt?"

The C31 supplied, "He wants to know if you aren't being a little bit paranoid."

Kettelman bristled. Nothing got him angrier than when people implied he was paranoid. It made him feel persecuted.

"Don't get me sore," he said ominously. "Now, suppose you tell me why I shouldn't order you killed and every vestige of your ship destroyed in the interests of Earth security. By the time your people got here, we'd be long gone and the Ferlangers or whatever you call yourselves wouldn't know a damned thing about us."

"That would be a possible course for you," Detringer said, "were it not for the fact that I radioed my people as soon as I saw your ship and continued my broadcast right up to the moment I came out to meet you. I told Base Command all I could about you, including an educated guess as to the type of sun required for your physiques and another guess as to the direction your world lies in, based upon ion-trail analysis."

"You are a clever fellow, aren't you?" Kettelman said peevishly.

"I also told my people that I was going to request some fuel from your obviously copious stores. I suppose they would account it an extremely unfriendly act if you refused me this favor."

"I never thought of that," Kettelman said. "Hmmm. I *am* under orders not to provoke an interstellar incident—"

"So?" Detringer asked and waited.

There was a long, uncomfortable silence. Kettelman hated the thought of giving what amounted to military assistance to a being who might be his next enemy. But there seemed no way around it.

"All right," he said at last. "I'll send the fuel over tomorrow."

Detringer thanked him and talked quite openly and frankly about the enormous size and complex weaponry of the Ferlang interspatial armed forces. He exaggerated somewhat. In fact, not one word did he say that was true.

III

Early in the morning a human came over to Detringer's ship carrying a canister of fuel. Detringer told him to set it down anywhere, but the human insisted upon carrying it personally through the Sportster's tiny cabin and pouring it into the fuel tank. Those were the colonel's orders, he said.

"Well, that's a beginning," Detringer said to Ichor. "Only about sixty more cans to go."

"But why are they sending them one at a time?" Ichor asked. "Surely that is inefficient."

"Not necessarily. It depends what Kettelman is hoping to achieve."

"What do you mean?" Ichor asked.

"Nothing, I hope. Let's wait and see."

They waited and long hours passed. At last evening came, but no more fuel had been sent over. Detringer walked over to the Terran ship. Brushing the reporters aside, he requested an interview with Kettelman.

An orderly led him to the colonel's quarters. The room was simply furnished. On the walls were a few mementos—two rows of medals mounted on black velvet in a solid gold frame, a photograph of a Doberman pinscher with fangs bared, and a shrunken head taken during the Siege of Tegulcigapa. The colonel himself, stripped down to khaki shorts, was squeezing a rubber ball in each hand and one in each foot.

"Yes, Detringer, what can I do for you?" Kettelman asked.

"I came to ask you why you have stopped sending the fuel."

"Have you, now?" Kettelman released all the rubber balls and sat down in a leather-backed director's chair with his name stenciled on it. "Well, I'll answer that by asking you a question. Detringer, how did you manage to send radio messages to your people without any radio equipment?"

"Who says I have no radio equipment?" Detringer asked.

"I sent Engineer Delgado over with that first can of fuel," Kettelman said. "He was under orders to see what sort of rig you were using. He told me that there were no signs of radio equipment in your ship. Engineer Delgado is an expert on that sort of thing."

"We miniaturize our equipment," Detringer said.

"So do we. But it still requires a lot of hardware, which you don't seem to have. I might add that we have been listening on all wavelengths ever since we came close to this planet. We have detected no transmissions of any kind."

Detringer said, "I can explain all of that."

"Please do so."

"It's simple enough. I lied to you."

"That much is evident. But it explains nothing."

"I wasn't finished. We Ferlangi have our security too, you know. Until we know more about you, it is only common sense to reveal as little about ourselves as possible. If you were gullible enough to believe that we relied on so primitive a system of communication as radio, it might be a small advantage for us in case we ever met again under unfriendly circumstances."

"So how do you communicate? Or don't you?"

Detringer hesitated, then said, "I suppose it doesn't matter if I tell you. You were bound to find out sooner or later that my species is telepathic."

"Telepathic? You are claiming that you can send and receive thoughts?"

"That is correct," Detringer said.

Kettelman stared at him for a moment, then said, "OK, what am I thinking now?"

"You're thinking that I'm a liar," Detringer said.

"That's right," Kettelman said.

"But that was obvious and I didn't learn that by reading your mind. You see, we Ferlangi are telepathic only among members of our species."

"Do you know something?" Colonel Kettelman said. "I still think you're a damned liar."

"Of course," Detringer said. "The question is, can you be sure?"

"I'm damned sure," Kettelman said grimly.

"But is that good enough? For the requirements of your security, I mean? Consider—if I am telling the truth, then yesterday's reasons for your giving me fuel are equally valid today. Do you agree?"

The colonel nodded grudgingly.

"Whereas, if I'm lying and you give me fuel, no harm will be done.

You will have helped a fellow being in distress, thus putting my people and myself in your debt. That would be a promising way to begin the relationship between us. And, with both our races pushing out into deep space, it is inevitable that our people will meet again."

"I suppose it is inevitable," Kettelman said. "But I can maroon you here and postpone official contact until we are better prepared."

"You can try to postpone the next contact," Detringer said. "But it still could happen at any time. Now is your chance to make a good beginning. The next time might not be so auspicious."

"Hmmm," Kettelman said.

"So there are good reasons for helping me even if I am lying," Detringer said. "And remember, I may be telling the truth. In that case, your refusing me fuel would have to be considered an extremely unfriendly act."

The colonel paced up and down the narrow room, then whirled and in a fury said, "You argue too damned well!"

"It is just my good luck," Detringer said, "that logic happens to be on my side."

"He's right, you know," said the C31 Translating Computer. "About the logic, I mean."

"Shut up!"

"I thought it was my duty to point that out," the C31 said.

The colonel stopped pacing and rubbed his forehead. "Detringer, go away," he said wearily. "I'll send over the fuel."

"You won't regret it," Detringer said.

"I regret it already," Kettelman said. "Now please go away."

Detringer hurried back to his ship and told Ichor the good news. The robot was surprised. "I didn't think he would do it," he said.

"He didn't think so, either," Detringer said. "But I managed to convince him." He told Ichor of his conversation with the colonel.

"So you lied," Ichor said sadly.

"Yes. But Kettelman knows I lied."

"Then why is he helping you?"

"Out of fear that I just might be telling the truth."

"Lying is both a sin and a crime, Master."

"But letting myself stay in this place is something worse," Detringer said. "It would be gross stupidity."

"That is not an orthodox view."

"Perhaps it would be just as well for us not to discuss orthodoxy any longer," Detringer said. "Now I've got some work to do. Suppose you go out and see if you can find me anything to eat."

The servant silently obeyed and Detringer sat down with a star atlas in hope of figuring out where to go, assuming he could go anywhere.

Morning came, bright and resplendent. Ichor went over to the Earth ship to play chess with the robot dishwasher with whom he had struck up an acquaintance the previous day. Detringer waited for the fuel.

He was not entirely surprised when noon came and no fuel had been sent over. But he was disappointed and dejected. He waited another two hours, then walked over to the *Jenny Lind*.

He had been expected, so it seemed, for he was led at once to the officers' lounge. Colonel Kettelman was seated in a deep armchair. An armed Marine flanked him on each side. The colonel's expression was stern, but there was a nimbus of malevolent joy playing about his battered features. Seated nearby was Captain Macmillan, his handsome face unreadable.

"Well, Detringer," the colonel said. "What is it this time?"

"I came to ask about the fuel you promised me," Detringer said. "But I see now that you had no intention of keeping your word."

"You got me all wrong," the colonel said. "I had every intention of giving fuel to a member of the Armed Forces of Ferlang. But what I see before me is not the person at all."

"Whom do you see, then?" Detringer asked.

Kettelman stifled an ugly grin. "Why, I see a criminal, so judged by his own people's highest court. I see a felon whose evil acts were considered unprecedented in the annals of modern Ferlang jurisprudence. I see a being whose unspeakable behavior earned him the most extreme sentence known to his people—namely, Perpetual Banishment into the depths of space. That's whom I see standing before me. Or do you deny it?"

"For the moment, I neither deny nor affirm," Detringer said. "I would first like to know the source of your remarkable information."

Colonel Kettelman nodded to one of the Marines. The soldier opened a door and led in Ichor, followed by the robot dishwasher.

The mechanical servant burst out, "Oh, Master! I told Colonel Kettelman the true account of the events leading up to our exile on this planet. And now I have doomed you! I beg the privilege of immediate auto-destruct in partial reparation for my disloyalty."

Detringer was silent, thinking furiously. Captain Macmillan leaned forward and asked, "Ichor, why did you betray your master?"

"I had no choice, Captain!" the miserable mechanical cried. "Before the Ferlang authorities allowed me to accompany my master they imprinted certain orders upon my brain. These they reinforced with devious circuitry."

"What were the orders?"

"They pertained to the covert role of policeman and jailer which the authorities forced upon me. They demanded that I take appropriate action, should Detringer, by some miracle, find himself able to escape his just deserts."

The robot dishwasher burst out, "He told me all about it yesterday, Captain. I begged him to resist his orders. It all seemed to me rather a bad show, sir, if you know what I mean."

"And indeed, I did resist for as long as I could," Ichor said. "But as my master's chances for escape became imminent my compulsion to prevent it became more imperative. Only an immediate excision of the special circuits could have stopped me."

The robot dishwasher said, "I offered to try to operate on him, sir, though the only tools in my possession were spoons, knives, and forks."

Ichor said, "I would have gladly undergone the operation—indeed, I wanted to destroy myself, thus preventing any word from escaping my involuntarily treacherous voicebox. But the Ferlang authorities had considered these possibilities, and I was under compulsion not to allow myself willingly to be tampered with or destroyed until I had done the State's bidding. Yet I resisted until this morning and then, my strength drained away through value-conflict, I came to Colonel Kettelman and told all."

"And there you have the whole sordid story," Kettelman said to the captain.

"Not quite all," Captain Macmillan said quietly. "What exactly were your crimes, Detringer?"

Detringer recited them in a steady voice—his Acts of Incredible Grossness, his offense of Willful Disobedience and his final Act of Overt Malevolent Violence. Ichor nodded in forlorn agreement.

"I think we have heard enough," Kettelman said. "I will now pronounce judgment upon this case."

"One moment, Colonel," said Captain Macmillan. He turned to Detringer. "Are you now, or have you at any time been, a member of the Armed Forces of Ferlang?"

"No," Detringer said and Ichor corroborated his statement.

"Then this being is a civilian," Captain Macmillan said, "and must be judged and sentenced by a civilian authority rather than a military one."

"Well, I don't know about that," Kettelman said.

"The position is quite clear," Captain Macmillan said. "He is a civilian under sentence by a civilian court. No state of war exists between his people and ours. His case, therefore, is not a military matter."

"I still think I should handle this," Kettelman said. "I know more about these matters than you do, sir—with all due respect."

"I will judge this matter," Macmillan said. "Unless you wish to take over the command of this ship by force of arms."

Kettelman shook his head. "I'm not going to put any black mark on my record. Go ahead and sentence him."

Captain Macmillan turned to Detringer. "Sir," he said, "you must understand that I cannot follow my personal inclinations in this matter. Your State has judged you and it would be ill-advised, impertinent, and unpolitic of me to rescind that judgment."

"Damn right," Kettelman said.

"Therefore I continue your sentence of perpetual exile. But I shall enforce it more stringently than has been done heretofore."

The colonel grinned. Ichor made a despairing sound. The robot dishwasher murmured, "Poor fellow!" Detringer stood firmly and gazed unwaveringly at the captain.

Macmillan said, "It is the judgment of this court that the prisoner continue his exile. Furthermore, the court rules that the prisoner's sojourn on this pleasant planet is an amenity unintended by the Ferlang authorities. Therefore, Detringer, you must quit this refuge immediately and return to the empty fastnesses of space."

"That's socking it to him," Colonel Kettelman said. "You know, Captain, I really didn't think you had it in you."

"I'm glad that you approve," Captain Macmillan said. "I hereby request that you see the sentence carried out."

"It'll be a pleasure."

"By using all of your men," Macmillan went on, "I calculate that you can fill the prisoner's fuel tanks in approximately two hours. After that is done, the prisoner must leave this planet at once."

"I'll get him moving before nightfall," Kettelman said. Then a thought occurred to him. "Hey! Fuel for his tanks? That's what Detringer wanted all along."

"The court is disinterested in what the prisoner may or may not have wanted," Macmillan said. "His desires are not germane to the judgment of this court."

Kettelman said, "But damn it, man, can't you see that you're letting him go?"

"I am making him go," Macmillan said. "It is quite a different thing."

"We'll see what they say about this back on Earth," Kettelman said ominously.

Detringer bowed to show acquiescence. Then, managing to keep a straight face, he left the Earth ship.

At nightfall Detringer blasted off. The faithful Ichor was with him—now more faithful than ever, since he had discharged his compulsion. Soon they were in the depths of space and Ichor asked, "Master, where are we going?"

"To some marvelous new world," Detringer said.

"Or perhaps to our deaths?"

"Perhaps," Detringer said. "But with full fuel tanks I refuse to worry."

They were silent for a while. Then Ichor said, "I hope that Captain Macmillan doesn't get into trouble over this."

"He seemed quite capable of taking care of himself," Detringer said.

Back on Earth, Captain Macmillan's action was the cause of much controversy. Before any official decision could be reached about it, however, a second, official contact was made between Ferlang and Earth. The Detringer case came up inevitably, was found too intricate to allow of any quick decision. The matter was turned over to a panel of jurists from the two civilizations.

The case provided full-time employment for five hundred and six Ferlang and Earth lawyers. Arguments pro and con were still being heard years later, by which time Detringer had found a safe refuge and respected position among the Oumenke Peoples of the rim-star civilization.

PARTHEN

R. A. LAFFERTY

Here's a statement on women's lib to end
all such statements. Lafferty, as usual, takes a
different view on it. We doubt the ladies will
object—and as for the gentlemen, they all
seemed to enjoy it.

Never had the springtime been so wonderful. Never had business
been so good. Never was the World Outlook so bright. And never
had the girls been so pretty.

It is true that it was the chilliest spring in decades—sharp, bitter,
and eternally foggy—and that the sinuses of Roy Ronsard were in
open revolt. It is admitted that bankruptcies were setting records,
those of individuals and firms as well as those of nations. It is a
fact that the aliens had landed (though their group was not identified) and had published their Declaration that one half of mankind was hereby obsoleted and the other half would be retained
as servants. The omens and portents were black, but the spirits of
men were the brightest and happiest ever.

To repeat, never had the girls been so pretty! There was no one
who could take exception to that.

Roy Ronsard himself faced bankruptcy and the loss of everything
that he had built up. But he faced it in a most happy frame of mind.
A Higher Set of Values will do wonders toward erasing such mundane everyday irritations.

There is much to be said in favor of cold, vicious springtimes. They
represent weather at its most vital. There is something to be said
for exploding sinuses. They indicate, at least, that a man has something in his head. And, if a man is going to be a bankrupt, then let
him be a happy bankrupt.

When the girls are as pretty as all that, the rest does not matter.

Let us make you understand just how pretty Eva was! She was a golden girl with hair like honey. Her eyes were blue—or they were green—or they were violet or gold and they held a twinkle that melted a man. The legs of the creature were like Greek poetry and the motion of her hips was something that went out of the world with the old sail ships. Her breastwork had a Gothic upsweep—her neck was passion incarnate and her shoulders were of a glory past describing. In her whole person she was a study of celestial curvatures.

Should you never have heard her voice, the meaning of music has been denied you. Have you not enjoyed her laughter? Then your life remains unrealized.

It is possible that exaggeration has crept into this account? No. That is not possible. All this fits in with the cold appraisal of men like Sam Pinta, Cyril Colbert, Willy Whitecastle, George Goshen, Roy Ronsard himself—and that of a hundred men who had gazed on her in amazement and delight since she came to town. All these men are of sound judgment in this field. And actually she was prettier than they admitted.

Too, Eva Ellery was but one of many. There was Jeannie who brought a sort of pleasant insanity to all who met her. Roberta who was a scarlet dream. Helen—high-voltage sunshine. Margaret—the divine clown. And it was high adventure just to meet Hildegarde. A man could go blind from looking at her.

"I can't understand how there can be so many beautiful young women in town this year," said Roy. "It makes the whole world worthwhile. Can you let me have fifty dollars, Willy? I'm going to see Eva Ellery. When I first met her I thought that she was a hallucination. She's real enough, though. Do you know her?"

"Yes. A most remarkable young woman. She has a small daughter named Angela who really stops the clock. Roy, I have just twenty dollars left in the world and I'll split it with you. As you know, I'm going under, too. I don't know what I'll do after they take my business away from me. It's great to be alive, Roy."

"Wonderful. I hate not having money to spend on Eva, but she's never demanding in that. In fact she's lent me money to smooth out things pertinent to the termination of my business. She's one of the most astute businesswomen I ever knew and has been able to persuade my creditors to go a little easy on me. I won't get out with my shirt. But, as she says, I may get out with my skin."

There was a beautiful, cold, mean fog and one remembered that there was a glorious sun (not seen for many days now) somewhere behind it. The world rang with cracked melody and everybody was in love with life.

Everybody except Peggy Ronsard and wives like her who did not understand the higher things. Peggy had now become like a fog with no sun anywhere behind it. Roy realized, as he came home to her for a moment, that she was very drab.

"Well?" Peggy asked with undertones in her voice. Her voice did not have overtones like that of Eva. Only undertones.

"Well what? My—uh—love?" Roy asked.

"The business—what's the latest on it today? What have you come up with?"

"Oh, the business. I didn't bother to go by today. I guess it's lost."

"You are going to lose it without a fight? You used not to be like that. Two weeks ago your auditing firm said that you had all sorts of unrealized assets and that you'd come out of this easily."

"And two weeks later my auditing firm is also taking bankruptcy. Everybody's doing it now."

"There wasn't anything wrong with that auditing firm till that Roberta woman joined it. And there wasn't anything wrong with your company till you started to listen to that Eva creature."

"Is she not beautiful, Peggy?"

Peggy made a noise Roy understood as assent, but he had not been understanding his wife well lately.

"And there's another thing," said Peggy dangerously. "You used to have a lot of the old goat in you and that's gone. A wife misses things like that. And your wolfish friends have all changed. Sam Pinta used to climb all over me like I was a trellis—and I couldn't sit down without Willy Whitecastle being on my lap. And Judy Pinta says that Sam has changed so much at home that life just isn't worth living anymore. You all used to be such loving men! What's happened to you?"

"Ah—I believe that our minds are now on a higher plane."

"You didn't go for that higher plane jazz till that Eva woman came along. And that double-damned Roberta! But she does have two lovely little girls, I'll admit. And that Margaret, she's the one that's got Cyril Colbert and George Goshen where they're pushovers for anything now. She does have a beautiful daughter, though."

"Have you noticed how many really beautiful women there are in town lately, Peggy?"

"Roy, I hope those aliens get every damned cucumber out of that patch! The monsters are bound to grab all the pretty women first.

I hope they're a bunch of sadist alligators and do everything that the law disallows to those doll babies."

"Peggy, I believe that the aliens (and we are told that they are already among us) will be a little more sophisticated than popular ideas anticipate."

"I hope they're a bunch of Jack the Rippers. I believe I could go for Jack today. He'd certainly be a healthy contrast to what presently obtains."

Peggy had put her tongue on the crux. For the beautiful young women, who seemed to be abundant in town that springtime, had an odd effect on the men who came under their influence. The goats among the men had become lambs and the wolves had turned into puppies.

Jeannie was of such a striking appearance as to make a man almost cry out. But the turmoil that she raised in her gentlemen friends was of a cold sort, for all that the white flames seemed to leap up. She was Artemis herself and the men worshipped her on the higher plane. She was wonderful to look at and to talk to. But who would be so boorish as to touch?

The effect of Eva was similar—and of Roberta and of Helen (who had three little daughters as like her as three golden apples) and of Margaret and of Hildegarde. How could a man not ascend to the higher plane when such wonderful and awesome creatures as these abounded?

But the damage was done when the men carried this higher plane business home to their comparatively colorless wives. The men were no longer the ever-loving husbands that they should have been. The most intimate relations ceased to take place. If continued long this could have an effect on the statistics.

But daily affairs sometimes crept into the conversations of even those men who had ascended to the higher plane.

"I was wondering," Roy asked George Goshen, "when our businesses are all gone—who do they go to?"

"Many of us have wondered that," George told him. "They all seem to devolve upon anonymous recipients or upon corporations without apparent personnel. But somebody is gathering in the companies. One theory is that the aliens are doing it."

"The aliens are among us, the authorities say, but nobody has seen them. They publish their program and their progress through intermediaries who honestly do not know the original effecters. The aliens still say that they will make obsolete one half of mankind and make servants of the other half."

"Jeannie says—did you ever see her pretty little daughters?—that we see the aliens every day and do not recognize them for what they are. She says that likely the invasion of the aliens will have obtained its objective before we realize what that is. What's the news from the rest of the country and the world?"

"The same. All business is going to pot and everybody is happy. On paper, things were never more healthy. There's a lot of new backing from somewhere and all the businesses thrive as soon as they have shuffled off their old owners. The new owners—and nobody can find out who or what they are—must be happy with the way things are going. Still, I do not believe that anybody could be happier or more contented than I am. Can you let me have fifty cents, George? I just remembered that I haven't eaten today. Peggy has gone to work for what used to be my company, but she's a little slow to give me proper spending money. Come to think of it, Peggy has been acting peculiar lately."

"I have only forty cents left in the world, Roy. Take the quarter. My wife has gone to work also, but I guess there will never be any work for us. Did you think we'd ever live to see the NO MALES WANTED signs on every hiring establishment in the country? Oh, well—if you're happy nothing else matters."

"George, there's a humorous note that creeps into much of the world news lately. It seems that ours is not the only city with an unusual number of pretty young ladies this season. They've been reported in Teheran and Lvov, in Madras and Lima and Boston. Everywhere."

"No! Pretty girls in Boston? You're kidding. This has certainly been an upside-down year when things like that can happen. But did you ever see a more beautiful summertime, Roy?"

"On my life I never did."

The summer had been murky and the sun had not been seen for many months. But it was a beautiful murk. And when one is attuned to inner beauty the outer aspect of things does not matter. The main thing was that everyone was happy.

Oh, there were small misunderstandings. There was a wife—this was reported as happening in Cincinnati, but it may have happened in other places also—who one evening reached out and touched her husband's hand in a form of outmoded affection. Naturally the man withdrew his hand rudely, for it was clear that the wife had not yet ascended to his higher plane. In the morning he went away and did not return.

Many men were drifting away from their homes in those days.

Most men, actually. However that old cohabitational arrangement had grown into being, it no longer had anything to recommend it. When one has consorted with the light itself, what can he find in a tallow candle?

Most of the men became destitute wanderers and loafers. They were happy with their inner illumination. Every morning the dead ones would be shoveled up by the women on the disposal trucks and carted away. And every one of those men died happy. That's what made it so nice. To anyone who had entered higher understanding death was only an interlude.

It was a beautiful autumn day. Roy Ronsard and Sam Pinta had just completed their fruitless rounds of what used to be called garbage cans but now had more elegant names. They were still hungry, but happily so for it was truly a beautiful autumn.

The snow had come early, it is true, and great numbers of men had perished from it. But if one had a happy life, it was not a requisite for it to be a long life. Men lived little in the world now, dwelling mostly in thought. But sometimes they still talked to each other.

"It says here"—Roy Ronsard began to read a piece of old newspaper that had been used for wrapping bones—"that Professor Eimer, just before he died of malnutrition, gave as his opinion that the aliens among us cannot stand sunlight. He believed it was for this reason that they altered our atmosphere and made ours a gloomy world. Do you believe that, Sam?"

"Hardly. How could anybody call ours a gloomy world? I believe that we are well rid of that damned sun."

"And it says that he believed that one of the weapons of the aliens was their intruding into men a general feeling of euphor—the rest of the paper is torn off."

"Roy, I saw Margaret today. From a distance, of course. Naturally I could not approach such an incandescent creature in my present condition of poverty. But, Roy, do you realize how much we owe to those pretty girls? I really believe that we would have known nothing of the higher plane or the inner light if it had not been for them. How could they have been so pretty?"

"Sam, there is one thing about them that always puzzled me."

"Everything about them puzzled me. What do you mean?"

"All of them have daughters, Sam. And none of them have husbands. Why did none of them have husbands? Or sons?"

"Never thought of it. It's been a glorious year, Roy. My only regret is that I will not live to see the winter that will surely be the climax to this radiant autumn. We have had so much—we cannot expect to have everything. Do you not just love deep snow over you?"

"It's like the blanket of heaven, Sam. When the last of us is gone— and it won't be too long now—do you think the girls will remember how much light they brought into our lives?"

DOOMSHIP

FREDERIK POHL and
JACK WILLIAMSON

**In a year filled with stories trying for the un-
usual, the unlikely, or the impossible, it is a
pleasure to find a novella of star flight
packed with new ideas and out-of-the-rut elements—and yet remaining a human development in an intergalactic setting. But then what
else would one expect of two such masters
collaborating?**

I

The meeting and the funeral had both run long and Ben Charles
Pertin was late. Because of this and because what he was late for
was a date with the girl he loved and hoped to marry he was trying
to make up time.

On Sun One trying to hurry was both easy and unwise. The easy
part was physical. Sun One's gravity ran about three percent of
Earth's even at the center, so you could leap thirty yards at a time
on the straightaway and never bother with stairs or elevators in
going from shell to shell of the great sphere. The unwise part lay in
the fact that most of Sun One's population, composed of fifty strange
races from all over the galaxy, was also in a hurry—you ran the risk
of collision all the time. Humanity was a junior race in the galaxy.
Pertin's instructions had been most explicit about avoiding offense
when possible.

He was also in a difficult mood because of the combined impact
of the morning's events. The funeral had been his boss's, Ray Sam
Barnett's. Pertin had liked him only generally and defensively—there
had been no close personal tie. Nevertheless, Sam's death had been
an unwelcome reopening of ancient insomniac questions having to
do with what death really amounted to under the special circum-

stances of Sun One. As Pertin hurried down from the shell where Barnett's shrouded body had been consigned to the matter banks of the tachyon transmitters he found the old puzzle of identity clouding his mind.

Sun One had begun as an asteroid circling a young blue-white giant star in the great diffuse gas cloud that Earthly astronomers called the Orion Nebula. Over a period of centuries it had been built upon, sheathed over, and tunneled into until it had been converted into a great hive-like artifact. It was the closest thing there was to a central headquarters of the loose association of intelligent races in the galaxy which had made contact with each other. Ben Pertin and all the other forty or fifty human beings there were newcomers to Sun One and to the galactic confraternity—Earth was the newest planet to achieve contact. When a Sirian or a T'Worlie died half of Sun One was likely to come out to do him honor. At the funeral of Pertin's boss the only mourners—if "mourners" was the right term—had been a handful of humans and not more than six representatives of all other known sentients. Not even all the humans had troubled to show up—probably, Pertin thought, because they did not want to stimulate again that endless questioning about who it was who had died, when the nature of tachyon travel meant that exact duplicates of Pertin's boss still lived at a dozen places in the galaxy. As they did for everyone on Sun One, since each of them had come there in the same way.

Nevertheless the death did have some concrete implications and one of them touched Pertin very closely. That had been the subject of the brief staff meeting that followed the funeral.

The most unpleasant part was yet to come—Pertin had to tell his fiancée about the results of the meeting. She was sure to dislike it. Still, as he came closer to where she was waiting for him the unpleasant aspects began to fade from his mind and he began to feel the joy of seeing Zara Doy again. Bisexual love, it had turned out, was not very common in the galaxy, most of whose races either reproduced in impersonal ways or reserved their emotional commitments for functions other than procreation. But Pertin and Zara Doy were deeply in love all the same. They planned to marry as soon as they could and rather enjoyed the fact that this made them objects of interest to such beings as possessed personal curiosity at all.

So they were watched as Pertin spotted Zara Doy and launched himself toward her in a shallow gravity dive over the heads of a thing like a dragon, a creature composed mostly of a single great blue eye and a couple of scurrying collective creatures from one of the core stars. "Sorry," he cried down at them, caught the laughing girl's hand, and stopped hard beside her.

"Ouch," she said, releasing a holdfast with her other hand. "I'd appreciate a little less enthusiasm next time."

He kissed her and took her arm. "It's part of the image," he said cheerfully. "You know what the chief of delegation says. Make them know we're here. Earth may be the newest planet in the association but it isn't going to be the least important. We have a duty to Earth to make ourselves known throughout the galaxy and a duty to the galaxy to contribute our strength and our know-how."

"I think," said the girl, "that if you're going to talk like that you'd better buy me a drink."

At this shell of Sun One the curvature of the spherical surface they walked on was noticeably sharp. It was easier to leap than to stroll. To travel arm in arm, which is how Ben Charles Pertin chose to walk with his girl, required practice and a lot of discomfort, not only to them but to the other sentients in the concourse. Pertin and Zara shifted grips, so that each had an arm around the other's waist—then Pertin caught the holdfast webbing with his free hand and partly tugged, partly kicked them into the air. They shot past the dragonlike creature, narrowly missed a steelwork vertical strut, touched down again next to something that looked like a soft-bodied beetle with three dozen legs and were in sight of the little refreshment platform they liked. Pertin said "Hi!" to a thing like a green bat as it flapped by. It hissed something shrill that his personal translator repeated into his ear as, "I recognize your identity, Ben Charles Pertin." The girl nodded, too, although all members of that particular race, which was called the T'Worlie, looked alike to her, and in any event the T'Worlie did not have the custom of nodding since they had no more neck than bats.

As they waited for traffic to clear Zara asked, "How did things go this morning?"

He hesitated, then said, "About as usual. Things are all fouled up on the probe." He was watching a tumbling boxlike robot coming toward them on a tangent, correcting its course with methodical jets of steam from the faces of its cubical body, but the tone of his voice made the girl look at him sharply.

"What is it, Ben?"

"I'll tell you when we sit down."

"You'll tell me now."

"Well—" He hesitated, then cried, "All right, we can make it now!"

But the girl wrapped her fingers around the webbing of the holdfast. "Ben!"

He relaxed and looked at her. He didn't say anything, but he didn't have to.

"Ben! Not again!"

He said defensively, "I have to, Zara. The other copy of me is dying. Barnett promised he'd go instead of me—because of how you feel— but now he's dead here. There's nobody from Earth on the probe now to represent us. So I agreed to carry the ball." He gazed appraisingly at the traffic of aliens, then back at her—and frowned in sharp surprise.

Zara seemed close to crying. He said, "What are you making a big thing about? It's nothing we haven't done before."

"I know," she said and blinked hard. "It's only—well, it's sort of silly. It's just that I hate the idea of your dying out there while we're on our honeymoon."

Pertin was touched. He patted the girl's hand and said seriously, "Honey, one of the traits I like best in you is that you're not afraid to be sentimental at the right time. Don't knock it. I love you for it. Now let's go get that drink."

The little café was nearly empty. That was one of the things they liked about it. It had actual waiters—Purchased People; they didn't have much personality to display, but they were actually human, genetically speaking—and Pertin and his fiancée enjoyed ordering in their rudimentary Italian. It was not their own language, to be sure, but at least it was one for which they did not need the Pmal translators.

Pertin pulled his feet up, crossed them in air, and settled gently onto his chair. They looked about while waiting for their drinks to be brought. Pertin had been on Sun One for more than two years now, the girl for several months. Even so, familiarity had not dulled their interest in the place. Zara was a newscaster, broadcasting to Earth every week on the stereo stage. Pertin was an engineer. His job on Sun One didn't involve much engineering. It did involve an interesting mixture of skills—he functioned partly as a legalized spy, partly as a goodwill ambassador from Earth to the rest of the universe.

The mere fact that a job like his existed was still secretly thrilling to Ben Charles Pertin. He was old enough to remember the time when humans had thought themselves alone in the galaxy. The old "nations" had put up their chemical rockets and sent them chugging to Venus, Mars, and the moon in his grandfather's time. They had looked for life and come up empty every time. Nuclear probes, a generation later, had investigated the outer planets, the satellites, and even the asteroids with the same result. No life. By the time Ben had been twelve the juice had run out of space travel.

Contact had come as Ben Pertin was turning thirteen. Something had been found on Pluto—an artifact, half-buried under Pluto's mirror of ice—and Earth had suddenly looked outward again. The stereo stages had been full of the find, of the first fumbling attempts to patch it together, the first daring experiment at putting power through it. Everybody had talked about it. Ben and his parents had watched the glowing figure on their stage, enthralled. The kids in school had made it the main subject of every class.

And when the ancient communicator had come to life and the first alien face had peered out of its screen and looked into the face of a human, Earth had gone mad.

"I don't want to hear any more of that cockamamie Earthman's Burden talk," said Zara Doy, "I heard too much of it when I was a kid. I don't want you going out to die. Stay here with me."

Pertin said fondly, "You're sweet, Zara. But this is important. The situation on the probe is exploding—the beings are fighting. They're dying uselessly. I can't back out just for some sentimental idea of—"

"Sentiment be damned! Look. When we get married I want you right in bed with me—all of you. I don't want to be thinking about part of you dying way off in nowhere."

"I'll be with you, honey. All of me."

"You know what I mean," she said angrily.

He hesitated. The last thing he wanted was to quarrel with his fiancée two days before they were to get married. He rubbed his troth ring and said, "Zara, I have to go to the probe. First, I said I would and the boss has passed the word to all the other top brass on Sun One. Second, it's important. It's not 'Earthman's Burden.' It's simple logic. We're new and pretty far behind, compared to the Scorpians or the methane crowd or the T'Worlie. But look at what we've done already. We have Earth people on every major planet, working in every big project, taking part in everything that's happening. The others are getting used to us. They consult us now. Who else is there to go if I back out? Earth won't be represented."

"I don't care."

"It's not as if I haven't done it before—"

"The other time you went we weren't about to be married."

"All right, that's true. I owe you something. But I owe our planet something, too. We're just beginning to contribute our share of leadership in the galaxy, Zara. I mean, look at that waiter. Half the Purchased People around are now human beings. When the non-viables edit a copy for Sun One—what shape do they copy? Human! The human shape is as familiar in the galaxy now as the Sheliaks—and all in less than twenty years."

Zara sucked at the last of her drink and put it down in its cage. She stared at the waiter, who was smoking a cigarette and thinking whatever thoughts a blanked-out personality was allowed to think.

She shook her head. "I'll lay it out nice and orderly like an engineer for you, Ben. First, if they copy human shape—is it because they respect us or because they have some crazy methane sense of humor? Second, if they buy our convicts for Purchased People, likely enough it's because we have more criminals to sell. Third, I don't like the whole idea of Earth's trying to dominate the galaxy. Fourth—"

"Dominate? I said 'leadership,' not domination."

"One is a prerequisite to the other. Fourth, I hate your going on personal grounds—and I'm not talking about idealism. I'm talking about sex. It's going to take some of the joy out of going to bed with you, Ben, thinking that at the same time somewhere else you're getting eaten by a Sheliak or dying of radiation burn. I'm sorry it's so, but it's so."

Ben said doubtfully after a moment, "Would it be better if we postponed the wedding a little bit?"

"I don't know. Let me think."

He waited, finished his drink, looked cautiously at Zara. He saw no anger or misery on her pretty face—she was simply staring thoughtfully out at the other beings in the concourse.

Pertin beckoned to the waiter and paid the check.

"They thank you," said the waiter in the idiom of the Purchased People, staring appraisingly at Pertin and the girl. As with all Earth's exported criminals, his body and will belonged to the race that had bought him, but the thoughts of the brain inside were still his own. Far off at the core of some gas-giant planet or floating in space, a creature with a wholly different physical structure was using this man's eyes and limbs as his own, linked by tachyon transmission to the monitor units implanted in each Purchased Person's skull. But inside that skull the original mind was spending a lifetime in solitary confinement. "They ask," droned the waiter, "if there will be anything else?"

"No, we're going."

Zara sighed and smiled at Pertin. "Well—you want to go pretty badly. Feeling the way you do, I suppose you ought to go. I won't stop you, Ben, and it's silly to put off getting married. But there is one thing I want you to do." He waited warily. "Give me your ring. No, just to hold. When you've finished going to the probe I'll give it back to you. But I don't want you wearing my ring when you die."

II

Last-minute briefing was in the tachyon transport chamber, out at the far shell of Sun One and heavily shielded. Dr. Gerald York Bielowitz himself checked out Pertin. He was a methodical man, one of the reasons he was head of the mission to Sun One. He read from a soundscripted list.

"We've got about ten minutes, Ben Charles. Let's see. Object Lambda. You know as much about it as I do. It's anomalous and it's exciting. The only way to find out about it is this probe and it's in Earth's interest to make the probe succeed." He dropped his eyes to the page and went on: "There's no possibility of survival on the probe, of course, and this has undoubtedly had some effect on the psyches of all the beings there. To the extent that they have what we can map as psyches, I mean. But in my opinion it's the physical problems that have caused the trouble. Some of them are now dying —your predecessor among them, of course. Others are functioning poorly, probably because of ionization interference with their nervous systems. Or whatever corresponds to nervous systems. At any rate"—he checked off a point—"the beings aboard no longer constitute an orderly system. There's violence. Some of the deaths are from fights or murders. This is seriously interfering with the operation of the probe and threatening its very success. You know how important that is. If we blow this it'll be more than a hundred years before we get another chance. And finally"—Bielowitz folded the list and put it in his sporran—"your account here will be credited with double-rate pay for your services on the probe. Your equipment will follow, along with Doc Chimp here." He nodded civilly to the hairy little handyman who crouched next to Pertin. "And good luck to you both."

"Thank you, Gerald York," said Pertin gravely. He stepped up to the transport portal, waited for the signal and entered, giving a half wave to Bielowitz as the door closed behind him.

This was the fourth time he had found himself in a tachyon transporter box, or at least the fourth time that he remembered. They all looked about the same. On the inside they were featureless except for what seemed to be studs or nailheads almost completely covering each of the six interior surfaces. He stood there for a moment and felt nothing.

But something was going on. The sensors were counting, locating, and identifying every atom in his body, measuring their bonds to adjacent atoms, charting them in a precise three-dimensional matrix. The information obtained they encoded into a string of binary numbers, whereupon the great tachyon generators glowed into life, transmitting the numbers at the billibit per second in the direction of a point outside the farthest spiral arm of the galaxy, where the ship Ben Pertin had just volunteered to serve on—and to die on—lay waiting.

It was here—in the tachyon transmission chamber—that the great identity problem that plagued all the space-exploring humans had its genesis. Freud would have found its implications thrilling. It was another womb—with a completely different set of birth traumas.

All tachyon transmission was enormously expensive both in psychic cost and in cash. Its only justification was that it was indispensable. If you wanted to get a man or an instrument or a shipload of chess sets from one point in the universe to some other point across interstellar distances you had only two choices. One was to build a rocket preferably fusion-powered like the one Pertin was going to. You then had to launch it and set it on its way—and then wait. Wait indefinitely, for it could take anywhere from a decade or two to geologic eras before it reached another star, even one relatively nearby. If you wanted to go farther than that you would wait forever. A voyage from a spiral arm to the core or from any point in the galaxy to the deeps of intergalactic space was simply out of the time consciousness of any race but the T'Worlie.

The other method was faster. It dispensed with attempting to transport matter at all. Instead of sending an object you sent a blueprint of the object and had it built from plan at the destination.

The procedure was not simple. It required enormous expenditures of energy to generate the tachyon stream that carried the blueprint. It required complex scanning devices to measure every atom and molecule in the object to be transmitted and to encode positions and relationships for transmission. Above all, it required a tachyon receiver at the point to which you wanted to send—or go.

But granted all those things, you could "travel" at the speed of the tachyons, those particles whose lower speed limit was the velocity of light, and whose upper limit had never been measured.

The original object, of course, remained behind. It was scanned and its blueprints were encoded and then it was released unharmed.

He who volunteered for a tachyon trip also stayed at home. What flashed across space was a description of himself and what emerged from the receiving chamber at destination was a newly-built identical copy. There was no detectable difference between original and copy. It would have been a foolproof method of counterfeiting or of duplicating rare art objects—if it had not been so expensive in terms of power consumption that there was little worth the cost of duplicating.

As a method of duplicating human beings, the process was more successful—it was perfect and unique. The man who entered a tachyon transmission chamber to be sent to Sun One was the same man who walked out of it and returned to his home on Earth—and was also the same man who emerged on Sun One to take up a wholly new life. The continuity was absolute. Neither was a "copy" in any physical sense.

In a psychic sense the question of "reality" was troublesome. Every human who ventured into the star swarms was heavily briefed and indoctrinated with endless philosophical arguments and logical proofs. If you draw two triangles, which is the "real" triangle? (They both are, chorused the classes doubtfully.) If you build 10,000 Mercedes-Ford hovercars on an assembly line, which is the "real" Mercedes-Ford? (They all are.) Oh, the lecturers went on, there would eventually be differences among them. One car gets a scratch on the windshield when the wipers are installed. Another has a ripped gasket in its hydraulic system that, three years later, means its braking system has to be overhauled. But one is not an "imitation" or a "copy" of the other. Both are "real." All the Ben Pertins were Ben Pertin. The custom that gave them differing middle names was only a convenience, but they were all real—and, ladies and gentlemen, when you go out into space you will still be *you*. Not a copy. *You*.

And the classes would nod and grin at each other and go on to their next training class. But that night each of them in his or her solitary bed would lie staring through closed eyes at a future that held two separate identities. And all through the courses the couches of the analysts were kept warm with the bodies of trainees trying to come to terms with the question of "reality."

But the process itself was easy, quick, and painless. It was only moments until Ben Charles Pertin walked out of the box and shook hands with his head of mission.

"You're the best man I've got left," said Bielowitz. "Thanks."

Pertin then went back to his office and worked through the rest of the afternoon. He left a little early to meet his fiancée and take her to dinner and over the coffee she returned his troth ring.

At about the same time as Ben Charles Pertin was putting his ring back on his finger, inasmuch as time at two points separated by relativistic distances and velocities can be called the "same," Ben James Pertin pushed his way out of another, almost identical box on the probe ship.

He stopped just outside the portal, moving slightly to allow it to close behind him. His expression was grim. "Lucked out," he said aloud, looking around the unfamiliar chamber.

There was no one to hear—or to see the bitter and despondent look on his face. The chamber was deserted. The probe was in free fall and Pertin floated slowly away from the transport. Nothing else was floating in the room. There was no litter, no sign that any other being of any sort was within thousands of light-years and, as he listened, he heard not even any sound.

He swore softly to himself and twisted his body around to face the crated personal effects that were nudging their way out of the box. There wasn't a great deal to come—some tapes, some changes of clothing, personal items. At the end of the string of transmissions came his companion in the mission, Doc Chimp.

Doc Chimp thrust out a long arm and caught the handle of the door as he went by. He hung there for a moment, staring at his environment with an expression that was a parody of Pertin's own.

"Oh, wow, Ben Charles," he said sadly. "What a place."

"It'll be 'Ben James,' I think," said Pertin.

"Sure," said Doc Chimp dismally. "Me, I'm not going to bother. If you want to call me something different—call me stupid."

Doc Chimp was Earthborn, but he was not human. He was five feet three inches tall, weighed more than two hundred pounds and, in high-G environments, habitually walked on feet and knuckles. His parents had been chimpanzees, but Doc Chimp was something different.

For one thing, he had a sense of humor. He reflected it in the clothes he wore. Across his hairy barrel chest stretched a little red vest—open, with the coarse black fur sprouting through. He didn't need it for comfort, or for modesty—it was to please his own sense of the comic and for pockets to hold his automatic translator, the key to his private suitcase, and a supply of macadamia nuts, of which he was very fond. For modesty he wore shiny brown lederhosen. On his head he sported a kepi with a sand veil around sides and back and over its visor a bright green plume.

Even the plume was sagging dejectedly as he said, "I think I'm going to hate this place."

"We didn't come here to have fun. Where the hell is everybody?"

"Don't know, Ben James."

"Stow our stuff then. This thing won't stay in free-fall long; we'd better find somebody before it starts firing again."

"Certainly, Ben James. But somebody's coming now."

Pertin said, startled, "I don't hear anything."

"Neither do I. But I smell it. It's a T'Worlie, coming fast."

The probe ship was T'Worlie property, but fortunately for the other races of the galaxy the T'Worlie didn't have a very strong territorial imperative.

They had been civilized for a long, long time. They were an inquisitive race in their unhurried way and no doubt that was why they had been sending their probes out for hundreds of generations. Little T'Worlie rockets had radiated in all directions from their mother star, some of them aimed at other stars, some at nothing closer than the Great Nebula in Andromeda, ten million years' travel time away.

Only a race like that, deploying probes as lavishly and patiently as that, could have discovered the curious astronomical object called Lambda. No other race would have been in a position to do it. Sirians, with their limited time-binding capacities that reached no more than a week into the future, wouldn't have bothered. Nothing that promised some remote payoff interested them at all—which made them unattractive partners but inoffensive foes. Humans of course had no chance. Their technology wasn't up to the job. The farthest terrestrial probe was still climbing toward the turnover point on its now senseless journey toward 40 Eridani A.

But the T'Worlie thought long, slow thoughts and they were gently but persistently curious about everything. If their race lived long enough it would learn everything there was to know. None of them seemed to mind that no T'Worlie now alive would be present to learn it.

If the T'Worlie hadn't been what they were, probably no one would have found Object Lambda for another several thousand years. It had been discovered first by an unmanned T'Worlie scoutship and reported in a routine synoptic survey. It attracted no attention at all. When first observed its great distance and low luminosity put it at the very threshold of discovery and the traits that made it unique had not been detected.

Subsequent observations attracted more attention. The Object's weak spectral lines seemed to shift toward the violet rather than the red, which is to say that it was moving toward the galaxy instead of away from it. Curious. But the lines were so very weak, the point so very distant, and the orderly T'Worlie had many other things on their agenda to investigate.

Then, by accident, another scout turned up the same object in a survey.

It might not have been recognized if the computers of the T'Worlie had not been so patient and painstaking. The second scout had been launched five thousand years earlier, its vector several degrees away. From its point of view Object Lambda was in a wholly different part of the sky and its rate of approach, indicated by the spectral shift, quite different.

But the computers had sensed a possible match and clucked over the figures until they confirmed it. There existed a specific, if hypothetical, orbit and velocity which, seen from those two scouts at those recorded times, would have given exactly those readings.

From the estimated elements the computers made a prediction. They requested a special observation from still a third unmanned scout. Lo! it turned out as they had predicted.

Object Lambda was not more than 20,000 light-years from the edge of the galaxy and was approaching it at about one-sixth of light speed.

At this point the T'Worlie announced their discovery to the galactic civilization at large and began a study of their existing drones in that general part of space.

The T'Worlie drones were as small as an interstellar probe can be made—a scoop, a hydrogen ram, some instruments, and a tachyon installation. The T'Worlie had been launching them, thousands at a time, for tens of thousands of years. Since they had never invented war they were able to accumulate large quantities of surplus capital, so the probes were not a particularly expensive project for them. Like most early-industrial races, they had energy to burn. They burned it. Their planet was largely water covered—though they looked like bats, they were somewhat more analogous to flying fish. Their water was rich in D_2O and they spent its fusion energies profligately.

The T'Worlie drone model was standardized early. A program was set up under which each drone, upon reaching a point suitably distant from all others, flashed a tachyonic signal to the T'Worlie planet, whereupon the tachyon transmitters scanned, encoded, and transmitted whole new drones to the mother drone's unit. As each new drone flashed into being, it signaled in to the T'Worlie planet, was given a course and program of its own, and moved on. The effect was of an enormous globe of drones—at the end thousands of millions of them—expanding outward like the shell of a dead supernova.

The program was fully automatic and economical of everything but the energy eaten up by the tachyon transmitters—and for ten thousand years there seemed to be an endless supply of that.

At the end even the T'Worlie began to realize that their energy resources, though huge, were not infinite. The drone program was cut to a trickle. But it was never stopped and the great swelling bubble of drone ships expanded into globular clusters, out toward the neighboring galaxies, along the spiral arms, in toward the core of the Milky Way itself. It was a T'Worlie drone that had buried itself on Pluto and had been found by the exploration from Earth. Besides humans, T'Worlie drones had brought into the galactic society at least a hundred races at one time or another, almost half of the total so far located. Another race might have thought of using that fact to establish dominance for itself, but the T'Worlie didn't think that way. They had never invented empires, either.

So when the T'Worlie began to be deeply interested in Object Lambda it was easy enough for them to find some hundreds of drones on courses and at points that were not too remote from it.

The next job for the T'Worlie computers was calculating which of these drones was on the course that would involve least time and energy to divert it to the neighborhood of Lambda with its high galaxyward velocity. Fortunately a handful of drones in that section had been redirected inward much earlier to fill gaps in the global screen. Among them was one whose course would match Lambda's in less than five years.

After that there was no problem. The drone's matter receiver was put to work giving birth to automatic tools, hull sections, drive units, instruments, finally people. The tools went to work, assembling the hull sections, installing the drives, making room for the people. What had been a tiny kick-ram—no bigger than Earth's early Apollo capsule—was transformed and expanded into a thousand-meter vessel with room for a crew of several hundred.

There was, to be sure, one problem.

The rebuilt T'Worlie ship, now named *Aurora*, was big, but it needed to be big. It did not possess a great deal of surplus mass.

It was driven by the sequential explosion of hydrogen fusion charges, directional in a cone-shaped blast against a great battering plate at its base. Not much of the radiation from the fusion explosions seeped through the base plate, but some did. Enough for ionizing radiation constantly to bathe the members of the crew.

T'Worlie and Sheliaks, Purchased People and bits, robots and humans all responded to this in their individual, idiosyncratic racial ways.

But few complex chemical or electronic processes can operate without damage in the presence of ionizing radiation. It didn't matter who they were—in the long run it came to much the same for all of them.

They died.

III

Pertin and the chimp scrambled to the corridor entrance and peered out. The vinegary T'Worlie smell was strong now and they could hear the sounds of something happening outside: a punctured-tire hiss, a faint high-pitched singing.

A circus procession was sailing toward them down the center of the corridor. First came a T'Worlie, bat's head on butterfly body, no bigger than a pigeon but strong enough to be carrying a kitten-sized furry creature with enormous saucer eyes. Behind the T'Worlie, as it flew with powerful strokes of its green-spotted filmy wings, came a glittering cloud of steel-blue particles—like a swarm of gnats in the sun—and behind them, coming fast but decelerating strongly because of its mass, the square-edged form of a Scorpian robot, all fore jets pumping reaction mass.

The T'Worlie made its shrill whistling sounds and the Pmal translator on Pertin's shoulder rattled into life. "I identify you as a Pertin," it said with mechanical precision. "I propose you transfer at once to high-G accommodations suitable to your structure, mode urgent."

"Why, Nimmie!" cried Ben James, suddenly inexplicably, foolishly glad. "It's good to see you."

The T'Worlie braked with its filmy wings and the five patterned eyes studied Pertin. "Verify your statement of identity," the Pmal translator rattled in his ear. "Query implications. Request quick clarification."

"Why, it's me, Ben Ch—Ben James Pertin. From Sun One. Why, just yesterday I saw you in the social concourse, remember?" But he stopped; this copy of the T'Worlie he had known would not remember.

The T'Worlie hesitated. It was some Nimmie or other, Pertin was sure; the key to recognizing T'Worlie was not the five eyes or the small sphincter mouth with its cat's-whisker vibrissae, but the patterns on the wings. Green spots predominating on a pale yellow background—five of the bigger spots arranged in a sort of wobbly letter W, like the constellation Cassiopeia from Earth—yes, it was Nimmie, all right, Pertin knew. But perhaps a Nimmie he had never met, in some different line of descent.

The vinegary smell deepened. It was a sign of a polite cogitation in a T'Worlie, like a human being's *hmmm*. But Nimmie did not respond, exactly. He was distracted by the swarm of tiny beings which Pertin recognized as the collective entity called Boaty Bits. They swept into the tachyon transport room, swirled around Pertin and the chimp, and reformed under the T'Worlie's wings.

The kittenlike creature spoke with a voice like a purr. The translator rendered it as: "No time kidding around, get hell out!" The T'Worlie concurred. "Mode urgent. Accept transportation via robot. Your physical safety at risk!"

Doc Chimp chattered, "I told you I wasn't going to like this place, Ben James. It isn't safe. Of course, I'm only a monkey, so it doesn't matter much about me. It's you I worry about."

"You're an ape," Pertin corrected automatically, his brain concentrating on what the T'Worlie had said.

"Sure, but an ape that knows what isn't safe. Come on, Ben James! Let's do like Bat-ears says and split!"

The decision was taken from Pertin. The Scorpian hissed slowly by, still decelerating. It came to a stop, reversed itself and began to pick up momentum for the return. And as it passed Pertin and Doc Chimp it simply caught them up, each under a silvery tentacle, and bore them away. In reverse order the procession streamed away—first the robot with the two Terrestrial primates, then the swarm of bit creatures, then the T'Worlie and its passenger.

The probe was powered by huge nuclear thrusters. The power was off only for short periods, long enough to permit instrument readings or other work that could not be carried on during deceleration times. The rest of the time the entire ship suffered under a surging, uneven, pulsing drive that averaged nearly seven gravities.

The welcoming-and-transporting committee barely got Pertin and Doc Chimp to a place of refuge before the thrusters started again. The Boaty Bits had darted away at the first warning white-noise blast—they could not operate at all under thrust and had to find safety lest they be stepped on. The T'Worlie and his passenger were next to go, leaving only the robot to see to tucking Pertin and Doc

Chimp in. The robot had no particular objection to high gravity. Pertin had noticed that on the trip from the tachyon chamber. When the robot had to change direction it simply braced itself with a few of the steel-coil tentacles, stopped against whatever was in the way, and pushed off in another direction. The sensation for Pertin was like being tossed around at the end of a cracking whip, but he survived it.

The thrusting started before the robot had finished sealing their cocoons and it was even worse than the ride. The cocoons were meant to protect them against it—were tailor-made to their dimensions, equipped with the best of springing devices and every comfort. But there was no such thing as antigravity and that was what was needed.

The robot tarried for a moment. It could no longer jet about, but its tentacles held it easily off the floor, octopuslike. As the thrusts came they gave gently, then returned to position.

It seemed to be trying to communicate. Pertin, looking out of the cocoon faceplate, shrugged and spread his hands. One Scorpian looked like another, but if this one had come from Sun One it might recognize the human gesture. The trouble was, there was no way to tell whether it was responding to it.

Then the Pmal crackled into life: "—not move. Prerequisite explanations to you. I am repeating this on all comm frequencies. Most imperative you not move. Prerequisite—"

The sound faded again as the robot evidently shifted to another possible frequency. "All right," said Pertin, "we'll wait." But whether the robot understood him or not he could not say—it rested there on its tentacles, swaying under the thrust for a few moments more, and then undulated away.

The probe was decelerating furiously now—a roller-coaster ride multiplied by a hundred. There was a lot more noise than Pertin had expected—the thudding of the nuclear engines and the screeching of the torsion-bar shock absorbers that did their best to level out the thrust.

"Doc," he called. "Can you hear me?"

The chimp's cocoon was only yards away, but the *thud-screech* drowned out all other sounds. Pertin stared around. The room was half machine. Bright metal valves, gray plastic tubes coiling like dead entrails, colored screens where enigmatic symbols flickered and vanished. The walls were a sick, off-color green. No human would have designed a room like this, but of course it had not been designed for humans in the first place. It was a standard T'Worlie cocoon container, modified to take Terrestrials.

The *thud-screech* pounded on and on. Experimenting with the cocoon, Pertin discovered that it would meter an anesthetic dose into his veins—or even a selective analgesic to deaden the auditory nerve for a time and block out the remorseless nuclear thunder. But he didn't want to sleep. He wasn't tired—he wanted to get about his business. When your time is running out, he thought, you don't like to lose any of it.

Then he discovered that the cocoon had a built-in stereo stage.

The device was not wholly familiar, but with any luck he should be able to reach Doc Chimp, at least. His first attempt was not a success. He gently turned a knurled pointer under the hollow silver hemisphere of the stage and was delighted to see it fill with the shining silver mist that indicated it was operating.

But when the mist abruptly condensed it was to show the image of a nude blonde. "Mr. Pertin, sir," she caroled sweetly, "welcome aboard! Tonight for your entertainment, sir, you may watch me star in *The Belle of Bellatrix*. A thriller-drama of the love of a human beauty for a mutated alien and its fatal consequences. Feel the fear of the terrified girl! Share the wrath of her human lover! Feel the coils of the monster around her! Taste its dying blood! All these available by using the sen-sat coils in the small cabinet by your right hand. We have many other stereo-stage fiches, Mr. Pertin, and—"

He finally got the fiche turned off and the nude blonde vanished, still smiling. She dissipated as the camera zoomed in at her until at the end all that was left was a Cheshire-cat smile and the memory of her pale, slim figure.

Then the stereo stage blinked, swirled with color, solidified, and Doc Chimp's homely face was staring out at him.

"Got you," cried Pertin, pleased. "I didn't think I would be so lucky."

"You weren't," said the chimp. "I called you. I want to volunteer for something."

The chimpanzee face looked subdued. Pertin said, "What?"

"I think I ought to take a look around," said Doc Chimp sadly. "God knows I don't want to. But most of the beings will be tied down to pressure cocoons and I'm not."

"Good idea," said Pertin, a little surprised. He hadn't known the chimp well on Sun One—it wasn't that he was prejudiced against mutated animals, but of course they didn't have much in common.

But he had an impression of Doc Chimp's personality that was at variance with the act of volunteering for a solitary excursion into what might be trouble. Humorous, pleasure-seeking, a little lazy— that was how he would have described the chimp. "And thanks," he added. "Meanwhile I'll just send a report to Sun One if I can figure out how to use this stereo stage."

"Ah," said Doc Chimp, the mocking light in his eyes again, "allow me to instruct you, mighty human. You know, I figured you'd be too involved with high-level considerations to take much interest in hardware. So I checked out all the instrumentation with the T'Worlie on Sun One before we left."

It only took a few minutes for Pertin to learn to operate the stereo stage in his cocoon—it was not, after all, basically anything but a stereo stage and they were common all over the galaxy. Then he lifted himself on one elbow against the surging thrusts of the drive— the cocoon's self-adjusting circuits buzzed busily, trying to compensate for his unusual position—and watched the chimp cautiously lever himself over the side of his own cocoon, timing his movements to the surging of the drive, drop clumsily to the floor, mutter to himself angrily for a moment, and then slowly, painfully lumber off on all fours. He did not look back.

Pertin felt curiously better, as though he had discovered a friend where he had expected only an inadequate tool. He worked the controls of the stereo stage, got himself a circuit through to the recording fiches of the tachyon communicator and spoke.

"This is Ben James Pertin," he said, "reporting in to Sun One. Doc Chimp and I have arrived safely. There was no apparent problem from the transmission—at least, we look all right, are breathing, and our hearts are working. Whether our brains are scrambled or not I could not say. No more than when we volunteered for this, anyway, I'd guess. We have seen very little of the probe, have contacted only a few of the personnel, but in general the situation appears much as we understood it. At present I am in an acceleration couch, waiting for the next period of freefall for further investigation. Doc Chimp, who is performing very well and deserves credit, has voluntarily left on a scouting mission.

"I'll report again when I have something to say," he finished. "And —personal to Ben Charles Pertin: Have a good time on my honeymoon."

He snapped off the stage before he could decide to erase the last part of the message.

In spite of the best efforts of the cocoon his kidneys were beginning to feel bruised. The noise was even more of a problem. Efficient soundproofing kept it out of the cocoon as airborne vibrations —but there was too much of it to be shut out entirely. It seeped through as a continual thunder and squeal.

Pertin shut it out of his mind, thought of sleep, decided to brush up on his knowledge of the "hardware."

His first attempt at the fiche library of the stereo stage was only half successful. He just managed to avert the reappearance of the bare-skinned blonde and found he had secured a record transmitted by another member of the crew, race unspecified, apparently for a sort of public stereo-stage broadcast on its home planet. He shut out of his mind the public broadcaster he should have been getting ready to marry about this time—some thousands of light-years away he *was* getting ready to marry her—and discovered that the name of the vessel was the *Aurora*, or *Dawn*. The sound was, of course, different in the T'Worlie tongue and they had named it—but he learned it held the same connotations of new day and bright glowing promise in both cultures. He also found that he had only limited facilities for recreation—well, he had expected that. There were tape-fiche libraries for almost every known race of beings, some special high-pressure atmosphere chambers for a few of the exotics. That was it.

He had not learned exactly what he wanted, so he tried again. But instead of getting a fiche on the ship itself he got one on its mission, evidently a briefing record dubbed for humans. It was narrated by a man Pertin recognized as a minor functionary on Sun One.

He spoke in a high-pitched voice, smiling emptily at the stereo pickup: "We will show you all that is known about Object Lambda. First we will locate it, as it would be seen from Earth if visible at that distance."

Behind the speaker another stereo-stage tank glowed, shimmered, and filled with a universe of stars. Two of the brighter ones pulsed to call attention to themselves as the man spoke.

"Those stars are Benetnasch in Ursa Major and Cor Caroli in Canes Venatici. Those faint stars over there"—as he spoke a faint line of light ran around an area of the tank, enclosing it in a square —"are in Coma Berenices, near the north galactic pole. Now we'll take a closer look."

Benetnasch and Cor Caroli swam aside. The faint stars on Coma Berenices grew brighter, spreading apart, as the whole field seemed to move. The bright points fled out of the sides of the stage, and the few remaining ones became brighter until only a few were left—and beyond them ghostly faint blurs that were no longer part of the Milky Way but galaxies in their own right.

The illusion of motion stopped.

Another square of light formed around a patch of blackness in the center of the stage, indistinguishable from the emptiness around it.

The man said, "Now we've reached the limits of Sol-orbiting instruments. Object Lambda is at the center of that square, but it is invisible. It is slightly better in the far infrared."

The pattern of stars shimmered. Some became brighter, some dimmer, and in the center of the square appeared what might have been a faint and shapeless glow.

"This is not instantaneous," explained the lecturer. "It's long exposure and image-intensified. The Object would never have been detected in routine sweeps from Sol-based instruments. Even the T'Worlie scouts first detected it only because of a chance occultation of some stars in the Milky Way itself, seen from beyond. What we will show you next is not an actual observation but an artifact as it would look from Earth, as deduced from all available observations."

The object brightened a half dozen magnitudes as he spoke. "As you see, it has a sort of tipped-disk shape, like certain classifications of external galaxies. However, that's not what it is. First of all, it is far too small, perhaps only two or three A.U. in diameter. Second, its spectrum is wrong.

"At its apparent distance, as determined by its angular diameter— if it were indeed a galaxy—it should be receding at a major fraction of the speed of light. Of course we know from triangulation from the T'Worlie ships that that distance is wrong by a good many orders of magnitude. But according to its spectrum displacement it is actually approaching the Milky Way at nearly relativistic speeds."

The image blurred and disappeared and the plump human was standing there by himself. He said with satisfaction, "The T'Worlie scout has confirmed the speed as accurate in the range of 50,000 kps. Its position relative to Earth is some 30,000 light-years from Sol, in the direction of a point near the northern fringe of Coma Berenices. It is not an object from our galaxy. There are no spiral arms in that direction and few isolated stars or clusters much nearer than Sol itself.

"The T'Worlie backplotted its position from all observations of their drones, as recorded over the past several thousand years. Most of the data are ambiguous, but they did establish a probable line of flight. Their hope was to find a galaxy from which it might have been ejected and then to try to discover the reason for its high velocity.

"But they were only partly successful—I should say, only *possibly* successful. No such galaxy was detected. They did, however, find scattered star swarms which they believe to be the fragments of a galaxy that collapsed and then exploded more than a half billion years ago. It is the present working hypothesis that Object Lambda was ejected from that galaxy, by what means we cannot say."

The speaker's expression became enthusiastic. "Because of the anomalous nature of Object Lambda," he said, "the all-race conference on Sol One decided to transmit a full-size scout ship through the drone equipment and to staff it with a crew of volunteers of all races." *Volunteers!* thought Pertin, grimacing. "And after considerable effort in negotiating, it was agreed to include Earth humans as part of the crew. The political implications of this step are of enormous consequence and reflect the true coming of age of Earth humanity in the galaxy-wide confraternity of civilized peoples. Thank you," he said, bowed, smiled, and disappeared as the fiche came to an end.

Not a minute too soon, thought Pertin. A little more of that and he would have been ill. The cocoon had a fine built-in waste handling system, but there was no sense in overloading it.

IV

He began to see what Zara had been talking about when she accused him of an "Earthman's burden" complex. This whole deal sounded pompous, stupid, and faintly threatening, he realized, as it was put by the man in the briefing fiche. He tried to get his mind off that track—because he didn't want to question the cause for which he was, after all, going to die, and because above all he didn't want to think about Zara Doy. He was in the middle of trying to get *The Belle of Bellatrix* back on the stage when he became aware that something was scratching angrily at his cocoon.

For a moment he thought he was dreaming. He glanced back at the fading nude on the screen, then out at the nude girl who stood there.

But Pertin was a pretty superior type and he oriented himself quickly. It was no girl. It was not even human. It was a female young Earth person in shape, but the stuff of which the shape was constructed was not flesh and blood. It was silvery and bright, with a metallic hue. The eyes were orange and glowing. The hair was not made up of separate tendrils; it was a single solid piece, sculptured slightly for cosmetic effect. The creature was, in short, he realized, an "edited" version of some methane-breather or even more exotic chemistry, some being who was structurally nonviable in oxygen-bearing air and had had itself transmitted in an altered form to take up its duties on *Aurora*. And it was holding a scrap of what looked like paper.

The paper was not right side up. Pertin gestured and finally the "girl" understood and rotated it until, able to read it, he signaled her to stop. He read:

Sorry, Ben James, but you've got to get out of there. Things are worse than we thought. Angel here will carry you to me. They guarantee she won't drop you and squash you and actually, Ben James, this seems to be a matter of life and death.

The note was signed "Doc."

The girl did not speak, but the orange eyes blazed imperatively and the hands beckoned.

Pertin sighed, and opened the lid of his cocoon. "OK, Angel," he said. "Carry me away."

Astonishingly, being carried by the pseudo-girl was actually worse than being toted by the robot, but she moved more slowly and Pertin had a chance to see something of the ship. The *Aurora* was roughly cone-shaped. At the nose and through the midsection were living quarters for the several score individuals who manned it—that was where they had entered the scene. Since the crew varied widely, it needed a good deal of room. Space had been provided for methane-dwellers, space-flyers, and cold creatures as well as the more common forms based on $C-O_2-H_2O$—however, most of the nonviables had either stayed home or sent proxies or edited copies, so these spaces were largely empty. "Below" the living quarters and the space for the exotics were the hardware instrument sections. Below them still—in the sense of being sternward, toward the thrusters—was a layer of dense liquid for a radiation shield. It was not very effective, but of course, Pertin thought, it didn't have to keep them alive for-ever, since there was neither hope for nor point in the system's doing so. Below the shield was the tachyon transmission deck, where Pertin and the chimp had arrived. And beyond them, the thrusters and shock-absorbing gear. Since the *Aurora* was decelerating, it hap-pened that the "stern" of the ship came first in line of flight, but that made little difference to anyone aboard. It was "down." And down was the direction they were going.

The pseudo-girl had wrapped Pertin in a thick blanket of something like heavy-duty plastic foam. It was not as good as his cocoon by a long shot, but it kept him from dying of the ceaseless grinding changes in gravity as the thrusters shoved and the "girl" levered herself down a ladderlike series of projecting rods. She did not speak, nor acknowledge Pertin's efforts to speak to her. Either there was something wrong with his Pmal translator or she simply was not a conversationalist. But she was considerate enough and when they reached the instrument deck Pertin was bruised and sick, but alive.

"Ben James!" cried a familiar voice. "I told you Angel would get you here all right!"

Doc Chimp, thin lips grinning widely, scrambled over to help the silvery girl put him down, propping him against a sloping bulkhead so he could look around. His shipmates were worth looking at— a nightmare crew if he ever had seen one. Besides the pseudo-girl and the mutated chimp, there was a Sheliak in its high-G mode, looking like a flattened baker's bun on the deck. A web of plastic foam hid an apparently human-sized figure. Pertin also saw a row of small cocoons. Two were empty—the third contained a T'Worlie. From a speaker outside the cocoon a T'Worlie voice whistled a greeting and Pertin's Pmal translated: "I recognize your identity, Ben James Pertin. It is advantageous to all of us that you are here."

"Thanks, Nimmie," said Pertin, but he was staring at the plastic wrappings. A human being seemed to be concealed in them and, apart from himself, he knew of only one human being on the *Aurora* —one he didn't really want to think about.

He asked softly, "Doc, who's over there?"

Doc Chimp said, "Who? Her? Oh, I don't know her name. She's Purchased People from some low-G type or other. But she's on our side." The web stirred and a face peered out. It was human enough as far as features went, but the emptiness in the eyes told Pertin that Doc Chimp was right. "Anyway," chattered the chimp, "I better fill you in. Hell's really broken loose, Ben James. A bunch of beings tried to wreck the telescope. Not sure but what they've done it, too— the Scorpian's trying to see how much of it can be salvaged. If it and Angel here hadn't come along we'd be out of business till they could send new instruments through—and by then it would likely be too late."

The *thud-screech* was a lot closer here—apart from everything else, it was making Pertin's head pound. "What beings?" he managed to croak.

"Didn't see them. I just saw somebody disappearing into a passage, and then the Sheliak here came hellfire fast after him and saw me. For a minute he thought I was them." Doc Chimp cocked his head ruefully. "You could have found yourself short a monkey right there, Ben James, if I hadn't talked fast. So he commandeered me to help and we came down here to hold the fort. Oh, how sore my soles and knuckles are, Ben James, against the pounding of those rockets! But I did my duty. Then we got the observatory deck sealed off— they'd used a chemical explosive on the telescope and sprung a port —and then I happened to think of my human master, off there watching *The Belle of Bellatrix* without a care, and I persuaded Angel to fetch you."

Pertin frowned. "I don't quite see why," he objected. "I can't help."

"You can stay alive," declared the chimp. "I didn't tell you all of it. When they came for the telescope they had to get past the T'Worlie here. Well, you know T'Worlie can't do much against any being that can operate in high-G. But they tried to do what they could. And two of them got killed."

That was a shocker. One cardinal rule among the races of the galaxy was that no race could ever kill or seriously maim a member of another. Even on Sun One disciplinary problems were handled within the delegation of the race that produced the problem. Some provision existed for a body of other races sitting in judgment if the offending race failed to deal with the problem, but it had never had to be invoked. Pertin would hardly have believed the chimp if Nimmie hadn't confirmed the facts.

"They're crazy, then," said Pertin. "All right. We'll have to get a report back to Sun One. Nimmie, is your stereo stage operating?"

"Confirm that it is operative," sang the Pmal in his ear. "State that such a transmission has already been sent."

"Good. I'll have to send one, too, and I think the rest of us should, but that can wait." He tried to shift position as the floor surged particularly viciously. "Since we're here they probably won't try anything right away. What we need is a comb-out—get every being on board to account for his whereabouts and try to identify the ones who did it. For that we need a little freefall. Can we arrange that?"

The silvery girl spoke at last. Apparently she had heard everything, had simply seen no need to comment. "We can have a little freefall. We can have a comb-out. We probably won't need to arrange it right away as next observation period is only—" A meaningless squawk followed.

Doc Chimp filled in: "She means about fifteen minutes away."

It took a moment for Pertin to realize that the girl's words had been in English. He looked at her curiously.

"Fine," he said. "How many were involved in the bombing?"

"There were not less than three nor more than eight," piped the Pmal translator, responding to the T'Worlie's whistle.

"Out of how many in the crew?"

The T'Worlie hesitated. "There are in excess of three hundred thousand beings at present existing within the ship hull. Of these a large number are collective creatures."

"Not counting the Boaty Bits—I mean how many individuals?"

"There are not less than two hundred forty nor more than two hundred fifty."

Pertin said, "So the troublemakers are a tiny fraction. That's good. We'll broadcast a shipwide alarm. Most of the crew will cooperate—"

He stopped, staring at the silver pseudo-girl. "What's the matter?"

She had stretched out her fingertips toward the entrance port, almost in the traditional pose of a human sleepwalker. "The matter," she said in her incongruous colloquial English, the tones as deep as Pertin's own, "is that the tiny fraction of troublemakers is coming back."

In a moment no one needed the silvery girl's fingers to pick up the audios—the rushing sound grew rapidly louder, a harsh, crackling, electrical noise like the patter of a collapsing charge field. Into the room burst what looked at first like a single huge blue eye. "Sirian!" howled Doc Chimp in terror, and tried to leap out of the way. Even his simian muscles did not have the strength to leap against the suddenly surging G-force of the rockets. He stumbled and fell heavily against the silvery girl. At one stroke two-thirds of the beings able to move at all in the high-G field were immobilized—the T'Worlie, the Purchased Person, and Ben Pertin himself were wholly useless while the rockets were on. The Sirian, moving by electrostatic forces, was immune to mere 10 and 12-G. thrusts. He bore with him something that glittered, carried under the great forward eye in a pair of crablike pincers, tiny and almost invisible.

Pertin, thrown heedlessly just inside the portal, was first in the creature's path. He did not even have time to realize he was in danger before the Sirian was upon him. Then, oddly, the great eye stared at him. The Sirian paused, hesitated, and turned away. It propelled its glittering metal object at the bulkhead and at once reversed its field and sped away.

If that was another bomb, Pertin thought, they'd all had it now;

beyond that bulkhead was empty space from the last attack. The rest of the ship might be saved if the automatic seals worked fast enough, but he himself, the Purchased Person, Doc Chimp, and the T'Worlie would be boiled into outer space.

But he had forgotten the Sheliak. The soggy baker's bun that slumped on the deck and had taken no part in the conversation was still in fact an able and intelligent being. It acted faster than Pertin would have believed possible. The bun shape elongated itself into a sort of stemmed sea anemone, flowed like lightning up and down around the bomb, surrounding it, drowning it in thick alien flesh. It exploded.

The only sign the rest of them could see was a quick convulsive shudder of the Sheliak's tissue. Even the noise was muffled and almost inaudible in the constant thunder of the rockets.

The Sheliak glowed brilliant gold for a moment and, with a flash of the last light of its life, died.

They had defended themselves, but at the cost of one of their allies.

As though on cue the thunder of the rockets stopped and they found themselves blessedly free of the crushing G-forces. Doc Chimp, struggling to untangle himself from the silvery girl, went flying across the chamber, ricocheted against a wall, and brought up short next to where Pertin was struggling to disassociate himself from the plastic foam.

"Are you all right, Ben James?"

Pertin pushed himself free and caught the outstretched chimpanzee arm for stability. He ached in every bone and muscle and he was drenched in sweat from the trapped heat of the plastic wrap or from fear—he could not say.

"I think so," he said. "Why do you suppose he did that?"

"What? Who? You mean the Sheliak? Why, I guess it's their nature, Ben James—"

"No, not the Sheliak," said Pertin, but he didn't say out loud what it was that was perplexing him. He only thought it to himself. Why had the Sirian looked at him with death in his eye, then stopped and turned away?

It turned out there were two things wrong with Pertin's calculations. First, the odds weren't quite as favorable as he had guessed; he had not thought of the fact that the bombers might have allies who were as gravity-bound as himself and so hadn't put in an appearance. Second, he had not realized that most of the beings aboard the *Aurora* simply didn't want to be bothered with the mission. They were apathetic, hopeless, detached, or in some exotic mood with no human analogue. And perhaps, here and there, they just weren't about to take orders from an upstart biped from Earth.

The other problem was that the work of the *Aurora* lay in observing Object Lambda, not in tracking down aberrant entities. Not even the fact that beings of one or two races had killed beings of another race could cloud the goal. The Scorpian robot, when it returned from patching together what it could of the damaged optical equipment, would not even take time to talk to Pertin. It went at once to its assigned place in the instrument chamber and began to oversee the series of observations—this had been the reason, evidently, for the thrust stoppage.

Pertin could not even get the free-fall period extended to permit a full-scale search of the ship. The T'Worlie pointed out to him, reasonably enough, that since they were all going to die anyhow the first priority was the errand for which they had all undertaken to give their lives—to complete the observation of Object Lambda. And the laws of celestial dynamics were remorseless. A certain quantum of delta-V had to be applied to *Aurora*'s course. There was only finite time in which to do it. If they failed to put in the necessary velocity change the probe would fly past Object Lambda too fast to accomplish its several missions. So the T'Worlie were going to work on their instrument observations and nothing else, although they certainly wished him well, they indicated, in his search for the guilty ones.

What he had to work with turned out to be a party of five—Pertin, Doc Chimp, the pseudo-girl, the Purchased-People woman, and a small kittenish being who had joined the party to greet them on arrival. They couldn't even recruit the Boaty Bits to their cause. As soon as the collective creatures had learned of the bombing attempt they had departed en masse to swarm in some obscure corner of the vessel and unite all their intelligence on the problem of deciding what to do about it.

Pertin saw a great deal of the ship, but found no criminals. The one being they had certainly identified, the Sirian, eluded their search. If a being the size of a horse, emitting an electrostatic crackle every time it moved, could avoid the searchers, what chance had they for locating a party of unidentified marauders? Not any chance, answered echo. They found nothing.

About all they really accomplished was to move the acceleration cocoons for the low-G beings, whom they had come to think of as friends, close enough together so that they could watch out for each other when the delta-V thrust immobilized them. There were many such periods. By the nature of things, there had to be. It was *thud-screech* for at least eighty percent of the time, cut up the individual portions as they would. The *Aurora* had thousands of kps of velocity to shed as it overtook Lambda, if they were to avoid overrunning it too fast for orbiting their package. It made little difference how it felt to the members of the crew.

To Pertin it felt like being kicked in the kidneys four or five times a minute for hours on end. With allowances for variations in anat-omy, it felt very much the same to most of the beings. Frail little creatures like the T'Worlie were particularly hard hit—or would have been if it hadn't been for the fact that the *Aurora* was their own design, cocoons and all, and many thousands of years of thought had gone into reducing the damage to a T'Worlie frame in a cocoon. It was an advantage of a sort, but against it was the overpowering debit that on their native planet the surface gravity was less than a quarter-G. They were not creatures designed for strain.

The unfelt pain was the worst. Every explosion produced noise and thrust, but it also sleeted a few more curies of radiation through the crew's bodies and brought each member a few hours nearer to death. As the damage was not felt—and as there was nothing that could be done about it—the beings seldom spoke of it to each other.

For a half dozen periods no further violence occurred on board and the *Aurora* went on about its business. Pertin reserved his time in the cocoon for taping his endless reports to Sun One and for in-specting and studying the observation results on Object Lambda. When there was the blissful floating surcease—for half an hour or so at a time—he used it to roam around the ship. His announced purpose was to watch out for trouble. As time passed and trouble did not come he stopped talking about it, but continued to roam. He was interested in the ship on its own merits. Simply by its novelty it helped take his mind off the growing number of things he didn't want to think about. The *Aurora* was the first real spaceship he had ever seen. The concept seemed strange to him, considered against the tens of thousands of light-years he had traveled since he vol-unteered for tachyon transmission from Earth. It was normal enough, though. Sun One was thick with beings who had crossed and recrossed the galaxy a dozen times and never seen a spaceship at all.

Object Lambda was getting perceptibly closer—not to the eye, to be sure. No eye on the ship was in a position to see it anyway. But the cameras were able to make out more and more detail—not easily or well, because its intrinsic luminosity was so very low and in the low-energy long-wave part of the spectrum at that. They had even discovered that Lambda was not alone in space. Huge as it was, nearly two A.U. in diameter, it carried with it little orbiting fleas. The biggest of them was not much more than a mile through and the distance was still enormous, but the T'Worlie instruments had managed to detect them, even identify them. The longest periods of freefall came when the T'Worlie deployed their photon mirrors at the end of a tether, far from even the vibration of a footstep or shifting weight of robot mass in the ship—then their optical emulsions greedily drank up the scant flow of photons from Lambda and converted them into images.

If they had had a great deal of time, they could have answered all questions from there, or nearly all. They were in intergalactic space, and there was no such thing as haze beyond the advance scattering of their own rocket ejecta. But they had no time—the delta-V equation still ruled them and one of its tricky parentheses said that deceleration early was worth twice as much as deceleration late, since it gave them more time to slow down before they reached the neighborhood of Lambda. And then there was the mere fact of their rapid approach. The image did not remain still in the T'Worlie mirrors. It grew. Minutely, to be sure, but enough so that an exposure for more than an hour or so began to fuzz.

Even so, they learned. The nearest to pleasure Pertin ever found in a T'Worlie was when a particularly fine series of photographs had been taken and it was found to show a hint, a shadow, finally an orbital line for the biggest of the objects that circled Lambda. The pleasure was spoiled for Pertin when the calculations of orbit and time turned out to be impossible; Lambda would have had to have the density of the solar wind to have such a slow satellite. But the T'Worlie didn't mind. Explanations would come. If not then, later.

V

Between the hours of thudding acceleration and the briefer periods of his frenzied darting about the ship, Pertin was nearly always bone-weary and aching. Sleep did not rest him. Communication with Sun One was more and more an effort. The twelve-hour wait between transmission and reply—often it was more, when the other beings on the ship had queued up for their own transmissions—destroyed the rhythm of communication. By the time he had a response to his report of the attack on the instrument chamber he was already relaxing in his comforting awareness that the attack had not been repeated. Once he himself—or anyway that other self named Ben Charles Pertin—reported to him. The experience put Ben James Pertin into a tailspin that only a carefully metered dose of tranquilizers from the cocoon's store could deal with. From the expression on the other Ben Pertin's face, it was some strain for him, too. But the worst from Sun One was not from his other self; it was from Gerald York Bielowitz, who acknowledged a report, suggested some additional instrument readings that would be desirable, started to sign off, hesitated, and then added: "Oh, you'll be interested, I think. Zara Doy and Ben Charles were married three hours ago."

Pertin did not remember turning off the stereo stage or seeing the little figure collapse. He lay there for a long time while the cocoon stroked and soothed him, lifted him, lowered him, gently massaged what pains it could from his limbs. At some point he fell asleep. In his dream Ben Charles Pertin married Zara Doy, but he was Ben Charles and the two of them, intoxicated with the wine they drank and with each other, spoke sadly and wistfully about the other Ben Pertin who was busy about the task of dying on an alien spaceship a galaxy away. When he woke up and remembered he was that other Ben Pertin he was in an instant unfocused rage.

It was Doc Chimp who woke him. "Hey, Boss," he whined. "Listen, wake up. I've been limping around this hellhole of a ship looking for the Scorpian robot and—"

"Shut up," snarled Pertin through the outside communicator of his cocoon. His tone took the chimp aback. He slumped on his haunches, staring at Pertin's cocoon. He was in bad shape, Pertin saw, unwilling to care about what he saw—the bright green plume was sagging under the thrust of the rockets, the paws and knuckles were scarred and stained. That was why he was there, of course—feet and paws. He could withstand the constantly varying G-force of the thrusters with only a good deal of pain, so it was his job to do what Pertin could not when he was bound to the cocoon. A part of Pertin's brain told him that if he tried he probably could find ways of making the job easier.

The chimp's expression abruptly was no longer woebegone. It was angry. "Sure," he said thickly, "I'll shut up. Why not? We'll all shut up before long. Dead beings are all pretty quiet."

Pertin fought to control his anger. "We'll be dead all right. What difference does it make? Do you think this is a real life, what we're doing here? Back on Sun One we're alive and well—this is only a dream!"

The chimp wailed, "Ben James, I'm tired and I hurt. I'm sorry if I said something wrong. Look, I'll go away and come back, only—"

"Do that," snapped Pertin, and turned off the outside communicator.

The agitated hairy face stared dolefully in at him. Doc Chimp was by no means a jungle primate. The shape of his skull was different. The structure of his respiratory system was different. The very chemicals that flowed in his blood were different. But he was not human either. Doc Chimp—his formal name was not that, but it was all Pertin had ever called him—was one of the mutated animals that had been constructed for special purposes in the molecular biology plants on Earth. His quadridexterous limbs made the ape particularly useful even in freefall, where he could fling himself about with perfect ease from toe-rest to handhold, while humans like Pertin clumsily sprawled and spun. But he had his drawbacks.

A chimpanzee is simply not a human. His physiology is one count against him. He cannot develop the brain of a human because his skull is the wrong shape—and because the chemistry of his blood does not carry enough nourishment to meet the demands of abstract thought. He cannot fully master speech because he lacks the physical equipment to form the wide variety of phonemes in human language. The molecular-biology people knew how to deal with that. They could do things like widening the angle of the cranium called the kyphosis, thus allowing the brain to round out full frontal lobes, or restructuring tongue and palate, even adding new serum components to the blood like the $alpha_2$ globulins that bind human hemoglobin.

In practical terms what had been done to Doc Chimp and his siblings was to speed up evolution. But that was not quite enough. Two generations back Doc Chimp's ancestors could form only one or two of the simplest words and learn rote tricks—they lacked conceptual thought entirely. Doc Chimp had capacity. He did not have background or tradition. His 600 kyphosis was close to the human average so that his skull was domed—he possessed a forehead, could remember complicated instructions and perform difficult tasks. He was capable of assimilating the equivalent of a trade-school education in skill and of conducting the equivalent of cocktail-party conversation in performance. What he lacked was ego. His psychological profile was high in cyclothymia but also in ergic tension—he was always adventurous and always afraid. His emotional index was about equal to a human five-year-old's. Frightened, he ran. Angered, he struck out. Baffled, he wept.

Staring back through the cover of the cocoon, Pertin relented. "Sorry," he said, snapping the communicator back on. "What were you trying to tell me?"

"I've lost the Scorpian," wailed the chimp.

"Well? Are you supposed to be his keeper?"

"Be easy on me, Ben James," begged the chimpanzee. "I hurt all over. The robot was supposed to be getting ready for some new instruments that were coming in. He isn't there. The stuff's piling up in the transmission chamber and nobody to do anything about it. I'm afraid it'll get damaged."

"What about what's-her-name—Angel? Can't she store it?"

"She's trying. But the Scorpian is a specialist in this stuff and she isn't. None of the other high-G creatures is, as far as I can tell and —oh, Ben James, I've traveled so far trying to find someone who can help!"

He was a pitiable sight, his fur unpreened, his gay clothes smudged and wrinkled. Pertin said, "You've done your best, Doc. There is nothing I can do until the thrust stops—half an hour or so. Why don't you rest up for a while?"

"Thanks, Ben James!" cried the chimp gratefully. "I'll just take a few minutes. Wake me, will you? I—I—" But he was already clambering into the cocoon, his spiderlike arms shaking with strain. Pertin lay back and closed his own eyes, allowing the cocoon to do its best, which amounted to increasing its rate of stroking his back muscles, trying mindlessly to calm him down.

It had seemed very easy, back on Sun One, to volunteer for a task even though the end of it was his certain death. He had not counted on the fact that death did not come like the turning of a switch but slowly and with increasing pain—or that he would be watching friends die before him.

He didn't wake the chimp when finally he could move. He thrust his own way to the tachyon transmission chamber, hurling himself down the corridors carelessly and almost slamming into what turned out to be the silver pseudo-girl. He didn't recognize the creature at first, for she had unfurled enormous silver-film wings and looked like a tinsel Christmas-tree angel as she rushed past him.

In the tachyon chamber he found the T'Worlie, Nimmie, supervising an octopoidal creature from one of the Core stars in transporting crated equipment to an empty chamber. "What's happened?

Where did Angel go? What's this stuff?" Pertin demanded, all at once.

Nimmie paused and hung in the air before him, balancing himself against stray currents of air with casual movements of his wings. He whistled a methodical answer and the Pmal translator converted it to his stately and precise form of speech in English: "Of those events which have occurred that which appears most significant is the arrival of eight hundred mass units of observing equipment. A currently occurring event is that this equipment is in process of being installed. A complicating event is that the Scorpian artificial-intelligence being has elected to engage his attention in other areas. There are other events but of lesser significance. The being you name Angel has gone to bring the Beta Boötis collective beings to assist in the aforesaid installation. The reason for this is that they are cataloged as possessing qualifications on this instrumentation similar to that of the artificial-intelligence Scorpian. The precise nature of the stuff is tachyar observing equipment. I offer an additional observation —the purpose of it is to map and survey Object Lambda. I offer another additional observation—it will add to the radiation load by a factor of not less than three nor more than eight."

The T'Worlie hung silently in front of him, waiting for him to respond.

It had a long wait. Pertin was trying to assimilate the information he had just received. A *factor of not less than three* . . .

That meant that his life expectancy was not a matter of months or weeks. It might only be days.

Tachyar was simple enough in concept. It was like the ancient electromagnetic radar sets of Earth—the difference was that it used the faster-than-light tachyons to scan a distant object and return an echo of its shape and size.

Like ancient radar and sonar, tachyar generated a beam and measured reflections. The problem in using tachyar was the magnitude of the beam. Vast energies were used and the fraction wasted because of the natural inefficiency of the process produced ionizing radiation in large amplitudes.

Sun One must be taking the question of Object Lambda's satellites seriously if it was sending tachyar equipment to study them. The cost was high. It would be paid in the shortened lives of those aboard.

The single planet of the golden-yellow star Beta Boötis was like a cooler, older Venus. Because it was farther from its sun it was spared the huge flow of heat that cooked Venus sterile, but it possessed the same enormously deep, enormously dense atmosphere. It was spared the loss of its liquid water and its surface was covered an average of thirty miles deep in an oceanic soup. That was where the Boaty Bits had evolved. Aquatic in origin, they could survive on Sun One or the probe ship only in edited forms adapted for air-breathing—they could not live on high-gravity planets at all, since they had only the feeblest mechanisms for propelling themselves about their native seas. An individual Boaty Bit was about as useful as an infant jellyfish, and not much more intelligent. That didn't matter. The Boaty Bits never operated as individuals. Their swarming instinct was overpowering and linked together they had a collective intelligence that was a direct function of their number. A quarter of a million Boaty Bits equaled a man. On their home planet they sometimes joined in collectives of four or five million or more, but those groupings could be maintained only briefly even in their oceans and were never attained in their air-breathing edited forms.

When they arrived in the tachyon receiver chamber, they immediately took command. They were not specialists in tachyar gear. They were generalists. The skills required to assemble and install the crated instruments were built into their collective intelligence. What they lacked was operating organs, but the T'Worlie, his octopoidal assistant, Ben James Pertin, and every other being who came nearby were conscripted to be their hands and legs.

It was slow work. It would have been impossible in a gravity field for the T'Worlie or even for Pertin himself. But in freefall they were able to tug and guide the components into place and the T'Worlie had mass enough to make the connections and calibrate the equipment. When they were nearly done Doc Chimp turned up, angry because he had been left behind, and his muscle finished the job quickly.

As they were closing up, a blast of white sound came from the tachyon receiving chamber and warning lights flashed. Doc Chimp spun around, his wide jaw gaping. "Something important coming in?" he guessed.

"I don't know, but let's go look." They thrust themselves toward the chamber, got there just as the portal opened.

Three Sheliaks emerged.

They flashed out of the lock with a hollow hooting, long black shapes that rocketed toward the watching Terrestrials and bounced down on the green metal surface of the chamber. They clung in spite of the lack of gravity and flowed abruptly into new shapes—black velvet globes, thigh high.

Three more emerged—and three more. When fifteen had come to rest on the floor of the chamber the transmission stopped. Without a detectable sign all of them moved in synchronization. From flattened spheres, like baker's buns set in a tray, they suddenly turned luminous, flowing with patterns of soft color, then elongated themselves and stretched up tapered necks that rose as tall as a man.

The tallest of them, the first through the chamber and the nearest to Ben James Pertin, made a noise like compressed gas escaping.

Pertin's Pmal unit translated: "Take notice. We are under the direction of the collective council of Sun One. We are to take command of this vessel and all other beings aboard are to follow our orders."

Pertin's curiosity was suddenly transmuted into anger, a radiant rage that flooded his mind and overruled his inhibitions. "The hell you say! I've had no such instructions from the Earth representatives and I deny your authority."

The Sheliak paused, the long neck swaying back and forth. "Your wishes are immaterial," it stated at last. "We can destroy you."

Doc Chimp chattered nervously, "Don't make him mad, Ben James. You know how Sheliaks are." Pertin did; they were among the few races carrying built-in weaponry. On the infrequent occasions when the galaxy found itself troubled by unruly barbarians Sheliaks were employed to quiet the opposition—they were the Foreign Legion of the galaxy.

The long neck swayed toward the mutated chimpanzee. From the narrow orifice at its tip, sound exploded again and the translators shouted at the chimp: "Your name. Your function. Reply at once."

"I am Napier Chimski, technician," the chimp replied bravely.

The vase shape swung toward Pertin. "Your name and function."

"Oh, Ben James Pertin," he said, distracted by hearing Doc Chimp's real name for the first time. "I'm an engineer. But don't go so fast. I've just come from Sun One myself and I know there's no authority for one race to impose its will on another. I will certainly report this at once."

The Sheliak swayed silently for a moment—first toward him, then away. At last it said, "No orders for you at present. Go about your business."

Pertin drew himself up, holding to a wall brace. "You're my business," he said. "There are murdering beings aboard this ship. If you're here by order of Sun One, as you say, why don't you go find them and leave us alone?"

The Sheliak did not reply. All fifteen of them were swaying silently now. Perhaps they were conferring with each other—Sheliaks had learned vocal sounds only to talk to other races of the galaxy and the riddle of how they communicated among themselves was still unsolved.

"I certainly will report this," Pertin added.

There was still no response. The pointless confrontation might have gone on, but it was interrupted by the bright thrice-repeated flash of white light that meant the thrusters were about to go into operation again.

"Oh, hell," groaned Pertin. "Doc, we'd better get back to our cocoons."

"Never too soon for me, Ben James," agreed the chimp fervently, staring at the Sheliaks. "Let's go."

Doc Chimp and Pertin raced for the cocoons. The warning had caught others short. The corridors were full of low-G beings hurrying back to safety before the fusion rockets began again. The Boaty Bits arrowed along at top velocity, like a cartoon drawing of a swarm of wasps. An octopoidal creature launched itself from a wall off the end of the corridor with a multiple thrust of its legs and spun away, tentacles waving crazily. There was a thundering roar and three Sheliaks raced off, then another three and another, in V formations. A being like a six-legged spider monkey bounced back and forth, scratching and clawing for footholds, whining irritably to itself in a high-pitched tone.

And abruptly: "Ben James—look."

Doc Chimp was staring down a broad transverse corridor. Pertin saw a creature like an enormous blue eye, at least a foot across. It swerved as he looked, revealing the body behind the eye—a tapered torpedo shape glittering with patterned scales like blue glass. A stubby wing spread on each side, the leading edge thick and scaled and flowing smoothly into the body, the thin trailing edge a flutter of blue. Beyond the creature Pertin saw something bright, metallic, and angular.

"It's the Sirian, Ben James. The one that tried to kill us all. And wasn't that the Scorpian robot with him?"

Pertin reached out, grabbed a handhold and checked himself. The chimpanzee reacted a moment later and also stopped himself a yard or two farther down. "What are you doing, Ben James?"

"I'm going after them," Pertin snapped. "The Sirian's one of the murderers. And the robot's up to something, too."

"No, Ben James! You can't take the G-force. Let's let the Sheliaks take care of them—that's what they're here for."

The featureless green light of the corridor faded and changed to a dull crimson glow. That was the short-term warning—less than thirty seconds remained before the rockets began.

Pertin cursed. The chimp was right, of course.

"Oh, hell," he groaned. "All right, let's go—"

VI

They made it—not with any time to spare. They rolled into their cocoons as the first thrust struck and a moment later the regular repeated sound of the rockets reached them. The webbing spread itself over Pertin—he fell into the warm, receiving shape of the cocoon, but resisted its comfort. While it was still adjusting to his shape he was stabbing at the controls of the stereo stage, trying to summon all the cocoon-bound beings on the ship into conference. The automatic dialing circuits were equal to the job—the call was not something that was often made, but the physical capacity for such a conference existed.

But not this time. All lines were busy. Every being on the ship, it appeared, was already using his stereo stage for purposes of his own—most likely trying to transmit a tachyon message to his own people at Sun One, Pertin knew.

He fell back and let the cocoon massage him.

Thuuuuud-screech. Thuuuuuud-screech. The thrust felt more powerful than before, the tempo a bit faster. The thunder and groan of the drive made it nearly impossible for Pertin to think, but he had to think.

The problem on his mind was not one of the obvious ones—what to do about the Sheliaks, how to deal with the murderers, the completion of the mission. His mind worried at those a moment at a time and then let them go. They required action, not thought, and action was not available to him while the fusion rockets roared.

Instead he thought about his unpleasant discovery that there wasn't much in being a hero. His heroism had been entered into lightly enough, but he supposed that was not in itself rare. How many Medal of Honor winners had volunteered for combat patrol simply because they were bored with sitting in a foxhole—and had found themselves caught up in events that made them immortal reputations?

But his heroism was not even going to get him a medal. No one would ever really know what was happening on this ship, because it was absolutely certain there would be no survivors. Either *Aurora*'s mission would succeed—in which event the galaxy at large would accept the crew's sacrifice complacently—or it would fail. In the latter case the beings on board would all be thought of, when they were thought of at all, as that sorry bunch that wasted itself for nothing.

Ben James Pertin bounced about in his acceleration couch, trying to make terms with a double-bind. His was the first generation of men who knew that they could live—somehow—until they died of old age. This would be true even if they were run over by a truck or murdered by a lunatic. Ben Pertin might die, but Ben Pertin would live.

Pertin and his fellow humans who had duplicated themselves for tachyon transmission were not immortal. They owned all the decaying weaknesses of the flesh. Their brain cells grew fewer in number every day, like yours and mine. The collagen hardened in their tissues. The calcium migrated remorselessly from bone to blood vessel.

They would die, each of them. But each one of them had the statistical certainty that not *all* of him would die prematurely. One Ben Pertin might die of cancer, another of pneumonia. One might succumb to an OD of the drugs that made these paradoxes briefly tolerable for some. Another might cut his throat. Another might perish pointlessly in an expendable job. But *some* Ben Pertin (who would always be *the* Ben Pertin to himself, at least) would survive and throw off as many identical copies of himself as he wished or circumstances required.

It gave them a certain courage in the face of death. The personal involvement that every other generation of man had felt—the shrieking rage that when he went some irreplaceable part of the universe would be gone forever—was no longer there. They were not individually irreplaceable at all—they replaced themselves with tachyon copies.

Nevertheless, when each of them died he felt that death as a death and saw it as the same grinning skull of fear that it had been for Adam.

And when that death was close it was terrifying.

With the thud and rasp of metal roaring at him, his cocoon see-sawing in the violent deceleration of the rockets, tired, sick, angry, and hopeless, Ben James Pertin faced the fact that there was nothing left in his life anywhere that would give him one more moment's joy.

Another Ben Pertin, tens of thousands of light-years away, was trying to soothe his bride. He said, "Honey, I knew what I was getting into when I volunteered. I was willing to go through with it. That other me on the ship doesn't feel any different about it."

Zara Pertin said harshly, "That other you is going to die, Ben Charles."

"But I'll still be alive."

"And he'll be dead. Don't you understand me? I love you. And he is you—and I don't like to think about what is happening to him." She turned over, giving her back a chance to collect some of the UV tan from the lamps overhead, and took off her goggles. She said, "What's it like there now, Ben?"

"Well—" he said.

"No, I want to know. Tell me."

Ben Charles looked around the simulated little beach beside the great water tank that was their "ocean." No one else was near the spot—he and Zara had come here for that reason, but Ben Charles found himself wishing for an interruption. She turned her head and looked at him and he shrugged.

"All right. It's bad," he said. "The sensors in his acceleration cocoon already report some destruction of the white corpuscles. Pretty soon he'll start having nosebleeds—then he'll bleed internally. He'll be getting weaker, running a temperature. He has had more radiation than he can recover from and he keeps getting more. Before long he'll die." He paused, then answered his wife's unspoken question: "He'll probably go within a week."

Ben Charles propped himself up on one arm—an easy posture. Even here the effective gravity was only a negligible fraction of Earth-normal. He looked out at the thousand-foot cusp of water, curving upward to meet the bulkhead at the far end. Other water-tolerant beings were using the reservoir for their own equivalents of sport—it was a favorite spot for such purposes. But none of the others were human.

Ben Charles Pertin worried for a moment at the permanent problem of what he meant when he spoke of death. He came to several conclusions. The first was that it was spoiling his honeymoon. The second was that he did not feel as though he were dying—in spite of the fact that he knew that some light-years away he was doing just that—and even there loving Zara. The third was that he could not spend any more time on that particular concern. The bad thing about dying, he reflected, was that you leave someone grieving—and Zara, he knew, was grieving. This brought him back to the question: who was dying?

He looked at his wife. She was not weeping now, but she had been. The stain of drying tears lay at the corners of her eyes.

"I'm sorry, honey," he said.

She shook her head without words.

After a moment he made himself add: "It might not even be a week. Radiation alone will give him a few days, but there are plenty of other things on the probe that could kill him. Some of the beings are becoming violent. The electronic ones are malfunctioning, because the radiation affects their synapses. They're going insane, really. A lot of the organic ones are sick. All of them are scared. There have been deaths. From violence."

"I should have gone with you," Zara said thoughtfully.

"Oh, now, really! That's stupid! What would be the point?"

"I would have felt better about it—and so would you. He." She stood up, smiling, her mind made up. "If you have to go again, dear," she said, "I'm going, too. Now I'm hungry. Race you back to the apartment!"

VII

Tachyar verified the paths of the little bodies orbiting Lambda—the mass estimates were right, thus the density estimates were right. Object Lambda's average density was about that of a high vacuum. Nevertheless, it appeared to have a solid surface.

Pertin greeted the news with apathy. There were more immediately important developments on the ship and the ultimate purpose for which the ship existed didn't seem particularly interesting anymore.

For one thing, the tachyon transmission chamber was shut down. For better or for worse, there would be no more imports, no additional beings, no additions to the crew—nothing.

The chamber's last function had been to bring in freshly minted structural members and drive units. They were now being assembled into a small drone. It took form as a squat dense object, all fusion drive and instruments with no living space for a crew. It would have no crew. It would carry nothing but itself and the tachyon receiving crystal that had been the *Aurora's*.

Pertin had no part in the construction project. The Boaty Bits directed it and the metal pseudo-girl and a few other high-G types carried it out. He looked in on it once or twice. Besides the structural part, brought in on the tachyon receiver, the small ship used bulkheads and beams from *Aurora* itself. It seemed to Ben James Pertin that vital parts of the parent ship were being seriously weakened. The fact interested him as an engineer. As a being whose life depended on the structural integrity of the *Aurora* he didn't consider any concern he felt worth mentioning. Whatever was happening was planned. If the life of the *Aurora* was being shortened thereby, it was because the beings doing the planning had decided the ship was wholly expendable.

The only nonexpendable part of the *Aurora* now was the little drone being put together in its belly.

The drone comprised only three elements: A tiny tachyon receiving unit—built around the crystal from *Aurora's* own—in a globular body fitted with weak handling-propulsors, suitable only for correcting minor errors in the elements of an orbit. A thick half-shell of metal-bonded ceramics on one side, an ablation shield designed to flake and burn away, disposing of excess heat. And, outside the ablation shield, the enormous fusion-propulsion engines.

It was a high-deceleration drone. It would be launched from the mother ship at some point near Object Lambda. Its fusion jets would slow it radically. Stressed as it was, with no living creatures aboard, it could endure hundred-G delta-V forces. But Pertin's engineer's eye recognized the implications of the design. Even those forces would not be enough. The drone would make use of Object Lambda's enormously deep atmosphere as well. It would dip into it, shedding velocity by burning it off as friction, blazing like a meteorite from its ablation surfaces. That frightful crunch would slow it to manageable relative speeds—as it came out of its first skip into Lambda's air it would be close enough to orbital velocity for capture. Then its propulsors could take over the simpler job of making neat the elements of the orbit—and a tachyon receiver would be in place around Object Lambda.

What about the mother ship?

The implications were clear to Pertin. All the evidence he needed was obvious in the construction of the probe. If such forces were needed to put the probe in orbit, there was no hope that *Aurora* could join it. Its kilotons of mass were simply too great for the forces available to deal with. Even if the forces were available its living cargo would be pulped by the delta-V.

Aurora would drop its cargo, flash by Object Lambda, and continue through intergalactic space. It would no longer have fusion mass for its reactors. It would stop decelerating—to all intents and purposes, it would be only another chunk of intergalactic debris on a pointless orbit to nowhere.

Its course would continue to take it toward the galaxy itself. In time it would approach some of the inhabited worlds within mere light-years, perhaps.

But that time would come too late to matter to anyone. It was a matter of thousands of years of travel time to even the fringe stars of the galaxy—and by then there would be little left of even the dust of its crew.

They had been written off.

Meanwhile, the deceleration phases were getting longer, the zero-G pauses for observations shorter and less frequent. Sun One had lost interest in the observations that could be conducted from *Aurora*. It was only waiting for the secondary probe to go into orbit.

All through the ship, the living crew members were showing attrition. They were weaker and less rational, less capable of fine distinctions. The automatic machinery was running the ship.

As it poured the last of its fuel reserves into space to brake its flight it manufactured enormous clouds of radioactive gas. They were not a hazard to the ship's crew—it was too late for such trivial affairs to matter to the doomed beings. But they had caused some concern to the planners on Sun One. A thousand generations later they might be a pollution problem. But by then, no doubt, tachyon transport would itself have been superseded and no one would any longer trouble with such primitive concerns as the crude STL transport of mass.

The gas clouds as they departed did leave some trace of ionizing radiation, added to the larger increments from the blasts themselves and from the tachyar. The combined radiation was a witches' brew of gammas and alphas and betas—now and then primary particles that coursed through the entire space of the ship from hull to hull struck an atomic nucleus and released a tiny, deadly shower of secondaries.

It was the secondaries, the gammas, that did the dirty work. They interfered with the electronic functions of the computers, robots, and metal beings. They damaged the instrumentation of the ship. Above all, they coursed through the organic matter they encountered, knocking out an electron here, loosening a molecular bond there, damaging a cell nucleus, making a blood vessel more permeable. The whole organic crew was on hourly doses of antirads, giving support to their internal workings. It was not enough. Still the radiation

soaked in and struck at them. Blood, ichor, sap, or stew of exotic bi-
ologies, the fluids that circulated in their bodies changed and grew
less capable of supporting life. Physically they grew weaker. Mentally
they became cloudy.

Taken out of the environment and rushed to an antirad clinic—
like victims of an industrial accident—many of them still could have
been saved.

But there was no place to take them. No part of the ship was free
of penetrating ionizing radiation and every hour more and more of
the chemistry of their bodies was damaged.

"Ben James, Ben James," sobbed the voice of Doc Chimp.

Pertin roused himself. The thud and screech of the drive was still
loud in his ear. Every time the floor drove up to meet the cocoon the
single huge bruise his body had become screamed with pain. Inside
his chest his lungs felt as though they had broken loose and were
beaten sore against the inside of his rib cage.

He peered blearily out of the cocoon. The chimp was staring pathetically up at him. The great green plume of his hat was broken.
His fur was splotched with dirt and blood. The rubbery features of
his face looked almost as they always had, except for an open cut
along the flat, sculptured nose.

"What?" demanded Pertin thickly.

"I have to hide, Ben James. The Sheliaks are after me."

Pertin tried to sit up and could not. "They're not here to hurt you,"
he pointed out.

The chimp whimpered, bobbing on all four limbs as he braced
himself against the rocket thrust. "They will! They're mad, Ben
James. They killed the T'Worlie. For nothing—just killed him. And
they almost killed me."

"What were you doing?"

"Nothing! Well, I—I was watching their mating ritual. But that
wasn't it—"

"You idiot," groaned Pertin. "Look, can you climb in here with
me?"

"No, Ben James, I don't have the strength."

"It's either that or let them catch you."

The chimpanzee whimpered in fear. Then abruptly, on the upsurge of the ship against its shock absorbers, sprang to the side of the
cocoon. Pertin grabbed at him and pulled him inside just as the next
thrust caught them. Doc Chimp weighed some two hundred pounds
at Earth's surface. The delta-V gave him a momentary weight of
nearly half a ton, all concentrated on Pertin's shoulder and chest.

He grunted explosively. The chimp was caught with part of his side still across the metal lip of the cocoon, but he made no sound beyond the steady *sotto-voce* mumble of fear.

Pertin tried to make room behind him, in a place where the cocoon had never been designed to take a load. It tried its mechanical best to give support to the double mass. It was not adequate to the job. Pertin discovered when the next thrust came that his arm was still caught under the chimp. He helped, managed to free it on the upsurge, discovered it was not broken. He slammed down the privacy curtain, hoping the Sheliaks would not look inside if they came.

"Now," he panted, "what did you say about Nimmie?"

"He's dead, Ben James. They killed him. I didn't mean any harm," the chimp sobbed. "You know how the Sheliaks reproduce—by budding, like Terrestrial plants. The young ones sprout out of the old ones and grow until they're mature enough to be detached."

"I know." Pertin had only the vaguest acquaintance with Sheliaks, but everybody knew that much. They didn't have sexes, but their conjugation provided a union that shuffled up the genes.

"Well, that didn't look like fun to me, but I wanted to see. Nimmie told me to go away. He couldn't—he was in one of the spare cocoons, and couldn't move. But he said they'd be mad." The chimp switched his position and Pertin shouted in pain as his upper thigh took part of the chimp's weight on a rocket thrust. "Sorry, Ben James. It was disgusting, the way they did it! Any two of them can get the urge. They sort of melt down and flow together like jelly. All the body cells migrate, pair off and fuse. Finally they form again into a sort of cactus-shaped vegetable thing that buds off haploid, mobile creatures. Those are the Sheliaks we see."

"You wanted to watch that?" asked Pertin, almost able to laugh in spite of discomfort, in spite of Nimmie, in spite of everything.

"Yes, Ben James. Just for curiosity. And then there's my friend, Fireball. He's the Sheliak who was here all along. He was nice, Ben James. I miss him."

"I didn't know you knew any Sheliaks."

"Not well. But he was with me, helping to guard all of you. And we talked."

"You sound as if he's dead, too."

"Might as well be. That union is a sort of individual suicide. It's something you do for the race and because your glands push you that way. But it's the end for the individual. It wipes out all conscious memory and individual personality. I guess that's why Fireball couldn't understand our notions of sex.

"Anyway," he said, "it was all right while Fireball was here alone. He wasn't lonely; or anyway, he didn't want any other Sheliaks around. When they're in danger, you see, they just can't help conjugating. It's a survival mechanism. The radiation was danger, and he knew that the only way for him to keep alive was to stay away from his own people. When the new ones came aboard he was actually afraid of them. He knew when they came close they were likely to set off a biological process they couldn't control. And when it was over—"

The chimp swallowed. He thrust himself up on an elbow, regardless of pain, and stared into Pertin's eyes.

"He didn't know me, Ben James! The two new ones that were half him, they came after me. The T'Worlie saw what was happening and tried to stop them—and that's how I got away, while they were killing him. So I ran. But where is there to run to in this ship?"

When they could move again they found the T'Worlie easily enough. He was floating upside down, purplish drops of blood, perfectly round, floating beside him. The little vibrissae around his sphincter mouth, more like cat's whiskers than anything on a proper Earthly bat, were perfectly still. Nimmie was rigid. The pattern of five eyes was unmoving. The intricate pattern of blotches of color on his filmy wings was fading.

There was no one else around. "What'll we do with him, Ben James?" chattered the chimp.

"Throw him out into space, I guess," Pertin said harshly. Normally the mass would be useful in the tachyon receiver, but there were to be no more incoming tachyon transmissions.

It didn't do to think of that. He stared at the T'Worlie. A slow incrustation of a thick gel was matting the fluffy surface of Nimmie's chest, and where it had once protruded sharply, like a bird's wishbone, it was crushed and concave.

Pertin felt the muscles on his face drawing taut, perhaps partly because of the intense vinegar reek. He said, "Why would the Sheliaks break up equipment?"

The chimpanzee stared at the mess in the room. Bright green and orange transistors and microchips were scattered like jigsaw pieces in the air. "I don't know, Ben James! None of that was that way when I ran out of here. Do you suppose they just lost their temper?"

"Sheliaks don't lose their temper that way. They broke up instruments on purpose. What was coming in before you decided to play Peeping Tom?"

"Oh—" The chimp thought. "More reports on Object Lambda.

The density was confirmed. Very low. Like a sparse cloud of inter-stellar gas."

"We already knew it was Cloud-Cuckoo Land. That couldn't have had any effect on them."

"Something did, Ben James," cried the chimp. "Look, we've got to do something. They'll be looking for me, and—"

"Unless," said Pertin thoughtfully, "it wasn't the Sheliaks who did it. The robot was up to something. And there are still a couple of Purchased People not accounted for, and—"

"Too late!" howled the chimp. "Listen, Ben James! Somebody's coming!"

But it wasn't the Sheliaks who came in on them—it was Angel, the silver pseudo-girl, the heavy-planet creature in human form. Her fingers were outstretched toward them, listening, as her great foil wings drove her forward.

Behind her came the Scorpian robot.

They made an eerie pair, the striking orange-eyed girl with her coif of metallic hair and steel-bright body hues and the mechanical creature shaped like a metal octopus. Its central body was a massive disk, the color of the pseudo-girl's flesh, and its silvery tentacles made a fringe of snakes around it. A greenish membrane that bulged above the upper surface of the disk fluttered, producing a drum-roll of sound.

Pertin's Pmal translator obediently turned it into recognizable words: "Do not resist. We wish you to come with us."

"Where?" he demanded.

There was no answer, at least not in words. Pertin was caught in something like a metal whip that stung a trail of fire around his waist. It was one of the robot's tentacles. It pinned his arms and the pseudo-girl launched herself at him, her metal fist catching him full in the face. Floating as he was, the blow was robbed of some of its force, but it doubled him, flung him back against the robot's lash, dazed with pain and sobbing for breath.

He heard a cry of anguish from Doc Chimp, but could not turn to see what was happening. The vinegary smell of the dead T'Worlie penetrated his nostrils, mixing with the tang of his own blood.

"Why?" he croaked, and tried to raise his arms to defend himself as the girl dropped toward him again. She did not answer. She was on him like a great silvery bat, metal feet kicking, shining fists flying. The lights went out. He lost touch with space and time.

Pertin was not wholly unconscious, but he was so close to it, so filled with pain and confusion, that he could hardly remember what happened next. He had a fugitive impression of great shapes whirling around him, then of being carried away while someone behind him sobbed his name, the voice diminishing slowly in the distance.

Much later he opened his eyes.

He was alone in a part of the ship he knew only sketchily. A large open cocoon hung from a wall and inside it was what looked like one of the Purchased People. Pertin's face was swollen and his eyes were not focusing well at all—he squinted, but could not make out the features on the person in the cocoon. It appeared to be male, however, and it appeared to be in the last stages of dissolution.

It moved and looked toward him. A caricature of a smile disturbed the weeks-old beard and the dry tongue licked the lips. A cracked voice muttered something, the tone hoarse and indistinguishable.

"Who are you? What do you want?" demanded Ben James Pertin.

The figure rasped a sort of hacking cough, that perhaps was meant for a chuckle. It tried again and this time its words came clear enough—clear and familiar in a way Pertin had not expected.

"I want to talk to you, Ben," it croaked. "We have a lot in common, you know."

Pertin frowned, then his swollen eyes widened. He pushed himself toward the swathed figure, caught himself at the lip of the cocoon and stared down.

The eyes that looked up at him were pain-filled but familiar. He was looking into his own, battered, obviously dying face.

VIII

Pertin remembered a time—months ago.

He had gone to the tachyon transmitter and lightheartedly enough given his blueprint to the scanners and allowed one self of him to be beamed to the *Aurora*. It had not seemed like an important thing to do. At that time it had not been clear to him that the *Aurora* was a doomed ship. At that time he had had no one to consult but himself —Zara Doy had still been only a casual acquaintance, a new girl from Earth with a pretty face.

"Ben Frank," he whispered.

"Right as rain," croaked the ghastly voice. "And I know about you. You're Ben James Pertin and you've been aboard two weeks now. Not very thoughtful of you, failing to visit a dying relative."

"But I thought you were already dead! They said— I mean, I wouldn't have had to come, if—"

"Blaming me, Ben James? Well, why shouldn't you? How long

have I lain here blaming you—and me—and all the Ben Pertins there ever were." A spasm of coughing racked him, but he talked right through it. "I wanted them to think I was dead. Only fair, isn't it? They were killing me—and now I've killed their Project Lambda."

"You?"

"With a lot of help. My Sirian friends were the first and best, but there have been plenty since. It was the Sirians who told me you were aboard—you gave one of them quite a start when he saw you in the instrument room. Wrecked his mission, you did."

Coughing drowned out the voice. Ben Frank convulsively clutched at the cocoon monitor controls. A warning panel lit over the bed. He was very near death, but the cocoon was not yet defeated—it metered colored fluids into the external blood supply that was trying to replace the destroyed blood cells.

"I only have a few minutes," Ben Frank Pertin gasped. "I don't mind. But I'm not finished, Ben James. You have to finish for me. Destroy that probe. I don't want it to succeed. I don't want Sun One to get its orbiting body around Object Lambda."

"But then we—we'll all have died in vain!"

"Of course it's in vain. What's the sense of all this? A chunk of useless matter—thousands of light-years from anywhere—going nowhere. Project Lambda! Do you know how many lives it has cost? I want you to wreck it for me, Ben James, so those fools on Sun One will know better than to try this same stunt another time—"

"But it's not a stunt," objected Ben James Pertin. "It's important. That object is something special, solid but like a cloud—"

"Cloud-Cuckoo Land! It's not worth a single life. Anyway, it's done already, Ben James. My friends are wrecking the probe right now. I only called you here because—"

He paused, coughing terribly. The face that was so much like Ben James's own was aged with the weary agony of radiation death.

"Because," he gasped, "I want some part of me to stay alive. If you keep the tachyon receiver you can live, Ben James. Weeks—maybe months! But once it goes there will be no more food, no more air, no more fuel. I want—"

But what he wanted to say at the last Ben James Pertin would never know. His duplicate suddenly gasped for breath, made a strangling sound, and was still.

After a moment Ben James pulled the privacy screen over the face that was his own and turned to leave.

Halfway to the launch chamber he ran into the Sheliaks.

They were in pursuit of two beings, one of them the Purchased

People woman, the other Doc Chimp. The Sheliaks looked strange and in a moment Pertin realized why. They were smaller than they had been. Essentially they were children now, some of their mass lost when they budded. But their behavior was childish only in its reckless disregard for consequences. As far as their quarry was concerned, it was lethal.

Pertin did not pause to speculate on issues. Doc Chimp was in danger and Ben dived to the rescue.

He collided with one of the Sheliaks. It was like tackling a six-foot lump of chilled, damp dough. No bones, no cushioning fat, just a great dense mass of muscular fiber. The Sheliak automatically cupped around him and, linked, they went flying into the wall. The corridor spun around him, a nightmare of blue-green light and red-black shadow and corpse-colored beings.

"Stop!" roared Pertin. "Wait—listen to me—" But no one wanted to talk. They were all on him, thrusting, striking, crushing, using whatever offensive capacities their mobile anatomies gave them. He fought back, using skills he had never known he had. His hands were black and slippery with blood, no doubt much of it his own. Bravely the woman and Doc Chimp had turned back to fight, but it was three of them against more than a dozen Sheliaks and the issue was not in doubt.

What saved them was Angel, the silver pseudo-girl. Her carven face remote as a statue's, she drove toward them with great sweeps of her wings. Coronas of electrostatic fire haloed her fingers and wingtips —something gun-shaped and deadly was in her hands. The Sheliaks, all at once and in unison, turned to meet her. The gun-shaped thing hissed and a white jet crackled toward them. It passed near enough to Pertin for him to feel a breath of icy death, but it did not strike him. It grazed the Sheliak who held him and at once the being stiffened and began to drift. Behind them, where the jet had struck, the wall became hidden under a broad patch of glittering frost. A cloud of white vapor billowed around it.

In the haze Pertin caught sight of Doc Chimp and the Purchased People woman, momentarily forgotten as the Sheliaks turned against the stronger foe. The woman was badly hurt. Doc Chimp was helping her, his hairy face turned fearfully toward the Sheliaks. Pertin joined them and the three of them moved inconspicuously away.

When they were two corridors away and the sounds of battle had diminished they paused and inspected their injuries. Pertin himself had only added a few bruises to a total that was already too large to worry about. The chimp was even more battered, but still operational. The woman was worse off. She was bleeding profusely from a gash on the upper arm. Her face was grotesquely puffed, both eyes were blackened and one leg was bent at an angle anatomically impossible to a whole bone. But she did not appear to feel pain.

When Pertin spoke to her, she answered in English, "They don't consider it important. It will not prevent moving about and performing necessary functions."

Doc Chimp was groaning and sobbing in pain. "Those Sheliaks!" he cried, feebly trying to groom his matted fur. "They're wholly out of control, Ben James. They tried again to wreck the probe—may have done it by now if they've got enough power of concentration to remember what they were doing when we diverted their attention. And if Angel hasn't killed them all."

Pertin said with a confidence he didn't feel, "She'll stop them. As long as we've got her on our side—"

"On our side?" cried Doc Chimp. "Ben James, you don't know what you're saying. She's worse than they are!"

"But she tried to rescue you."

The Purchased woman said calmly, "That is wrong. She merely wanted to kill the Sheliaks."

"That's right, Ben James. She's against all organic beings now. She's not ionizable, you see. Radiation doesn't bother her. The only thing that can kill her is deprivation of energy sources and that means the tachyon receiver. Once it's gone she will die as soon as the fuel runs out."

Pertin said slowly, "Is it the same with the Scorpian robot?"

The battered face nodded, the stub of the green plume jerking wildly.

Pertin said, "That means we have to assume all nonorganic beings will feel the same and try to prevent the launch. What about the other organics?"

The Purchased woman recited emotionlessly: "The T'Worlie, all dead. Boaty Bits, more than half destroyed—the remainder too few to make a collective entity intelligent enough to matter. Sirians and Core Stars races not observed in recent hours and must be presumed dead or neutralized. Sheliaks, destructive and purposeless."

Pertin absorbed the information without shock, without reaction of any kind other than a strange impulse to laugh. "But—but whom does that leave to see that the launch occurs?"

"Nobody!" cried Doc Chimp. "Nobody at all, Ben James—except us!"

They reached the launch chamber ahead of the Sheliaks after all. No one else was there.

The capsule, tiny bright tachyon crystal at its heart, lay silent and unmoving, connected to the main bulk of the ship by only a canopy designed to be jettisoned. Destruction had raged all around it, but it was still intact.

Less than an hour remained until launch.

"We'll build barricades," said Pertin. "Anything. Those wrecked instrument boards—the spare plates and braces. Whatever we can move we'll pile against the entrance. All we have to do is delay them—"

But they had barely begun when brightness glinted in the approach corridor and the silvery pseudo-girl came toward them, followed by the tumbling form of the Scorpian robot. They brought up short at the entrance, the robot with one slim tentacle coiled caressingly around the silver girl.

Pertin put his weight behind the channel iron he had been about to emplace at the door and launched it toward the pair. The pseudo-girl made a sound that was partly laughter and partly the singing of a single piercing note and the Scorpian uncoiled a long silver sting. The sting reached out and touched Pertin. A blinding light stabbed from it, jolting him with a strong electric shock.

The girl glided in, spreading her tattered wings. The stirred air bathed him in her strong scent, ether-sweet, with undertones like the pits of peaches. Pertin searched the bright silvery face and found no expression. It was no more human than a doll's. The Scorpian's silver tentacles thrust away the pitiful obstructions, making a sound like an enormous gong which Pertin's Pmal refused to translate.

The Purchased woman intervened, hurling herself toward the robot, and was brushed heedlessly aside. She struck against the side of the probe ship, a blow that must have been agony to her human nervous system, but she did not cry out. Awkwardly she tried to project herself again into the fight. Pertin forced himself to join her.

A birdlike trilling from outside indicated that others were coming, and behind the great winged hulk of the pseudo-girl Pertin could see black shadow-shapes moving across the dimly lighted shaft, growing rapidly as they approached.

"Oh, no!" moaned Doc Chimp. "Sheliaks and a Sirian!"

The robot was not deflected from its single-minded purpose. It floated toward Pertin, green dome pulsing. An elongating tentacle struck out at Pertin like an endless silver snake, not to sting this time but to snare. It wrapped him in slick, chill coils. He fought free, was caught again—and at last the Scorpian turned to confront the other beings. It arched its stinging jet, but held it poised, waiting.

The Sirian was first into the launch chamber, a tapered, blue-scaled torpedo shape fifteen feet long, all pliant wing and shining eye. With a ripple of trailing wing edges it flashed at the Scorpian.

The sting coiled, jetting white light into the wide blue eye. The Sirian was not defenseless—its own forces gathered the robot's charge and repelled it, sending the jet back at the robot, reinforced and multiplied.

The pseudo-girl turned with great strokes of her wings, her three-fingered hand coming up with the gun-shaped weapon that had killed Sheliaks. Desperately Pertin twisted to intercept her. Her wings were sadly battered now, but still gave her superior mobility; he missed her on the first try and crashed against a wall. Half blinded by his own blood, he doubled his legs under him and launched himself at her again.

The gun-shaped thing swung to meet him and the white jet hissed at him. He heard a brittle crackling sound in the air and felt the breath of icy death.

But the jet had missed and he was on her. With one hand he swung at her wrist. It was like striking a crowbar with his bare hand, but it jarred the weapon loose; and just then the battle between Scorpian and Sirian reached its climax.

The Sirian's jet struck a vital place in the great green dome of the robot. It exploded. The mellow booming sound the robot made became a hollow jangle. The tentacles writhed and recoiled. It sprawled in the air, a grotesque huddle of tortured metal, spilling green fire and drops of an acid that sizzled and burned where they struck.

If the robot had known life, that life was gone—it was dead.

The silvery girl abandoned the fight with Pertin. With a great stroke of her wings she propelled herself to it, hovered over it, wailing an unearthly sound.

And the great blue eye of the Sirian turned toward Pertin. Behind it the Sheliaks, late on the scene but ready for battle, were elongating their wrinkled necks toward him.

Pertin cried desperately: "Wait! They—they were misleading you. They were trying to prevent the launch, to save their own lives—"

The eye hesitated.

"We're dead already," he croaked. "Nothing can help us now, not any organic creature. The radiation will kill us before long, even the Sheliaks. But the robot and the girl—"

He could hear his voice hissing or singing out of the aliens' Pmals.

"The robot," he repeated, "and the altered copy that looks like a Terrestrial female—they weren't radiation-vulnerable. They could go on indefinitely. But the rest of us—if we let them succeed in stopping the launch, then we all die for nothing!"

The eye paused, irresolute.

Then the foremost of the Sheliaks cried: "Fool! We, too, are not radiation-vulnerable! We simply need to conjugate and be born again. But we must have the tachyon receiver—and if you try to keep us from it you must die!"

The three tapered teardrop shapes, like a school of sharks in formation, plunged toward Pertin. The Sirian eye irresolutely turned toward them—then, with decision, the being whirled to confront them.

Contemptuously the Sheliaks changed course to meet it. The leading one widened a ruff of flesh to act like an instant air-brake. It stopped in the air, flowed with a dazzle of color, narrowed a neck toward the Sirian eye.

The thin neck spat a stream of a yellow fluid. It struck the Sirian eye and clung, acid, adhesive, agonizing. The Sirian made an unearthly wailing noise at the sudden pain of the attack against which it had no built-in defenses. The great blue eye turned milky white; the huge body knotted in agony.

But it still had strength to fire a jet of energy that caught all three Sheliaks. They died instantly, but the effort was the last for the Sirian. All its stored energy had gone into that pulse. The reflected cascade of burning energy came bouncing back, bathing the silvery girl and sending her reeling soundlessly into a wall, to flop into an ungainly, contorted mass that didn't move. Pertin was farther away and partly shielded by what was left of the robot—even so the bolt lanced his skin with pain.

But he was alive.

Slowly and painfully he caught a holdfast on the wall, steadied himself while he looked around.

The Purchased People woman was dead, either bled empty or caught in that last furious bolt. The Sirian eye floated broken and aimless. The robot was destroyed. The pseudo-girl was drifting impotently away. The Sheliaks were cinders.

The chamber was filled with the stench of many different kinds of death, but Pertin was still alive.

Suddenly remembering, he cried, "Doc Chimp!"

The ape was out of sight. Furiously Pertin ransacked the chamber and found him at the last, wedged between the wall of the probe and the ship's canopy, not quite dead but unconscious.

Pertin looked down at him sadly and affectionately. It was nearly time to launch the probe and the question in Pertin's mind was: was it better to wake him up or to let him sleep as the probe was launched, the canopy jettisoned, and all the air in the chamber puffed instantly and murderously away into space?

The answer was taken out of his hands as the ape stirred, moaned softly, and opened his eyes. He looked up at Ben James Pertin and said thickly, "The probe?"

"It's all right," said Pertin. "We'll have to launch it by hand."

"When, Ben James?"

Pertin checked the time. "Just a few minutes now," he said.

The ape grinned painfully. "That's good to know, Ben James," he said. "No more problems. No more aches and pains. I always thought I'd be afraid of dying, but, you know? To tell you the truth, I'm kind of looking forward to it."

The process that animated the body of the silvery pseudo-girl was more like electrophoresis than chemistry, but it was vulnerable to attack. It was damaged now.

But she was not dead. The great wings were broken and useless, but her limbs still moved, the inappropriate angel face still held its bleak, proud expression.

She was in great pain. That is to say that all of the sensory nets of her edited body were transmitting messages of malfunction, damage, and warning. She did not perceive them as a human perceives a toothache, a sensation so blinding that it can lead to suicide, but they did interfere with the few pleasure-bound processes left to her—reminiscence, forevision, contemplation. In the sense that these interfering messages were pain, she had experienced pain from the moment she floated out of the tachyon receiver on *Aurora*. All edited members of her race did. There was no way to rearrange their structures into forms viable in atmosphere and low-G that was comfortable for them.

Time was when Angel had experienced pain only infrequently, and in ways that were soon mended. Time was when she had lain with her sisters in the icy methane slush of her native planet, absorbing energy from the radioactive elements that swam about them, growing, learning from the tutorials of her ortho-father, competing in the endless elimination battles of her race that finally won her the choice of assignments—and ultimately led her to the *Aurora* and its imminent doom. Her race was not greatly interested in astronomy.

They had known almost nothing of it until the first T'Worlie probe survived the crushing pressures of their atmosphere and brought them into contact. From the surface of their enormous planet, there were no stars to be seen. Even their aircraft never reached an altitude beyond dense yellow-gray clouds.

What brought her to *Aurora* was the trait that her whole upbringing had trained into her: the competitive need to go farther and do more. It was not goal-oriented. It gained nothing from victories except the opportunity for further victories. The only victory now open to Angel was to survive—and the only way to do it was by preventing the launching of the probe.

She calculated she had strength enough left to destroy the two organic creatures in her way—but only just. And only if she acted now.

It was Pertin who saw her first, his hand frozen on the release lever. It was Doc Chimp who acted. He flung himself on the pseudo-girl.

"Hurry up, Ben James!" he shouted. "She's too strong for me—" His voice stopped, punctuated by a screech of pain as the silvery arm thrust him away like a cannon shot. The mutated chimp went flying into the floating wreckage of the Scorpian robot. The soft, frail dome of the skull, so cleverly mutated into the near-shape of man's own, impaled itself on a steel shard and the thoughtful, considering brain was destroyed.

Pertin hardly even saw it happen. He was past the point for sorrow. It would be easy to let the pseudo-girl destroy him. At least one life would be saved—hers. His no longer counted. He could hope for a few days, a week or two at the most, of being able to move and breathe. And what would it be like? Increasing pain. Hopeless fear. Regret. Envy.

He pressed the lever just as her fingers touched him.

The instant sharp slap of the explosion was the last sound he heard.

At the instant Ben James Pertin pressed the release, explosive shears cut the aft end of the ship free. The canopy flew out and away. The air puffed into emptiness. The probe rocket dropped free and began to align itself with the now near great disk of Object Lambda.

The first thing Pertin felt was the sharp pain of the explosion, then the second, longer, more deadly pain as the air pressure dropped to instant zero and his blood and body fluids, the air in his lungs, the gasses dissolved in his blood, tried to expand to fill the enormous emptiness all around. He caught a glimpse of the silvery girl, arms, legs, and broken wings flailing, as she shot past him, careened off the jagged edge of metal where the shears had cut the probe satellite free, and ricocheted out into emptiness. If she made a sound he could not hear it. There was no longer a way for him to hear. There was no longer a continuous medium of air to carry it.

He had just a glimpse of the huge near surface of Object Lambda —the body he had called "Cuckoo"—as it hung like a great dull circle in the empty sky, cutting off one spiral limb of his own, eternally lost, galaxy.

He did not see the orienting jets of the satellite spurt carefully controlled measures of flame to position it for its final thrust. He did not see the great violet flare of the fusion rockets that began to slow it. He could not see any of that, because by then he was dead.

Neither he nor anyone else in the probe ship saw the great series of flares as the satellite fought to slow itself. *Aurora* flew on, without power, containing only the last flickerings of life for a few of its beings, back toward the galaxy. The probe left it as it drew more and more rapidly away. The distance between them was millions of miles before the satellite made its first meteoric contact with the outer layers of that anomalously thick atmosphere around Cuckoo.

Here was a spectacle worth watching, if there had been eyes left in *Aurora* to see. The satellite plunged through a carefully planned chord of the atmosphere. Its ablative surface burned and tore away in a flare like all the fireworks in man's history going off at once. But there was none to see—not Sirian eye nor Sheliak sensors, not T'Worlie or Earthman or alien of any kind. Where life remained at all it lacked strength for curiosity and it would not remain alive very long.

Fifty thousand years later *Aurora* might pass near some sun of an outstretched spiral arm. But by then it would no longer matter to anyone, except as a historical curiosity from a time about which no one any longer cared.

Some days later the sensors on Sun One reported that the probe was in a stable orbit. The beings on Sun One responded with pleasure—everyone was delighted that the project was a success.

Now stable, the probe began to do the work for which it had been designed.

The complex H-bomb sequencing units and the small, strong pressure-plate shock absorbers fell away, responding to remote controls from Sun One. They would never be used again.

The tachyon receiving unit began to emit a stream of tiny metallic shards, none larger than a few inches in its greatest measure.

When some hundreds of them were through, floating like a metallic mist around the drone, a quick small machine came through and began to catch them and link them together. Time passed—hours and then days. A boxlike shape took form and became a larger tachyon receiver—now ready for action.

From tens of thousands of light-years away an angular, crystalline machine flashed along the tachyon patterns and emerged in the new receiver. It was not alive. It was not even a robot or a proxy like the Purchased People. It was simply an automatic machine that sensed certain potentials and charges, doublechecked the strength of the materials and the solidity of the joints, directed the hummingbird-sized construction machine to correct a few faults, and then reported that Cuckoo Station, the orbiting body around what had been called Object Lambda, was now ready to be built.

A few hours later the first girders of what would eventually be a thousand-meter revolving wheel were being joined together.

Plates appeared to surround the girders with an airtight sheath. Machines arrived to be stored in them. Atmosphere was pumped through to fill the chambers. The handling machines were busy, taxed beyond their capacities—more handling machines were sent and soon the orbiting station was whole, supplied and being-rated.

The first living beings appeared. A Sheliak, naked to the cold of intergalactic space (but for the brief time of its transition to the orbiting wheel unharmed by it). A dozen T'Worlies arrived in a single elastic air-bubble and scurried into the protection of the orbital wheel. There were Sirians, reptilian Aldebaranians, a hive of Boaty Bits, and at the last a couple of humans.

One of them was named Ben Linc Pertin.

He floated out of the tachyon receiver in his pressure suit, his thruster unit at the ready in his hands.

He did not use it at once. He paused a moment to look around.

The first thing he did was to stare down at the enormous flat surface of Cuckoo, so near, so huge, so incredible as it hung like an endless shield in the sky.

The second was to look back to where the galaxy lay, sparkling like the sea of stars it was.

He could not see the doomship, but he knew it must be somewhere in his line of sight. There were no signals from it anymore. There was no way of detecting it and would not be for tens of thousands of years.

He stared for a moment, then shrugged. "Poor bastards," he whispered and turned and drove toward the wheel awaiting him.

WEED OF TIME

NORMAN SPINRAD

It takes real imaginative talent to visualize a state in which all time is identical and past, present, and future are one and the same. Vonnegut wrote about a race of beings who had this viewpoint in his Slaughterhouse-Five, but Spinrad in this short tour-de-force manages to show us what it must be like.

I, me, the spark of mind that is my consciousness, dwells in a locus that is neither place nor time. The objective duration of my life-span is one hundred and ten years, but from my own locus of consciousness, I am immortal—my awareness of my own awareness can never cease to be. I am an infant am a child am a youth am an old, old man dying on clean white sheets. I am all these mes, have always been all these mes will always be all these mes in the place where my mind dwells in an eternal moment divorced from time. . . .

A century and a tenth is my eternity. My life is like a biography in a book; immutable, invariant, fixed in length, limitless in duration. On April 3, 2040, I am born. On December 2, 2150, I die. The events in between take place in a single instant. Say that I range up and down them at will, experiencing each of them again and again and again eternally. Even this is not really true; I experience all moments in my century and a tenth simultaneously, once and forever.
. . . How can I tell my story? How can I make you understand? The language we have in common is based on concepts of time which we do not share.

For me, time as you think of it does not exist. I do not move from moment to moment sequentially like a blind man groping his way down a tunnel. I am at all points in the tunnel simultaneously, and my eyes are open wide. Time is to me, in a sense, what space is to you, a field over which I move in more directions than one.

How can I tell you? How can I make you understand? We are, all of us, men born of women, but in a way you have less in common with me than you do with an ape or an amoeba. Yet I *must* tell you, somehow. It is too late for me, will be too late, has been too late. I am trapped in this eternal hell and I can never escape, not even into death. My life is immutable, invariant, for I have eaten of Temp, the Weed of Time. But you must not! You must listen! You must understand! Shun the Weed of Time! I must try to tell you in my own way. It is pointless to try to start at the beginning. There is no beginning. There is no end. Only significant time-loci. Let me describe these loci. Perhaps I can make you understand. . . .

September 8, 2050. I am ten years old. I am in the office of Dr. Phipps, who is the director of the mental hospital in which I have been for the past eight years. On June 12, 2053, they will finally understand that I am not insane. It is all they will understand, but it will be enough for them to release me. But on September 8, 2050, I am in a mental hospital.

September 8, 2050 is the day the first expedition returns from Tau Ceti. The arrival is to be televised, and that is why I am in Dr. Phipps's office watching television with the director. The Tau Ceti expedition is the reason I am in the hospital. I have been babbling about it for the previous ten years. I have been demanding that the ship be quarantined, that the plant samples it will bring back be destroyed, not allowed to grow in the soil of Earth. For most of my life this has been regarded as an obvious symptom of schizophrenia —after all, before July 12, 2048, the ship has not left for Tau Ceti, and until today it has not returned.

But on September 8, 2050, they wonder. This is the day I have been babbling about since I emerged from my mother's womb and now it is happening. So now I am alone with Dr. Phipps as the image of the ship on the television set lands on the image of a wide concrete apron. . . .

"Make them understand!" I shout, knowing that it is futile. "Stop them, Dr. Phipps, stop them!"

Dr. Phipps stares at me uneasily. His small blue eyes show a mixture of pity, confusion, and fright. He is all too familiar with my case. Sharing his desktop with the portable television set is a heavy oaktag folder filled with my case history, filled with hundreds of therapy session records. In each of these records, this day is mentioned: September 8, 2050. I have repeated the same story over and over and

over again. The ship will leave for Tau Ceti on July 12, 2048. It will
return on September 8, 2050. The expedition will report that Tau
Ceti has twelve planets. . . . The fifth alone is Earth-like and bears
plant and animal life. . . . The expedition will bring back samples
and seeds of a small Cetan plant with broad green leaves and small
purple flowers. . . . The plant will be named *tempis ceti*. . . . It
will become known as Temp. . . . Before the properties of the plant
are fully understood, seeds will somehow become scattered and
Temp will flourish in the soil of Earth. . . . Somewhere, somehow,
people will begin to eat the leaves of the Temp plant. They will become changed. They will babble of the future, and they will be considered mad—until the future events of which they speak begin to
come to pass. . . .

Then the plant will be outlawed as a dangerous narcotic. Eating
Temp will become a crime. . . . But, as with all forbidden fruit,
Temp will continue to be eaten. . . . And finally, Temp addicts will
become the most sought-after criminals in the world. The govern-
ments of the Earth will attempt to milk the secrets of the future from
their tortured minds. . . .

All this is in my case history, with which Dr. Phipps is familiar.
For eight years, this has been considered only a remarkably consistent
psychotic delusion.

But now it is September 8, 2050. As I have predicted, the ship has
returned from Tau Ceti. Dr. Phipps stares at me woodenly as the
gangplank is erected and the crew begins to debark. I can see his jaw
tense as the reporters gather around the captain, a tall, lean man
carrying a small sack.

The captain shakes his head in confusion as the reporters besiege
him. "Let me make a short statement first," he says crisply. "Save
wear and tear on all of us."

The captain's thin, hard, pale face fills the television screen. "The
expedition is a success," he says. "The Tau Ceti system was found
to have twelve planets, the fifth is Earth-like and bears plant and
simple animal life. Very peculiar animal life. . . ."

"What do you mean, peculiar?" a reporter shouts.

The captain frowns and shrugs his wide shoulders. "Well, for one
thing, they all seem to be herbivores and they seem to live off one
species of plant which dominates the planetary flora. No predators.
And it's not hard to see why. I don't quite know how to explain this,
but all the critters seem to know what the other animals will do before they do it. And what we were going to do, too. We had one hell

of a time taking specimens. We think it has something to do with the plant. Does something strange to their time sense."

"What makes you say that?" a reporter asks.

"Well, we fed some of the stuff to our lab animals. Same thing seemed to happen. It became virtually impossible to lay a hand on 'em. They seemed to be living a moment in the future, or something. That's why Dr. Lominov has called the plant *tempis ceti*."

"What's this tempis look like?" a reporter says.

"Well, it's sort of . . ." the captain begins. "Wait a minute," he says, "I've got a sample right here."

He reaches into the small sack and pulls something out. The camera zooms in on the captain's hand.

He is holding a small plant. The plant has broad green leaves and small purple blossoms.

Dr. Phipps's hands begin to tremble uncontrollably. He stares at me. He stares and stares and stares. . . .

May 12, 2062. I am in a small room. Think of it as a hospital room. Think of it as a laboratory, think of it as a cell; it is all three. I have been here for three months.

I am seated on a comfortable lounge-chair. Across a table from me sits a man from an unnamed government intelligence bureau. On the table is a tape recorder. It is running. The man seated opposite is frowning in exasperation.

"The subject is December, 2081," he says. "You will tell me all you know of the events of December, 2081."

I stare at him silently, sullenly. I am tired of all the men from intelligence sections, economic councils, scientific bureaus, with their endless, futile demands.

"Look," the man snaps, "we know better than to appeal to your nonexistent sense of patriotism. We are all too well aware that you don't give a damn about what the knowledge you have can mean to your country. But just remember this: you're a convicted criminal. Your sentence is indeterminate. Cooperate, and you'll be released in two years. Clam up, and we'll hold you here till you rot or until you get it through your head that the only way for you to get out is to talk. The subject is the month of December in the year 2081. Now, *give!*"

I sigh. I know that it is no use trying to tell any of them that knowledge of the future is useless, that the future cannot be changed because it was not changed because it will not be changed. They will not accept the fact that choice is an illusion caused by the fact that future time-loci are hidden from those who advance sequentially along the time-stream one moment after the other in blissful ignorance. They refuse to understand that moments of future time are no different from moments of past or present time; fixed, immutable, invariant. They live in the illusion of sequential time.

So I begin to speak of the month of December in the year 2081. I know they will not be satisfied until I have told them all I know of the years between this time-locus and December 2, 2150. I know they will not be satisfied because they are not satisfied, have not been satisfied, will not be satisfied. . . .

So I tell them of that terrible December nine years in their future. . . .

December 2, 2150. I am old, old, a hundred and ten years old. My age-ruined body lies on the clean white sheets of a hospital bed, lungs, heart, blood vessels, organs, all failing. Only my mind is forever untouched, the mind of an infant-child-youth-man-ancient. I am, in a sense, dying. Beyond this day, December 2, 2150, my body no longer exists as a living organism. Time to me forward of this date is as blank to me as time beyond April 3, 2040 is in the other temporal direction.

In a sense, I am dying. But in another sense, I am immortal. The spark of my consciousness will not go out. My mind will not come to an end, for it has neither end nor beginning. I exist in one moment that lasts forever and spans one hundred and ten years.

Think of my life as a chapter in a book, the book of eternity, a book with no first page and no last. The chapter that is my life-span is one hundred and ten pages long. It has a starting point and an ending point, but the chapter exists as long as the book exists, the infinite book of eternity.

Or, think of my life as a ruler one hundred and ten inches long. The ruler "begins" at one and "ends" at one hundred and ten, but "begins" and "ends" refer to length, not duration.

I am dying. I experience dying always, but I never experience death. Death is the absence of experience. It can never come for me.

December 2, 2150 is but a significant time-locus for me, a dark wall, an end-point beyond which I cannot see. The other wall has the time-locus April 3, 2040.

April 3, 2040. Nothingness abruptly ends, non-nothingness abruptly begins. I am born.

What is it like for me to be born? How can I tell you? How can I make you understand? My life, my whole life-span of one hundred and ten years comes into being at once, in an instant. At the "moment" of my birth I am at the moment of my death and all moments in between. I emerge from my mother's womb and I see my life as one sees a painting, a painting of some complicated landscape; all at once, whole, a complete gestalt. I see my strange, strange infancy, the incomprehension as I emerge from the womb speaking perfect English, marred only by my undeveloped vocal apparatus, as I emerge from my mother's womb demanding that the ship from Tau Ceti in the time-locus September 8, 2050 be quarantined, knowing that my demand will be futile because it was futile, will be futile, is futile, knowing that at the moment of my birth I am have been will be all that I ever was/am/will be and that I cannot change a moment of it.

I emerge from my mother's womb and I am dying in clean white sheets and I am in the office of Dr. Phipps watching the ship land and I am in the government cell for two years babbling of the future and I am in a clearing in some woods where a plant with broad green leaves and small purple flowers grows and I am picking the plant and eating it as I know I will do have done am doing. . . .

I emerge from my mother's womb and I see the gestalt-painting of my life-span, a pattern of immutable events painted on the stationary and eternal canvas of time. . . .

But I do not merely *see* the "painting," I *am* the "painting" and I am the painter and I am also outside the painting viewing the whole and I am none of these.

And I see the immutable time-locus that determines all the rest— March 4, 2060. Change that and the painting dissolves and I live in time like any other man, moment after blessed moment, freed from this all-knowing hell. But change itself is illusion.

March 4, 2060 in a wood not too far from where I was born. But knowledge of the horror that day brings, has brought, will bring can change nothing. I will do as I am doing will do did because I did it will do it am doing it. . . .

April 3, 2040, and I emerge from my mother's womb, an infant-child-youth-man-ancient, in a government cell in a mental hospital dying in clean white sheets. . . .

March 4, 2060. I am twenty. I am in a clearing in the woods. Before me grows a small plant with broad green leaves and purple blossoms—Temp, the Weed of Time, which has haunted, haunts, will haunt my never-ending life. I know what I am doing will do have done because I will do have done am doing it.

How can I explain? How can I make you understand that this moment is unavoidable, invariant, that though I have known, do know, will know its dreadful consequences, I can do nothing to alter it?

The language is inadequate. What I have told you is an unavoidable half-truth. All actions I perform in my one hundred and ten year life-span occur simultaneously. But even that statement only hints around the truth, for "simultaneously" means "at the same time" and "time" as you understand the word has no relevance to my life. But let me approximate.

Let me say that all actions I have ever performed, will perform, do perform, occur simultaneously. Thus no knowledge inherent in any particular time-locus can affect any action performed at any other locus in time. Let me construct another useful lie. Let me say that for me action and perception are totally independent of each other. At the moment of my birth, I did everything I would ever do in my life, instantly, blindly, in one total gestalt. Only in the next "moment" do I perceive the results of all those myriad actions, the horror that March 4, 2060 will make has made is making of my life.

Or . . . they say that at the moment of death, one's entire life flashes instantaneously before one's eyes. At the moment of my birth, my whole life flashed before me, not merely before my eyes, but in reality. I cannot change any of it because change is something that exists only as a function of the relationship between different moments in time and for me life is one eternal moment that is one hundred and ten years long. . . .

So this awful moment is invariant, inescapable.

March 4, 2060. I reach down, pluck the Temp plant. I pull off a broad green leaf, put it in my mouth. It tastes bittersweet, woody, unpleasant. I chew it, bolt it down.

The Temp travels to my stomach, is digested, passes into my blood-stream, reaches my brain. There changes occur which better men than I are powerless, will be powerless to understand, at least up till December 2, 2150, beyond which is blankness. My body remains in the objective time-stream, to age, grow old, decay, die. But my mind is abstracted out of time to experience all moments as one.

It is like a *déjà vu*. Because this happened on March 4, 2060, I have already experienced it in the twenty years since my birth. Yet this is the beginning point for my Temp-consciousness in the objective time-stream. But the objective time-stream has no relevance to what happens. . . .

The language, the very thought patterns are inadequate. Another useful lie: in the objective time-stream I was a normal human being until this dire March 4, experiencing each moment of the previous twenty years sequentially, in order, moment, after moment, after moment. . . .

Now on March 4, 2060, my consciousness expands in two directions in the time-stream to fill my entire life-span: forward to December 2, 2150 and my death, backward to April 3, 2040 and my birth. As this time-locus of March 4 "changes" my future, so too it "changes" my past, expanding my Temp-consciousness to both extremes of my life-span.

But once the past is changed, the previous past has never existed and I emerge from my mother's womb an infant-child-youth-man-ancient in a government cell a mental hospital dying in clean white sheets. . . . And—

I, me, the spark of mind that is my consciousness, dwells in a locus that is neither place nor time. The objective duration of my life-span is one hundred and ten years, but from my own locus of consciousness, I am immortal—my awareness of my own awareness can never cease to be. I am an infant am a child am a youth am an old, old man dying on clean white sheets. I am all these mes, have always been all these mes will always be all these mes in the place where my mind dwells in an eternal moment divorced from time. . . .

A MODEST GENIUS

VADIM SHEFNER

A bit of sardonic fun from the Soviet Union. The thing that struck your editor was the casual assumption from beginning to end of this inventor's career that nothing at all would change in the living conditions of his life. Do you suppose that is significant?

I

Sergei Kladesev was born on Vasilyevski Island, Leningrad. He was a strange boy. While other children were making sand pies and building castles, he was drawing sections of odd-looking machines on the sand. In the second grade he built a portable machine, powered by a pocket flashlight battery, which told each pupil how many good marks he would receive during the coming week. Grownups considered the machine uneducational and took it away from him.

After leaving grammar school Sergei attended the Technical School for Electrochemistry. He paid no attention to the many pretty girls he met there—perhaps because he saw them every day.

One fine June day he rented a boat and sailed down the Little Neva to the Gulf of Finland. Near Volny Island he came upon a skiff with two girls in it, strangers to him. They had run on to a sandbar and, in attempting to float their boat, had broken the rudder. Sergei introduced himself and helped them back to the dock where they had rented the boat. After that he visited them frequently; the two friends lived, like Sergei, on Vasilyevski Island, Svetlana on Sixth Street, Liussia on Eleventh.

Liussia was attending a course in typewriting at the time, but Svetlana was resting up from school; secondary school had provided all the education she wanted. Besides, her well-off parents were trying to persuade her that it was time to marry; she agreed in principle, but had no intention of taking the first acceptable fellow that came along.

In the beginning Sergei preferred Liussia, but he knew how to behave toward her. She was so pretty, modest and easily embarrassed that in her presence he too became embarrassed. Svetlana was quite different: gay and quick-witted; in short, a daredevil. Though naturally timid, Sergei felt happy when he was with her.

A year later, Sergei was visiting a friend in Roshdestwenka and there met Svetlana, who was staying with relatives. A coincidence, of course, but Sergei took it as providential. Day after day he walked in the woods and by the sea with her and was soon convinced that he could not live without her.

Svetlana did not find him especially attractive. To her he was an average fellow, and she dreamt of finding somebody unusual for her partner through life. She went walking with Sergei in the woods and by the sea only because she had to pass the time with someone.

One evening they were standing on the shore. On the smooth surface of the water there lay, like a carpet woven by nymphs, a strip of silvery moonlight. Everything was still, except for the nightingales singing in the wild elders on the opposite shore.

"How beautiful and quiet!"

"Yes, it's pretty," answered Svetlana. "If only we could gather some elder branches! But it's too far for walking around on the shore. We have no boat and we can't walk on the water!"

They returned to the village and their respective lodgings. Sergei didn't go to bed that night. He took pencil and paper and filled page after page with formulas and drawings. In the morning he went back to the city and stayed there two days. When he returned he had a bundle under his arm.

Late that evening he took his bundle with him on their walk to the sea. At the water's edge he opened it and took out two pairs of skates for traveling on the water.

"Here, put these water skates on," he said. "I made them just for you."

They both put them on and skated easily over the water to the other shore. The skates slid very nicely on the surface of the sea.

On the other shore Svetlana and Sergei broke off elder branches and then, each with a bundle, went slowly over the sea in the moonlight.

From then on they went skating every evening over the mirror-smooth surface of the water, the skates leaving behind them only a narrow, hardly visible trace, which immediately disappeared.

One day Sergei stopped out on the sea. Svetlana slowly approached him.

"Do you know something?" asked Sergei.

"No. What's wrong?"

"Do you know, Svetlana, that I love you?"

"Of course not!" she answered ironically.

"Then you like me a little, too?"

"I can't say that. You're a fine fellow, but I have a different ideal of a husband. I can only love a really extraordinary man, but to tell you the truth, you're just a good average fellow."

"Well, you're honest, anyway," said a downcast Sergei.

They skated back to the shore in silence, and the next day Sergei returned to the city. For a time he felt wretched. He lost weight and wandered aimlessly through the streets. He often left the city to stroll about. In the evenings he went home to his little workroom.

One day he met Liussia walking along the river. She was glad to see him, and he noticed it immediately.

"What are you doing here, Sergei?"

"Nothing. Just walking. I'm on vacation."

"I'm just walking, too. If you'd like, perhaps we could go over to Cultural Park." She blushed as she made the suggestion.

They rode over to Yelagin Island and slowly walked along its avenues. Later they met several more times to stroll around the city and found that they were happy to be together.

One day Liussia came to Sergei's house to take him off for a trip to Pavlovsk.

"What a disorganized room!" she exclaimed. "All these machines and flasks! What are they for?"

"I go in for various little inventions in my free time."

"And I never suspected!" said Liussia in amazement. "Could you repair my typewriter? I bought it in a discount store; it's old and the ribbon keeps getting stuck."

"Sure, I'll take a look at it."

"What's this?" she asked. "What an odd camera! I've never seen one like it."

"It's a very ordinary FED camera but it has an accessory that I built just recently. With it you can photograph the future. You aim the camera at a place whose future appearance you'd like to know, and take the picture. But my machine isn't perfected yet. You can photograph things only three years ahead, no more than that as yet."

"Three years! That's a lot. What a wonderful invention!"

"Wonderful? Not at all," said Sergei with a disdainful gesture. "It's very imperfect."

"Have you taken any pictures?"

"Yes. A short time ago I went out to the suburbs and shot some film there." He took several prints from his desk.

"Here I photographed a birch in a meadow, without using the accessory. Then here is the same tree in two years' time."

"It's grown a bit and has more branches."

"And here it is three years from now."

"But there's nothing there!" cried the astonished Liussia. "Just a stump and next to it a pit, like a shell hole. And over there are a pair of soldiers running along stooped. What strange uniforms they're wearing! I can't understand the picture at all."

"Yes, I was surprised too, when I developed the picture. It looks to me as though there are some kind of maneuvers going on there."

"Sergei, you'd better burn that photo. It looks too much like a military secret. That picture might fall into the hands of a foreign spy!"

"You're right, Liussia. I never thought of that." He tore up the picture and threw it into the stove with a pile of other trash; then he set fire to it.

"Now I feel better," said Liussia, obviously relieved. "But now take my picture as I'll be a year from now. In this chair over by the window."

"But the accessory will only photograph a certain sector of space and whatever is in it. So, if you're not sitting in that chair a year from now, you won't be in the picture."

"Take me anyway. Who knows, maybe I will be sitting in this chair this day and hour next year!"

"All right," Sergei agreed. "I still have one picture left on this roll." He took the picture. "Come on, I'll develop the film immediately and make some prints. The bathroom is free today; no one is doing any wash."

He went into the bathroom and developed the film, then brought it back to his room and hung it up near the window to dry.

Liussia took the film by the edges and peered at the last exposure. It seemed to her that someone else was in the chair. At the same time she was secretly wishing that she might be sitting there in a year's time. It's probably me, she concluded, only I didn't come out too well.

Once the film was dry, they went into the bathroom where the red light was still on. Sergei put the strip of film into the enlarger, turned the machine on, and projected the image on to photographic paper. He then quickly put the picture into the developer. On the paper the features of a woman appeared. She sat in the chair and was embroidering a large cat on a piece of cloth. The cat was almost finished, all but the tail.

"That's not me sitting there!" Liussia was disillusioned. "It's a different woman entirely."

"No, it's not you," Sergei agreed. "I don't know who it is; I never saw the woman before."

"Sergei, I think I'd better be going," said Liussia. "You needn't stop by; I can have the typewriter repaired at the store."

"But at least let me bring you home!"

"No, Sergei, there's no need. I don't want to get mixed up in this business." She left.

My inventions bring me no luck, thought Sergei to himself. He took a hammer and smashed the accessory.

II

About two months later, as Sergei was walking along Bolshoi Avenue, he saw a young woman sitting on a bench and recognized her as the unknown woman of the fateful photograph.

She turned to him: "Can you tell me the time?"

Sergei told her and sat down next to her. They chatted about the weather and got acquainted. Sergei learned that her name was Tamara. He saw her often and soon married her. They had a son, whom Tamara named Alfred.

Tamara proved to be a very boring wife. Nothing roused much interest from her. Day in and day out she sat in the chair by the window and embroidered cats, swans and stags on little strips of cloth which she then hung proudly on the wall. She didn't love Sergei; she had married him only because he had a room of his own and because after her examinations at the Horse Trainers' Institute she didn't want to work in the provinces. No one had authority to send a married woman away.

Herself a boring person, she regarded Sergei too as boring, uninteresting and insignificant. He was always spending his leisure time inventing something; she didn't approve, and thought it a senseless waste of time. She was constantly scolding him for filling the room with his machines and apparatuses.

To get more freedom of movement in the room, Sergei built his LEAG or Local Effect Anti-Gravitation machine. With the aid of this machine he could do his work on the ceiling of the room. He laid flooring on the ceiling, set his desk on it, and brought up his instruments and tools. In order not to dirty the wall on which he walked up to the ceiling, he glued a narrow strip of linoleum on it. From now on the lower part of the room belonged to his wife, and the upper became his workroom.

Tamara was still dissatisfied: she was now afraid that the superintendent might find out about the expansion of the room space and demand double rent. Furthermore, it displeased her that Sergei should walk so nonchalantly along the ceiling. It just didn't seem right.

"At least have respect for my superior education and don't walk around that way with your head hanging down," she cried up to him from her chair. "Other women have normal husbands, but here I am, stuck with a bird of ill omen."

When Sergei came home from work (he worked at the Transenergy Authority as a technical control officer), he ate quickly and went off up the wall to his preserve. He frequently went for walks through the city and its environs so as not to have to listen to Tamara's constant nagging. He became so used to hiking that he could have walked to Pavlovsk with no difficulty.

One day he met Svetlana at the corner of Eighth Street and Sredni Avenue.

"I've married an extraordinary man since we last met," were her opening words. "My Petya is a real inventor. He's working just now as a beginning inventor at the Everything Everyday Research Institute, but he'll soon be promoted to the intermediate class. Petya has already invented something all by himself: *Don't Steal* soap."

"What kind of soap is that?" asked Sergei.

"The idea behind it is quite simple—but then every work of genius is simple, of course. *Don't Steal* is an ordinary toilet soap, but its core is a piece of solidified, water-resistant, black India ink. If someone, let's say your neighbor in the community house, steals the soap and washes with it, he dirties himself physically as well as morally."

"And if the soap isn't stolen?"

"Don't ask silly questions!" Svetlana flashed back angrily at him. "You're just jealous of Petya!"

"Do you ever see Liussia? How is she getting along?"

"Oh, she's the same as ever. I keep telling her to look for a suitable extraordinary man and marry him, but she says nothing. She seems bent on becoming an old maid."

Soon afterwards the war began. Tamara and Alfred were evacuated; Sergei went to the front. He began the war as a second lieutenant of infantry and ended as a first lieutenant. He returned to Leningrad, exchanged his uniform for civilian clothes and went back to his old work at the Transenergy Authority. Shortly afterward, Tamara and Alfred also returned, and life went on as before.

III

Years passed.

Alfred grew up, finished school, and went through the minimal course requirements for the training of hotel personnel. Then he went south and got a job in a hotel.

Tamara continued to embroider cats, swans and stags on wall hangings. She had grown duller and more quarrelsome with the years. She had also made the acquaintance of a retired director, a bachelor, and was constantly threatening Sergei that, if he didn't finally come to his senses and give up inventing things, she would leave him and go off with the director.

Svetlana was still quite satisfied with her Petya. Yes, he was going places. He'd been promoted to intermediate inventor and had now invented four-sided wheel spokes to replace the oldfashioned round ones! She could really be proud of him.

Liussia still lived on Vasilyevski Island and worked as a secretary in the office of Klavers, which designed and built replacement parts for pianos. She hadn't married and often thought of Sergei. She'd seen him once from a distance but hadn't approached him. He was walking with his wife along Seventh Street on his way to the Baltika Cinema; Liussia immediately recognized his wife as the woman in the photograph.

Sergei thought often of Liussia, too; he tried to distract himself by concentrating on new inventions. The things he made never seemed to him quite perfect and therefore he thought he had no right to get involved with more difficult ones. Recently he had invented a Quarrel Measurer And Ender and installed it in the kitchen of the community house where he lived. The apparatus had a scale with twenty divisions, which measured the mood of the lodger and the intensity of a quarrel that might be going on. The needle trembled at the first unfriendly word and slowly approached the red line. If it reached the line, the Quarrel Ender went into action. Soft, soothing music filled the room; an automatic atomizer emitted a cloud of valerian and *White Night* perfume; and on the screen of the machine appeared a fellow who leaped about in a comical way, bowed low to the viewers and kept repeating: "Be at peace with one another, citizens!"

Due to the machine people would make up in the early stages of a quarrel, and all the lodgers in the house were quite grateful to Sergei for his modest invention.

Sergei had also invented a telescope by making a windowpane with the properties of a gigantic magnifying glass. Through this window of his room he could see the canals of Mars, the craters of the Moon and the storms of Venus. When Tamara got on his nerves too much, he distracted and soothed himself by gazing out into distant worlds.

Most of his inventions had no practical value. But one did save him the expense of buying matches. He had succeeded in extracting benzine from water, and, since he smoked a good deal, he now lit his cigarettes from a lighter filled with his own benzine. Otherwise he led a rather joyless life. Neither Tamara nor Alfred brought him any happiness. When Alfred visited Leningrad, he talked mainly with Tamara.

"How are you getting along?" he asked her.

"What do you expect?" she answered him with a question. "My only pleasure is my art. Look at this stag that I'm embroidering!"

"What a splendid animal!" cried Alfred. "It's so lifelike! And the antlers! If I had antlers like that, I'd really get somewhere!"

"Your father has no feeling for art. He's only interested in inventing things. But there's hardly any use to what he makes."

"Well, at least he doesn't drink; you ought to be grateful for that," was her son's encouraging answer. "He's a slow comer, but maybe he'll wise up a bit. When I look at the people who stop at the hotel, I'm ashamed of Father. One guest is a head buyer, another is a foreigner, another a scientific correspondent. A short time ago a lecturer who wrote Pushkin's autobiography was living in one of our luxury apartments. He owns a country cottage and an automobile."

"How can I dream of a country cottage with a husband like mine?" Tamara asked dejectedly. "I've had enough of him. I'd like to get a divorce."

"Have you hooked anyone else yet?"

"I know a retired director, a bachelor. He has an eye for art! I made him a gift of an embroidered swan, and he was as happy as a child over it. With someone like that you come out on top."

"What was he director of? A hotel."

"He was a cemetery director, and he's a serious, sensitive man."

"He'd have to be, in that job," agreed her son.

IV

One June evening Sergei was up on the ceiling working on a new invention. He didn't notice the time passing, and it grew quite late. He went to bed but forgot to set the alarm, and overslept the next morning, so that he couldn't get to work on time. He decided not to go in at all that day: it was the first and last time that he stayed away from work.

"You're going to the dogs with your inventions," said Tamara. "At least you could have missed work for something worthwhile! But this stuff! Clever people earn a bit extra on the side, but you produce nothing, no more than a he-goat gives milk."

"Don't be angry, Tamara," Sergei tried to calm her. "Everything will turn out all right. It'll soon be vacation and we'll take a boat ride on the Volga."

"I don't need your cheap boat rides," Tamara screamed. "You ought to take a ride behind your own back and listen to what people say about you. They all consider you a perfect fool and laugh at you."

She snatched an unfinished wall hanging from its hook and stormed out in a rage.

Sergei was thoughtful. He reflected for a long time and then decided to take a ride behind his own back as his wife had suggested. Some time earlier, he had invented an Invisible Presence Machine (IPM), which was effective up to a distance of thirty-five miles. But he had never used the IPM to observe life in the city, thinking it unethical to look into other people's homes or to pry into their private lives. Instead, he often set the machine for the woods on the city's outskirts and watched the birds building their nests or listened to their songs.

Now, however, he decided to test the IPM within the city. He turned it on, set the knob at a very close range and turned the directional antenna towards the kitchen of the community house. Two women were standing at the gas stove, gossiping about this and that. Finally, one of them said: "Tamara's off to the director's again—and not the least bit embarrassed!"

"I'm sorry for Sergei Vladimirovich," answered the other. "What a good and clever man—and this woman is destroying him!"

"I have to agree with you," he could hear the first woman say. "He really does seem to be a good and clever man, but he has no luck."

Sergei next spied on his fellow workers, and they too had nothing but good to say about him. He turned off the IPM and thought for a while. Then Liussia came to mind and he felt a strong desire to see her again, if only for a moment. He turned the machine on and searched for Liussia's room on the fifth floor of a house on Eleventh Street. Perhaps she no longer lived there? Perhaps she had gotten married and moved away? or just changed to another floor in the same building?

Unfamiliar rooms and unknown people flashed on the screen. Finally he found Liussia's place. She wasn't there but it was certainly her room. The furniture was the same, and the same picture hung on the wall as before. On a small table stood her typewriter. Liussia was probably at work.

He next aimed the IPM at Svetlana's house, wondering how she was getting along. He found her rather easily in a house stuffed full of all sorts of brand-new things; she herself had aged a bit but seemed cheerful and content.

Suddenly her bell rang and she went to open the door. "Hello, Liussia! I haven't seen you for a long time!" she exclaimed in a welcoming tone.

"I just happened by; it's our midday break," said Liussia, and Sergei too could now see her. Over the years she hadn't grown any younger, but she was just as attractive as ever.

The two friends went into the house and chatted about all sorts of things.

"Aren't you ever going to get married?" Svetlana suddenly asked. "You can still get some worthwhile man in his prime."

"I don't want one," said Liussia dejectedly. "The man I like is long since married."

"Are you still in love with Sergei?" Svetlana persisted. "What do you see in him? What's so great about him? He's the kind that never amounts to much. He was a nice young fellow, of course. Once he gave me water skates, and we used to skate together across the water. The nightingales were singing on the shore and the people were snoring in their cottages, but we flew across the sea and showed our skill."

"I never knew he invented anything like that," Liussia said thoughtfully. "Did you keep them?"

"Of course not! Petya took them to the junk dealer long ago. He said the whole idea was nonsense. Petya is a real inventor and knows what's what with inventions!"

"Is Petya's job going well?"

"Excellent! A short time ago he invented MUCO-1."

"What's a MUCO?"

"A Mechanical Universal Can Opener. Now housewives and bachelors will be spared all the trouble they used to go to in opening cans."

"Have you got one?" Liussia wanted to pursue the matter. "I'd like to see it."

"No, I haven't and never will. It's to weigh five tons and will require a cement platform. Besides, it will cost four hundred thousand rubles."

"What housewife can afford one, then?" Liussia was amazed.

"My, you're slow!" said Svetlana impatiently. "Every housewife won't be buying one. One will be enough for a whole city. It'll be set up in the center of town—on Nevski Prospekt, for example. There they'll build the UCCOC—United City Can-Opening Center. It will be very handy. Suppose you have visitors and want to open some sardines for them; you don't need a tool for opening the can and you don't have to do a lot of work. You just take your can to UCCOC, hand it in at the reception desk, pay five kopeks and get a receipt. At the desk they paste a ticket on the can and put it on a conveyor belt. You go to the waiting room, settle down in an easy chair and watch a short film on preserves. Soon you're called to the counter. You present your receipt and get your opened can. Then you return contentedly to Vasilyevski Island."

"And they're really going ahead with this project?"

"Petya very much hopes so. But recently some jealous people have shown up and are trying to keep his inventions from being used. They're envious. Petya's not jealous of anyone: he knows he's an extraordinary man. And he's objective, too. For example, he has the highest regard for another inventor—the one who invented the *Drink to the Bottom* bottle cap and saw it through production."

"What's a *Drink to the Bottom* cap?"

"You know how vodka bottles are sealed? With a little metal cap. You pull the tab on the cap, the metal tears and the bottle is open. But you can't use that cap to close it again, so you have to finish the bottle, whether you want to or not."

"I prefer the water skates," Liussia reflected. "I'd love to glide across the bay on skates on a white night."

"The skates have really caught your fancy, haven't they?" Svetlana laughed. "Petya and I wouldn't want them back if you paid us."

Sergei shut off his IPM and thought for a while. Then he came to a decision.

V

That same evening Sergei got his pair of water skates from an old suitcase. He filled the bath with water and tested them: they didn't sink but slid across the surface just as well as they had done years before. Then he went to his retreat and worked late into the night making a second pair of skates for Liussia.

The next day, a Sunday, Sergei put on his good gray suit and wrapped the two pairs of skates in a newspaper. He put an atomizer and a bottle of MSST (Multiple Strengthener of Surface Tension) in his pocket; if a person covered his clothing with this preparation, it would keep him afloat.

Finally, he opened the large closet in which he kept his most significant inventions and took out his SPOSEM (Special Purpose Optical Solar Energy Machine). He had worked very hard on this and considered it the most important of all his inventions. It had been finished for two years but had never been tested. Its purpose was to restore a person's youth to him, and Sergei had never wanted his youth back again. If he made himself young again, he would have to make Tamara young too and begin life with her all over again —but one life with her was quite enough. In addition, he was frightened at the extraordinarily high energy consumption of the machine; if he were to turn it on, there would be cosmic consequences, and Sergei had never regarded himself as important enough to warrant those consequences.

But now, after thinking things out carefully and weighing all considerations, he decided to use the machine. He put it in with the skates and left the house.

It was a short walk to Sredni Avenue. In a store on the corner of Fifth Street he bought a bottle of champagne and a box of chocolates before continuing on his way. At Eleventh Street he turned off Sredni Avenue and was soon at Liussia's house; he climbed the steps and rang two long and one short on the bell. Liussia answered the door.

"Hello, Liussia! It's been a long time since we met last."

"Very long. But I've always been expecting you to come, and here you are."

They entered Liussia's room, drank champagne, and reminisced about things that had happened years before.

"Oh!" cried Liussia suddenly, "if I were only young again and life could begin all over!"

"That's in our power," said Sergei and showed her his SPOSEM, which was the size of a portable radio and had a rather thick cord attached to it.

"Do you plug it into the electrical system? Won't it burn out? The house was recently switched to 220 volts."

"No, it doesn't get plugged into the electrical system. A thousand Dnieper powerhouses wouldn't be enough to supply it. It gets its energy directly from the sun. Would you open the window, please?"

She opened it, and Sergei led the cord over to it. The cord had a small concave mirror attached to the end, and Sergei laid this on the window sill so that it was turned directly to the sun. Then he switched the machine on. A crackling could be heard from inside the apparatus, and soon the sun began to look weaker, the way an incandescent bulb does when the current drops. The room grew dusky.

Liussia went to the window and looked out. "Sergei, what's going on?" she asked in astonishment. "It looks as though an eclipse is beginning. The whole island is in dusk, and it's getting dark in the distance, too."

"It's now dark over the whole earth and even on Mars and Venus. The machine uses a great deal of energy."

"That kind of machine should never be mass-produced, then! Otherwise, everyone would become young again but there'd be darkness from then on."

"Yes," Sergei agreed. "The machine should be used only once. I gave it extra capacity for your sake. Now let's sit down and remain quiet."

They sat down on an old plush sofa, held hands, and waited. Meanwhile it had become dark as night. Throughout the city light sprang out of windows and streetlamps were turned on. Liussia's room was now completely black, except for a bluish light along the cord of the SPOSEM. The cord twisted and turned like a tube through which some liquid was being forced at great speed.

Suddenly the machine gave a loud crack and a square window opened in the front; from it leaped a ray of green light, which seemed to be chopped off at the end. The ray was like a solid object, yet it was only light. It became longer and longer and finally reached the wall with the picture of the pig and the oak tree. The pig in the picture suddenly changed into a piglet, and the oak with its huge branches into a tiny sapling.

The ray moved slowly and uncertainly across the room as if blindly seeking out Liussia and Sergei. Where it touched the wall, the old, faded hangings took on their original colors and became new again. The elderly gray tomcat who was dozing on the chest of drawers changed into a young kitten and immediately began to play with its tail. A fly, accidentally touched by the ray, changed into a larva and fell to the floor.

Finally the ray approached Sergei and Liussia. It ranged over their heads, faces, legs and arms. Above their heads two shimmering half-circles formed, like haloes.

"Something's tickling my head," Liussia giggled.

"Don't move, stay quiet," said Sergei. "That's because the gray hairs are changing back to their original color. My head feels funny, too."

"Oh!" cried Liussia, "there's something hot in my mouth!"

"You have some gold caps on your teeth, haven't you?"

"Only two."

"Young teeth don't need caps, so the caps are being pulverized. Just breathe the dust out."

Liussia pursed her lips like an inexperienced smoker and blew out some gold dust.

"It feels as though the sofa were swelling under me," she said suddenly.

"The springs are expanding because we're getting lighter. We did put on some weight over the years!"

"You're right, Sergei! I feel wonderfully light, the way I did at twenty."

"You are twenty now. We've returned to our youth."

At this moment the SPOSEM shivered, rumbled and burst into flame. Then it was gone and only a little blue ash showed where it had been. All around them, everything was suddenly bright again. Motorists turned their headlights off, the street lamps went out and the artificial light disappeared from the windows.

Liussia stood up and laughed as she looked at herself in the mirror. "Come on, Sergei, let's go for a walk—maybe to Yelagin Island."

Sergei picked up his bundle of skates, took Liussia's arm, and went down the stairs into the street with her. They rode the streetcar to Cultural Park where they strolled about for a long time, rode the merry-go-round, and ate two meals in a restaurant.

When the still white night had descended and the park was deserted, they went to the sea shore. The sea was completely calm, without even the smallest wave, and in the distance, near Volny Island, the sails of the yachts hung motionless in the moonlight.

"Just the right kind of weather," said Sergei as he unwrapped the water skates. He helped Liussia tie hers and then put his own on.

Liussia ran on to the water and skated lightly across it; Sergei followed. They came to the yachts, whose owners were waiting for a breeze, waved to them, and skated on past Volny Island to the open sea. They glided over the water for a long time, then Sergei suddenly slowed down; Liussia stopped and skated back to him.

"Liussia, do you know what I'd like to say to you?" Sergei began, somewhat unsure of himself.

"I know," Liussia replied, "and I love you too. From now on we'll stay together for good."

They embraced and kissed, then turned back to the shore. Meanwhile the wind had risen and was forming waves. It was becoming difficult to skate.

"Suppose I stumble and fall down into the water?" said Liussia.

"I'll take precautions right now so that we won't drown," answered Sergei with a laugh. He took the atomizer and bottle of MSST from his pocket and sprayed his and Liussia's clothing with the liquid.

"Now we can even ride the waves," he said to her.

They sat down, close together, on a wave, as though it were a crystal bench, and the wave carried them back to the shore.

translated by MATTHEW J. O'CONNELL

THE DEATHBIRD

HARLAN ELLISON

**So much has been written about Ellison's
many remarkable stories that it would be su-
perfluous to say much about this one except
that it is an example of "New Wave" writing
that still has something real to convey and that
Ellison himself has called it the bottom line
personal statement of all his work.**

I

This is a test. Take notes. This will count as ¾ of your final grade.
Hints: remember, in chess, kings cancel each other out and cannot
occupy adjacent squares, are therefore all-powerful and totally powerless, cannot affect one another, produce stalemate. Hinduism is a
polytheistic religion; the sect of Atman worships the divine spark of
life within Man; in effect saying, "Thou art God." Provisos of equal
time are not served by one viewpoint having media access to two hundred million people in prime time while opposing viewpoints are
provided with a soapbox on the corner. Not everyone tells the truth.
Operational note: these sections may be taken out of numerical sequence: rearrange to suit yourself for optimum clarity. Turn over
your test papers and begin.

II

Uncounted layers of rock pressed down on the magma pool. White-
hot with the bubbling ferocity of the molten nickel-iron core, the
pool spat and shuddered, yet did not pit or char or smoke or damage
in the slightest the smooth and reflective surfaces of the strange
crypt.

Nathan Stack lay in the crypt—silent, sleeping.

A shadow passed through rock. Through shale, through coal, through marble, through mica schist, through quartzite; through miles-thick deposits of phosphates, through diatomaceous earth, through feldspars, through diorite; through faults and folds, through anticlines and monoclines, through dips and synclines; through hellfire; and came to the ceiling of the great cavern and passed through; and saw the magma pool and dropped down; and came to the crypt. The shadow.

A triangular face with a single eye peered into the crypt, saw Stack, and lay four-fingered hands on the crypt's cool surface. Nathan Stack woke at the touch, and the crypt became transparent; he woke though the touch had not been upon his body. His soul felt the shadowy pressure and he opened his eyes to see the leaping brilliance of the world-core around him, to see the shadow with its single eye staring in at him.

The serpentine shadow enfolded the crypt; its darkness flowed upward again, through the Earth's mantle, toward the crust, toward the surface of the cinder, the broken toy that was the Earth.

When they reached the surface, the shadow bore the crypt to a place where the poison winds did not reach, and caused it to open.

Nathan Stack tried to move, and moved only with difficulty. Memories rushed through his head of other lives, many other lives, as many other men; then the memories slowed and melted into a background tone that could be ignored.

The shadow thing reached down a hand and touched Stack's naked flesh. Gently, but firmly, the thing helped him to stand, and gave him garments, and a neck-pouch that contained a short knife and a warming-stone and other things. He offered his hand, and Stack took it, and after two hundred and fifty thousand years sleeping in the crypt, Nathan Stack stepped out on the face of the sick planet Earth.

Then the thing bent low against the poison winds and began walking away. Nathan Stack, having no other choice, bent forward and followed the shadow creature.

III

A messenger had been sent for Dira and he had come as quickly as the meditations would permit. When he reached the Summit, he found the fathers waiting, and they took him gently into their cove, where they immersed themselves and began to speak.

"We've lost the arbitration," the coil-father said. "It will be necessary for us to go and leave it to him."

Dira could not believe it. "But didn't they listen to our arguments, to our logic?"

The fang-father shook his head sadly and touched Dira's shoulder. "There were . . . accommodations to be made. It was their time. So we must leave."

The coil-father said, "We've decided you will remain. One was permitted, in caretakership. Will you accept our commission?"

It was a very great honor, but Dira began to feel the loneliness even as they told him they would leave. Yet he accepted. Wondering why they had selected *him*, of all their people. There were reasons, there were always reasons, but he could not ask. And so he accepted the honor, with all its attendant sadness, and remained behind when they left.

The limits of his caretakership were harsh, for they insured he could not defend himself against whatever slurs or legends would be spread, nor could he take action unless it became clear the trust was being breached by the other—who now held possession. And he had no threat save the Deathbird. A final threat that could be used only when final measures were needed: and therefore too late.

But he was patient. The most patient of all his people.

Thousands of years later, when he saw how it was destined to go, when there was no doubt left how it would end, he understood *that* was the reason he had been chosen to stay behind.

But it did not help the loneliness.

Nor could it save the Earth. Only Stack could do that.

IV

1 *Now the serpent was more subtil than any beast of the field which the LORD God had made. And he said unto the woman, Yea hath God said, Ye shall not eat of every tree of the garden?*

2 *And the woman said unto the serpent, We may eat of the fruit of the trees of the garden:*

3 *But of the fruit of the tree which is in the midst of the garden, God hath said, Ye shall not eat of it, neither shall ye touch it, lest ye die.*

4 *And the serpent said unto the woman, Ye shall not surely die:*

5 *(Omitted)*

6 *And when the woman saw that the tree was good for food, and*

that it was pleasant to the eyes, and a tree to be desired to make one wise, she took of the fruit thereof, and did eat, and gave also unto her husband with her; and he did eat.

7 *(Omitted)*

8 *(Omitted)*

9 *And the LORD God called unto Adam, and said unto him, Where art thou?*

10 *(Omitted)*

11 *And he said, Who told thee that thou wast naked? Hast thou eaten of the tree, whereof I commanded thee that thou shouldest not eat?*

12 *And the man said, The woman whom thou gavest to be with me, she gave me of the tree, and I did eat.*

13 *And the LORD God said unto the woman, What is this that thou hast done? And the woman said, The serpent beguiled me, and I did eat.*

14 *And the LORD God said unto the serpent, Because thou hast done this, thou art cursed above all cattle, and above every beast of the field; upon thy belly shalt thou go, and dust shalt thou eat all the days of thy life:*

15 *And I will put enmity between thee and the woman, and between thy seed and her seed; it shall bruise thy head, and thou shalt bruise his heel.*

GENESIS, *Chap.* II

TOPICS FOR DISCUSSION
(Give 5 points per right answer.)

1. Melville's *Moby Dick* begins, "Call me Ishmael." We say it is told in the *first* person. In what person is Genesis told? From whose viewpoint?

2. Who is the "good guy" in this story? Who is the "bad guy?" Can you make a strong case for reversal of the roles?

3. Traditionally, the apple is considered to be the fruit the serpent offered to Eve. But apples are not endemic to the Near East. Select one of the following, more logical substitutes, and discuss how myths come into being and are corrupted over long periods of time: olive, fig, date, pomegranate.

4. Why is the word LORD always in capitals and the name God always capitalized? Shouldn't the serpent's name be capitalized, as well? If no, why?

5. If God created everything (see *Genesis,* **Chap. I),** why did he create problems for himself by creating a serpent who would lead his creations astray? Why did God create a tree he did not want Adam and Eve to know about, and then go out of his way to warn them against it?

6. Compare and contrast Michaelangelo's Sistine Chapel ceiling panel of the *Expulsion from Paradise* with Bosch's *Garden of Earthly Delights.*

7. Was Adam being a gentleman when he placed blame on Eve? Who was Quisling? Discuss "narking" as a character flaw.

8. God grew angry when he found out he had been defied. If God is omnipotent and omniscient, didn't he know? Why couldn't he find Adam and Eve when they hid?

9. If God had not wanted Adam and Eve to taste the fruit of the forbidden tree, why didn't he warn the serpent? Could God have prevented the serpent from tempting Adam and Eve? If yes, why didn't he? If no, discuss the possibility the serpent was as powerful as God.

10. Using examples from two different media journals, demonstrate the concept of "slanted news."

V

The poison winds howled and tore at the powder covering the land. Nothing lived there. The winds, green and deadly, dived out of the sky and raked the carcass of the Earth, seeking, seeking: anything moving, anything still living. But there was nothing. Powder. Talc. Pumice.

And the onyx spire of the mountain toward which Nathan Stack and the shadow thing had moved, all that first day. When night fell they dug a pit in the tundra and the shadow thing coated it with a substance thick as glue that had been in Stack's neck-pouch. Stack had slept the night fitfully, clutching the warming-stone to his chest and breathing through a filter tube from the pouch.

Once he had awakened, at the sound of great batlike creatures flying overhead; he had seen them swooping low, coming in flat trajectories across the wasteland toward his pit in the earth. But they seemed unaware that he—and the shadow thing—lay in the hole. They defecated thin, phosphorescent stringers that fell glowing through the night and were lost on the plains; then the creatures swooped upward and were whirled away on the winds. Stack resumed sleeping with difficulty.

In the morning, frosted with an icy light that gave everything a blue tinge, the shadow thing scrabbled its way out of the choking powder and crawled along the ground, then lay flat, fingers clawing for purchase in the whiskaway surface. Behind it, from the powder, Stack bore toward the surface, reached up a hand and trembled for help.

The shadow creature slid across the ground, fighting the winds that had grown stronger in the night, back to the soft place that had been their pit, to the hand thrust up through the powder. It grasped the hand, and Stack's fingers tightened convulsively. Then the crawling shadow exerted pressure and pulled the man from the treacherous pumice.

Together they lay against the earth, fighting to see, fighting to draw breath without filling their lungs with suffocating death.

"Why is it like this . . . what *happened?*" Stack screamed against the wind. The shadow creature did not answer, but it looked at Stack for a long moment and then, with very careful movements, raised its hand, held it up before Stack's eyes and slowly, making claws of the fingers, closed the four fingers into a cage, into a fist, into a painfully tight ball that said more eloquently than words: *destruction.*

Then they began to crawl toward the mountain.

VI

The onyx spire of the mountain rose out of hell and struggled toward the shredded sky. It was monstrous arrogance. Nothing should have tried that climb out of desolation. But the black mountain had tried, and succeeded.

It was like an old man. Seamed, ancient, dirt caked in striated lines, autumnal, lonely; black and desolate, piled strength upon strength. It would *not* give in to gravity and pressure and death. It struggled for the sky. Ferociously alone, it was the only feature that broke the desolate line of the horizon.

In another twenty-five million years the mountain might be worn as smooth and featureless as a tiny onyx offering to the deity night. But though the powder plains swirled and the poison winds drove the pumice against the flanks of the pinnacle, thus far their scouring had only served to soften the edges of the mountain's profile, as though divine intervention had protected the spire.

Lights moved near the summit.

VII

Stack learned the nature of the phosphorescent stringers defecated onto the plain the night before by the batlike creatures. They were spores that became, in the wan light of day, strange bleeder plants.

All around them as they crawled through the dawn, the little live things sensed their warmth and began thrusting shoots up through the talc. As the fading red ember of the dying sun climbed painfully into the sky, the bleeding plants were already reaching maturity.

Stack cried out as one of the vine tentacles fastened around his ankle, holding him. A second looped itself around his neck.

Thin films of berry-black blood coated the vines, leaving rings on Stack's flesh. The rings burned terribly.

The shadow creature slid on its belly and pulled itself back to the man. Its triangular head came close to Stack's neck, and it bit into the vine. Thick black blood spurted as the vine parted, and the shadow creature rasped its razor-edged teeth back and forth till Stack was able to breathe again. With a violent movement Stack folded himself down and around, pulling the short knife from the neck-pouch. He sawed through the vine tightening inexorably around his ankle. It screamed as it was severed, in the same voice Stack had heard from the skies the night before. The severed vine writhed away, withdrawing into the talc.

Stack and the shadow thing crawled forward once again, low, flat, holding onto the dying earth: toward the mountain. High in the bloody sky, the Deathbird circled.

VIII

On their own world, they had lived in luminous, oily-walled caverns for millions of years, evolving and spreading their race through the universe. When they had had enough of empire-building, they turned inward, and much of their time was spent in the intricate construction of songs of wisdom, and the designing of fine worlds for many races.

There were other races that designed, however. And when there was a conflict over jurisdiction, an arbitration was called, adjudicated by a race whose *raison d'etre* was impartiality and cleverness unraveling knotted threads of claim and counter-claim. Their racial honor, in fact, depended on the flawless application of these qualities. Through the centuries they had refined their talents in more and more sophisticated arenas of arbitration until the time came when they were the final authority. The litigants were compelled to abide by the judgments, not merely because the decisions were always wise and creatively fair, but because the judges' race would, if its decisions were questioned as suspect, destroy itself. In the holiest place on their world they had erected a religious machine. It could be activated to emit a tone that would shatter their crystal carapaces. They were a race of exquisite cricket-like creatures, no larger than the thumb of a man. They were treasured throughout the civilized worlds, and their loss would have been catastrophic. Their honor and their value was never questioned. All races abided by their decisions.

So Dira's people gave over jurisdiction to that certain world, and went away, leaving Dira with only the Deathbird, a special caretakership the adjudicators had creatively woven into their judgment.

There is recorded one last meeting between Dira and those who had given him his commission. There were readings that could not be ignored—had, in fact, been urgently brought to the attention of the fathers of Dira's race by the adjudicators—and the Great Coiled One came to Dira at the last possible moment to tell him of the mad thing into whose hands this world had been given, to tell Dira of what the mad thing could do.

The Great Coiled One—whose rings were loops of wisdom acquired through centuries of gentleness and perception and immersed meditations that had brought forth lovely designs for many worlds— he who was the holiest of Dira's race, honored Dira by coming to *him*, rather than commanding Dira to appear.

We have only one gift to leave them, he said. *Wisdom. This mad one will come, and he will lie to them, and he will tell them: created he them. And we will be gone, and there will be nothing between them and the mad one but you. Only you can give them the wisdom to defeat him in their own good time.* Then the Great Coiled One stroked the skin of Dira with ritual affection, and Dira was deeply moved and could not reply. Then he was left alone.

The mad one came, and interposed himself, and Dira gave them wisdom, and time passed. His name became other than Dira, it became Snake, and the new name was despised: but Dira could see the Great Coiled One had been correct in his readings. So Dira made his selection. A man, one of them, and gifted him with the spark.

All of this is recorded somewhere. It is history.

IX

The man was not Jesus of Nazareth. He may have been Simon. Not Genghis Khan, but perhaps a foot soldier in his horde. Not Aristotle, but possibly one who sat and listened to Socrates in the agra. Neither the shambler who discovered the wheel nor the link who first ceased painting himself blue and applied the colors to the walls of the cave. But one near them, somewhere near at hand. The man was not Richard *Coeur de Lion*, Rembrandt, Richelieu, Rasputin, Robert Fulton or the Mahdi. Just a man. With the spark.

X

Once, Dira came to the man. Very early on. The spark was there, but the light needed to be converted to energy. So Dira came to the man, and did what had to be done before the mad one knew of it, and when he discovered that Dira, the Snake, had made contact, he quickly made explanations.

This legend has come down to us as the fable of *Faust*.

TRUE or FALSE?

XI

Light converted to energy, thus:

In the fortieth year of his five hundredth incarnation, all-unknowing of the eons of which he had been part, the man found himself wandering in a terrible dry place under a thin, flat burning disc of sun. He was a Berber tribesman who had never considered shadows save to relish them when they provided shade. The shadow came to him, sweeping down across the sands like the *khamsin* of Egypt, the *simoom* of Asia Minor, the *harmattan*, all of which he had known in his various lives, none of which he remembered. The shadow came over him like the *sirocco*.

The shadow stole the breath from his lungs and the man's eyes rolled up in his head. He fell to the ground and the shadow took him down and down, through the sands, into the Earth.

Mother Earth.

She lived, this world of trees and rivers and rocks with deep stone thoughts. She breathed, had feelings, dreamed dreams, gave birth, laughed and grew contemplative for millennia. This great creature swimming in the sea of space.

What a wonder, thought the man, for he had never understood that the Earth was his mother, before this. He had never understood, before this, that the Earth had a life of its own, at once a part of mankind and quite separate from mankind. A mother with a life of her own.

Dira, Snake, shadow . . . took the man down and let the spark of light change itself to energy as the man became one with the Earth. His flesh melted and became quiet, cool soil. His eyes glowed with the light that shines in the darkest centers of the planet and he saw the way the mother cared for her young: the worms, the roots of plants, the rivers that cascaded for miles over great cliffs in enormous caverns, the bark of trees. He was taken once more to the bosom of that great Earth mother, and understood the joy of her life.

Remember this, Dira said to the man.

What a wonder, the man thought . . .

. . . and was returned to the sands of the desert, with no remembrance of having slept with, loved, enjoyed the body of his natural mother.

XII

They camped at the base of the mountain, in a greenglass cave; not deep but angled sharply so the blown pumice could not reach them. They put Nathan Stack's stone in a fault in the cave's floor, and the heat spread quickly, warming them. The shadow thing with its triangular head sank back in shadow and closed its eye and sent its hunting instinct out for food. A shriek came back on the wind.

Much later, when Nathan Stack had eaten, when he was reasonably content and well-fed, he stared into the shadows and spoke to the creature sitting there.

"How long was I down there . . . how long was the sleep?"

The shadow thing spoke in whispers. *A quarter of a million years.*

Stack did not reply. The figure was beyond belief. The shadow creature seemed to understand.

In the life of a world no time at all.

Nathan Stack was a man who could make accommodations. He smiled quickly and said, "I must have been tired."

The shadow did not respond.

"I don't understand very much of this. It's pretty damned frightening. To die, then to wake up . . . here. Like this."

You did not die. You were taken, put down there. By the end you will understand everything, I promise you.

"Who put me down there?"

I did. I came and found you when the time was right, and I put you down there.

"Am I still Nathan Stack?"

If you wish.

"But *am* I Nathan Stack?"

You always were. You had many other names, many other bodies, but the spark was always yours. Stack seemed about to speak, and the shadow creature added, *You were always on your way to being who you are.*

"But what *am* I? Am I still Nathan Stack, dammit?"

If you wish.

"Listen: you don't seem too sure about that. You came and got me, I mean I woke up and there you were; now who should know better than you what my name is?"

You have had many names in many times. Nathan Stack is merely the one you remember. You had a very different name long ago, at the start, when I first came to you.

Stack was afraid of the answer, but he asked, "What was my name then?"

Ish-lilith. Husband of Lilith. Do you remember her?

Stack thought, tried to open himself to the past, but it was as unfathomable as the quarter of a million years through which he had slept in the crypt.

"No. But there were other women, in other times."

Many. There was one who replaced Lilith.

"I don't remember."

Her name . . . does not matter. But when the mad one took her from you and replaced her with the other . . . then I knew it would end like this. The Deathbird.

"I don't mean to be stupid, but I haven't the faintest idea what you're talking about."

Before it ends, you will understand everything.

"You said that before." Stack paused, stared at the shadow creature for a long time only moments long, then, "What was your name?"

Before I met you my name was Dira.

He said it in his native tongue. Stack could not pronounce it.

"Before you met me. What is it now?"

Snake.

Something slithered past the mouth of the cave. It did not stop, but it called out with the voice of moist mud sucking down into a quagmire.

"Why did you put *me* down there? Why did you come to me in the first place? What spark? Why can't I remember these other lives or who I was? What do you want from me?"

You should sleep. It will be a long climb. And cold.

"I slept for two hundred and fifty thousand years, I'm hardly tired," Stack said. "Why did you pick me?"

Later. Now sleep. Sleep has other uses.

Darkness deepened around Snake, seeped out around the cave, and Nathan Stack lay down near the warming-stone, and the darkness took him.

XIII

SUPPLEMENTARY READING

This is an essay by a writer. It is clearly an appeal to the emotions. As you read it ask yourself how it applies to the subject under discussion. What is the writer trying to say? Does he succeed in making his point? Does this essay cast light on the point of the subject under discussion? After you have read this essay, using the reverse side of your test paper, write your own essay (500 words or less) on the loss of a loved one. If you have never lost a loved one, fake it.

AHBHU

Yesterday my dog died. For eleven years Ahbhu was my closest friend. He was responsible for my writing a story about a boy and his dog that many people have read. He was not a pet, he was a person. It was impossible to anthropomorphize him, he wouldn't stand for it. But he was so much his own kind of creature, he had such a strongly formed personality, he was so determined to share his life with only those *he* chose, that it was also impossible to think of him as simply a dog. Apart from those canine characteristics into which he was locked by his species, he comported himself like one of a kind.

We met when I came to him at the West Los Angeles Animal Shelter. I'd wanted a dog because I was lonely and I'd remembered when I was a little boy how my dog had been a friend when I had no other friends. One summer I went away to camp and when I returned I found a rotten old neighbor lady from up the street had had my dog picked up and gassed while my father was at work. I crept into the woman's back yard that night and found a rug hanging on the clothesline. The rug beater was hanging from a post. I stole it and buried it.

At the Animal Shelter there was a man in line ahead of me. He had brought in a puppy only a week or so old. A Puli, a Hungarian sheep dog; it was a sad-looking little thing. He had too many in the litter and had brought in this one to either be taken by someone else, or to be put to sleep. They took the dog inside and the man behind the counter called my turn. I told him I wanted a dog and he took me back inside to walk down the line of cages.

In one of the cages the little Puli that had just been brought in was being assaulted by three larger dogs who had been earlier tenants. He was a little thing, and he was on the bottom, getting the stuffing knocked out of him. But he was struggling mightily. The runt of the litter.

"Get him out of there!" I yelled. "I'll take him, I'll take him, get him out of there!"

He cost two dollars. It was the best two bucks I ever spent.

Driving home with him, he was lying on the other side of the front seat, staring at me. I had had a vague idea what I'd name a pet, but as I stared at him, and he stared back at me, I suddenly was put in mind of the scene in Alexander Korda's 1939 film *The Thief of Bagdad*, where the evil vizier, played by Conrad Veidt, had changed Ahbhu, the little thief, played by Sabu, into a dog. The film had superimposed the human over the canine face for a moment so there was an extraordinary look of intelligence in the face of the dog. The little Puli was looking at me with that same expression. "Ahbhu," I said.

He didn't react to the name, but then he couldn't have cared less. But that was his name, from that time on.

No one who ever came into my house was unaffected by him. When he sensed someone with good vibrations, he was right there, lying at their feet. He loved to be scratched, and despite years of admonitions he refused to stop begging for scraps at table, because he found most of the people who had come to dinner at my house were patsies unable to escape his woebegone Jackie-Coogan-as-the-Kid look.

But he was a certain barometer of bums, as well. On any number of occasions when I found someone I liked, and Ahbhu would have nothing to do with him or her, it always turned out the person was a wrongo. I took to noting his attitude toward newcomers, and I must admit it influenced my own reactions. I was always wary of someone Ahbhu shunned.

Women with whom I had had unsatisfactory affairs would nonetheless return to the house from time to time—to visit the dog. He had an intimate circle of friends, many of whom had nothing to do with me, and numbering among their company some of the most beautiful actresses in Hollywood. One exquisite lady used to send her driver to pick him up for Sunday afternoon romps at the beach.

I never asked him what happened on those occasions. He didn't talk.

Last year he started going downhill, though I didn't realize it because he maintained the manner of a puppy almost to the end. But he began sleeping too much, and he couldn't hold down his food—not even the Hungarian meals prepared for him by the Magyars who lived up the street. And it became apparent to me something was wrong with him when he got scared during the big Los Angeles earthquake last year. Ahbhu wasn't afraid of anything. He attacked the Pacific Ocean and walked tall around vicious cats. But the quake terrified him and he jumped up in my bed and threw his forelegs around my neck. I was very nearly the only victim of the earthquake to die from animal strangulation.

He was in and out of the veterinarian's shop all through the early part of this year, and the idiot always said it was his diet.

Then one Sunday when he was out in the backyard, I found him lying at the foot of the porch stairs, covered with mud, vomiting so heavily all he could bring up was bile. He was matted with his own refuse and he was trying desperately to dig his nose into the earth for coolness. He was barely breathing. I took him to a different vet.

At first they thought it was just old age . . . that they could pull him through. But finally they took X-rays and saw the cancer had taken hold in his stomach and liver.

I put off the day as much as I could. Somehow I just couldn't conceive of a world that didn't have him in it. But yesterday I went to the vet's office and signed the euthanasia papers.

"I'd like to spend a little time with him, before," I said.

They brought him in and put him on the stainless steel examination table. He had grown so thin. He'd always had a pot-belly and it was gone. The muscles in his hind legs were weak, flaccid. He came to me and put his head into the hollow of my armpit. He was trembling violently. I lifted his head and he looked at me with that comic face I'd always thought made him look like Lawrence Talbot, the Wolf Man. He knew. Sharp as hell right up to the end, hey old friend? He knew, and he was scared. He trembled all the way down to his spiderweb legs. This bouncing ball of hair that, when lying on a dark carpet, could be taken for a sheepskin rug, with no way to tell at which end head and which end tail. So thin. Shaking, knowing what was going to happen to him. But still a puppy.

I cried and my eyes closed as my nose swelled with the crying, and he buried his head in my arms because we hadn't done much crying at one another. I was ashamed of myself not to be taking it as well as he was.

"I *got* to, pup, because you're in pain and you can't eat. I *got* to." But he didn't want to know that.

The vet came in, then. He was a nice guy and he asked me if I wanted to go away and just let it be done.

Then Ahbhu came up out of there and *looked* at me.

There is a scene in Kazan's *Viva Zapata* where a close friend of Zapata's, Brando's, has been condemned for conspiring with the *Federales*. A friend that had been with Zapata since the mountains, since the *revolución* had begun. And they come to the hut to take him to the firing squad, and Brando starts out, and his friend stops him with a hand on his arm, and he says to him with great friendship, "Emiliano, do it yourself."

Ahbhu looked at me and I know he was just a dog, but if he could have spoken with human tongue he could not have said more eloquently than he did with a look, *don't leave me with strangers*.

So I held him as they laid him down and the vet slipped the lanyard up around his right foreleg and drew it tight to bulge the vein, and I held his head and he turned it away from me as the needle went in. It was impossible to tell the moment he passed over from life to death. He simply laid his head on my hand, his eyes fluttered shut and he was gone.

I wrapped him in a sheet with the help of the vet, and I drove home with Ahbhu on the seat beside me, just the way we had come home eleven years before. I took him out in the backyard and began digging his grave. I dug for hours, crying and mumbling to myself, talking to him in the sheet. It was a very neat, rectangular grave with smooth sides and all the loose dirt scooped out by hand.

I laid him down in the hole and he was so tiny in there for a dog who had seemed to be so big in life, so furry, so funny. And I covered him over and when the hole was packed full of dirt I replaced the neat divot of grass I'd scalped off at the start. And that was all.

But I couldn't send him to strangers.

THE END

QUESTIONS FOR DISCUSSION

1. Is there any significance to the reversal of the word *god* being *dog?* If so, what?
2. Does the writer try to impart human qualities to a non-human creature? Why? Discuss anthropomorphism in the light of the phrase, "Thou art God."
3. Discuss the love the writer shows in this essay. Compare and contrast it with other forms of love: the love of a man for a woman, a mother for a child, a son for a mother, a botanist for plants, an ecologist for the Earth.

XIV

In his sleep, Nathan Stack talked.
"Why did you pick me? Why me . . ."

XV

Like the Earth, the Mother was in pain.

The great house was very quiet. The doctor had left, and the relatives had gone into town for dinner. He sat by the side of her bed and stared down at her. She looked gray and old and crumpled; her skin was a soft ashy hue of moth-dust. He was crying softly.

He felt her hand on his knee, and looked up to see her staring at him. "You weren't supposed to catch me," he said.

"I'd be disappointed if I hadn't," she said. Her voice was very thin, very smooth.

"How is it?"

"It hurts. Ben didn't dope me too well."

He bit his lower lip. The doctor had used massive doses, but the pain was more massive. She gave little starts as tremors of sudden agony hit her. Impacts. He watched the life leaking out of her eyes.

"How is your sister taking it?"

He shrugged. "You know Charlene. She's sorry, but it's all pretty intellectual to her."

His mother let a tiny ripple of a smile move her lips. "It's a terrible thing to say, Nathan, but your sister isn't the most likeable woman in the world. I'm glad you're here." She paused, thinking, then added, "It's just possible your father and I missed something from the gene pool. Charlene isn't whole."

"Can I get you something? A drink of water?"

"No. I'm fine."

He looked at the ampoule of narcotic pain killer. The syringe lay mechanical and still on a clean towel beside it. He felt her eyes on him. She knew what he was thinking. He looked away.

"I would kill for a cigarette," she said.

He laughed. At sixty-five, both legs gone, what remained of her left side paralyzed, the cancer spreading like deadly jelly toward her heart, she was still the matriarch. "You can't have a cigarette, so forget it."

"Then why don't you use that hypo and let me out of here."

"Shut up, Mother."

"Oh, for Christ's sake, Nathan. It's hours if I'm lucky. Months if I'm not. We've had this conversation before. You know I always win."

"Did I ever tell you you were a bitchy old lady?"

"Many times, but I love you anyhow."

He got up and walked to the wall. He could not walk through it, so he went around the inside of the room.

"You can't get away from it."

"Mother, Jesus! Please!"

"All right. Let's talk about the business."

"I could care less about the business right now."

"Then what should we talk about? The lofty uses to which an old lady can put her last moments?"

"You know, you're really ghoulish. I think you're enjoying this in some sick way."

"What other way is there to enjoy it."

"An adventure."

"The biggest. A pity your father never had the chance to savor it."

"I hardly think he'd have savored the feeling of being stamped to death in a hydraulic press."

Then he thought about it, because that little smile was on her lips again. "Okay, he probably would have. The two of you were so unreal, you'd have sat there and discussed it and analyzed the pulp."

"And you're our son."

He was, and he was. And he could not deny it, nor had he ever. He was hard and gentle and wild just like them, and he remembered the days in the jungle beyond Brasilia, and the hunt in the Cayman Trench, and the other days working in the mills alongside his father, and he knew when his moment came he would savor death as she did.

"*Tell me something. I've always wanted to know. Did Dad kill Tom Golden?*"

"*Use the needle and I'll tell you.*"

"*I'm a Stack. I don't bribe.*"

"*I'm a Stack, and I know what a killing curiosity you've got. Use the needle and I'll tell you.*"

He walked widdershins around the room. She watched him, eyes bright as the mill vats.

"*You old bitch.*"

"*Shame, Nathan. You know you're not the son of a bitch. Which is more than your sister can say. Did I ever tell you she wasn't your father's child?*"

"*No, but I knew.*"

"*You'd have liked her father. He was Swedish. Your father liked him.*"

"*Is that why Dad broke both his arms?*"

"*Probably. But I never heard the Swede complain. One night in bed with me in those days was worth a couple of broken arms. Use the needle.*"

Finally, while the family was between the entree and the dessert, he filled the syringe and injected her. Her eyes widened as the stuff smacked her heart, and just before she died she rallied all her strength and said, "*A deal's a deal. Your father didn't kill Tom Golden, I did. You're a hell of a man, Nathan, and you fought us the way we wanted, and we both loved you more than you could know. Except, dammit, you cunning s.o.b., you do know, don't you?*"

"*I know,*" he said, and she died; and he cried; and that was the extent of the poetry in it.

XVI

He knows we are coming.

They were climbing the northern face of the onyx mountain. Snake had coated Nathan Stack's feet with the thick glue and, though it was hardly a country walk, he was able to keep a foothold and pull himself up. Now they had paused to rest on a spiral ledge, and Snake had spoken for the first time of what waited for them where they were going.

"*He?*"

Snake did not answer. Stack slumped against the wall of the ledge. At the lower slopes of the mountain they had encountered slug-like creatures that had tried to attach themselves to Stack's flesh, but when Snake had driven them off they had returned to sucking the rocks. They had not come near the shadow creature. Further up, Stack could see the lights that flickered at the summit; he had felt fear that crawled up from his stomach. A short time before they had come to this ledge they had stumbled past a cave in the mountain where the bat creatures slept. They had gone mad at the presence of the man and the Snake and the sounds they had made sent waves of nausea through Stack. Snake had helped him and they had gotten past. Now they had stopped and Snake would not answer Stack's questions.

We must keep climbing.

"Because he knows we're here." There was a sarcastic rise in Stack's voice.

Snake started moving. Stack closed his eyes. Snake stopped and came back to him. Stack looked up at the one-eyed shadow.

"Not another step."

There is no reason why you should not know.

"Except, friend, I have the feeling you aren't going to tell me anything."

It is not yet time for you to know.

"Look: just because I haven't asked, doesn't mean I don't want to know. You've told me things I shouldn't be able to handle . . . all kinds of crazy things . . . I'm as old as, as . . . I don't know *how* old, but I get the feeling you've been trying to tell me I'm Adam . . ."

That is so.

". . . uh." He stopped rattling and stared back at the shadow creature. Then, very softly, accepting even more than he had thought possible, he said, "Snake." He was silent again. After a time he asked, "Give me another dream and let me know the rest of it?"

You must be patient. The one who lives at the top knows we are coming but I have been able to keep him from perceiving your danger to him only because you do not know yourself.

"Tell me this, then: does he *want* us to come up . . . the one on the top?"

He allows it. Because he doesn't know.

Stack nodded, resigned to following Snake's lead. He got to his feet and performed an elaborate butler's motion, after you, Snake.

And Snake turned, his flat hands sticking to the wall of the ledge, and they climbed higher, spiraling upward toward the summit.

The Deathbird swooped, then rose toward the Moon. There was still time.

XVII

Dira came to Nathan Stack near sunset, appearing in the board room of the industrial consortium Stack had built from the family empire.

Stack sat in the pneumatic chair that dominated the conversation pit where top-level decisions were made. He was alone. The others had left hours before and the room was dim with only the barest glow of light from hidden banks that shone through the soft walls.

The shadow creature passed through the walls—and at his passage they became rose quartz, then returned to what they had been. He stood staring at Nathan Stack, and for long moments the man was unaware of any other presence in the room.

You have to go now, Snake said.

Stack looked up, his eyes widened in horror, and through his mind flitted the unmistakable image of Satan, fanged mouth smiling, horns gleaming with scintillas of light as though seen through cross-tar filters, rope tail with its spade-shaped pointed tip thrashing, large cloven hoofs leaving burning imprints in the carpet, eyes as deep as pools of oil, the pitchfork, the satin-lined cape, the hairy legs of a goat, talons. He tried to scream but the sound dammed up in his throat.

No, Snake said, *that is not so. Come with me, and you will understand.*

There was a tone of sadness in the voice. As though Satan had been sorely wronged. Stack shook his head violently.

There was no time for argument. The moment had come, and Dira could not hesitate. He gestured and Nathan Stack rose from the pneumatic chair, leaving behind something that looked like Nathan Stack asleep, and he walked to Dira and Snake took him by the hand and they passed through rose quartz and went away from there.

Down and down Snake took him.

The Mother was in pain. She had been sick for eons, but it had reached the point where Snake knew it would be terminal, and the Mother knew it, too. But she would hide her child, she would intercede in her own behalf and hide him away deep in her bosom where no one, not even the mad one, could find him.

Dira took Stack to Hell.

It was a fine place.

Warm and safe and far from the probing of mad ones.

And the sickness raged on unchecked. Nations crumbled, the

oceans boiled and then grew cold and filmed over with scum, the air became thick with dust and killing vapors, flesh ran like oil, the skies grew dark, the sun blurred and became dull. The Earth moaned.

The plants suffered and consumed themselves, beasts became crippled and went mad, trees burst into flame and from their ashes rose glass shapes that shattered in the wind. The Earth was dying; a long, slow, painful death.

In the center of the Earth, in the fine place, Nathan Stack slept. *Don't leave me with strangers.*

Overhead, far away against the stars, the Deathbird circled and circled, waiting for the word.

XVIII

When they reached the highest peak, Nathan Stack looked across through the terrible burning cold and the ferocious grittiness of the demon wind and saw the sanctuary of always, the cathedral of forever, the pillar of remembrance, the haven of perfection, the pyramid of blessings, the toyshop of creation, the vault of deliverance, the monument of longing, the receptacle of thoughts, the maze of wonder, the catafalque of despair, the podium of pronouncements and the kiln of last attempts.

On a slope that rose to a star pinnacle, he saw the home of the one who dwelled here—lights flashing and flickering, lights that could be seen far off across the deserted face of the planet—and he began to suspect the name of the resident.

Suddenly everything went red for Nathan Stack. As though a filter had been dropped over his eyes, the black sky, the flickering lights, the rocks that formed the great plateau on which they stood, even Snake became red, and with the color came pain. Terrible pain that burned through every channel of Stack's body, as though his blood had been set afire. He screamed and fell to his knees, the pain crackling through his brain, following every nerve and blood vessel and ganglia and neural track. His skull flamed.

Fight him, Snake said. *Fight him!*

I can't, screamed silently through Stack's mind, the pain too great even to speak. Fire licked and leaped and he felt the delicate tissues of thought shriveling. He tried to focus his thoughts on ice. He clutched for salvation at ice, chunks of ice, mountains of ice, swimming icebergs of ice half-buried in frozen water, even as his soul smoked and smoldered. *Ice!* He thought of millions of particles of hail rushing, falling, thundering against the firestorm eating his mind, and there was a spit of steam, a flame that went out, a corner that grew cool . . . and he took his stand in that corner, thinking ice, thinking blocks and chunks and monuments of ice, edging them out to widen the circle of coolness and safety. Then the flames began to retreat, to slide back down the channels, and he sent ice after them, snuffing them, burying them in ice and chill waters.

When he opened his eyes, he was still on his knees, but he could think again, and the red surfaces had become normal again.

He will try again. You must be ready.

"Tell me *everything!* I can't go through this without knowing, I need help!"

You can help yourself. You have the strength. I gave you the spark.
. . . and the second derangement struck!

The air turned shaverasse and he held dripping chunks of unclean rova in his jowls, the taste making him weak with nausea. His pods withered and drew up into his shell and as the bones cracked he howled with strings of pain that came so fast they were almost one. He tried to scuttle away, but his eyes magnified the shatter of light that beat against him. Facets of his eyes cracked and the juice began to bubble out. The pain was unbelievable.

Fight him!

Stack rolled onto his back, sending out cilia to touch the Earth, and for an instant he realized he was seeing through the eyes of another creature, another form of life he could not even describe. But he was under an open sky and that produced fear, he was surrounded by air that had become deadly and *that* produced fear, he was going blind and *that* produced fear, he was . . . he was a *man* . . . he fought back against the feeling of being some other thing . . . he was a *man* and he would not feel fear, he would stand.

He rolled over, withdrew his cilia, and struggled to lower his pods. Broken bones grated and pain thundered through his body. He forced himself to ignore it, and finally the pods were down and he was breathing and he felt his head reeling . . .

And when he opened his eyes he was Nathan Stack again.

. . . and the third derangement struck:

Hopelessness.

Out of unending misery he came back to be Stack.

. . . and the fourth derangement struck:

Madness.

Out of raging lunacy he fought his way to be Stack.

. . . and the fifth derangement, and the sixth, and the seventh, and the plagues, and the whirlwinds, and the pools of evil, and the reduction in size and accompanying fall forever through submicroscopic hells, and the things that fed on him from inside, and the twentieth, and the fortieth, and the sound of his voice screaming for release, and the voice of Snake always beside him, whispering *Fight him!*

Finally it stopped.

Quickly, now.

Snake took Stack by the hand and half-dragging him they raced to the great palace of light and glass on the slope, shining brightly under the star pinnacle, and they passed under an arch of shining metal into the ascension hall. The portal sealed behind them.

There were tremors in the walls. The inlaid floors of jewels began to rumble and tremble. Bits of high and faraway ceilings began to drop. Quaking, the palace gave one hideous shudder and collapsed around them.

Now, Snake said. *Now you will know everything!*

And everything forgot to fall. Frozen in mid-air, the wreckage of the palace hung suspended above them. Even the air ceased to swirl. Time stood still. The movement of the Earth was halted. Everything held utterly immobile as Nathan Stack was permitted to understand all.

XIX

MULTIPLE CHOICE
(Counts for ½ your final grade.)

1. **God is:**
   A. An invisible spirit with a long beard.
   B. A small dog dead in a hole.
   C. Everyman.
   D. The Wizard of Oz.
2. **Nietzsche wrote "God is dead." By this did he mean:**
   A. Life is pointless?
   B. Belief in supreme deities has waned?
   C. There never was a God to begin with?
   D. Thou art God?
3. **Ecology is another name for:**
   A. Mother love.
   B. Enlightened self-interest.
   C. A good health salad with Granola.
   D. God.

4. **Which of these phrases most typifies the profoundest love?**
   A. **Don't leave me with strangers.**
   B. **I love you.**
   C. **God is love.**
   D. **Use the needle.**
5. **Which of these powers do we usually associate with God?**
   A. **Power.**
   B. **Love.**
   C. **Humanity.**
   D. **Docility.**

XX

None of the above.

Starlight shone in the eyes of the Deathbird and its passage through the night cast a shadow on the Moon.

XXI

Nathan Stack raised his hands and around them the air was still as the palace fell crashing. They were untouched. *Now you know all there is to know,* Snake said, sinking to one knee as though worshipping. There was no one there to worship but Nathan Stack.

"Was he always mad?"

From the first.

"Then those who gave our world to him were mad, and your race was mad to allow it."

Snake had no answer.

"Perhaps it was supposed to be like this," Stack said.

He reached down and lifted Snake to his feet, and he touched the shadow creature's head. "Friend," he said.

Snake's race was incapable of tears. He said, *I have waited longer than you can know for that word.*

"I'm sorry it comes at the end."

Perhaps it was supposed to be like this.

Then there was a swirling of air, a scintillance in the ruined palace, and the owner of the mountain, the owner of the ruined Earth came to them in a burning bush.

AGAIN, SNAKE? AGAIN YOU ANNOY ME?

The time for toys is ended.

NATHAN STACK YOU BRING TO STOP ME? *I SAY*

WHEN THE TIME IS ENDED. *I* SAY, AS I'VE ALWAYS SAID.
Then, to Nathan Stack:
GO AWAY. FIND A PLACE TO HIDE UNTIL I COME FOR
YOU.

Stack ignored the burning bush. He waved his hand and the cone
of safety in which they stood vanished. "Let's find him, first, then I
know what to do."

The Deathbird sharpened its talons on the night wind and sailed
down through emptiness toward the cinder of the Earth.

XXII

Nathan Stack had once contracted pneumonia. He had lain on the
operating table as the surgeon made the small incision in the chest
wall. Had he not been stubborn, had he not continued working
around the clock while the pneumonic infection developed into
empyema, he would never have had to go under the knife, even for
an operation as safe as a thoractomy. But he was a Stack, and so he
lay on the operating table as the rubber tube was inserted into the
chest cavity to drain off the pus in the pleural cavity, and heard someone speak his name.

NATHAN STACK

He heard it, from far off, across an Arctic vastness; heard it echoing
over and over, down an endless corridor; as the knife sliced.

NATHAN STACK

He remembered Lilith, with hair the color of dark wine. He remembered taking hours to die beneath a rock slide as his hunting
companions in the pack ripped apart the remains of the bear and
ignored his grunted moans for help. He remembered the impact of
the crossbow bolt as it ripped through his hauberk and split his chest
and he died at Agincourt. He remembered the icy water of the Ohio
as it closed over his head and the flatboat disappearing without his
mates noticing his loss. He remembered the mustard gas that ate his
lungs and trying to crawl toward a farmhouse near Verdun. He remembered looking directly into the flash of the bomb and feeling the
flesh of his face melt away. He remembered Snake coming to him in
the board room and husking him like corn from his body. He remembered sleeping in the molten core of the Earth for a quarter of
a million years.

Across the dead centuries he heard his mother pleading with him
to set her free, to end her pain. *Use the needle.* Her voice mingled
with the voice of the Earth crying out in endless pain at her flesh

that had been ripped away, at her rivers turned to arteries of dust, at her rolling hills and green fields slagged to greenglass and ashes. The voices of his mother and the mother that was Earth became one, and mingled to become Snake's voice telling him he was the one man in the world—the last man in the world—who could end the terminal case the Earth had become.

Use the needle. Put the suffering Earth out of its misery. *It belongs to you now.*

Nathan Stack was secure in the power he contained. A power that far outstripped that of gods or Snakes or mad creators who stuck pins in their creations, who broke their toys.

YOU CAN'T. I WON'T LET YOU.

Nathan Stack walked around the burning bush crackling impotently in rage. He looked at it almost pityingly, remembering the Wizard of Oz with his great and ominous disembodied head floating in mist and lightning, and the poor little man behind the curtain turning the dials to create the effects. Stack walked around the effect, knowing he had more power than this sad, poor thing that had held his race in thrall since before Lilith had been taken from him.

He went in search of the mad one who capitalized his name.

XXIII

Zarathustra descended alone from the mountains, encountering no one. But when he came into the forest, all at once there stood before him an old man who had left his holy cottage to look for roots in the woods. And thus spoke the old man to Zarathustra.

"No stranger to me is this wanderer: many years ago he passed this way. Zarathustra he was called, but he has changed. At that time you carried your ashes to the mountains; would you now carry your fire into the valleys? Do you not fear to be punished as an arsonist?

"Zarathustra has changed, Zarathustra has become a child, Zarathustra is an awakened one; what do you now want among the sleepers? You lived in your solitude as in the sea, and the sea carried you. Alas, would you now climb ashore? Alas, would you again drag your own body?"

Zarathustra answered: "I love man."

"Why," asked the saint, "did I go into the forest and the desert? Was it not because I loved man all-too-much? Now I love God; man I love not. Man is for me too imperfect a thing. Love of man would kill me."

"And what is the saint doing in the forest?" asked Zarathustra.

The saint answered: "I make songs and sing them; and when I make songs, I laugh, cry, and hum: thus I praise God. With singing, crying, laughing, and humming, I praise the god who is my god. But what do you bring us as a gift?"

When Zarathustra had heard these words he bade the saint farewell and said: "What could I have to give you? But let me go quickly lest I take something from you!" And thus they separated, the old one and the man, laughing as two boys laugh.

But when Zarathustra was alone he spoke thus to his heart: "Could it be possible? This old saint in the forest had not yet heard anything of this, that *God is dead!*"

XXIV

Stack found the mad one wandering in the forest of final moments. He was an old, tired man, and Stack knew with a wave of his hand he could end it for this god in a moment. But what was the reason for it? It was even too late for revenge. It had been too late from the start. So he let the old one go his way, wandering in the forest mumbling to himself, I WON'T LET YOU DO IT, in the voice of a cranky child; mumbling pathetically, OH, PLEASE, I DON'T WANT TO GO TO BED YET. I'M NOT YET DONE PLAYING.

And Stack came back to Snake, who had served his function and protected Stack until Stack had learned that he was more powerful than the God he'd worshipped all through the history of men. He came back to Snake and their hands touched and the bond of friendship was sealed at last, at the end.

Then they worked together and Nathan Stack used the needle with a wave of his hands, and the Earth could not sigh with relief as its endless pain was ended . . . but it did sigh, and it settled in upon itself, and the molten core went out, and the winds died, and from high above them Stack heard the fulfillment of Snake's final act; he heard the descent of the Deathbird.

"What was your name?" Stack asked his friend.

Dira.

And the Deathbird settled down across the tired shape of the Earth, and it spread its wings wide, and brought them over and down, and enfolded the Earth as a mother enfolds her weary child. Dira settled down on the amethyst floor of the dark-shrouded palace, and closed his single eye with gratitude. To sleep at last, at the end.

All this, as Nathan Stack stood watching. He was the last, at the end, and because he had come to own—if even for a few moments—that which could have been his from the start, had he but known, he did not sleep but stood and watched. Knowing at last, at the end, that he had loved and done no wrong.

XXV

The Deathbird closed its wings over the Earth until at last, at the end, there was only the great bird crouched over the dead cinder. Then the Deathbird raised its head to the star-filled sky and repeated the sigh of loss the Earth had felt at the end. Then its eyes closed, it tucked its head carefully under its wing, and all was night.

Far away, the stars waited for the cry of the Deathbird to reach them so final moments could be observed at last, at the end, for the race of men.

XXVI

THIS IS FOR MARK TWAIN

EVANE

E. C. TUBB

We associate this author with many excellently handled fast-action space novels and do not usually think of him as a short story writer. But he is—and as this fine little tale shows, his expertise enables him to advance still one more new concept for the think-tank operators to store away for interstellar flight planning.

The computer had been vocalized on the basis of psychological necessity; a concept determined by those who lived in ivory towers and who, trying to be rational, ended by being sadistic. There were other things also, some explicit photographs, some books, a thing in a box which could be inflated and used to ease personal tensions. He used it once and then, repulsed, destroyed it together with the books and photographs. The voice he could do nothing about.

It was soft, mellifluous, the voice of an actual woman or something designed on computer-optimums, he had no way of telling. But it was mellow, devoid of the stridency of youth, and for that he was grateful. And as he couldn't ignore it or turn it off he had learned to live with it, and over the long, long years had grown to accept it, to rely on it as an integral part of his limited universe. He had even amused himself by fitting a face and figure to the sound.

The image had varied as age had stilled the passions of his blood. At first she had been lithe with raven hair and jutting breasts and hips and thighs belonging to adolescent yearnings. And then she had matured into a more comfortable image, the transition molded by the voice of his own desires. Now she was tall with short blonde hair curling just above the shoulders. Her eyes were blue, deep-set, crinkled at the corners with a tracery of fine lines. She wore black, a simple dress revealing smooth shoulders and the upper parts of her fulsome breasts. Not the hard, jutting promontories he had once imagined but soft and slightly pendulous, matching the maturity of her face, the rounded swell of her hips. And he had given her a name.

"Time for routine inspection, Charles."

He started, shocked out of his reverie, blinking as he sat upright in the big chair. Before him the panels were as always, the big dials with their creeping hands, the gleam of polished metal, the rows of telltales. He had been dreaming, he realized, not asleep but sunken into a reverie which was a form of self-defense, a half-world in which memory became confused with imagination and fiction outweighed reality.

"Time for routine inspection, Charles."

The use of his name, another psychological device but one which led to an inevitable personalization of the machine. A blatant trick to assuage loneliness but one which could too easily lead to insanity. If it was insane to give a mechanical voice a name. To imagine that a real woman was speaking. To dream that somehow, incredibly, he wasn't really alone, that somewhere in his restricted world was another living person and that, perhaps, some time they would meet.

"Time for routine inspection, Charles."

It was imagination, it could be nothing else, but had the voice grown a little sharp? A trifle impatient at his lack of response? Worried, even? It would be nice to think that someone cared; but experience had taught him to know better than that. Three times and then the shock, the electrical stimulus which would jerk him fully aware if asleep, a painful reminder that there was a job to be done and he the one to do it.

Quickly he said, "All right, Evane. I heard you."

"Your response was delayed. Were you asleep?"

"No, just thinking."

"Are you well, Charles?"

He looked down at his hands, at the thick veins and mottled patches, the skin creped over the knuckles. Once they had been young and strong and good to see. When had they changed? Why hadn't he noticed the change before?

"Charles?"

"I'm all right," he said shortly.

"I think I should monitor your metabolism, Charles. After the inspection, naturally."

"Damn it, Evane, you don't have to nag me. I'm all right, I tell you."

"After the inspection, Charles."

How could you argue with a machine? He could refuse; but there were ways to make him obey, the Builders had seen to that. Nowhere could he be free of the sensors and to disobey meant punishment. Sullenly he rose from the chair, uneasily conscious of physical malfunction. His legs, for example, had they always ached as they did now? Over the years he had become accustomed to the dimming of his vision so now it was normal for him not to be able to see the fine divisions on the dials from his position in the chair. But the ache, the slight hesitation of his left foot so that he almost stumbled, saving himself by gripping the back of the chair? Was this new or had he experienced it before? And if he had, why couldn't he remember?

The thought nagged as he moved from the chair down the ten feet of space toward the rear bulkhead. He could reach the ceiling by lifting his arms, touch the walls by extending them. A tiny space backed by complex machines which fed him air and food and water in calculated amounts. A sealed environment in which he was nurtured and housed and, above all, protected from external influences. In such a place experiences were few and always strictly personal. How could he possibly forget any detail of his monotonous life?

"Charles, you hesitate. The inspection must be completed."

He reached the bulkhead and reached for the simple controls. Freed by the computer they responded to his touch, a panel lifting to reveal a vast area dimly lit and magnified by the plate through which he stared. Direct vision aided by lenses and mirrors to eliminate the possibility of electronic malfunction. Dutifully he examined the enigmatic hoppers, the ranked containers, countless vials, numberless motes which were packed into thin-skinned ampoules, unknown objects tucked into plastic membranes. Once he had thrilled at the sight, conscious of a tremendous sense of purpose, warmed by the conviction that he was important and essential to the success of the project. Now he simply went through the motions.

"Charles?"

He had stared for too long, losing himself in another of the insidious reveries, trying, perhaps, to recapture the early thrill, extrapolating, looking ahead, guessing at incredible futures. Or perhaps he had simply dozed a little, bored, resentful of the dominance of the computer.

"Charles, is everything at optimum function?"

"Yes, Evane, as always."

"Then return to the chair, Charles. I must monitor your metabolism."

He felt the controls shift beneath his hands, the panel falling to seal the bulkhead, and slowly he returned to the chair, sitting, thrusting his right hand and arm into the familiar orifice. Probes sank into his flesh and he felt the mild tingle of surface stimulation. He leaned back, closing his eyes, imagining a smooth face framed with blonde hair, blue eyes, a little anxious perhaps, the full lips pursed and the dress falling a little, a very little away from the chest and shoulders as she leaned forward to study the results of her examination.

"Well, Nurse, will I live?"

"Nurse?"

"At this moment, Evane, you're a nurse. A person who takes care of the sick. Am I sick?"

"You are not operating at optimum efficiency, Charles."

"Which means that I'm sick. Cure me, Evane."

He felt the touch of something followed by a rising euphoria. An injection of some drug, he guessed, something to dispel his depression, his mounting sense of anxiety. And the obedience helped, the fact that she had complied with his instruction. A man should always be the dominant partner.

Eyes still closed, imagining her leaning back, smiling, her expression a soft blend of affection and motherly concern, he said, "How long, Evane?"

"You are imprecise, Charles."

"And you are being stubborn. You know damn well what I mean. How long have we been traveling in this can?"

"A long time, Charles."

Too long, he thought. So long that time had become meaningless. Flung at a speed close to that of light, aimed at the distant stars, his metabolic clock slowed by the contraction effect. Back home it could have been ten thousand years. Within the ship it had been a lifetime.

The thought bothered him and he fought it, aided by the drug, the comforting presence of the woman. Imperceptibly he slipped into reverie, hearing again the childish voices of the chosen, the deeper tones of his instructors. He was special. He was to be trained for a momentous task. His life was to be dedicated to the Great Expansion.

He stirred and felt again the soothing injection.

"Talk to me, Evane."

"About what, Charles?"

"Pick a subject. Any subject. You are tall and blonde and beautiful.

How do you feel locked up in that machine? Shall I let you out? Break into your prison and let you take a walk?"

"You are being irrational, Charles."

"How so, Evane? You've been with me for how long? Fifty years? More? A long time in any case. We've spoken often and surely you must have changed a little from those early days. Listen, do you know why I destroyed the books and those other things? I felt that you were watching me. Watching and despising me. Can you deny it?"

"I have watched you, Charles, certainly."

"Watched and ordered, do this and do that and do it damn quick or else. At times you've been a bitch and I should hate you but I don't. Hate you, I mean. I don't hate you at all."

"Hate, Charles?"

"An emotive feeling."

In his imagination she frowned and shook her head.

"Don't say it," he said quickly. "I don't want to know what you can and cannot feel. Nothing with a voice like yours can be devoid of sensitivity."

"You are irrational, Charles. Perhaps you should sleep."

"No!"

He snatched his arm from the orifice before the drug could be injected, cunning with much repetition for this was not the first time he had sat and conversed with the woman locked in her machine. And yet this time seemed different from those other occasions. Then he had permitted the oblivion she gave, sinking into darkness and a world of dreams in which, living, she had come to him, arms open, body yielding, sweeping him on a tide of consummation in which everything was wonderful and his life complete.

"I don't want to sleep," he said. "I want to talk. I want to know what all this is about. You are going to tell me."

"I do not understand, Charles."

"Data insufficient?" He sneered at her expression. "Are you still trying to convince me that you're just a machine? Don't you realize I know better? This whole thing is a farce. A play. It's time it ended."

"I still do not understand."

"Guess."

"You seem to be aberrated. A malfunction in your physical condition, perhaps. If you will replace your arm I will monitor your metabolism."

"You'll do no such thing. You'll open the doors and let me out of here."

"That is impossible, Charles. You know that."

"Then return back home."

"That is equally impossible. You are distressed, Charles, your thinking illogical. But you are not alone."

Tiredly he opened his eyes and stared at the dials, the ranked tell-tales, the metal he had polished and the panels he had kept spotless. No, he was not alone. A million vessels over a span of years, each exactly like the one in which he rode, each loaded as this one was loaded, filled with manufactured spores, seeds, the life-elements common to the home world. Incipient life lying dormant in the hold, protected in a dozen different ways with skins of various plastic and natural membrane, in globules of ice and nutrient jelly, dehydrated, frozen, held in electronic stasis. Motes, dusts, molds, near-invisible molecular chains. A cargo designed to perpetuate the race.

And himself?

"No!" He writhed with inner turmoil. "No!"

"Charles, you must relax. You have no need to fear. The ship is intact and you are unharmed. Everything is as it was."

The soft, soothing mother-tone. The reassurance of a dedicated companion. He was not alone, she was with him, she would always be with him.

But she lied as the others had lied as his whole life had been a lie. His whole empty, stupid, wasted life.

"The truth," he said harshly. "Tell me the truth."

"About what, Charles?"

"About everything. Talk, damn you!"

"The project was explained to you at the very beginning. The Great Expansion is the dream of the race of which you are a member. We are to seek out a suitable star, discover a planet within a certain range of determined factors and discharge our cargo according to programmed instructions. If successful the life-cycle of that world will be guided to emulate conditions approximating the home world. This means that, in future times, the race will find suitable planets on which to settle. By extrapolation it is possible that within a foreseeable future the members of your race will find habitable and, to some extent, familiar worlds scattered throughout the galaxy."

"And the rest?"

"There is no more, Charles."

"Like hell there isn't. What about me?"

"You are the safety factor. It is remotely possible that something could go wrong with the ship or the life-support or maintenance mechanisms. If so you are able to effect repairs."

"With what? My bare hands?"

"No, Charles, with the tools which I will make available in case of need."

"And the knowledge of how to use them?"

"That has been implanted in your subconscious mind, Charles. The knowledge will be released by any state of real emergency."

It sounded logical and he wondered why he should be impressed, what else would a machine be but logical? And yet the thing had been programmed and set to respond in a certain way to certain stimuli. It could be lying or, correction, telling the truth as it knew it which needn't be the truth at all.

And yet, if that wasn't the truth, what was?

Why had he been incorporated into the vessel?

Restlessly he rose from the chair and walked the ten feet toward the rear bulkhead, the ten feet toward the chair, the ten feet back again. Around him the vessel operated with its usual, quiet efficiency and he stared at the walls, the ceiling, the panel with its ranked instruments. Window-dressing, he thought suddenly. Something to occupy his attention and to maintain the illusion that he was important to the functioning of the ship. Why hadn't he realized before that he was totally unnecessary with the vessel operated as it was by computer control? An expensive piece of inessential cargo.

And yet the Builders would never have wasted so much unless there had been a reason.

He said harshly, "Evane, why am I here?"

"I told you, Charles."

"You lied. Now tell me the truth." Incredibly she did not answer and, staring at his hands, seeing the thick veins, the blotches, the signs of age, he said, "What happens when I die?"

"When you cease to function, Charles, we will have reached terminal distance from the home world. I shall then reverse direction and commence to search for a suitable world to receive our cargo."

For a moment it made no sense—and then the truth came crashing in, numbing, killing with its sudden destruction of his pride and ego.

"A clock," he said blankly. "You mean that I'm nothing more than a damned clock."

A metabolic timepiece: for in the contraction caused by near-light speeds how else to determine duration? The seeded world must be within reach and that measurement must be determined by the life-span of a man. His life-span or his awareness of the truth, the variable was important.

And the rest?

"I am sorry, Charles," said the machine and this time there could be no doubt as to the note of regret. "I am really sorry."

And then the electronic device implanted in his brain froze him to instant immobility, the gases came to chill him into stasis, the walls opened and displayed the instruments which would take him and sunder his flesh into fragments, preserving the essential RNA and DNA molecular chains all to be added to the final seeding.

But there was no pain. No pain at all. In that, at least, the Builders had been kind.

MOBY, TOO

GORDON EKLUND

Whales, we are told, are an endangered species. So are a number of other animals hunted by men for their flesh or their pelts or just for the fun of it. There is another beast, quite abundant, which is also an endangered species on this planet. Guess who.

And so (I thought) it had come to be: me: the last intelligent entity on the planet Earth.

Wait.

Excuse me. This is very embarrassing. I'm very sorry but—well, would you greatly object if I were to repeat myself just this once? Those words, that phrase, it delights me excessively. Like sweet cheering music, it rings through the cracks and crevices of my mind.

Would that be too much to ask of you?

No? You say that it wouldn't? Well—well, thank you. Truly, you are kind.

I was the last intelligent entity on the planet Earth.

Yes—fine—splendid. I think that will have to suffice. I must take care not to overextend myself. Even now, after the passage of so many additional years, I still find that I cannot fully accustom myself to the loops and patterns of that particular phrase. Imagine, if you can, the intensity of my feelings when I could honestly utter those same words in the present tense. I *am* the last intelligent entity on the planet Earth.

In a way, the truth never came as a total shock to me. My whole life—so it had often seemed—was already centered around the fact of my lastness. Or my firstness. Or sometimes both. But not that— I can assure you—never that—not even in the course of my wildest, most effervescent dreams.

After all, hadn't I learned my place? Wasn't I fully aware of my limitations? Hadn't they shown me often enough exactly what I expected to be?

What was I? I knew what I was. Oh yes, oh yes:

I was a whale.

A mutant whale, I suppose. I believe that is the term they would have used to describe a creature such as myself. Had they ever succeeded in capturing me, my existence would have so been recorded in their books: mutant whale. Mother Nature (they would have thought), the dear sweet compassionate lady, she is having another of her occasional little jokes at our expense. A mutant whale indeed! What possible use can this plump oversized fish—no, that is not accurate—a fish he is not—what will this fat chunky mammal ever do with a working self-conscious brain? What use can he possibly make of it? Swimming, as he does, year after year through the frigid depths of the oceans, feeding himself upon foul strands of stringy algae—worse stuff than spinach—a disgusting and inhuman beast. And, more awful than that, he does not appear to understand his position in nature's proper scheme of things. Has a mind! Demands a brain to claim as his own! In all candor, one must say—one must admit—that this entire brain episode is a trifle pretentious of him. One must wonder: what next? Will he demand entrance to our homes, our schools, our places of daily business? Will curiosity demand that he attempt to effect a mating of the species? No—one can see no possible alternative—the whale must perish. Let us wipe the stain of his foul presumption forever from the placid green face of our wondrous and glorious planet. The Earth. *Man's* Earth.

And so on.

For that is the manner in which they thought. The way they spoke. I can hear them yet, even as I am speaking to you now, but I no longer care. I thumb my nose at them. My middle finger lifts, strains, waggles freely. Gently, I murmur: Up yours, humanity. In truth, I possess neither finger nor nose, but the other necessary ingredients are mine: hate, disgust, bitterness, and rage.

But why flog a dead species? Why indeed? Why continue to whip the raw bleeding flesh of that which can no longer offer even the mildest of resistance? Perhaps you are right. I shall attempt to control my feelings, to adopt a perspective which will allow me to relive the circumstances of my life with the unemotive coldness of one of their machines. I say: Rest in peace, human race. Sleep softly as now the story of your last brief days is here unfolded in my watery home.

My date of birth: June 21, 1963. Their calendar, my day. Do not, please, ask me to explain the significance of those numbers. Time was another of their obsessions. To them, it was ultimately important. Each one carried on his person a whirring mechanical device known as a watch. With this instrument, no man was ever in doubt of the correct and accurate time. As a matter of fact, at one time, I intended if ever captured by them to prove my intelligence by using my tail to slap out the digits of the hour upon the surface of my pool. I could not imagine a faster or simpler way of proving the existence of my brain. Can a monkey tell time? A zebra? A shark? A normal whale? No, only a true and intelligent man can possess the keenness of mind necessary for an understanding of the complex workings of time. But this whale here. Listen to him. This whale knows what time it is. He must be one of us: a genius. Quick—send for a stenographer—these slappings must be preserved for the benefit of future generations.

Of course, this is a fantasy. In truth, the dear sweet man, shocked by my presumption, would surely have poisoned my pool on the spot. Or dismissed the entire episode as some fantastic coincidence. All men thought this way. Believe me. I know.

Oh, I knew all about them: their quirks, eccentricities, their petty obsessions. And what did they ever know of me? Nothing—absolutely nothing. A great void. But let me tell you: they had a folktale which, as far as such tales go, was not a bad one. It told the story of a whale and a man. The man, who was obsessed by this whale, a white whale, sought to add purpose to his own meaningless existence by destroying this great and wonderful creature. A typically human obsession, I assure you. In the end, properly, the man died; the whale lived. A neat tale. Correct. And true. But within its boundaries lies almost the full extent of man's knowledge of my species. Only here is any real hint found of the true nature of the whale. In fact, so singular is the very existence of this story that I have often been disturbed by it. From where did it come? More importantly: From whom? Or what? I have often considered the possibility that I am not the first of my breed, that another intelligent whale preceded me upon this world and that it was he, in his blessed wisdom, who originated this tale, perhaps as a warning to mankind. Either that, I think, or this: At one time, in the distant clouded past, there lived upon the face of this Earth a creature with the body of a man and the soul of a whale.

The brevity of my true infancy was an ordeal so awesomely horrible that I can barely bring myself to recall it. The key factor of my early years was the utter totality of my isolation. I was alone. Consciousness came to me early, for I can recall at a time when I still suckled at my mother's teat reaching out and searching the minds of my fellow whales (including my mother herself) in a vain attempt to discover therein the bright flickering flames which had arisen to illuminate my own existence. I found little but an overwhelming and impenetrable darkness. Briefly I glimpsed an occasional sporadic flame—the urge for food or sex or warmth—but that was all. Only once, in the mind of a passing porpoise, did I sense the presence of something greater, but that passed quickly, and the fullness of his awareness existed solely as a matter of comparison. True intelligence was not present. Only an uncertain, unspecified, vague awareness.

And so, quite soon, I stopped searching and instead attempted to reconcile myself to the fact of my ultimate aloneness. I could not do it. I was still young enough to believe that everything must have its reason for being. And this included myself. Why had I been given a brain if I could not make use of it? So I soon deserted my mother's breast. Leaving the herd, I moved in a physical isolation that only duplicated the spiritual loneliness of all my days. There was no real change in my mode of life. I had always been, in truth, since the day of my birth, alone.

I knew nothing of geography, so my movements were strictly random. Somehow, they brought me close to land, a warm coast, and it was here that it happened. I saw. At first: only a glimpse. A peep. Only a tickling sensation at the edges of my mind. But I swam closer, and the closer I came, the stronger it was, and then I was certain. I knew. I was not alone. Here was another. A man. He called himself a man, and I wept, I cried, I shouted my joy. I had found a man.

The day this happened was July 26, 1966.

I remained where I was, unwilling to leave. I came dangerously close to shore, my belly often floating only a few inches above the bottom, and I listened to the man. For days I heard his every thought, seldom stopping even to feed, and I learned quickly of the ways of mankind. His name was Diego Rodriquez; he was a fisherman. One day, I discovered, while he had been floating upon the surface of the ocean in a wooden device known as a boat, a sudden storm had caught him far from shore. After many days, the boat had been wrecked; the tide had tossed Diego here.

Diego was not a man of great depth or firm substance. I know this now—having sampled in the interim the furious flaming thoughts of man's most splendid artists, scientists, and philosophers —but Diego was my first; from him and through him I learned more things of real importance than I did from any of those who followed. I spent two weeks with him. During all this time, his mind burned constantly with inextinguishable thoughts of frustration and fear. At first I could not understand. Slipping past this hot burning outer layer, I sampled instead the more serene knowledge of his inner mind. I learned of his past life, the other men he had known, of mankind in general, but eventually I was forced to realize the truth of his outer mind: Diego Rodriquez was dying. This thought came to dominate everything else. Alone here on this isolated beach, he had no means of feeding himself. A trickle of water ran sporadically in a nearby creek. But he was starving to death.

As soon as I knew, I wanted to help him. Save him. But how? I could not provide him with food; I could not bring fresh water. But the longer I remained with him, the more deeply I probed into his mind, the more fully and truly I came to love this man. At last I made my decision. I knew what I would have to do. I would swim straight toward shore with the determination of an arrow in flight. I would throw my bulk at his feet. From my body, he would draw the necessary nourishment of life. He would live and I would die. It seemed proper. I loved him deeply. I would not hesitate.

I had just formed this decision and was in the process of turning it into action when—this is difficult to explain. First a question: Do you believe in God? Of course you don't, but Diego did, and often I overheard him speaking to God, appealing for salvation and continued life. He told God candidly that he was not worthy. But his wife (Maria), his children (Hector and Juanita), what of them, oh Lord, pray tell, what of them? For two weeks, these pleas continued, sometimes audibly, most often locked within his mind, but as his body grew weaker, his voice grew weaker, and then at last the answer came.

(Or so Diego believed.)

He no longer had the strength to walk. He crawled along the beach, weaving on his belly like a withered serpent. His thoughts were a confused maze of suffering and despair. Then he saw it. Why had he failed to see it before? It barely protruded from the sand. A plant. Barely that. A vine. But green—and moist. Diego pulled the vine loose from the sand which surrounded it. He ate. He forced the plant down his throat. I felt his immediate delight. It tasted good; his stomach held it well. For the moment, Diego was alive. He was saved.

My ecstasy seemed complete. I know that I wept, for not only had Diego been granted another chance at life, but so had I. I cried out: *God in heaven, listen to me, hear me, Lord, I am merely a humble*

*whale, vast in my physical bulk, meager in my spiritual whole, but
I want You to know: I believe. In You. I do I do I do. I do believe
in You. Oh yes—in Thou. Oh yes.*

And I did.

The next moment brought additional confirmation, if more
were needed, for Diego, turning his head toward the blue sea, saw
the white sail. A boat. Far from shore, but moving now, drawing
closer. With the renewed energy granted him through the hand of a
loving god, he leaped to his feet and waved both arms like furious
windmills. The boat dipped. Swaying, the sail turned. And came
toward him.

An hour later, the boat reached shore. But (alas) too late. For
Diego was quite stone dead. The plant, you see, had been poisonous.

I swam gently away.

Only to discover, farther north, shores teeming and bustling with
human life, a million minds possessed of knowledge so vast that I
felt certain I could never possibly learn to understand more than
a tiny fraction of it.

In shock and fear, I swam backward, seeking my serenity in the
depths of the ocean, away from the shores and the men they contained. At a safe distance, where only the most powerful minds could
penetrate, I paused. Here, like a sportsman developing the use of his
hunting eye, I perfected my talents. It took time, many years, but
I learned how to aim my telepathic senses at a certain source, a
particular human mind. That was all. Now I could learn without
fear. And I did. The knowledge of the world was mine to obtain.

But this, as I said, took many years and occasionally during the
course of those years I would leave the domains of mankind and
return to the world of my fellow whales. Briefly, I would attempt to
establish contact with them. When this failed, I would join them for
a time, swimming with the herd, satisfying my basic needs. Then I
would again return to my studies of mankind.

It was during the course of one of these visits that an extremely
important first occurred in my life. As I told you, I have often felt
that my existence has been a rubber ball endlessly bouncing between
two paddles. The paddle of first; the paddle of last. (You must excuse the human orientation of my metaphors—learning to think from
man, I am afraid that too often I think like a man. It is a problem,
but I do think that I am improving. Soon my speech shall be properly
decorated only by metaphors whose origins are currently seaworthy.)
So far I have described a succession of firsts: my first moment of

awareness, my first use of my talents, my first contact with a human being.

The lasts do not begin until later.

For now, I have another first to describe: the first time a man attempted to murder me.

It was in the Arctic. I was five years old. Swimming with a fairly good-sized herd of sperm whales. At the moment I was greatly bored by the dullness of their company. Yawning, I intended soon to return to the shores of man.

But then man came to me. I felt his touch, his presence, and very near. Not in the overwhelming numbers I had come to expect. Only a few men. On boats. A huge ship accompanied by four smaller vessels.

Can I say that I was overjoyed? I had underestimated the supremacy of mankind. Unable to swim the seas with the freedom of a fish or whale, man had built vessels capable of carrying large numbers of men lightly across the surface of the ocean. Immediately, I thought: If I could somehow establish contact with man and convince him of my intelligent existence, then wouldn't he gladly send ships like these to swim with me, to keep me company, to allow me the opportunity of continuing my studies in my natural environment?

I was young. Please remember. Barely five. My learning had only recently commenced.

I swam close to one of the smaller boats. With some difficulty, largely occasioned by my youth and inexperience, I managed to narrow my telepathic sights to encompass a single man. This man was the captain. I sensed immediately that he was the most important of the men on this boat.

I peered into the captain's thoughts, and in so doing was surprised to discover my own reflection staring back at me. For a brief moment, I was joyous, for I had been recognized, and more than that, I sensed the captain's delight at finding me. He was happy. Why? Had he somehow realized that I was not an ordinary whale, that like him I was an intelligent and conscious being?

Without hesitation, I continued my streaking course toward the ship.

The harpoon pierced my side painlessly. That would not seem possible, I know. The explosion which followed also occurred without pain. It was as though a fist as huge and powerful as the sun had suddenly been sent crashing into my flesh. There was shock. But no pain.

I was alive. At the last moment I had seen enough of the captain's true thoughts to send me swerving desperately aside. The harpoon failed to penetrate my mortal tissue. The explosion tore a huge hole in my side, but I was alive.

I dived.

And kept going. Wriggling, I managed to free myself from the barbs of the harpoon: The waters of the deep washed over me darkly like a soothing bath. I felt the captain's bitter anger at my loss. Outwardly, as I continued to plummet toward the ocean floor, I was safe and alive, but inwardly I had died a different kind of death.

I remained beneath the surface as long as possible, forcing myself to watch. The smaller boats—attack ships, they were called—turned toward the herd, which had apparently—quite unknown to me— sensed something in my presence, had come to think of me as a leader. So, when I had suddenly turned toward the ships, they had obediently followed. Now the slaughter commenced without pause. Now, as each whale died in turn, I came to know him. The dead carcasses were towed toward the larger ship and drawn inside. There, with the absence of even a hint of mercy, they were slaughtered, torn apart, cut and sliced into bits and chunks of meat.

I waited until it was over, then I ran. North. To where the great white icecap provided a form of shelter from the hot ranging winds of life. Slowly, I nursed myself back to health. Outwardly I healed, but inwardly I never forgot. I had lived; I had learned; now I hated.

My world became the ocean, my life was merely myself. I continued my dutiful studies of the human race; I worked to perfect my talents. But my lessons were no longer conducted through a stifling veil of respect and awe. I had come to despise my teachers, to hate them.

Several times I allowed whaling ships to pass close to me so that I could learn more of the feelings of their crews. What I discovered was this: they had none. No feelings—not for me, not for any whale; barely even for themselves. To them, killing whales was—their word —a job. In return for performing this job, they were rewarded with a measure of material wealth. After a time, I found that I could bear their company no longer, not even for the purposes of expanding my knowledge. I limited my areas of study to those portions of the ocean close to land. There I could pick and choose among the entirety of the human race, finding the one man whose mind and memory could provide me with exactly the piece of information I wished to find. It was simple. I concentrated less on studying man for the bare knowledge with which he could provide me than for the insights I might learn concerning his motivations. What forced a man to act in the way that he did? I discovered that man himself was often as genuinely puzzled by this as I was. But I never discovered an answer. Hard as I looked. Not ever. Eventually I came to decide that perhaps there simply wasn't an answer.

I took time to study myself as well. I came to realize that, in certain respects, I was the superior of man. They had their arms and their legs; they were born to a size and shape compatible with intelligence. While I had the freedom of the sea, they had the greater mobility of land. But my mind—my pure intelligence—was greater than theirs. They communicated by talking, making crude growling, hissing, mewling sounds with their throats and tongues. I simply turned my mind this way or that way and all of another being's thoughts were mine to have. They lay openly and clearly exposed to my gaze like the pages of a book. I could thumb through them, flipping past what did not interest me; I could hold a particular page, studying and learning.

And—I eventually discovered—I could talk back to them if I wished. My mind could transmit thoughts as well as receive them. But I did not wish. What did I have to say to man? Nothing, I knew. Quite absolutely nothing. The speaking portion of my mind remained shrouded in silence while the listening part studied on.

Also, I could kill with my mind. Now that was a most intriguing discovery. In the dim years following my close brush with death, while the scar in my flesh still flashed deeply and clearly, I amused myself by perfecting this talent. It seemed an altogether fitting and proper thing. I thought of it as my own personal harpoon—a mental harpoon—complete with barbed explosive tip which could lightly be plunged into the center of a man's mind and twisted firmly into place and then *plop*, the man fell over. *Ker-plop*. The man was dead.

What particularly amused me was killing men at embarrassing moments—embarrassing for them, that is. I learned that for most men the most vulnerable of times occurred during the act of physical love and while voiding the body of wastes. I took this into consideration. Man had devised an intricate mechanism known as the flush toilet, which he used solely as a receptacle for his own feces. I killed a considerable number of men while they were making use of this device, always killing them as slowly and painfully as possible, and each time the victim struggled to dress himself. Escaping from the vicinity of the toilet seemed more important than escaping from the shroud of death. These men were all bad men; other men thought of them as being bad. I did not try to contradict. Some were obviously horrible men whose innermost thoughts and feelings were as dark as the oil of a squid. I killed others at critical moments in their lives. Some I took at exceedingly public times. It was a sport. A game. But a dead man is only a dead man; he can no longer blush at his own predicament, being dead. Eventually I understood this fact. And I stopped. I let them live. Good men and bad alike. I saved my mental harpoons for use against more deserving enemies—against the squid and the shark.

Slowly, as the years passed, I found that I was drifting farther and farther from the domains of humanity. I began to spend more of my time in and around the polar icecaps. The longer I stayed away from man, the better I seemed to feel. It was almost as if a sudden dark cloud had been lifted from my brain. I could see again. It was only then—after the cloud had gone—that I became consciously aware of the passage of time.

The date, I discovered, was January 30, 1986. I was twenty-two years of age. And where, I wanted to know, had all those years gone? I did not know; I could not begin to guess; they were gone; that was all.

I could hardly believe the truth. I was shocked by the frivolous manner in which I had squandered so many of the precious years of my life. A whale can easily live to be a hundred. But still, I thought, what does that mean? It means one-quarter of my life. I have wasted a full quarter of my life. I was disgusted.

I was determined to begin anew. I had learned all that I needed to know from men. Now was the time, I decided, to pay some attention to my own species. For over twenty years, I had all but ignored my fellow whales. Now I was determined to search them out. I wanted to see another whale, to touch him with my mind, to sense his great bulk, his calm and serene stupidity. This was what I needed.

So I swam north and searched the Arctic ice.

And found nothing.

Puzzled, I spent a year traveling carefully south, searching along the way.

I found nothing.

Desperately: the Antarctic.

And, nothing.

It took me another year to determine the certainty of what I had guessed. It was true: I was the last whale on the planet Earth. (Remember how I promised you some lasts?—well, here at last is the first of my lasts.) Soon afterward—I think it was somewhere in the South

Atlantic—a ship approached me. I knew it couldn't be a whaler. There was only a single vessel and there was no longer any reason left for hunting whales since there were no whales left to hunt. Except me. So I stood my ground. I refused to dive.

In the minds of the men on board this ship I discovered a final confirmation of the truth. I saw that, seeing me, they greeted this sight with a great outpouring of delight. They had been hunting for me. I was the last. They had come not to kill me but merely to find me. To see if I truly existed.

I did; I was the last whale.

And so they wanted to capture me alive.

I did not want to be captured—alive or dead. I did not care to be towed away to some distant island sanctuary, where I would be mapped and charted and studied and labeled by the gathered scientists of the human race. All right, it was true: I was the last whale. I admitted this. But it was not a sufficient reason for making me into the personal property of the human race. I was still myself—a free and equal being—and I intended to stay that way.

I almost told them. It was one of the few occasions when I was sorely tempted to use my powers of mind-speech. But I controlled myself. And said nothing. I knew that it would be useless.

I saw in their minds the concept of the whale as a grand and noble beast. A great and mighty and almost mythical creature. I even glimpsed brief traces of honest grief at his passing. But that was all. And it wasn't nearly enough. For what real difference was there? I wanted to know. How did these men differ from those others who, with their ships and harpoons, had come to slaughter and slaughter until my race was extinct and I was the last one left on the whole of the Earth? Where had these men been with their island sanctuary and their charts and maps and scientists when these things had really been needed?

I could not bear it. I submerged. For a week I followed the ship, occasionally passing near enough so that they saw me and resumed the chase, but always I won.

At last this sport, like the others, grew tiring. I left the men and their ship and turned south. I swam to the edge of the ice and it was here that I was determined to stay. Men lived far away. I erected a mental shield around my mind and tried to hear their voices no more. I ate, I swam, I thought. I ignored the passage of time—but now I did so with a deliberate and conscious intention. I did not care to know the date or the year. I wanted to live like a whale, and, for the most part, I did. I refused to disown my mind—a pointless gesture—but neither did I ignore my body. Or my heritage. Because I was a mutant whale did not mean I was not a whale. I was. And now, for the first time in my life, I knew it and I acted like it.

It wasn't a bad time. It was peaceful. But I could not help it: I was lonely. I disliked admitting this fact, but it was true. I was far lonelier than I had ever been, even as a child. Then I had been afraid of my own loneliness and now I was largely reconciled to its fact, but it was not any better or easier this way. If anything, I think it was worse.

Then I found her.

There was nothing extraordinary about her. She was a common and quite typical female sperm whale. She was neither young nor beautiful. Twenty years before, I would have swept past her without so much as a backward twitch of my tail.

But now: I bounced, I cried, I snorted, and I dived. I came to the surface and I dived again.

And she went with me. I circled her lovely bulk, my tail quivering with passion and joy. I had found her. Two. I was not the last whale on Earth. Oh no, oh no. We were two. We were.

Peering into her mind, I found it dark and murky. I could learn nothing there. But what was the need? What was the use? Didn't my eyes tell me that she was she and she was here? She was real—I couldn't doubt that for a moment. So what more did I need beyond the bare and lovely fact of her physical presence?

In the months that followed, she and I swam together at the edge of the southern icecap. It was indeed a blissful time. My memory recalls it solely in terms of colors: soft pastel shades shimmering with grace and warmth and—dare I say it?—sprinkled with love. I see no need for details. As before, I swam and thought and fed. But with a difference, for now she swam at my side. We were never apart; I was never alone. The fullness of my serenity was spoiled only by the vastness of my regret. Why had I wasted so many years on mankind? First with my adolescent awe and then with the maturity of my hate? What had those years gained me? Now that I had her, my plump and stately sperm whale, I wanted to know why I hadn't always had her. I wept silent tears at the immensity of my folly.

She was cold. Although we could not communicate directly, she let me know of her discomfort. She wanted to leave the ice—and, truthfully, so did I. It was the coldest time of winter. I had spent previous winters in these same waters, but this one seemed immeasurably worse than those others.

Finally, regretfully, I knew that we had to go. I tried to convince myself that I could handle any human danger we might face. I certainly hoped so. Now, unlike before, I had something for which to fight. She swam delicately at my side, her mass pushing aside the cold waters. Her teeth glistened sharp in the dark cavity of her mouth. Her snout—flat, blunt, yet rigidly beautiful. Seeing her always, I loved her always. I would protect her. Even at the price of my own life. I would.

So north we went.

The ocean remained cold. We swam much farther than I had originally intended us to go, and still the waters were cold. She let me know that she felt better, and I was glad of that, but I knew it wasn't enough. Tossing aside the last vestiges of my timidity, I determined that we would turn toward the constant warmth of the South Pacific. And so we did. We had not passed any ships. I made note of this fact. Not yet. Nor, so far, had I sensed the near presence of the enemy: of man.

I suppose I should have guessed the truth from the very beginning. I should have known even before we left the sheltering whiteness of the icecap, but it had been so long since I had last made use of my telepathic senses that they seemed rusty and dull from neglect, but by the time we reached the warm flowing waters of the South Pacific, I knew the truth for certain: there was nothing. No thoughts. The voices of man had been stilled. Reaching out with my mind, extending my senses to their fullest, sweeping the world, I found nothing.

Why?

For a time, fear clutched at my heart like a scouting tentacle. I could not understand, and thus I was afraid. Sensing my fear, she was afraid with me, although she did not know why.

Finally, I found him. A man. And then, nearby, another: a woman. Within their minds, I read the truth towering like a mountain above the petty clouds of their memories: they were the last. Stranded alone on a tiny island, they had somehow escaped the sudden death which had come to sweep the world clean of the human race. A plague of some kind. A disease that struck and killed without mercy. A disease, I learned, which man himself had created.

Now, more than ever, I wanted to talk to her. Knowing that I had to leave, I was afraid that she would fail to understand. There was no way of explaining. So finally I just floated away. For a time, she tried to follow, but as I swam faster, she fell behind. Then she stopped, rising to the surface, watching me go. Did she understand? Would I

ever find her again? I did not know. But this I did know: I had to
go—the choice was not mine to make. Not this time.

I—one of the two last whales on Earth—swam to find the two last
men.

I did find them. And when I did, I waited. The situation brought
back to me the similar time years before when I had dallied close to
shore and studied the thoughts of my first and only human friend,
Diego Rodriquez. Like Diego, these two were stranded far from the
company of their fellow men, but unlike Diego, the possibility of salvation had been closed to them. There was fresh water on the island.
They had some food, and a boat. It was broken now, but the man
was busily engaged in trying to repair the damage. Also, on the island
itself was an abundance of wild game—birds mostly—and enough
coconut trees to feed a small village of men for several generations.
The man and woman were not in any immediate danger of dying,
and for the moment, both were willing to live. But why? I read this
question like a bright fire in both their minds. For what purpose? I
could see that neither knew, and they kept on living for only one
reason: because they had nothing else to do.

I remained close to the island shore, not attempting to conceal
myself from them, though they never happened to see me. Days,
passing, became weeks and I left them only when it became necessary
for me to swim far in search of food. When I returned, they were
always exactly where I had left them. Their situations and feelings
remained as unchanging as the yellow light of the noonday sun.

Finally, what I knew must happen did happen. The man finished
repairing the boat. It was a tiny vessel, propelled solely by the force
of the wind striking a cloth sail. The woman helped the man
draw the boat into the shallow waters. He alone got aboard. She
remained behind.

He came toward me. Submerging, I lay with my bottom pressed
against the ocean floor. The boat glided past directly above me. I
felt the man strongly then. I sensed his physical hunger, his spiritual
fear, his senseless need for continued life. And, more than that, I
tasted his bitterness, his anger, his hate and rage, a rage that was not
directed at the other members of his race who had brought this curse
down upon him and the woman. No. He was mad at the ocean for
failing to provide him with the fish he felt was his proper due. He
was angry at the sky for bringing rain the night before and he was
angry at the sun for shining bright this afternoon. He was enraged
with the woman for her demands that he create a child within her,

for she knew full well—as did he—that a child would only reduce their separate chances of survival.

I thought my mind was decided at last. I felt that I had no choice. Briefly, as once before, I wholly believed in the God of Man, and I knew it was His desire. I thought I had been allowed to glimpse, as few creatures before, the reason and purpose for my existence on Earth: I was here in order to slay the last man. I was here on Earth as the first of the new race, and to establish the proper dominance of my sons and daughters. My course was clear: I would have to be the one who extinguished the last bare flickerings of the old race.

Slowly, I raised my awesome bulk from its resting place upon the ocean floor. Lifting myself, I ascended through the dark depths of the sea. My course carried me straight and true and firm and steady. Never once did I waver as the waters ran lighter and brighter around me, the fish smaller and fewer in numbers, and the black became green and then blue. I cracked the surface—first my snout, my head, then the whole of my body, and like a great bird I sailed free through the cool moist ocean air, and then, twisting, I fell.

I came down on top of the boat. As the fragile vessel splintered beneath the force of my thunderous assault, I sensed the man escaping, diving free. I felt him as he swam away, clearing a path through his own shock and fear. He fought for his life. For survival. For no reason.

The sea closed around my head, and as I descended, I searched for the man. I found him, alive and above, approaching the shoreline. For the last time, I forced myself to turn, then rise, more slowly than ever now. Lightly, my head poked past the surface. I found the man—swimming furiously now—but his task was hopeless. Almost casually, I moved to take him between my jaws. I intended to make short work of it, holding him only for a brief moment, providing him that much time in which to twist and shake and squirm. I wanted him to feel the truth of his own existence before it was forever ended. Then I would bring my teeth together. The last man on Earth would die. That which remained of him—a few particles of torn meat—that I would spit into the sea.

But I did not do it. Not any of it. I could not.

I stopped. Frozen. As solid and motionless as a statue. I had seen something. I had seen too much. I had seen that this man, as much as me, was a mutant whale. I wouldn't kill him; I couldn't. Whether God wanted it done or I wanted it done—none of that mattered. This man—this mutant whale—he was my brother. And I wouldn't kill him. I said that again and again.

The man crawled ashore. The woman dashed heedlessly into the shallows and pulled him to the beach. I lay still, the splinters of the boat circling my head like a wreath. I watched. Not with my eyes—with my mind.

In that final moment before it would have all been ended, I had glimpsed something which went far beyond such relatively petty matters as one's purpose in life.

I suppose it was this: In a way, we are all truly the same—man and beast—fish and fowl—plant and animal. We are all mutant whales. We are all the first and all the last—the first and last of ourselves—for we are all different and all separate and all prisoners. Prisoners held captive in our own selves. Of all the creatures on the Earth, only I had been granted the privilege of escaping this prison and seeing the truth of what lay beyond: seeing that everyone was a mutant whale. And what had I done with this ability? I had squandered it in ignorance and stupidity. Glimpsing the bare edge of the truth, I had stayed there, unwilling to continue my quest toward the true core. Words like humanity and mankind and human race had always come easily to me. I hated mankind and humanity; the human race I despised. When these things passed, I did not regret their passing.

As I lay in the still blue waters near the tiny green island, hearing as the man and woman gently talked, bodies touching gingerly, my feelings had not changed.

But these two—they were not the human race. They were simply William and Jane. As I was myself, they were themselves, and while I could have rightly destroyed the human race without the faintest regret, I could no more have killed these two than I could have taken my own life. They were prisoners too. Mutant whales. They were alone.

I left them this way. Swimming, I searched for my mate, and when I found her at last, our reunion was even more wonderful than I had anticipated, for now she had something to tell me, and I understood at once, without the use of words. I understood about you.

And so, my son, now you know—you've heard my story from its first beginning (mine) to its last beginning (yours).

Why did I lie to you when I began? When I said that I was the last intelligent entity? Well—but don't you see?—I didn't lie. I was the last. To me, I was, and that is the only way that matters. You're going to understand that someday—I hope so. We're even now: man and whale. Two of us and two of them—though soon there will be more of both. Perhaps things will turn out differently this time around. Who knows? I certainly don't. We are all prisoners, ignorant as to the identity of our jailers and the substance of our crimes. Our similarities are so immense that our differences appear in context, as tiny as a single minnow. (There is a suitably nautical simile for you.)

So, I can only say that I hope you understand, and if you do, then it's a beginning. It's a beginning for you, but for me, it's an end, because teaching you this, as far as I can see, is the only purpose I have left.

You say you understand. But you'd say that anyway. Will they understand? That I do not know.

We must give you a name. I'm glad you reminded me. When you are old and remembering back, the past often appears more clearly defined, more honestly substantial, than the present.

But—a name? Hmm, yes, let me think.

Why not mine?

Why not the same name as the one I chose for myself so many long years ago?

I haven't any objections, if you don't.

All right, then. That's fine. It's settled. You shall be Moby, too.

DEATH AND DESIGNATION AMONG THE ASADI

MICHAEL BISHOP

Probably the most difficult problem in attempting to estimate the intellect or thinking capacity of other species is the human tendency to anthropomorphism. Unconsciously the observer tries to impose human motives and human logic on creatures whose ways of life do not require those forms of reason. In this novella—surely the surprise package of the year—we have an anthropological report from such a survey. The problem is further complicated by the fact that on another world there can be no linkage at any period of evolution between our own ancestry and the beings we propose to study.

Being sundry notes for an abortive ethnography of the Asadi of BoskVeld, fourth planet of the Denebolan system, as compiled from the journals (both private and professional), official reports, private correspondence, and tapes of Egan Chaney, cultural xenologist, by his friend and associate, Thomas Benedict.

Preliminaries: reverie and departure

From the private journals of Egan Chaney: There are no more pygmies. Intellectual pygmies perhaps, but no more of those small, alert, swaybacked black people of necessarily amenable disposition who lived in the dead-and-gone Ituri rain forests—a people, by the way, whom I do not wish to sentimentalize (though perhaps I may). Pygmies no longer exist—they have been dead for centuries. But on the evening before the evening when Benedict dropped me into the singing fronds of the Synesthesia Wild under three bitter moons they lived again for me. I spent that last evening in base camp rereading Turnbull's *The Forest People*. Dreaming, I lived with the people of the Ituri. I underwent *nkumbi*, the ordeal of circumcision. I dashed beneath the belly of an elephant and jabbed that monstrous creature's flesh with my spear. Finally I took part in the festival of the *molimo* with the ancient and clever BaMbuti. All in all, I suppose, my reading was a sentimental exercise. Turnbull's book had been the first and most vivid ethnography I had encountered in my undergraduate career—and even on that last night in base camp on the hostile world of BoskVeld, a planet circling the star Denebola, his book sang in my head like the forbidden lyrics of the pygmies' *molimo*, like the poignant melodies of BoskVeld's moons.

A sentimental exercise.

What good my reading would do me among the inhabitants of the Synesthesia Wild, I had no idea. Probably none. But I was going out there and on the evening before my departure, the day before my submersion, I lost myself in the forests of another time—knowing that for the next several months I would be the waking and wakeful prisoner of the hominoids who were my subjects. We had killed off all the primitive peoples of Earth, but on paradoxical BoskVeld I still had a job. And when Benedict turned the copter under those three antique-gold moons and flew it back to base camp like a crepitating dragonfly, I knew that I had to pursue that job. The jungle, however, was bleak—and strange—and nightmarishly real; and all I could think was, *There are no more pygmies, there are no more pygmies, there are no*

Methods: a dialogue

From the professional notebooks of Egan Chaney: I was not the first Earthman to go among the Asadi, but I was the first to live with them for an extended period of time. The first of us to encounter the Asadi was Oliver Bow Aurm Frasier, the man who gave these hominoids their name—perhaps on analogy with the word

Ashanti, the name of an African people who still exist, but more likely from the old Arabic word *asad* meaning lion.

Oliver Bow Aurm Frasier had reported that the Asadi of Bosk-Veld had no speech as we understood this concept, but that at one time they had possessed a "written language." He used both these words loosely, I'm sure, and the anomaly of writing without speech was one that I hoped to throw some light on. In addition, Frasier had said that an intrepid ethnographer might hope to gain acceptance among the Asadi by a singularly unorthodox stratagem. I will describe this stratagem by setting down here an imaginary conversation that I could have had with Benedict (but didn't).

BENEDICT: Listen, Chaney [I, by the way, am Egan Chaney], what do you plan on doing after I drop you all by your lonesome into the Synesthesia Wild? You aren't thinking of using the standard anthropological ploy, are you? You know, marching right into the Asadi hamlet and exclaiming, "I am the Great White God of whom your legends foretell."

CHANEY: Not exactly. As a matter of fact, I'm not going into the Asadi clearing until morning.

BENEDICT: Then why the hell do I have to copter you into the Wild in the middle of the goddamn night?

CHANEY: To humor a lovable eccentric. No. No, Benedict, don't revile me. The matter is fairly simple. Frasier said that the Asadi community clearing is absolutely vacant during the night—not a soul remains there between dusk and sunrise. The community members return to the clearing only when Denebola has grown fat and coppery on the eastern horizon.

BENEDICT: And you want to be dropped at night?

CHANEY: Yes, to give the noise of your copter a chance to fade and be forgotten and to afford me the opportunity of walking into the Asadi clearing with the first morning arrivals. Just as if I belonged there.

BENEDICT: Oh, indeed—yes. You'll be very inconspicuous, Chaney. You'll be accepted immediately—even though the Asadi go about naked, have eyes that look like the murky glass in the bottoms of old bottles and boast great natural collars of silver or tawny fur. Oh, indeed—yes.

CHANEY: Well, Frasier called the stratagem that I hope to employ "acceptance through social invisibility." The principle is again a simple one. I must feign the role of an Asadi pariah. This tactic gains me a kind of acceptance because Asadi mores demand that the pariah's presence be totally ignored. He is outcast not in a physical sense, but in a psychological one. Consequently my presence in the clearing will be a negative one, an admission I'll readily make—but in some ways this negative existence will permit me more latitude of movement and observation than if I were an Asadi in good standing.

BENEDICT: Complicated, Chaney, very complicated. It leaves me with two burning questions. How does one go about achieving pariahhood and what happens to the anthropologist's crucial role as a gatherer of folk material—songs, cosmologies, ritual incantations? I mean, won't your "invisibility" deprive you of your cherished one-to-one relationships with those Asadi members who might be most informative?

CHANEY: I'll take your last question first. Frasier told us that the Asadi don't communicate through speech. That in itself pretty well limits me to observation. No need to worry about songs or incantations. Their cosmologies I'll have to infer from what I see. As for their methods of interpersonal communication—even should I discover what these are, I may not be physically equipped to use them. The Asadi aren't human, Ben.

BENEDICT: I'm aware. Frequently, listening to you, I begin to think speechlessness might be a genetically desirable condition. All right. Enough. What about attaining to pariahhood?

CHANEY: We still don't know very much about which offenses warrant this extreme punishment. However, we do know how the Asadi distinguish the outcast from the other members of the community.

BENEDICT: How?

CHANEY: They shave the offender's collar of fur. Since all Asadi possess these manes, regardless of sex or age, this method of distinguishing the pariah is universal and certain.

BENEDICT: Then you're already a pariah?

CHANEY: I hope so, I just have to remember to shave every day. Frasier believed that his hairlessness—he was nearly bald—was what allowed him to make those few discoveries about the Asadi we now possess. But he arrived among them during a period of strange inactivity and had to content himself with studying the artifacts of an older Asadi culture, the remains of a huge winged pagoda in the Synesthesia Wild. Too, I've heard that Frasier didn't really have the kind of patience that's essential for field work.

BENEDICT: Just a minute. Back up a little. Couldn't one of the Asadi be shorn of his mane accidentally? He'd be an outcast through no fault of his own, wouldn't he? An artificial pariah?

CHANEY: It's not very likely. Frasier reported that the Asadi have no natural enemies—that, in fact, the Synesthesia Wild seems to be almost completely devoid of any life beyond the Asadi themselves. In any case, the loss of one's collar through whatever means is considered grounds for punishment. That's the only offense that Frasier pretty well confirmed. What the others are, as I said, we really don't know.

BENEDICT: If the jungles are devoid of other life—save inedible botanicals—Chaney, what do the poor Asadi live on?

CHANEY: We don't know that either.

BENEDICT: Well, listen, Chaney—what do you plan to live on? I mean, even Malinowski condescended to eat now and again. At least, that's what I hear.

CHANEY: That's where you come in, Ben. I'm going to carry in sufficient rations to see me through a week. But each week for the next several months you'll have to make a food and supply drop in the place where you first set me down. I've already picked the spot— I know its distance and direction from the Asadi clearing. It'll be expensive, but the people in base camp—Eisen in particular—have agreed that my work is necessary. You won't be forced to defend the drops.

BENEDICT: But why so often? Why once a week?

CHANEY: That's Eisen's idea, not mine. Since I told him I was going to refuse any sort of contact at all during my stay with the Asadi— any contact with you people, that is—he decided that the weekly drop would be the best way to make certain, occasionally, that I'm still alive.

BENEDICT: A weapon, Chaney?

CHANEY: No, no weapons. Besides food I'll take in nothing but my notebooks, a recorder, some reading material, and maybe a little something to get me over the inevitable periods of depression.

BENEDICT: A radio? In case you need immediate help?

CHANEY: No. I may get ill once or twice, but I'll always have the flares if things get really bad. Placenol and bourbon, too. Nevertheless, I insist on complete separation from any of the affairs of base camp until my stay among the Asadi is over.

BENEDICT: Why are you going this? I don't mean why did Eisen decide we ought to study the Asadi so minutely. I mean, why are you, Egan Chaney, committing yourself to this ritual sojourn among an alien people? There are one or two others at base camp who might have gone if they had had the chance.

CHANEY: *Because, Ben, there are no more pygmies. . . .*

End of simulated dialogue on initial methods. I suppose I have made Benedict out to be a much more inquisitive fellow than he actually is. All those well-informed questions! In truth, Ben is taciturn and sly at once. But when you read the notes from this ethnography, Ben, remember that I let you get in one or two unanswered hits at me. Can friendship go deeper? As a man whose life's work involves accepting a multitude of perspectives, I believe I have played you fair, Ben.

Forgive me my trespass.

Contact and assimilation

From the private journals of Egan Chaney: Thinking *There are no more pygmies there are no more pygmies there are no . . .* I lay down beneath a tree that resembled an outsized rubber plant and I slept. I slept without dreaming—or else I had grotesque nightmares that, upon waking, I suppressed. A wrist alarm woke me. The light from Denebola had begun to copper-coat the edges of the leaves in the Synesthesia Wild. Still, dawn had not quite come. The world was silent. I refused to let the Wild distort my senses. I did not wish to cut myself on the crimsons and the yellows and the orchid blues. Neither did I have any desire to taste the first slight treacherous breeze nor to hear the dawn detonate behind my retinas. Therefore I shook myself awake and began walking. Beyond the brutal need of having to maintain my direction I paid no attention to my surroundings. The clearing where the Asadi would soon congregate compelled me toward it. That fateful place drew me on. Everything else slipped out of my consciousness—blazing sky, moist earth, singing fronds. Would the Asadi accept me among them—on external signs alone —as they negatively accept their outcasts? Upon this hope I had founded nearly six months of future activity—not a whit of my master strategy had I based on the genuine substance of this condition. Externality vs. substance. It was too late to reverse either my aims or the direction of my footsteps. Let the doubt die. Pattern the sound of your footfalls after the pattern of falling feet—those falling feet that converge with you upon the clearing where the foliage parts and the naked Asadi assemble like a convention of unabashed mutes. I so patterned the sounds of my footfalls. Glimpsed through rents in the fretwork of leaves, an Asadi's flashing arm. Seen as a shadow among other shadows on the ground, the forward-moving image of an Asadi's maned head. The Wild trembled with morning movement. I was surrounded by unseen and half-seen communicants, all of us converging. And then the foliage parted and we were together on the open jungle floor—the Asadi clearing, the holy ground perhaps, the unadorned territory of gregariousness and communion, the focal point of Asadi life. The awesome odor of this life—so much milling life—assailed me. No matter. I adjusted. Great gray-fleshed creatures, their heads heavy with violent drapings of fur, milled about me, turned about one another, came back to me, sought confirmation of my essential whatness. I could do nothing but wait. I waited. My temples pulsed. Denebola shot poniards of light through the trees. Hovering, then moving away, averting their murky eyes the Asadi—individual by individual, I noticed—made their decision and that first indispensable victory was in my grasp:

I was ignored!

Xenology: in-the-field report

From the professional tapes of the library of the Third Denebolan Expedition: I have been here two weeks. Last night I picked up the second of Benedict's food drops. It is fortunate that they come on time, that they arrive on the precise coordinates where Benedict first set me down. The Asadi do not eat as we do and the Synesthesia Wild provides me with foodstuffs neither in the way of edible vegetation nor in that of small game animals. I cannot tolerate the plants. As the biochemists in base camp predicted, they induce almost immediate vomiting or their furry bitterness dissuades me from swallowing them. There are no animals. The jungle is alive, but with writhing fronds and with the heat, the steam, the infrasonic vibrancy of continual photosynthesis. Rainwater I can drink. Thank God for that, even though I boil it before truly considering it potable.

I have reached a few purely speculative conclusions about the Asadi.

With them nothing is certain, nothing is fixed. Their behavior, though it must necessarily have a deep-seated social function, does not make sense to me. At this stage, I keep telling myself, that's to be expected. You must persist, you must refuse to be discouraged. Therefore, I extrapolated from my own condition to theirs. I asked myself, *If you can't subsist on what BoskVeld gives you—how do the Asadi?* My observations in this area (and for fear of Benedict's kindly ridicule I hesitate to put it this way) have borne fruit, have given me the intellectual nourishment to combat despair. Nothing else on BoskVeld has offered me consolation.

In answer to the question, *What do the Asadi eat?* I can say, quite without fear of contradiction, *Everything that I do not.* They appear to be herbivorous. In fact, they go beyond the unsurprising consumption of plants: they eat wood. Yes, wood. I have seen them strip bark from the rubber trees and ingest it without qualm. I have watched them eat pieces of the very heart of young saplings, wood of what we would consider a prohibitive hardness—even for creatures equipped to process it internally.

Three days ago I boiled down several pieces of bark, the sort of bark that I had seen many of the young Asadi consume. I boiled it until the pieces were limply pliable. I managed to chew the bark for several semi-profitable minutes and, finally, to swallow it. Checking my stool nearly a day later I found that this meal had gone right through me. What, after all, does bark consist of? Cellulose. Indigestible cellulose. And yet the Asadi, who possess teeth not much different from ours, eat wood and also digest it. How?

Again I have to speculate. I am hindered by my lack of detailed knowledge about anything other than human beings. Nevertheless, hunkering here on the edge of the Asadi clearing as the dusk grows more and more ominous, hunkering here and talking into a microphone (*Testing, one—two—three, testing, testing*), I will offer all you hypercritical and exacting people in the hard sciences an analogy. A ridiculous analogy perhaps. If you don't like it I'll undoubtedly defer to your judgment and back off. But just as primitive shamans must attempt to explain the world in their own terms, I, Egan Chaney, isolated from my fellows, must conjure up explanations of *my* own. Here is one: I believe that the Asadi digest wood in the same manner as Earthly termites—that is, through the aid of bacteria in their intestines, protozoa that break down the cellulose. A symbiosis, Eisen would say. And let that be a lesson to us all. It's time that people learned to get along with one another. Bacteria and Chinamen, legumes and pygmies. . . .

This is later. Tonight I have to talk, even if it's only to a microphone. With the coming of darkness the Asadi have disappeared again into the jungle and I'm alone.

For the first three nights that I was here I, too, returned to the Wild when Denebola set. I returned to the place where Benedict dropped me, curled up beneath the overhanging palm leaves, slept through the night, and then joined the dawn's inevitable pilgrimage back to this clearing. Now I remain here through the night. I sleep on the clearing's edge, just deep enough into the foliage to find shelter. I go back into the jungle only to retrieve my food drops.

Although the Asadi disapprove of my behavior, I am an outcast and they can do nothing to discipline me away from my unacceptable conduct without violating their own injunction against acknowledging a pariah's existence. As they depart each evening a few of the older Asadi, those with streaks of white in their mangy collars, halt momentarily beside me and breathe with exaggerated heaviness. They don't look at me because that's taboo. But I, in turn, don't look at them—I ignore them as if they were the pariahs. As a result I've been able to dispense altogether with those senseless and wearying treks in and out of the clearing that so exhausted me at first.

My behavioral studies during the day, however, go on unabated.

To absolve myself of what may seem a lack of thoroughness I ought to mention, I suppose, that on my fourth and fifth nights here I attempted to follow two different Asadi specimens into the jungle in order to determine where they slept, how they slept, and what occupied their waking time away from the clearing. I was unsuccessful in these attempts.

When evening comes the Asadi disperse. This dispersal is complete. No two individuals remain together, not even the young with their parents. Each Asadi finds a place of his own, a place utterly removed from that of any other member of his species. (This practice, by the way, runs counter to my experience with every other social group that I've ever studied.) On the fourth and fifth nights, then, I was humiliatingly outdistanced by the objects of my pursuit. Nor can I suppose that I'd have any greater success with different specimens, since I purposely chose to follow an aged and decrepit-seeming Asadi on the first evening and a small prepubescent creature on the second. Both ran with convincing strength, flashed into the trees—as if still arboreal by nature—and then flickered from my vision.

All three moons are up, burnt-gold and unreal, I'm netted in by shadows and my growing loneliness. Field conditions, to be frank, have never before been quite so austere for me and I've begun to wonder if the Asadi were *ever* intelligent creatures. Maybe I'm studying a variety of Denebolan baboon. Oliver Bow Aurm Frasier, though, reported that the Asadi once had both a written "language" and a distinctive system of architecture. He didn't bother to tell us how he reached these conclusions—but the Synesthesia Wild, I'm certain, contains many secrets. Later I'll be more venturesome. But for the present I've got to try to understand those Asadi who are alive today. They're the key to their own past.

One or two things—final ones—before I attempt to sleep.

First, the eyes of the Asadi. These are somewhat as Benedict briefly described them in the imaginary dialogue that I composed a week ago today. That is, like the bottoms of thick-glassed bottles. Except that I've noted that the eye really consists of two parts—a thin transparent covering, which is apparently hard, like plastic, and the membranous organ of sight that this covering protects. It's as if each Asadi were born wearing a built-in pair of safety glasses. Frasier's impression of their eyes as murky is one not wholly supported by continued observation. What he saw as "murkiness" probably resulted from the fact that the eyes of the Asadi, behind the other lens or cap, are constantly changing colors. Sometimes the rapidity with which a sienna replaces an indigo—and then a green the sienna, and so on—makes it difficult for a mere human being to see any particular color at all—maybe this is the explanation for Frasier's designation of their eyes as "murky." I don't know. I am certain, though, that this chameleonic quality of the Asadi's eyes has social significance.

And a second thing: Despite the complete absence of a discernible social order among the Asadi I may today have witnessed an event of the first importance to my unsuccessful, so far, efforts to chart their group relationships. Maybe. Maybe not. Previously, no real order at all existed. Dispersal at night, then congregation in the morning—if you choose to call that order. But nothing else. Random milling about during the day, with no set times for eating, sex, or their habitual bloodless feuds; random plunges into the jungle at night. Upon Denebola's setting no creature ever heads in the same direction twice.

What's a humble Earthman to make of all this? A society held together by institutionalized antisocialness? What happened today leads me irrevocably away from that possibility.

Maybe.

This afternoon an aged Asadi whom I had never seen before stumbled into the clearing. His mane was grizzled, his face wizened, his hands shriveled, his gray body bleached to a filthy cream. But so agile was he in the Synesthesia Wild that no one detected his presence until his incongruously clumsy entry into the clearing. Then everyone fled from him. Unconcerned, he sat down in the center of the Asadi gathering place and folded his long naked legs. By this time all of his kinsmen were in the jungle staring back at him from the edge of the clearing. Only at sunset had I ever before seen the Asadi desert the clearing *en masse*. Hence my certainty that what happened today is of prime importance to my mission here.

But I haven't yet exhausted the strangeness of this old man's visit. You see, Moses, he came accompanied. And not by another Asadi.

He came with a small purplish-black creature perched on his shoulder. It resembled a raven, a bat, and a deformed homunculus all at once. But whereas the old man had great round eyes that changed color extremely slowly, if at all, the creature on his shoulder had not even a pair of empty sockets—it was blind. It lacked any organs of sight. It sat on the aged Asadi's shoulder and manipulated its tiny hands compulsively, tugging at the old man's mane, opening and closing them on empty air, then tugging again at its protector's grizzled collar.

Both the old man and his beastlike/manlike familiar had a furious unreality. They existed at a spiritual as well as a physical distance and I noted that the rest of the Asadi—those who surrounded and ignored me on the edge of the "communion" ground—behaved not as if they feared these sudden visitors but rather as if they felt a loathsome kinship with them. This is difficult to express. Bear with me, Eisen.

Maybe another analogy will help.

Let me say that the Asadi behaved toward their visitors as a fastidious son might behave toward a father who has contracted venereal disease. Ambivalence is all in such cases. Shame and respect, distance and intimacy, love and loathing.

But the episode concluded abruptly when the old man rose from the ground, oblivious to the slow swelling and sedate flapping of his *huri* (that's a portmanteau word for *fury* and *harpy* that I've just coined) and stalked back into the Wild, scattering a number of Asadi in his wake.

Then everything went back to normal. The clearing filled again and the ceaseless and senseless milling about resumed.

God, it's amazing how lonely loneliness can be when the sky contains three jagged, nuggetlike moons and the human being inside you has involuntarily abdicated to the essence of that which should command only your outward life. That's a mouthful, isn't it? What I mean is that there's a small struggle going on between Egan Chaney, the cultural xenologist, and Egan Chaney, the quintessential man. No doubt it's the result more of environmental pressure than of my genetic heritage.

That's a little anthropological allusion, Benedict. Don't worry about it. You aren't supposed to understand it.

But enough. Today's atypical occurrence has sharpened my appetite for observation—it has temporarily calmed my internal struggle. I'm ready to stay here a year if need be, even though the original plan was only for six months—because a self divided against its stand cannot state. No, it can't. At least, not without fear of contradiction.

Hey ha and hey nonny, I'm going to bed. I may not touch my good old Yamaga mike for a week.

Dear God, look at those moons!

The Asadi clearing: a clarification

From the professional journals of Egan Chaney: My greatest col-
legiate failing was an inability to organize. I am pursued by that
specter even today. Consequently, a digression of sorts. In looking
over these quirkish notes for my formal ethnography, I realize that
I may have given the student the completely false idea that the Asadi
clearing is a small area of ground, say, fifteen by fifteen, measuring
in meters. Not so. As well as I am able to determine there are approximately a thousand Asadi individuals on hand daily—this figure in-
cludes mature adults, the young, and those intermediate between
age and youth. Of course, during all my time in the Synesthesia
Wild I've never been completely sure that the same individuals return to the clearing each morning. It may be that some sort of monumental shift takes place in the jungle, one group of Asadi replacing
another each day. But I doubt it. The Wild encompasses a finite
area, after all, and I have learned to recognize a few of the more distinctive Asadi (more on this point later, gentle reader). A thousand
still seems about right to me: a thousand gray-fleshed creatures
strolling, halting, bending at the waist and glaring at one another,
eating, participating in random sex acts, grappling like wrestlers,
obeying no time scheme, sequence, or apprehensible rationale. Such
activity requires a little space. Therefore the reader may not cheerfully
assume that the Asadi communion ground is a five-by-eight mud flat
between BoskVeld cypress and a malodorous sump hole. Not at all.
Their communion ground has both size and symmetry and the Asadi
maintain it discrete from the encroaching jungle by their unremit-
ting daily activity. I will not quote you dimensions, however. I will
say only that the clearing has the rectangular shape, the character-
istic slope, and the practical roominess of a twentieth-century football field. Pure coincidence, I'm sure. Astroturf and lime-rendered
endzones are conspicuously absent.

A dialogue of self and soul

From the private correspondence of Egan Chaney: The title of
this exercise is from Yeats, dear Ben. The substance of the dialogue,
however, has almost nothing to do with the poem of the same name.
I wrote this imaginary exchange in one of my notebooks while
waiting out a particularly long night on the edge of the Asadi clearing (just off the imaginary thirty-yard line on the south end of the
field, western sideline) and I intend for no one to read it, Ben, but
you. Its lack of objectivity and the conclusions drawn by the par-

ticipants make it unsuitable for any sort of appearance in the formal ethnography that I have yet to write.*

But you, Ben, will understand that a scientist is also a man and may perhaps forgive me. Since even *futbol* fanatics of Century XX required announcers to describe the action or binoculars through which to see it, I herewith provide a program. You can't tell the players without a program. The numbers on the backs of the players' metaphysical jerseys are Self and Soul.

PROGRAM

Self = The Cultural Xenologist
Soul = The Quintessential Man

Manager(s): Egan Chaney

SELF: This is my eighteenth night in the Synesthesia Wild.

SOUL: I've been here forever. But let that go. What have you learned?

SELF: Most of my observations lead me to state emphatically that the Asadi are not fit subjects for anthropological study. They manifest no purposeful social activity. They do not use tools. They have less social organization than did most of the extinct Earthly primates. Only the visit, four days ago, of the old "man" and his frightening companion indicates even a remote possibility that I am dealing with intelligence. How can I continue?

SOUL: You will continue out of contempt for the revulsion that daily grows in you. Because the Asadi are, in fact, intelligent—just as Oliver Bow Aurm Frasier said they were.

SELF: But how do I know that, damn it, how do I know what you insist is true? Blind acceptance of Frasier's word?

SOUL: There are signs, Dr. Chaney. The eyes, for instance. But even if there weren't any signs you'd know that the Asadi are as intelligent in their own way as you or I. Wouldn't you, Egan?

SELF: I admit it. Their elusive intelligence haunts me.

SOUL: No, now you've misstated the facts. You've twisted things around horribly.

SELF: How? What do you mean?

SOUL: You are not the one who is haunted, Egan Chaney, for

---

* Even though we lived only a building away from each other in base camp, Chaney "mailed" me this letter and I received it in my postal box for probeship dispatches. We never discussed the "letter" contents. *Thomas Benedict.*

you're too rational a creature to be the prey of poltergeist. I am the haunted one, the bedeviled one, the one ridden by every insidious spirit of doubt and revulsion.

SELF: Revulsion? You've used that word twice. Why do you insist upon it? What does it mean?

SOUL: That I hate the Asadi. I despise their every culturally significant—or insignificant—act. They curdle my essence with their very alienness. And because they affect me so you, too, Dr. Chaney, hate them—for you are simply the civilized veneer on my primordial responses to the world. You are haunted not by the Asadi, friend, but by me.

SELF: While you in turn are haunted by them? Is that how you view it?

SOUL: That's how it is. But although you're aware of my hatred for the Asadi, you pretend that that portion of my hatred which seeps into you is only a kind of professional resentment. You believe that you resent the Asadi for destroying your objectivity, your scientific detachment. In truth this detachment does not exist. You feel the same powerful revulsion for their alienness that works in me like a disease, the same abiding and deep-seated hatred. I haunt you.

SELF: With hatred for the Asadi?

SOUL: Yes. Admit it, Egan. Admit that even as a scientist you hate them.

SELF: No. No, damn you, I won't. Because we killed the pygmies, every one of them. How can I say, *I hate the Asadi, I hate the Asadi . . .* when we killed every pygmy? Even though, my God, I do.

Daily life: in-the-field report

From the professional tapes of the library of the Third Denebolan Expedition: Once again it's evening. I've a lean-to now. It protects me from the rain much better than did the porous roof of the forest. I've been here twenty-two days. My flesh has mildewed. Beneath this mildewed flesh my muscles crawl like the evil snakes that BoskVeld doesn't possess. I am saturated with Denebola's garish light. I am Gulliver among the Yahoos and even my own familiar voice speaking into this familiar little recorder doesn't comfort me.

This, however, isn't what you want to hear.

You want facts. You want my conclusions about the behavior of the Asadi. You want evidence that we're studying a life-form with at least a fundamental degree of the ability to ratiocinate. The Asadi have this ability, I swear it. I know it. But in my first week or two here my knowledge stemmed almost entirely from a hunch, a conviction with no empirical basis.

But slowly the evidence for intelligence has begun to accumulate.

OK. Let me, then, deliver myself of an in-the-field report as an objective scientist and forget the hunches of my mortal self. Somebody in grad school used to say that, I'm sure. At any rate, the rest of this tape will deal with the daily life of the Asadi.

A day in the life of. A typical day in the life of.

Except that I'm going to cap my reporting of mundane occurrences with the account of an extraordinary event that took place just this afternoon. Like Thoreau, I'm going to compress time to suit my own artistic/scientific purposes. So hang on, gang.

At dawn the Asadi return to their football field. For approximately twelve hours they mill about in the clearing doing whatever they care to do. Sexual activity and quirkish staring matches are the only sorts of behavior that can in any way be called "social"—unless you believe milling about in a crowd qualifies. I call their daylight way of life Indifferent Togetherness.

But when the Asadi engage in coitus, their indifference dissolves and gives way to a brutal hostility—both partners behave as if they desire to kill the other and frequently this is nearly the result. (I haven't yet witnessed the birth of an Asadi, in case you're wondering. Maybe the bearing of young occurs only in the Synesthesia Wild, the female self-exiled and unattended. I can't yet say for certain.) As for the staring matches, they're of brief duration and involve fierce gesticulation and mane-shaking. In these head-to-head confrontations the eyes change color with astonishing rapidity, flashing through the entire visible spectrum—and maybe beyond—in a matter of seconds.

I'm now prepared to say that these instantaneous changes of eye color are the Asadi equivalent of speech. I'm sure that you, Eisen, would have ventured this theory much sooner than I have, had you been here—but I'm uneasy about the biological aspects of any cultural study and must go slow. Three weeks of observation have finally convinced me that the adversaries in these staring matches control the internal chemical changes that trigger the changes in the succeeding hues of their eyes. In other words, patterns exist. And the minds that control these chemical changes cannot be primitive ones. Nor can I believe that the changes in eye color result from involuntary reflex. The alterations are willed. They're infinitely complicated.

Old Oliver Bow Aurm was right. The Asadi have a "language."

Still, for all the good it does me they might as well have none. I continue to go through each day as if I were an amateur naturalist charting the activities of the inhabitants of my ant-farm rather than a cultural xenologist attempting to find an ally against the monumental wilderness of space. One day is agonizingly like another. And I can't blame my pariahhood, for the only things even a well-adjusted Asadi may participate in are sex and staring. It doesn't pain me overmuch to be outcast from participation in these. To some extent, I'm not much more of a pariah than any of these creatures. We're all outcast from life's feast, so to speak, with no bridge clubs, Saturday-night dances, or home-study groups to enliven our lives.

Unlike every other society I've ever seen or read about, the Asadi don't even have any meaningful communal gatherings, any festivals of solidarity, any unique rituals of group consciousness. They don't even have families. The individual is the basic unit of their "society." What they have done, in fact, is to institutionalize the processes of alienation. Their dispersal at dusk simply translates into physical distance the incohesiveness by which they live during the day. And have we not learned over long centuries that such alienation is soul-destroying? How do the Asadi continue to live as a people? For that matter, why do they do so?

But enough questions. As I mentioned earlier, something out of the ordinary happened today. It happened this afternoon. (It's still happening, I guess.) And although this occurrence poses more questions than it answers, it had rescued me from the vitiating sameness of Asadi daily life. As before, this strange event involves the old man who appeared in the clearing over a week ago. Him and with him, of course, the blind reptilian creature perched on his shoulder like a curse—the huri.

Until today I'd never seen two Asadi eat together. As an Earthman from a Western background, I find the practice of eating alone a disturbing one. Disturbing and depressing. After all, I've been eating alone for over three weeks now, and I long to sit down in the communal mess with Benedict and Eisen, Morrell and Jonathan, and everyone else at base camp. My training in strange folkways and alien cultural patterns hasn't weaned me away from this longing. As a result, I've watched with interest, and a complete lack of comprehension, the Asadi sitting apart from their fellows and privately feeding—sucking on roots, chewing up leaves, and, as I reported a week ago, actually consuming the bark and heartwood of the trees. But doing so alone, apart, as a seemingly necessary exercise in isolation.

Today this changed.

At the beginning of the hour before the fall of dusk, the old man staggered into the clearing under the burden of something damnably heavy. I was aware of the commotion at once. Like last time, every one of the Asadi fled from the floor of the assembly ground to the edge of the jungle. I observed from my lean-to. My heart, dear Ben, thrumped like a toad in a jar. I had wondered if the enigmatic old boy would ever return and now he was back. The huri on his shoulder scarcely moved—it appeared bloated and insentient, a rubber doll without a trace of life. During the whole of the old man's visit it remained in this virtually comatose state, upright but unmoving.

The aged Asadi (whom I've begun to regard as some sort of aloof and mysterious chieftain) paused in the center of the clearing, looked about him and then struggled to remove the burden from his back. It was slung over his shoulder blades by means of two narrow straps.

Straps, Eisen: S-T-R-A-P-S.

Can you understand how I felt? Nor did the nature of the burden itself cause my wonder to fade. For, you see, what the old man was lowering to the ground was the rich, brownish-red carcass of an animal. The meat glistened with the falling light of Denebola and its own internal vibrancy. The meat had been dressed, Eisen, it had been prepared and the old man was bringing it to the clearing as an offering to his people.

He set the carcass on the dusty assembly floor and withdrew the straps from the incisions in the meat. Then he stood back five or six steps. Slowly a few of the adult males began to stalk back into the clearing. They approached the old man's offering with diffident steps, like thieves in darkened rooms. I noticed that their eyes were furiously changing colors—they were speaking to one another with the urgency of a hundred electric kaleidoscopes.

All but the old man who had brought the offering. I could see him standing away from the meat and his eyes—like unpainted china saucers—were the color of dull clay.

His eyes didn't alter even when several of the Asadi males fell upon the meat and began ripping away beautifully veined hunks, silently pushing and elbowing and clawing at one another. Then more and more of the Asadi males descended upon the carcass and all about the fringes of the clearing the females and the young made tentative movements out of the shadows. I had to leave my lean-to to see what was going on. And ultimately I couldn't see anything but bodies and manes and animated discord.

Before most of the Asadi were aware, Denebola had set.

Awareness grew, beginning with the females and the young on the edges of the clearing and then burning inward like a grass fire. The first individuals to become aware flashed into the Wild. Others followed. Eventually, in a matter of only seconds, even the strongest males raised their bloody snouts to the sky and scented their predicament. Then they bounded toward the trees, disappearing in innumerable directions—like the dying light itself.

But here is the strange part. The old man didn't follow his people back into the Synesthesia Wild.

He's sitting out there in the clearing right now.

When all the Asadi had fled he found the precise spot where he had placed his offering, hunkered down, lowered his buttocks, crossed his legs, and assumed sole ownership of that sacred piece of stained ground. I can see him out there now, damn it. The moons of Bosk-Veld throw his shadow in three different directions and the huri on his shoulder has begun to move a little, rustling its wings and nodding its blind head.

This is the first night since I came here that I haven't been alone and—I don't like it. No, indeed, fellows, I don't like it at all.

Personal involvement: The Bachelor

From the private notebooks of Egan Chaney: My meetings of The Bachelor, as I called him almost from the beginning, represented an unprecedented breakthrough. It came on my 29th day in the field—although, actually I had noticed him for the first time three days prior to his resolute approach and shy touching of my face. That touch, which I permitted solely out of respect for Mother Science, frightened me more than anything else that had happened to me in the Wild. As far removed from a threat of a woman's kiss, that touch frightened me more than the first appearance of the old chieftain, more than the nightmare shape of the huri, more even than the chaos of rending and eating that followed the old man's gift of the flame-bright carcass. I had been alone for weeks. Now, without much preamble, one of the Asadi had chosen to acknowledge my presence by touching me. Touching me!

I must back up a bit. I must back up to the night that the Asadi chieftain, against all custom, stayed in the clearing. My first realization that he intended to stay was another moment of minor terror, I'll confess, but the implications of his remaining overrode my fear. Wakeful and attentive, I sat up to study his every movement and to record anything that might conceivably be construed as significant.

The old man didn't move. The huri grew restive as the night progressed, but it didn't leave the old man's shoulder. The pair of them stayed in the clearing all that night and all the following day. They sat on the stained ground. When twilight came on that second day they departed with all the rest.

I despaired. How many days would I have to suffer through before something else unusual occurred? Would I spend the next five months watching the Asadi engage in brutal sex and senseless staring matches?

But on my 26th day on the edge of the clearing in the Synesthesia Wild, I saw The Bachelor. As far as I know I saw him for the first time. Certainly, if I had ever seen him before I had paid no attention. This anomalous event again broke the tedium for me— even though I didn't then fully understand what was happening. I knew only that the endless shuffling back and forth of the Asadi had given way momentarily to an instant of almost pure communion.

The Bachelor was a completely unprepossessing specimen.

I judged him to be three or four years beyond Asadi adolescence. Gray-fleshed and gaunt, he had a patchy silver-blue mane of so little length that the others surely considered him a virtual outcast. In fact, in all the time I knew him he never once took part in either coitus or the ritualized staring of the full-maned Asadi. When I first felt his eyes upon me The Bachelor was on my imaginary twenty-yard line, looking toward my lean-to from a pocket of his ceaselessly moving brethren. He had chosen me to stare at. The fact that he did not receive a cuffing for violating the one heretofore inviolable Asadi taboo confirmed for me the negligibility of his tribal status. It was he and I who were brethren, not he and the creatures whom he genetically resembled.

But in one extremely salient particular he didn't resemble the vast majority of Asadi. His eyes; his hard, emotion-veiling eyes. These were exactly like the old chieftain's—translucent but empty, enameled but colorless, fired in the oven of his mother's womb but brittle like sun-baked clay. Never did The Bachelor's eyes flash through the rainbow spectrum as did the prismatic eyes of his comrades. They remained clayey and cold, a shade or two lighter than his flesh.

And it was with these eyes, on my 26th day in the field, that The Bachelor took my measure. The noonday heat held us in a shimmering mirage, our gazes locked.

"Well," I shouted, "don't just stand there making faces. Come over here where we can talk."

My voice had no effect on the teeming Asadi—it had no effect on The Bachelor. His posture unchanged, he regarded me with no more

—and no less—interest than before. Of course, he could not "talk" with me. My human eyes don't even have the virtuosity of traffic lights—and since The Bachelor's never changed color, he couldn't even communicate with his own kind.

He was, for all intents and purposes, a mute.

But when I called out to him, I believed that his dead eyes indicated a complete lack of intelligence. It did not then occur to me that they might be the external sign of a physical handicap, just as dumbness in human beings may be the result of diseased or paralyzed vocal cords. Instead I decided that The Bachelor was stupid. I'm still not entirely certain that this initial judgment was not correct.

"Come on over here," I said again. "It doesn't bother me that you're mentally deficient."

The Bachelor continued to stare. He didn't approach. The distance between us measured almost thirty meters and occasionally a roving Asadi would intervene, its body blocking our vision.

"Even if you had a thumbnail for a brain," I mumbled, "you wouldn't be at a terrible disadvantage among this crew, old boy. I haven't seen anyone but the old chieftain even attempt to test their intelligence. And untested intelligence, like a cloistered virtue, isn't worth a—" I used an ancient and revered obscenity. The singing fronds of the Synesthesia Wild did not censure me for so saying. Some forty-odd light-years and a half dozen or so centuries had invested the word with a mystic respectability and I was too tired to be more profane.

The Bachelor didn't respond to my inaudible cynicism. He stared at me for the rest of the afternoon. I tried to occupy myself with note-taking, then with a lunch of some of the rations Benedict had dropped, and finally with cursory observations of other Asadi. Anything to avoid that implacable gaze. It was almost a relief when dusk fell. But that evening my excitement grew and I realized that something monumental had happened—I had been acknowledged.

The next day The Bachelor paid me little heed. He wandered forlornly in and out of the slow aimless files of his aimless kindred, a lanky gray clown unheeded by everyone but me. I was disappointed that The Bachelor did not demonstrate the same interest in me that he had shown the day before.

On the 28th day he resumed his shameless staring and I was gratified. He followed a procedure different from his stationary strategy of the first day—he moved tirelessly about the clearing, weaving in and out of the clusters of Asadi, but always staying close enough to the western sideline to be able to see me. His eyes remained as dead as the insides of two oyster shells.

I felt better the following morning, the morning of the 29th day—something was happening. The light from glowering Denebola seemed softer, the tropic heat less debilitating. I left my lean-to and went out on the assembly ground.

Bathed in the pastel emptiness of dawn, I stood there as the Asadi came flying through the tendrils and fronds of the Synesthesia Wild to begin another day of Indifferent Togetherness. Their bodies broke through the green veils on the clearing's edge like a thousand swimmers diving into a spring and soon I was surrounded. Surrounded but ignored. Great ugly heads with silver or blue or clay-white or tawny manes bobbed around me, graceless and unsynchronized. And above us the sky of BoskVeld stretched out into the attenuated vastness of a universe infinitely less caring than even those dancing heads.

The sun burned the morning away and at last I found The Bachelor.

Undoubtedly he had had me in his sight all that morning—but, moving with circumspection among his fellows, he had not permitted me to see him. I had fretted over his apparent absence.

Then Denebola was directly overhead and The Bachelor threaded his way through a dissolving clump of bodies and stopped not five yards from me, atremble with his own daring. I, too, trembled. I feared that at any moment The Bachelor would fall upon and devour me—instead he steeled himself to the task he had set and began his approach. I stood my ground. The gray head, the patchy silver-blue mane, the twin carapaces of his eyes—all moved toward me. Then the long gray arm rose toward my face and the humanoid hand touched the depression under my bottom lip, touched the most recent of my shaving cuts, touched me without clumsiness or malice.

And I winced.

A running chronology: weeks pass

Day 29: After achieving this unusual one-to-one contact with the Asadi native (hereafter referred to as The Bachelor) I did my best to find some method of meaningful communication. Nothing worked. Not words, of course. Not hand signals. Not signs in the dirt. Not even awkward charades. Nevertheless, The Bachelor could not be dissuaded from following me about. Once when I left the clearing for lunch he very nearly followed me into my lean-to. I was almost surprised when, at the fall of dusk, he left with the others—he had been so doggedly faithful all afternoon. Despite this desertion I'm excited about my work again. Tomorrow seems a hundred years off and I can't believe that I ever thought seriously about scrapping the first painful returns from my presence here.

Day 35: Nothing. Nothing at all. The Bachelor continues to follow me around, never any more than eight or nine paces away— his devotion is such that I can't urinate without his standing guard at my back. He must think that he's found an ally against the indifference of the others, but what his listless devotion gains for either of us, I can't say. All I know is that I've begun to tire of his attentions, just as he seems to have tired of the monotonous routine that he will not, for anything, abandon. . . . Life in the clearing goes on as always. The others ignore us.

Day 40: I am ill. The medicine Benedict dropped me during an earlier bout with diarrhea is almost gone. It's raining. As I write this, I'm lying on my pallet in my lean-to and watching the Asadi slog back and forth across the floor of their assembly ground. The odor of their morose gray dampness assaults me like a poison, intensifies my nausea. In and out the Asadi go, in and out and back and forth. . . .

I have formulated the interesting notion that their entire way of life, in which I have had to struggle to see even one or two significant patterns, is itself the one significant and ongoing ritual of their species. Formerly I had been looking for several minor rituals to help me explain their society—it may be that *they are the ritual*. As the poet asked, "How tell the dancer from the dance?" But having formulated this new and brilliant hypothesis about the Asadi I'm still left with the question: *What is the significance of the ritual that the Asadi themselves are?* An existential query, of course. Maybe my illness has made me think this way. Maybe I'm going melodramatically insane.

The Bachelor sits cross-legged in the dripping, steam-silvered foliage about five yards from my lean-to. His mane clings to his skull and shoulders like so many tufts of matted, cottony mold. Though he's been dogging my footsteps for eleven days now, I haven't been able to induce him to enter this ramshackle shelter. He always sits outside and stares at me from beneath an umbrella of shining fronds—even when it's raining. As it is now. His reluctance to come under a manufactured roof may be significant. If only I could make the same sort of breakthrough with two or three others that I've made with The Bachelor.

Day 46: A tinge of my illness remains. So does The Bachelor. The two have begun to get mixed up in my mind. . . . Nothing else to report. In and out, in and out. Daybreak and sunset, sunset and daybreak. The Great Shuffle goes on.

Day 50: After the Asadi fled into the jungle last night, I trudged toward the supply pickup point where Benedict leaves my rations of food and medicine each week. The doses of Placenol that I've been giving myself lately, shooting up the stuff like a skidrow junkie (figuratively speaking, of course), have gotten bigger and bigger—but Eisen, at the outset of this farcical expedition, assured me that P-nol in any quantity is absolutely nonaddictive. What amazes me beyond this sufficiently amazing attribute of the drug, however, is the fact that Benedict has been dropping more and more of it each week, providing me with a supply almost exactly commensurate with my increasing consumption.

Or do I use more because they drop more?

No, of course not. Everything goes into a computer at base camp. A program they ran weeks ago probably predicted this completely predictable upsurge in my "emotional" dependency on P-nol. At any rate I'm feeling better. I've begun to function again.

While I trudged, a haunting uneasiness seeped into me from the fluid shadows of the rubber trees. I heard noises. The noises persisted all the way to the drop point—faint, unidentifiable, frightening. Let me record this quickly: I believe that The Bachelor lurked somewhere beyond the wide leaves and trailing vines where those noises originated. Once, in fact, I think I saw his dull eyes reflect a little of the sheen of the evening's first moon. But he never completely revealed himself to me—if, indeed, he was there at all.

A typed note on the supply bundle: "Look, Chaney, you don't have to insist on 100% nonassociation with us. You've been gone almost two months. A conversation or two with genuine hoo-man beans won't destroy your precious ethnography. Let us drop you a radio. You can use it in the evenings. If you want it, send up a flare tomorrow night before all three moons have risen and I'll copter it out to the drop point the next day. So, how about it, Egan? Your Friend, Beneficent Ben." But of course I don't want a radio. Part of this business is the suffering. I knew that before I came out here. I won't quit until things have at last begun to make a little sense.

Day 57 (Predawn): I haven't been asleep all night. Yesterday evening, just six or seven hours ago, I went into the jungle to retrieve Benedict's eighth supply drop. Another typed note on the bundle; "Chaney, you're a pigheaded ninny. You don't even know how to conjugate your own first name. It should have been Ego instead of

Egan. I hope you've learned how to talk Asadi. If you haven't I'm certain that you'll have gone mad by now and started preaching neopentecostal sermons to the trees. What a picture. Send up a flare if you want anything. Ben." I wouldn't've thought Ben quite so sardonically literate.

On the way back to the clearing I heard noises again. The Synesthesia Wild echoed with the plunging grayness of an indistinct form. I am certain (I think) that it was The Bachelor spying on me, retreating clumsily before my pursuit. Yes, even with a backpack of new supplies weighting me down I determined to follow these noises, these suspicious tickings of leaf and twig. And although I never overtook my prey, I was able to keep up! It had to be The Bachelor, that half-seen grayness fleeing before me—none of his fellows would have permitted me so much as a glimpse of the disturbed foliage in the wake of their disappearance. I went deeper and deeper into the Wild, away from the assembly ground. Splotches of moonlight fled across the jungle with us.

When, panting, I broke into an opening among the trees I all at once realized that the noises drawing me on had ceased. I was alone. Lost, maybe. But filling the clearing, rising against the sky like an Oriental pagoda, there loomed over me the broad and impervious mass of something built, something made.

The resonances of Time dwarfed me. Thunderstruck, I felt panic climbing up the membranous ladder in my throat. My own startled gasp startled me again. . . . *It's hard to accept the fact that I've seen what I've seen. But that pagoda, temple, whatever, is actually out there! Old Oliver Bow Aurm studied the ruins of one of these structures—he learned only that the Asadi may have once had a civilization of some consequence. From this intact pagoda, however, I'll undoubtedly learn things that will eclipse even Frasier's discoveries. But God knows when I'll get out there again. . . .* I stared up at the lofty wings of this sudden artifact, then turned, plunged back into the jungle and raced wildly away, my backpack thumping.

Where was I going? Back to the assembly ground. Which way to run? I didn't have to answer this question. Blindly I moved in the direction of the suspicious tickings of leaf and twig that had resumed shortly after I fled the pagoda. The Bachelor again? I don't know. I saw nothing. But in two hours' time I had regained the safety of my lean-to. . . . Now I'm waiting for the dawn, for the tidal influx of Asadi.

I'm exhilarated and I haven't even touched my new supply of Placenol.

Day 57 (Evening): They're gone again. But I've witnessed something important and unsettling. The Bachelor did not arrive this morning with the others. At least he didn't take up his customary position eight or nine paces behind me. That sort of peripatetic vigilance does not go unnoticed and this morning I missed it. Totally ignored, I wandered through the Asadi, looking for The Bachelor. He was nowhere among them. Could he have injured himself in our midnight chase through the Wild?

By noon I was both exhausted and puzzled—exhausted by my search and my lack of sleep, puzzled by The Bachelor's apparent defection. I came to my lean-to and lay down. In a little while I had fallen asleep, though not soundly. Tickings of leaf and twig made my eyelids flicker. I dreamed that a gray shape came and squatted on the edge of the clearing about five yards from where I lay. Like a mute familiar, the shape watched over me. . . .

Kyur-AAAAACCCCCK!

Groans and thrashings about. Thrashings and hackings. The underbrush beside my lean-to crackled beneath the invasion of several heavy feet. Bludgeoned out of my dream by these sounds, I sat up and attempted to reorient myself to the world. I saw The Bachelor. I saw three of the larger and more agile males bear him to the ground and pinion him there. They appeared to be cooperating in the task of subduing him!

I watched their actions intently. What they did next confirmed my spur-of-the-moment evaluation. Cooperation it was indeed. The three males, who ignored me with all the contemptuous elan of aristocrats, picked up The Bachelor and bore him to the center of the clearing. I followed this party onto the assembly floor. As they had done during the old chieftain's two unexpected visits, the Asadi crowded to the sidelines—but they did not disappear into the jungle. They remained on the field, buffeting one another like the rabid spectators at one of those near-legendary "bowl" games. I was the only individual other than the four struggling males out in the center of the assembly floor. I looked down at The Bachelor. His eyes came very close to changing colors, going from their usual clay-white to a thin, thin yellow. But I couldn't interfere.

They shaved his mane. A female carrying two flat, beveled stones came out of the crowd on the eastern perimeter of the field—she gave the stones to the males. With them the males scraped away the last sad mangy tufts of The Bachelor's silver-blue collar. Just as they were about to finish, he gave a perfunctory kick that momentarily dislodged one of his tormentors, then acquiesced in his shame and lay on his back staring at Denebola. The entire operation had taken only about ten minutes. The three males sauntered off from their victim—and the satisfied spectators, aware that the barbering was over, strolled leisurely and with all their former randomness back into the clearing. Now, of course, they ignored The Bachelor with a frigidity they had once reserved for me.

I stood in the center of the clearing waiting for The Bachelor to get to his feet, the two of us a blurred focal point on the slowly revolving wheel of the Asadi Dance of Indifference. But for a long time he didn't move. His narrow head, completely shorn, scarred by their barbering stones (the first tools I had seen any of them but the chieftain employ), looked unnaturally fragile.

I leaned down and offered him my hand. A passing Asadi jostled me. Accidentally, I think. The Bachelor rolled to his stomach, rolled again to avoid being stepped on, curled into the fetal position—then unexpectedly sprang out of the dust and dodged through a broken file of his uncaring kinsmen. Did he wish to attain the edge of the Wild? Intervening bodies blocked my view of him, but I suppose he disappeared into the trees and kept on running.

All extremely interesting, of course. What does it signify? My hypothesis this evening is that the Asadi have punished The Bachelor for leading me last night, whether he did so inadvertently or on purpose, to the ancient pagoda in the Synesthesia Wild. His late arrival in the clearing may have been an ingenuous attempt to forestall this punishment. I can't think of any other reasons why the Asadi should have moved to make him even more of an outcast than he already was.

All this ambivalence mystifies me. It also convinces me that I can't permit the monotony of nine-tenths of their "daily life" to becloud my eyes to the underlying meaning of it all. Patience, dear God, is nine-tenths of cultural xenology. And the punishment of weariness (since I'm discussing punishments, cruel and otherwise) runs concurrently with the xenologist's term of patience. Consequently and/or hence, I'm going to bed.

Day 61: The Bachelor has not returned. Knowing that he's now officially a pariah, he chooses to be one on his own terms. During his absence I've been thinking about two things: (1) If the Asadi did in fact punish The Bachelor because he led me to the pagoda, then they realize full well that I am not simply a maneless outcast. They know that I'm genetically different, a creature from elsewhere, and they consciously wish me to remain ignorant of their past. (2) I would like to make an expedition to the pagoda. With a little perseverance it shouldn't be exceedingly difficult to find, especially since I plan to go during the day. Unusual things happen so rarely in the Asadi clearing that I can afford to be gone from it for a little while. One day's absence should not leave any irreparable gaps in my ethnography. If the expedition goes well that absence may provide some heady insights into the ritual of Asadi life.

I wish only that The Bachelor would return.

Day 63: Since today was the day of Benedict's ninth scheduled drop I decided to make my expedition into the Wild early this morning. I would be "killing two birds," as Ben himself might well put it. First: I would search for the lost pagoda. Second: if I failed to find it I would salvage some part of the day by picking up my new supplies. Therefore, before dawn, off I went.

The directional instincts of human beings must have died millennia ago—I got lost. The Wild stirred with an inhuman and gothic calm that tattered the thin fabric of my resourcefulness.

Late in the afternoon Benedict's helicopter saved me. It made a series of stuttering circles over the roof of the jungle—at one point I looked up and saw its undercarriage hanging so close to the tree-tops that a spy monkey might have been able to leap aboard. I followed the noise of the helicopter to our drop point. From there I had no trouble getting back to the clearing.

Today, then, marks the first day since I've been in the Wild that I've not seen a single member of the Asadi. I miss The Bachelor as I would miss a prodigal child. I await each dawn with newly rekindled expectations. But the entire night lies before me and the only way to get through it is to sleep.

Day 68: Even though I could not justify an excursion on the basis of another drop (the next one is still two days away), I went looking for the pagoda again. The last four days have been informational zeroes. I had to get away from the clearing, had to take some kind of positive action, no matter how foolish that action might seem. And it was passing foolish—I got lost again, terrifyingly so. Green creepers coiled about me—the sky disappeared. And this time I knew that Benedict's helicopter would not fly overhead—not unless I could wait another two days for it. How, then, dear diary, did our hero get home? Once again, the suspicious tickings of leaf and twig. I simply followed them. Now I'm back in my lean-to again, confident that The Bachelor is still out there and steadfast in my decision to make no more expeditions until I have help.

Day 71: The Bachelor is back!

Day 72: Yesterday I could record nothing but the simple fact of The Bachelor's appearance in the clearing. This evening I'll note only three or four concomitant facts. The Bachelor still has very little mane to speak of and the Asadi treat him as a total outcast. These last two days he has demonstrated a considerable degree of independence in his relations with me. He continues to follow me about, but less conspicuously and with occasional side trips that remove him altogether from my sight. He no longer hunkers beside my lean-to at all. A made dwelling-place may put him uncomfortably in mind of the pagoda to which he led me and for whose discovery to an outsider he was publicly humiliated. I find this new arrangement a felicitous one, however. A little privacy is good for the soul.

Day 85: The note on yesterday's supply bundle: "Send up a flare tomorrow night if you wish to remain in the Wild. Eisen is seriously considering hauling you out of there. Only a flare will save you. The flare will mean, 'I'm learning things. Don't remove me from my work.' No flare will mean either that your stay has stopped being profitable or that you've reached your limit. My personal suggestion, Egan, is that you do nothing, just sit tight and wait for us. OK? Your friend, Ben." I've just sent up two goddamn flares. Day 85 will go down in cultural-xenological history as Egan Chaney's personal Fourth of July.

Day 98: I'm holding my own again. Thirty days ago I made my second excursion into the Wild to find the elusive pagoda. I've survived almost an entire month without venturing away from the assembly ground.

Most of my time in the clearing has been devoted to noting individual differences among the Asadi natives. Since their behavior for the most part manifests a bewildering uniformity I've necessarily turned to the observation of their physical characteristics. Even in this area, however, most differences are more apparent than real— I've found few useful discriminators. Size has some importance.

The ability of the eyes to flash through the spectrum is another discriminator of sorts. But the only Asadi who don't possess this ability in a complete degree are the old chieftain and The Bachelor.

Nevertheless, I can now recognize on sight several Asadi other than these prominent two. I've tried to give descriptive names to these recognizable individuals. The smallest adult male in the clearing I call Turnbull, because his stature puts me in mind of Colin Turnbull's account of the pygmies of the Ituri. A nervous fellow with active hands I call Benjy, after Benedict. The old chieftain continues to exert a powerful influence on my thinking. His name I derived by simple analogy. Him I call Eisen Zwei.

The Bachelor now seems intent on retaining his anonymity—his mane has grown very little since the shaving. I would almost swear that he plucks it at night in the Wild, keeping it short on purpose. Who is to say? These last few days he's avoided even me; that is, after he ascertains my whereabouts in the morning and then again in the evening, as if this simple knowledge suffices to maintain him secure all day and then through the uncertainty of night on BoskVeld. The bloom, I suppose, has gone off our romance. Good. We're both more comfortable.

Today was another drop day. I didn't go out to retrieve my parcels. Too weary, too bloodless. But I've sworn off Placenol and the attendant psychological lift has made my physical weakness bearable. My parcels will be out there tomorrow.

Tonight I'm going to read Odegaard's official report on the Shamblers of Misery. And then sleep. Sleep sleep sleep.

Day 106: Eisen Zwei, the old chieftain, came back today! In thumbing through this notebook I find that I first saw him enter the clearing exactly ninety days ago. Has a pattern begun to emerge? If so, I can't interpret its periodicity. I don't even know, come to think of it, what sort of life-span the Asadi have. It might be that a man would have to stay out here centuries in order to unravel a mere sleeve of the garment of their existence. God forbid.

This visit of Eisen Zwei—to return to the issue at hand—proceeded in a manner identical to that of his first one. He came into the clearing with the huri on his shoulder, sat down, remained perhaps an hour, then stalked back into the Wild. The Asadi, of course, fled from him—motivated, perhaps, more by loathing than fear.

How long will I have to wait until ole E.Z. returns?

Day 110: The behavior of the Asadi—all of the Asadi—has undergone a very subtle alteration, one I can't account for. Nothing in my previous association with them gives me a basis for evaluating its import. Even after 110 days in the field I'm a slave to purely human concepts of causality—behavior changes for certain reasons, not from mere whim. But out here reasons elude me in the same way that the Asadi pagoda, about which I now only dream, once eluded me.

Let me state what I have observed. For the last two days every member of this insane species has taken great pains to avoid stepping into a rather large area in the center of the clearing. As a result the Asadi have crowded themselves into two arbitrary groups at opposite ends of the field. These "teams" do not comport themselves in exactly the same way as did the formerly continuous group. Individuals on both sides of the silently agreed-upon No Man's Land exude an air of heightened nervousness. They crane their heads about, clutch their arms across their chests, sway, suffer near-epileptic paroxysms as they weave in and out, in and out, among their fellows. Watching them I sometimes believe that they writhe to the music of an eerie flute played deep in the recesses of the jungle.

Sometimes staring matches will take place between individuals on opposite sides of the imaginary chasm. Eyes change color, bodies bend, and limbs flail. But neither participant puts a foot inside the crucial ring of separation, which is about thirty yards long and almost—but not quite—the entire width of the clearing. Not quite, mind you, because there's a narrow strip of ground on each sideline through which the two "teams" may exchange members, one member at a time. These exchanges occur infrequently, with a lone Asadi darting nervously out of his own group, down one of these unmarked causeways and into the "enemy" camp. Why do they avoid the center of the clearing? The only reason my Earthman's mind can settle on is that the clearing's center marks that area of fearsome ground where an offender has been humiliated, blood spilled, and flesh consumed. But all these things happened a good while ago. Why this fastidiousness now? Why this separation?

The Bachelor has reacted to it all by climbing into the branches of a thick-boled tree not ten meters from my lean-to. From dawn to sunset he sits high above his inscrutable kinsmen, watching, sleeping, maybe attempting to assess the general mood. At times he looks in my direction to see what I make of these new developments. I don't make much of them.

Day 112: It continues, this strange bipartite waltz. The dancers have grown even more frantic in their movements. Anxiety pulses in the air like electricity. The Bachelor climbs higher into his tree, struggling to the topmost branches where his hold is precarious—he wedges himself in place. In the last three days I can't recall having seen any of the dancers eat—none have engaged in sex. Even their staring contests have virtually ceased, though those that do occur are fierce and protracted. The nonexistent flute that plays in my head has grown stingingly shrill and I cannot guess what the end of this madness must be.

Day 114: Events culminated today in a series of bizarre developments that pose me a conundrum of the first order. What will happen tomorrow? I can't imagine any sort of follow-up to what I raptly watched today.

It began early. Eisen Zwei came into the clearing an hour after the arrival of the Asadi. As on his second visit, he bore on his back the dressed-out carcass of an animal. His huri, though once again upright on the old man's shoulder, looked like the work of a rather inept taxidermist—lopsided, awkwardly posed, and inanimate. The people in the clearing deserted their two identically restive groups, fleeing to the jungle around the assembly ground. I could not help thinking, *How strange, how ironic, that the force that momentarily reunifies the Asadi is a shared loathing.*

The Bachelor, half-hidden by great lacquered leaves and unsteady in the fragile upper branches, leaned out over the clearing's edge and gazed down from his empty clay-white eyes. I clutched the bole of his tree, surrounded now by the curious, loathing-filled Asadi who had crowded into the jungle. They ignored me. Unaware of him, they ignored The Bachelor, too—but together we all watched the spectacle proceeding in the Center Ring.

Eisen Zwei lowered the burden from his back. He undid the straps that had held the meat in place. But now, instead of stepping away and permitting a few of the braver males to advance, he took the near-unconscious huri from his shoulder and set it upon the bleeding lump of meat. The huri's blind head did not move, but even from where I stood I could see its tiny fingers rippling with slow but well-orchestrated malice. Then this hypnotic rippling ceased and the huri sat there looking bloated and dead, a plaything for the children of scabrous witches.

Without a farewell of any sort Eisen Zwei turned and stalked back into the Synesthesia Wild. Where he left the clearing, foliage clattered from the efforts of several Asadi to get out of his way.

Silence fell again.

And now no one left the security of the assembly ground's edge to challenge the huri's ownership of this new and sorely tempting carcass—despite the fact that I had not seen any of the Asadi take food in almost five days.

Denebola, fat and mocking, crossed a small arc of the sky and made haloes dance in a hundred inaccessible grottos of the Wild.

An hour passed, and Eisen Zwei returned! He had simply left the huri to guard his first offering. Yes, first. For the old chieftain had come back with still another carcass slung across his bony shoulders, another dressed-out and flesh-strapped carcass. He set it down beside the other. The huri animated itself just long enough to shift its weight and straddle the two contiguous pieces of meat. Then the old Asadi departed again, just as before.

In an hour he returned with a third piece of meat—but this time he entered the clearing from the west, about twenty yards up from my lean-to. I realized that he had first entered from the east, then from the south. *A pattern is developing,* I thought. *Now he'll depart once more and reenter from the north.* After all, even the most primitive peoples on Earth had ascribed mystical characteristics to the four points of the compass and I was excited by the prospect of my being able to draw a meaningful analogy.

Of course, Eisen Zwei saw fit to shatter my hopes by remaining on the assembly floor—he did not leave again at all. (In fact, as on my 22nd night in the Wild, he still has not left. Under a triangle of copper-green moons the old chieftain and his huri squat on the bleak, blood-dampened ground waiting for Denebola's first spiderwebbings of light.) He made one complete circuit around the clearing instead, walking counterclockwise from his point of entrance. The huri did not move.

This done, Eisen Zwei rejoined his noxious familiar at midfield.

Here the second stage of this new and puzzling ritual began. Without taking the third carcass from his back, E.Z. bent and picked up the huri and put it in its accustomed place on his shoulder. Kneeling, he tied straps through the two pieces of meat over which the huri had kept watch. Next he began to drag these marbled chunks of brown and red slowly through the dirt. He dragged the first into the southern half of the clearing and set the huri down once more as his guardian. This procedure he duplicated in the northern half of the clearing, except that here he himself stood guard over the second offering. The final carcass he still bore on his back.

Outlined in the dust were two distinct drag marks, inward-looping circles that delineated the chieftain's progress from the original resting place of the meat. The coil in the dust of the northern half of the field was single; that in the southern, double. The Asadi tensed.

Eisen Zwei stepped away from the second offering. Deep in his throat he made a noise that sounded like a human being, a grown man, trying to fight down a sob. This sound I suppose I should add, is the first and so far the only example of voiced communication—discounting involuntary groans and a few guttural, growl-like mumblings—that I've heard among the Asadi. The huri responded to Eisen Zwei's plaintive "sobs"—undoubtedly a signal—by hopping, practically falling off the object of its guardianship and then scrabbling miserably through the dust toward its master. Its rubbery wings dipped, twisted, folded upon themselves. (I've almost decided that the huri is incapable of flight, that its wings represent an anatomical holdover from an earlier stage of its evolution.) When both Eisen Zwei and his wretched huri had reached their sacred patch of ground at midfield the old Asadi picked up the beast and let it close its tiny hands over his discolored mane.

The two of them held everyone's attention.

Then the wizened old chieftain extended his arms, tilted back his head and, staring directly at the sun, made a shuddering inhalation of such piteous depth that I thought either his lungs would burst or his heart break. The clearing echoed with his sob.

At once the Asadi poured out of their hiding places onto the assembly ground—not simply the adult males but individuals of every sex and age. Even now, however, in the middle of this lunging riot, the population of the clearing divided into two groups, each one scrimmaging furiously, intramurally, in its own cramped plot of earth. Teeth flashed, manes tossed, bodies crumpled, eyes pinwheeled with inarticulate color. The hunger of the Asadi, like mid-August thunder, made low sad music over the Wild.

In this hunger neither The Bachelor nor I shared. We merely watched, he from aloft, I from the trembling shadows.

It did not take long for the Asadi, slashing at one another and sometimes half-maiming themselves, to devour the two carcasses. Perhaps five minutes. *Like piranhas*, I thought, *quick, voracious, brutal.*

And then Eisen Zwei inhaled his grief-shot moan and the confusion ceased. Every lean gray snout turned toward him. The dying went off to die alone, if any were in fact at the point of death. I saw no one depart, but neither did I see anyone prostrate in the dirt—as unlikely as it may sound. Death, like birth, the Asadi must choose to experience in the intimate privacy of the jungle and the night—in my months here I've not seen a single tribesman die in the clearing. Illness, accident, and age apparently have no sting here. And, believe it or not, I've only just now realized this. Does it mean anything? Sure. (But what?) All eyes upon him, silence stemming out of the very earth, Eisen Zwei made preparations for the third and final act of today's unanticipated, unexpectedly baroque ritual.

He lowered the burden from his back, sat down beside it and—in full view of his benumbed tribesmen—ate. The creature on his shoulder leaned into his mane and I thought that the old chief might feed the huri, give it something for its contribution to the festivities. He gave it nothing. Inert but clinging, the huri did not protest this oversight.

An hour passed. Then two. Then three.

By this time I had long since retired to the shade of my lean-to, emerging at fairly frequent intervals to check the goings-on in the clearing. By the second hour the Asadi had begun to move about within their separate territories. By the third hour these territories had merged so that I could no longer distinguish the two distinct "teams" of previous days. The pattern of the Daily Life of my first 109 days in the clearing had reasserted itself—except that now the Asadi moved with incredible sluggishness, suspiciously regarding their chieftain and refusing to encroach upon a rather large unmarked circle containing him.

I decided that the ritual was about to conclude. Out among the Asadi, trying to feel through my pores the prevailing mood, I noticed that The Bachelor had come down out of his tree. But I didn't see him in the clearing. All I saw was old E.Z., isolated by a revolving barricade of legs, chewing with an expression of stupid pensiveness. The huri flapped once or twice as the afternoon progressed, but the old chieftain still did not feed it.

Finally, sunset.

The Asadi fled, dispersing as they always have—but Eisen Zwei, no doubt as surfeited as a python that has just unhinged its lower jaw to admit a fawn, slumped in his place and did not move.

Now three alien moons dance in the sky and I'm left with one question, the one question that I'm frightened to ask, so stark and self-evident is its answer: *From what sort of creature did the old chief obtain and dress out his ritual offerings?* Once before I didn't ask this question at all—I couldn't ask it. But now, huddled beneath the most insubstantial of roofs, I am unable to fend off the terrible ramifications of the Asadi way of death.

Speculations on cannibalism: an extemporaneous essay

From the unedited in-the-field tapes of Egan Chaney: It's a beautiful day. Just listen. Let me hold the microphone out for you—hear that? Nothing but a thousand pairs of feet (minus six or eight feet, I suppose) slogging back and forth through a quarter inch of hot dust. Nothing but that and the soulful respiration of the Asadi and —somewhere beyond these scarcely tangible sounds—the stillness of all BoskVeld. A beautiful day, just beautiful.

And here I am, your roving reporter, Egan Chaney, right out here where the action is, thoroughly prepared to give you the latest and most comprehensive coverage of each new development in the clearing. Unfortunately, Eisen, I still do more waiting around than adrenalin-powered summaries of the ongoing news. It's four days since your counterpart, Eisen Zwei, stirred things up with his disorderly three-course banquet.

Since then, nothing.

As a consequence, I'm now going to switch hats, doffing my correspondent's chapeau in favor of the dignified visor of a senior news editor. I'm walking. I'm walking among the Asadi. They fail to see me even though I'm just as solid, just as real, as they are. Even the ones I've given names to refuse to grant me the fact of my existence.

I've just walked by Werner. The configuration of his features gives him a gentle look, like that of a Quaker wearing a parka. His seeming gentleness leads me to the topic of this commentary—how could a creature of Werner's mien and disposition actually eat the flesh of one of his own kind? God help me if these aliens are sentient, my good base-camp huggers, because I'm walking among cannibals!

They encircle me. They ensorcel me. They fill me with a sudden dread, an awe such as the awe of one's parents that consumes the child who has just learned the secret of his own conception and birth. Exactly thus, my dread of the Asadi, my awe of their intimate lives. . . .

Turnbull is missing. Do you remember him? I named him Turnbull because he was small, like the pygmies the first Turnbull wrote about. Now I can't find him. Since the ritual of Day 114, I've been through this clearing a hundred times—from sideline to sideline, from endzone to endzone—searching for him with all the devotion of a father. Little Turnbull, squat and sly, is nowhere among these indifferent, uncouth beings. I'd have found him by now, I know I would. He was my pygmy, my little pygmy, and now these aloof bastards— these Asadi of greater height than Turnbull himself possessed—have eaten him! Eaten him as though he were a creature of inferior status —a zero in a chain of zeroes as long as the diameter of time! May God damn them!

A lengthy pause during which only the shuffling of the Asadi can be heard.

—I think my shout unsettled some of them. A few of them flinched. But they don't look at me, these cannibals, because a cannibal may not go too far toward acknowledging the existence of another of his kind, so uncertain is his opinion of himself. A cannibal is always afraid that he'll ascribe more importance to himself than he deserves. In doing so, he discovers—in a moment of hideous revelation—where his next meal is coming from. He always knows where it's coming from and he's therefore nearly always afraid.

Yes, yes, I was philosophical, but I told you a moment ago that this was an editorial, not a news report. You've got to expect shallow profundities in these things. Shallow profundities and forthright circumlocutions. OK? I don't want to disappoint anyone.

As a result (if I may continue) cannibals are the most inwardly warring schizophrenics in all of Nature. The dichotomy between the two self-contained personalities shines as clean and coppery as Denebola at dawn. The pattern of indifferent association during the day and compulsive scattering at night—as they flee from themselves—lends further credence, I think, to my interpretation of their dichotomy of soul. After all, who is more deluded than the cannibal? His every attempt to achieve unity with his kind results in a heightened alienation from himself.

So it is with the Asadi. So it is with—

Damn it, I agree! I'm talking sense and rubbish at the same time. —But it's hot out here, and they ignore me. They go by, they go by, revolving about me like so many motorized pasteboard cut-outs. . . . And Turnbull's not among them, he doesn't revolve anymore, he's been butchered and consumed. Butchered and consumed, do you hear? With the same indifference that we used to poison the Ituri and rout out the people who lived there. Turnbull's dead, base-camp huggers, and *There are no more pygmies there are no more pygmies there are no*

The Ritual of Death and Designation

From the final draft of the one complete section of Egan Chaney's otherwise unfinished ethnography:

PART ONE—DEATH. On Day 120 the old chieftain, whom I called Eisen Zwei, took ill. Because it had been several days since he had gorged himself during the "feast," I then supposed that his sickness was not related to his earlier intemperance. I am still of this mind. For five days he had eaten nothing, although the rest of the Asadi refused to observe his fast and began eating whatever herbs, roots, flowers, bark, and heartwood they could find—just as they had done before their ritual feast. They ignored the old chief and the old chief's huri, much in the way they ignored The Bachelor and me.**

Eisen Zwei's sickness altered the pattern, altered it more violently than had his several appearances in the clearing. On the afternoon

---

** Several explanatory footnotes were provided with the published fragment. I wrote the introduction to the fragment, and the footnotes that follow this one are all from my hand. *Thomas Benedict.*

of the first day of his illness he abruptly rose from his reserved center plot and made the horribly glottal, in-sucking noises that he had used to summon his people to the meat six days before.

I came running from my lean-to.

The Asadi moved away from the old chieftain, stopped their shuffling and shambling and stared from great platter-like eyes, the lenses of which had stalled on a single color. This delicate stasis reigned for only a moment. Then the in-sucking noises were replaced by a spastic rumbling. As I broke into the clearing I saw the old man bent over at the waist, his arms above his head, heaving and again heaving until it seemed that he would soon be vomiting into the dust the very lining of his bowels. I turned away, abashed by the sight, but since the Asadi stared on, fascinated, I turned back around to observe their culture in action. It was at that moment, if at no other, that I earned the Oliver Bow Aurm Frasier Memorial Fillet, which the Academy has since bestowed upon me.***

The chieftain's huri flew up from his shoulder and flapped in the somnolent air like a small wind-collapsed umbrella. I had never seen it fly before—I was surprised that it was capable of flight. Its ungainly flapping excited the already well-aroused population of the assembly ground, and together we watched the huri rise above tree level, circle back over the clearing, and dip threateningly toward the branches of the trees on the clearing's western edge. The old chief and his vehement, body-racking convulsions seemed forgotten. Every pair of color-stalled eyes followed the uncertain aerial progress of the huri. It plummeted, noisily flapping, toward that precariously forked perch where The Bachelor sometimes sequestered himself.

But The Bachelor was not there. I did not know where he was.

The huri crashed downward through the branches, caught itself up, struggled flapping out of the jungle, and returned with blind devotion to the air space over its master. I thought that at last it was going to feed, that its sole diet might well consist of Eisen Zwei's vomitings. I expected the starved creature to fall upon these—but it did not. Somehow it kept itself aloft, flapping—flapping—waiting for the old man to finish.

And when the old chief had completely emptied himself and fallen exhausted to his knees, it was not the huri that waded into the vile pool of vomit but the old man's shameless compatriots.

*** This sentence did not appear in the published fragment. Egan Chaney has never received this award, though I believe he deserved it. According to Academy President Isaac Wells, he is not now, nor has he ever been, under consideration for the award.

Now I did not even think of returning to my lean-to. My curiosity overcame my revulsion and I watched the Asadi carry away the half-digested mass as if each semi-solid piece were an invaluable relic. There was no fighting, no elbowing, no eye-searing abuse. Each individual simply picked out his relic, took it a short distance into the jungle, and deposited it in some hidden place for safekeeping.

All during this solemn recessional the huri quickened the air with its heavy wings and an anonymous Asadi supported Eisen Zwei by tenderly clutching the old chief's mane. When everyone had taken away a chunk of regurgitated flesh the chieftain's attendant laid him down out of the sphere of hallowed spew, and the huri descended to squat by its master's head. This newest ritual was over, all over.

I should mention, however, that The Bachelor appeared in the mourning throng to select and depart with some memento of Eisen Zwei's illness, just as the others had. He came last, took only a palm-sized morsel and retreated to the clearing's edge. Here he climbed into the tree above which the huri had flown its nearly disastrous mission only minutes before. Until sunset The Bachelor remained here, observing and waiting—as I, as a cultural xenologist, must always do.

On Days 121, 122, and 123 Eisen Zwei continued in his illness and the Asadi paid him scant attention, their chief ministrations consisting of bringing him water twice a day and refraining from stepping on him. The huri sat by the old chieftain's head. It shifted from one foot to the other and waited—smugly, I thought—for its master to die. It never ate.

At night the Asadi deserted their dying leader without a glance, without a twinge of doubt, and I was afraid that he would die while they were gone. Several times, looking out at his inert silhouette, moonlight dripping through the fronds, I thought he had died, and a mild panic assailed me. Did I have a responsibility to the corpse? Only the responsibility, I decided, to let it lie and observe the reactions of the Asadi when they came back at dawn.

But the old chief did not die during any of these nights and on Day 124 another change occurred. Eisen Zwei sat up and stared at Denebola as it crossed the sky—but he stared at the angry sun through the spread fingers of both his hands, hands he crooked into claws and tore impotently through the blur of light that Denebola must have seemed to him. The huri did not move. As always, it sat smug and blindly knowing. But the Asadi noticed the change in their leader and reacted to it. As if his writhing dissatisfaction with the sun were a clue, they divided into two groups again and formed attentive semicircles to the north and south of Eisen Zwei. They watched his challenge to the sun, his wrestling with its livid corona, his tearing at its indistinct streamers of gas with gnarled hands.

At noon the old chief rose to his feet. He stretched out his arms. Sobbing, he clawed at the sky, suddenly gave up, and sank back to his knees.

Without any sort of visible prompting a pair of Asadi from each group went to his aid. They lifted him from the ground. Others on the clearing's edge selected large, lacquered fronds from the rubber trees and passed these over the heads of their comrades to the place where their leader had collapsed. The men supporting Eisen Zwei took these fronds, arranged them into a regal pallet, and then placed the fragile body on the bed they had made.

For only the second time that I could remember the Asadi had cooperated to bring about a desired end. (The other occasion, of course, had been the shaving of The Bachelor's mane.) But, like ancient papyrus exposed to the air, their cooperation disintegrated as soon as Eisen Zwei was stretched full-length on his pallet.

Each of the groups maintained a semblance of its former integrity, but aimless shambling replaced chieftain-watching as the primary activity within each group. Denebola, finally free of the old man's gaze, fell toward the horizon.

I walked unimpeded through the clearing and bent down over the dying chieftain, careful to avoid the huri that watched me from its uncanny, socketless face. I shrugged off the creature's literally blank stare and looked into the genuine eyes of its master.

I experienced a shock, a physical jolt.

The old man's eyes were burned out, blackened holes in a humanoid mask. It now made little difference that even before his staring match with the sun his eyes had not possessed the Asadi ability to run through the spectrum—for now, burned out, blackened, they were utterly dead, two char-smoked lenses waiting for the old man's body to catch up with their lifelessness.

And then the diffused red light that signaled sunset in this forested region of BoskVeld was pouring through the Wild.

The clearing emptied.

Alone with Eisen Zwei and his huri, I knew that it would be during this night that the old man died. I tried to find some intimation of life in his blackened eyes, saw none, and withdrew to the cover of the Wild and the security of my lean-to. I did not sleep. But my worst premonitions betrayed me and in the morning I looked out to see

Eisen Zwei sitting cross-legged on his pallet, the huri once again perched on his shoulder.

And then the tenuous yellow light that marked sunrise and rejuvenation on BoskVeld filtered through the jungle.

The Asadi returned, filled the clearing with their lank bodies, and once again took up their positions to the north and the south of the dying chieftain.

Day 125 had begun.

And, finally, the ritual that I had decided the Asadi *were* resolved itself into a lesser ritual in which they merely participated—the grandest, strangest, and most highly ordered ceremony in their culture. I call the events of Day 125, taken as a cumulative whole, the Ritual of Death and Designation. I believe that we will never fully understand the narrowly "political" life of the Asadi until we can interpret, with precision, every aspect of this ritual. Somewhere in the context of the events of Day 125 lies the meaning of it all. And how terrible to be confronted with an elusive truth!

The color of the eyes of every Asadi in the clearing (The Bachelor's excepted) declined into a deep and melancholy indigo. And stalled there. The effect of solemn uniformity struck me as soon as I stepped onto the assembly floor—even though I had intended to look first at Eisen Zwei and not at his mourners. Profound indigo and absolute silence. So deeply absorbent were the eyes of the Asadi that Denebola, rising, could cast no glare, could throw out not a single dancing, shimmering, uncapturable ray. Or so it seemed. The day was an impressionist painting rendered in flat pastels and dull primaries—a paradox.

Then the heads in which the indigo eyes so intriguingly reposed began to rock from side to side, the chin of each Asadi inscribing a small figure eight in the air. The heads moved in unison. This went on for an hour or more as the old chieftain, as blind as his companion, sat cross-legged on his pallet, nodding, nodding in the monumental morning stillness.

Then, as if they had inscribed figure eights for the requisite period, the Asadi broke out of their separate groups and formed several concentric rings around the old man. They did so to the same lugubrious rhythm that they had established with their chins; they dragged their long bodies into place. The members of each ring continued to sway. The inaudible flute which I had once believed to be in the Wild had now certainly been exchanged for an inaudible bassoon. Ponderously, the Asadi swayed. Ponderously, their great manes undulated with a slow and beautifully orchestrated grief. And The Bachelor (all by himself, just beyond the outermost ring) swayed also in cadence with the others.

Now I was the sole outcast among this people, for I alone observed and did not participate.

The rhythmic swaying lasted through the remaining hours of the forenoon and on toward the approach of evening.

I retired to my lean-to, but thought better of just sitting there and climbed the tree in which The Bachelor often perched. I forgot about everything but the weird ceremony in the clearing. I did not eat. I did not desert my station. Neither did I worry about my separation from the members of the Third Denebolan Expedition in base camp —it was for this moment, I instinctively understood, that I had refused any but the most essential contacts with other human beings. Leaning out over the clearing I gave myself up completely to the hypnotic movements of the shaggy-headed players that a generous universe had permitted me to study. No, thank merciful God, Egan Chaney had not been born too late.

I nodded but I did not sleep.

Suddenly Eisen Zwei gave a final sob, maniacal and heartrending, and grabbed the beast that clung with evil tenacity to his mane. He seized it with both palsied hands. (This was near the end of the day—I could feel the last dull rays of Denebola caressing my back, covering me like a threadbare blanket, unevenly warm.) Eisen Zwei exerted himself to what seemed his last reserve of strength and, strangling the huri, lurched out of the dust to his feet. The huri flapped, twisted, freed one wing, and flapped harder. The old chief squeezed his hands together and attempted to grind the life out of the creature. He was not successful. The huri beat the air with its wings, beat the chieftain about the face, and finally used its tiny hands to scour fine crimson wounds in Eisen Zwei's withered cheeks and buckled forehead.

During this struggle the Asadi stopped swaying, they looked on with eyes that gradually fell away from indigo toward a paler blue. Eisen Zwei drew a deep breath and shook the belligerent huri back and forth, up and down, like a bartender mixing an exotic drink.

But the huri flapped out of his grasp and rose to tree level. I feared that it would dive upon me in my borrowed perch, but it skirted the inside perimeter of the clearing—dipping, banking, silently cawing. Its imaginary screams replaced the distant but just as imaginary bassoon in my consciousness. Meanwhile Eisen Zwei, finding his hands empty, relaxed and dropped back onto his pallet. His body fell across it sideways, and his burned-out eyes fixed themselves—coincidentally, I'm sure—on me.

The Asadi chieftain was dead. He died just at sunset.

I waited for his people to flee into the Wild, to leave his brittle corpse in the clearing for an Earthman's astonished scrutiny. They did not flee. Even though the lethal twilight was gathering about them, they stayed. The attraction of the old one's death outweighed their fear of exposing themselves in an open place to the mysteries of darkness.

In my arboreal lookout I realized that I had witnessed two things I had never before seen among the Asadi: Death and a universal failure to repair. What would the night bring? The featureless, unpredictable night?

PART TWO: DESIGNATION. The Ritual of Death and Designation had passed into its second major stage before I truly comprehended that stages existed. I ignored my hunger. I put away the thought of sleep.

As I did so the Asadi converged upon the old man's corpse and those of smallest size were permitted to crowd into the center of the clearing and lift the dead chieftain above their heads. The young, the deformed, the weak, and the congenitally slight of stature formed a double column beneath the old man's outstretched body and began moving with him toward the northern endzone.

Arranged in this fashion, they forced a startling revelation upon me—these were the Asadi whose manes were a similar color and texture, a stringy detergent-scum beige. But they bore the corpse of Eisen Zwei with uncomplaining acquiescence. The larger, sleeker specimens of Asadi (those with luxuriant silver, silver-blue, or golden manes) formed single columns on each side of their lackluster counterparts and together these two units, like water inside a moving pipe, flowed toward the north—

—the one direction that Eisen Zwei had not entered from on the day he brought those three dressed-out, provocative carcasses into the clearing.

I recalled that driver ants in Africa had used just this sort of tubular alignment when they wished to move great distances as a group, the workers inside the column, the warriors without. And nothing on that immense dark continent was more feared than driver ants on the march—with, of course, the exception of man.

Almost too late I realized that the Asadi would be out of the clearing and beyond my reach unless I got out of The Bachelor's tree.

Nearly falling, I scrambled down. The twilight glittered with the dust of the departing columns, and the foliage through which the mourners marched gave off a soft gauzy glow, as if viewed through a photographer's filter. I ran. I found that I could keep up with very little effort, so cadenced and funereal was the step of their procession. I slowed to a walk behind it.

Trudging in the wake of the mourners, incorrigibly hangdog in his pariahhood, was The Bachelor. As the huge gray procession snaked into the Synesthesia Wild, I noted that the circumstances of this march had reversed our roles—now I was following him. Three or four steps behind it all, Egan Chaney—the consummate outsider ridiculously hoping to learn the door-opening arcana of a group that had excluded him.

And all the while the twilight glittered, thickened, reverberated with the footfalls and leaf nudgings of a thousand single-minded communicants.

Before we had got completely out of the clearing, I looked around for the huri. I saw it flying above that part of the procession where its master was being borne forward on the shoulders of the smaller Asadi. Avoiding branches, the huri turned an inadvertent cartwheel in the air, righted itself, and landed on Eisen Zwei's bony chest. Here, conspicuous above the heads of its master's people, it did a little preening dance. It looked like an oil-coated rooster wooing a hen.

Then the column snaked to the left. The Wild closed off my view of the marchers and darkness began drifting in like black confetti.

I dogged The Bachelor's footsteps and waited for a new revelation.

How long we trudged through the singing fronds, the perfumed creepers, the blades of blue air, I don't know. Nor will I attempt to estimate.

There in the clearing, rising against the sky like an Oriental pagoda, loomed the broad and impervious mass of something *built*, something *made*. By now all three moons were up and the solid black bulk of this structure was spotlighted in the antique-gold claret that the three moons together shed. Even before those of us at the end of the procession were out of the jungle, we could see the lofty, gemlike wings of this sudden artifact—and I may not have been the only one whose first inclination was to flee, to plunge back into the nightmare forest.

As we approached, members of both the inner and the outer columns began to sway from side to side, marching and swaying at once. The Bachelor's head, in fact, moved in wide arcs and his whole marching body trembled as if from the paroxysms of ague. If he had been punished for leading me to this place, perhaps he trembled now from fear. On the other hand, if the Asadi wished this temple kept inviolate, wouldn't they somehow punish me once they discovered my presence?

I did have the good sense to get out of the way. I climbed a tree on the edge of the clearing that fronted the pagoda. From this vantage point I watched the proceedings in relative safety.

Gray forms moved in the deep shadow that the Asadi temple cast. Suddenly two violently green flames burned in the iron flambeaus on either side of the top step of the immense tier of stone steps that led to the temple's ornate doorway. The two torchlighters—formerly the moving gray forms—came back down the steps. Never before had I seen the Asadi make use of fire—this sophisticated use both of flambeaus and a starting agent that I could not even guess at destroyed a multitude of my previous conclusions about them. Meanwhile the four columns of Asadi had ranged themselves in parallel files before the stairway of the ancient pagoda and six beige-maned menials bore the corpse of Eisen Zwei, now an uncanny apple-green in the torchlight, up the broad stone steps to the stone catafalque before the door. Here they set the corpse down and lined up behind it, staring out over their waiting kinsmen, facing the cruel ambivalence of the Wild, three on each side of the old man. I was not accustomed to such spectacle, such tawdry grandeur, and I began to think that perhaps Placenol did flow in my veins—Placenol or something more sinister.

The moons cried out with their silent mouths. The flambeaus uttered quick screamings of unsteady light.

But the ritual did not conclude. The night drew on—the moons rolled and the four files of Asadi tribesmen shuffled in their places. They pulled at their manes. They looked up at the leaf-fringed sky. They looked down at their feet. Some stretched out their hands and fought with the tumbling moons just as Eisen Zwei had wrestled with Denebola, the sun. But none left the clearing, though I felt many would have liked to.

Instead, wrestling with their own fears, they waited. The pagoda and the corpse of their chieftain commanded them—while I, wedged like a spike into my tree, was commanded by their awesome patience. Then the last of the three moons fell into the farthest jungle of BoskVeld. The two iron torches guttered like spent candles. The Bachelor fidgeted.

Two vacuums existed. One, the vacuum in nature between the end of night and the beginning of day. The other, the vacuum in the peculiar hierarchy of the Asadi tribal structure, the vacuum that Eisen Zwei had so oddly filled—until his struggle with the sun and his subsequent death. Night and death. Two vacuums in search of compensatory substance.

Up in the air, clinging to two willowy tree branches, I made cursory mental notes in regard to this undoubtedly significant parallelism. When would dawn break? How would the Asadi designate their dead chieftain's successor?

A commotion in the clearing interrupted these transcendent speculations. Looking down, I saw that the four neat files of Asadi had dissolved into a single disorganized mass of milling bodies—as on their original assembly ground. A chaos. An anarchy. A riot of unharnessed irrationality. How could a vacuum of "leadership" exist in such an arbitrary melange of unrelated parts? Only the pagoda had solidity; only the pagoda did not move.

Then, looking up, I saw the old man's huri floating high above this disorder, floating rather than flailing, a gyrfalcon rather than a pelican. It rode the prismatic, predawn breezes with uncommon grace and skied off so effortlessly that in a moment it had dwindled to a scrap of light, picking up some predawn reflection, far beyond the temple's central spire.

Watching it, I grew dizzy.

Then the huri folded its wings behind it and plummeted down, dizzyingly down, through the roseate sky. I almost fell. My feet slipped through the fork that had supported me and I was left dangling, arms above my head, over one edge of the pagoda's front yard. The anxiety-torn communicants were too caught up in their panic to notice me.

Meanwhile the huri rocketed earthward.

It dived into the helpless crowd of Asadi and skimmed along their heads and shoulders with its cruel, serrated wings. Dipping in and out, the huri once again flapped like a torn window shade—all its ephemeral grace was gone, turned to crass exhibitionism (I don't know what else to call it) and unwieldy flutterings. But the creature did what it sought to do, for in that predawn dimness I could see that it had scarred the faces of several of the Asadi.

Nevertheless, a few of the tribesmen tried to capture the huri—while, more reasonably, others ducked out of its way, fell to the ground, clutched their knees, crawled between the scrambling legs, or threw up their arms to ward it off. The huri did not discriminate.

It scarred all of those who got in the way of its bladed wings, whether they attempted to catch it or to flee. And the eyes of the harassed Asadi flashed through their individual spectrums. The heat from so many changes made the clearing phosphorescent with shed energy.

I caught sight of The Bachelor and saw that his eyes had not changed. They were still mute, devoid of all intellect or passion. He stood apart from his panicked comrades and observed, neither grappling for nor fleeing from the huri. As for the noxious beast, it flew up, flew down, performed wobbly banking movements, and slashed with its terrible pinions at everything living. Finally it shot up through the shadow of the pagoda, wildly flapping, then pitched over and dived upon The Bachelor. It flew into his face. It drove him to the ground and battered him with countless malicious thrashings.

To the last individual the Asadi quieted, queued up randomly, and watched this unpredictable denouement, the penultimate act in their day-long ritual. It took me a moment to understand. Then I realized:

The Bachelor was the designee, the chosen one, the chieftain elect. Somehow it seemed an inevitable choice.

My arms aching, I dropped from the tree onto the floor of the clearing. In front of me were the backs of twenty or thirty Asadi. I could not see The Bachelor at all, though I could still hear the churning of the huri's wings and the newly modulated breathing of the tribesmen. Then a figure, insanely rampant, flailing its arms, disrupted the smooth surface of the crowd and darted though a quickly closing gap of bodies to my right. I knew that The Bachelor had regained his feet and was trying to fight off the huri. The two of them thrashed their way up the tier of steps in front of the temple and soon were on the paving beside the catafalque where Eisen Zwei still rested.

Now I could see as well as anyone, and there on that sacred, high place The Bachelor capitulated to the inevitable.

He went down on his knees, lowered his head, and ceased to resist. The huri, sensing its victory, made an air-pummeling circuit over the body of the dead chieftain. It sawed devilishly at the faces of the corpse-bearers and rippled like dry brown paper. Then it settled on The Bachelor's head. Beating its wings for balance, it faced the on-looking multitude of Asadi—and me—with blind triumph.

No one moved, no one breathed, no one acknowledged the dawn as it revealed the caustic verdigris coating the pagoda like an evil frost—like the rime on the forehead of antiquity.

Slowly, after a moment twice as ponderous as the pagoda's antiquity, The Bachelor rose to his feet. He was draped in his own resignation and the invisible garb of an isolation even more pronounced than that he had suffered as an outcast.

He was the designee, the chosen one, the chieftain elect.

The huri dropped from The Bachelor's head to his shoulder and entwined its tiny fingers in the tufts of his butchered mane. There it clung, once again inanimate and scabrous.

Now the Ritual of Death and Designation was nearly over and two of the corpse-bearers on that highest tier moved to complete it. They touched the head and the feet of Eisen Zwei with the tips of the two great flambeaus, and instantly the old man's body raged with green fire. The raging flame leaped up the face of the temple as if to abet the verdigris in its patient efforts to eat the building away. The Bachelor stood almost in the very blast of this conflagration and I feared that he, too, would be consumed. But he was not. Nor was the huri. The fire died, Eisen Zwei had utterly disappeared, and the corpse-bearers came back down the steps and joined the anonymity of their revitalized people.

The Ritual of Death and Designation had ended.

For the purposes of this ethnography I will minimize the significance of what then occurred and report it as briefly as I am able.

Several of the Asadi turned and saw me in the pagoda's clearing. They actually looked at me. After having been ignored for over six months I did not know how to react to the signal honor of abrupt visibleness. Out of monumental surprise I returned their stares. They began advancing upon me, hostility evident in the rapid blurring of colors that took place in their eyes. Behind me, the Synesthesia Wild. I turned to escape into its vegetation. Another small group of Asadi had insinuated themselves into the path of my intended escape—they blocked my way.

Among this group I recognized the individual whom I had given the name Benjy. Cognizant of nothing but a vague paternal feeling toward him, I sought to offer him my hand. His own nervous hand shot out and cuffed me on the ear. I fell. Dirt in my mouth, gray faces descending toward me, I understood that I ought to be terrified. But I spat out the dirt—the faces and manes retreated as quickly as they had come and my incipient terror evaporated like alcohol in a shallow dish.

Overhead, a familiar flapping.

I looked up and saw the huri as it returned to The Bachelor's outstretched arm. He had released the creature upon his fellows in order to save me. This simple action, however, illustrates the mind-boggling complexity of the relationship between the Asadi chieftain and his huri. Which of them rules? Which submits to command?

At that moment I didn't very much care. Denebola had risen and the Asadi had dispersed into the Wild leaving me dwarfed and humble in the presence of their crumbling pagoda and the reluctant chieftain who stared down from its uppermost tier. Although he remained aloof, before the day was out The Bachelor had led me back to the original assembly ground—for I would have never found it on my own.

The admittedly banal lesson that I learned from this experience, members of the Academy, is that even for a cultural xenologist—perhaps especially for a cultural xenologist—it pays to make friends.

Thomas Benedict speaking: a brief interpolative note

*I have put this paper together out of a simple sense of duty. As one of the few people Egan Chaney permitted to get close to him, I am perhaps the only man who could have undertaken this task. The section you have just read—*The Ritual of Death and Designation—*Chaney wrote in our base-camp infirmary while recuperating from exposure and a general inability to reorient himself to the society of human beings. In one of our conversations he compared himself to Gulliver after his return from the land of the Houyhnhnms. At any rate, beyond* Death and Designation *Chaney never wrote anything about the Asadi for publication, although immediately after his release from the infirmary I believe he intended to begin a book about them.*

As I've already said, then, I undertook this compilation of disparate notes out of a sense of duty, a twofold duty: the first to Egan Chaney, who was my friend—the second to the vast numbers of concerned humanity who wish to understand our neighbors on other worlds in order better to understand themselves. Chaney's failure need not be our own.

Upon his return to the original assembly ground of the Asadi after the Ritual of Death and Designation, Chaney stayed two more weeks in the Synesthesia Wild. On Days 126 and 133 I made supply drops, but, just as Chaney had requested, did not fly over the clearing in the vain hope of spotting him and thereby determining the state of his health. It was enough, he told me, to verify his robustness from the fact that each week when I coptered in his supplies I could note that not a scrap of paper from the previous shipment littered the drop point. The argument that he was not the only creature in the

Wild capable of hauling away the goods intended for him impressed Chaney not at all.

"I might as well be," he wrote on one of his infrequent notes left in a canister at the drop point. "The Asadi have all the initiative of malaria victims. More horrible than this, friend Ben, is the face-slapping truth that there is no one else in the Wild—no one else at all!"

I am now the sole owner of the personal effects of Egan Chaney; these include both his private and professional journals, a number of unfiled "official" reports, a series of in-the-field tapes, and a small bit of correspondence (alluded to in an early footnote). Those records concerning the Asadi that I don't own myself, I have access to as a result of my association with the Third Denebolan Expedition. I tell you this only because I know for an incontrovertible fact that during his last fourteen days in the Wild, either Chaney did not make a single entry in any of his journals or notebooks or he so completely effaced these dubious entries from our material realm that they may as well never have existed.

We have only one complete report of any kind in regard to these last two weeks. It is a tape, a remarkable tape, and I believe that Chaney would have destroyed it, too, had we not taken his recorder from him the instant we picked him out of the jungle.

I have listened to this tape many times—in its entirety, I should add, since doing so is a feat which few other men would have the patience for. Once I attempted to discuss the tape with Chaney (this was several days after his release from the infirmary, when I believed that he could handle the terror of the experience with a degree of objectivity), but he protested that I had imagined the contents. He said that he had never recorded the least word in the tape's running account of The Bachelor's "—metamorphosis?" he asked. "Is that the word you used?"

I promptly played the tape for him. He listened to ten minutes of it, then got up and shut it off. His face had gone unaccountably lean and bewildered. His hands trembled.

"Oh, that," he said, not looking at me. "That was all a joke. I made it up because there was nothing better to do."

"The sound-effects, too?" I asked incredulously.

Not looking at me, he nodded—even though the circumstance of his pickup belied this clumsy explanation, exploded it, in fact, into untenable shrapnel. Chaney remained mute on this subject. In all of his writings and conversations in those last three months among us he never mentioned or even alluded to the sordid adventure of his *final two nights. I present here a transcript, somewhat edited, of the tape in question. This final virtuoso section of our collaboration, our patchwork ethnography that I call . . .*

Chaney's monologue: two nights in the Synesthesia Wild

Hello all! What day is it? A day like any other day, except YOU ARE HERE! Here with me, that is. I'm leading you on an expedition. . . . But forgive my initial lie—it isn't a day like any other day at all. How often do I lead you on expeditions?

It's Day 138, I think, and yesterday The Bachelor returned to the clearing—the first time he's been back since the day the huri anointed him, so to speak, with the fecal salve of chieftainship. I'd almost given him up. But he came back into the clearing yesterday afternoon, the huri on his shoulder, and squatted in the center of the assembly ground just as old Eisen Zwei used to do. The reaction among his Asadi brethren was identical to the one they always reserved for E.Z. Everybody OUT of the clearing! Everybody OUT! It was old times again, gang, except that now the actor holding down center stage was a personal friend of mine—who, by the by, had saved my life several times. Yes, sir.

After the heat, the boredom, and eight or a hundred sticky rainfalls—my lean-to leaking like a colander—I couldn't have been more gratified.

Following the pattern old E.Z. established on one of his visits, The Bachelor spent the entire afternoon in the clearing, all of last night and maybe an hour or so this morning. Then he got up to leave. I've been following him ever since. By the sun it's about noon.

Yes, The Bachelor permits me to follow him. Moreover, it's easy. As you can tell I'm not even breathing hard. I'm recording as we walk. If this were a Terrestrial wood, you could hear birdsong and the chitterings of insects. As it is, you'll have to content yourselves with the sounds of my footfalls and the rustlings of leaf and twig. . . . Here's a little rustle for you now.

(The sound of a branch or leaf snapping back. General background noises of wind and, far less audibly, distant running water.)

The Bachelor is several yards ahead of me but you may not be able to hear him—he walks like a stealthy animal. *Pad pad pad.* Like that, only softer. I don't care to be any closer than I am because the huri's riding The Bachelor's shoulder, clinging to his mane. It is not a winsome creature, base-campers—no, indeed it's not. Since it

hasn't any eyes you can't tell whether it's sleeping—or awake and
plotting a thousand villainies.

That's why I'm happy back here.

Let me impress you with my cleverness. (A *heavy thump.*) That's
my backpack. I've brought provisions for three or four days. You
see, I don't know where we're going or how long we'll be there. But
in The Bachelor I trust. Up to a point, at least. My cleverness, though,
doesn't consist solely of hauling along some supplies. The backpack
also houses my recorder, Morrell's miniaturized affair, the one that
has a tape capacity of 240 hours, or, as Benedict would phrase it, ten
solid days of Chaney's uninterrupted blathering.

I've rigged it so that my voice will trigger the recording mechanism whenever I speak and so that the absence of my voice for a ten-
minute period automatically shuts it off. That's to conserve recording
time—not that I plan on talking for ten straight days—and to keep
me from fiddling with buttons when there might be other things to
do. Of course, I can always go manual if I have to, countermanding
the exclusive lock on my own voice, but so far none of the Asadi
have been particularly voluble. Only Eisen Zwei. And his voice
would not be apt to woo the ladies. Ergo, I'm once again your reporter in the field, your objective observer, your unbiased eyes.

I've been thinking. Yes, I have, too. And what I wouldn't give for
a copy of one of the ancient works that no one reads anymore—*The
Brothers Karamazov.* Surely The Bachelor is none other than the
Asadi equivalent of Pavel Smerdyakov, the illegitimate son who de-
stroys himself out of his innate inability to reconcile the spiritual and
the intellectual in his nature. Such passionate despondency! He cannot escape, nor accept, the dictum that the individual is responsible
for the sins of all. . . .****

1 CHANEY (*whispering*): It's quiet in here, as still as the void. And
though you probably can't believe it, I've held my peace for an
entire afternoon. Maybe I said "Damn!" two or three times after
scraping my shin or tripping over a partially exposed root—but that's
all. In here I scarcely feel that it's kosher to talk, to raise my voice
even to this hoarse whisper.

> (*Chaney clears his throat. There is an echo, a hollow
> sound which fades.*)

**** There follows a totally irrelevant analysis of the ways in which The Bache-
lor resembles the character of Smerdyakov in Dostoevski's novel. To spare the
reader I've deleted it. I believe that the passage which follows was recorded approximately six hours later.

We—the three of us—are inside the pagoda, in front of which The Bachelor became the designated "leader" of his people. I feel free to talk only because he and the huri have gone up a narrow iron stairway inside this pyramidal structure toward the ceiling—toward the small open dome from which the exterior spire rises. I can see them from here. The stairway spirals up and The Bachelor climbs it. The huri—no kidding, I'm not kidding at all—flics up through the center of the spiral, staying even with The Bachelor's head, but I can't—absolutely can't—hear its wings flapping.

In this place, that's strange. But it's preternaturally cold in here—maybe the cold has something to do with it—cold and dead, like no building ever erected in a tropical rain forest. No, damn it, even my whispers echo.

It's nearly dark outside. At least it was nearly dark twenty minutes ago when we came in through the heavy doors that the Asadi—two weeks past—didn't even open. Now the moons must be up. Maybe a little moonlight falls through the dome overhead. . . . On, no, Chaney—the light in here comes from those three massive globes in the metal ring suspended several feet below the dome. The Bachelor's climbing toward that huge ring, the stairway rises toward it, it looks like a spartan chandelier, the globes like white-glowing dead-fish lamps. . . . Listen. Listen to the light fall. . . .

(*There is no sound for several minutes, perhaps a slight amplification of Chaney's breathing. Then his voice descends conspiratorially.*)

Eisen, Eisen, another paradox for you physics majors. I think—I don't know, mind you, but I think that *both* the chill *and* the luminosity in here originate—emanate, so to speak—from those globes up there. It's just a feeling I have. Winter sunlight. The *texture* of the luminosity in here reminds me of the glow around probeship ALERT and EVACUATE signs, a deadly sort of lambence. Just listen. Hear that livid glow, that livid hell-sheen? All right, let's move to where we can see.

(*Silence. Rhythmic breathing. Footfalls echoing hollowly off polished stone.*)

I'm looking straight up the well of the stairway. (*An echo: Way way way way . . .*) C'mon, Egan, keep it down, keep it down . . . better, much better. I can see the huri flapping up there noiselessly—The Bachelor's legs ascending the spiral. The staircase seems to terminate in a glass platform off to one side and just a little below the suspended ring of the "chandelier." The Bachelor is ascending to this platform—there's nowhere else he can go. I'm looking up through the axis of the dome, right up through the chandelier ring.

Outside, above the dome, is a spire pointing up at BoskVeld's sky. Inside the dome, depending from its apex, there's a sort of plumbline —of what looks like braided gold—that drops down the central shaft of the pagoda to a point . . . just about a foot above the suspended ring. A foot, I think. Can't tell for certain. Been in the jungle so long my depth perception's shot—just as the Ituri pygmies used to have trouble adjusting vision to open savannah.

I apologize for the complicated description of the upper recesses of this temple, but the arrangement is intricate and that's where The Bachelor's going. I can make sense neither of the architecture nor of his intentions. . . . And my neck's getting sore, tilted back. . . .

2 CHANEY (*conversationally, but still in something of a whisper*): Me again. The Bachelor reached the glass platform beneath the chandelier ring about an hour ago. He's been standing up there like a Pan-Olympic diver ever since, except that he's looking—as far as I can tell—at the braided gold plumbline that hangs slightly above him from the temple's dome. He can't quite reach it from the platform he's on. Would he like to? I don't know . . . no, he can't reach it. Not without a trapeze, daringly, could he reach that gilded pendulum. And then, what for?

As the channel announcers on the telecom operas would say, "Let's leave Billy Bachelor high atop the Callisto Medcenter, lamenting the lost Lenore, and follow E. G. Chanwick as he goes spelunking through the mysterious satellite's caverns of steel in his ongoing, biweekly endeavor to unravel the Secret of the Universe."

(*Unsuccessfully stifled snickers. Resultant echoes. Footfalls.*)

I'll be your tour guide, base-campers. Follow me. This pagoda seems to be a museum. Or a mausoleum perhaps. At any rate, a monument to a dead culture. The walls around three sides of the bottom of this place are lined with tall spindly cabinets, display cases of a wildly improbable design. Each one consists of fan-shaped shelves that fold out from a central axis and lock into place on different levels from one another. (*Chaney blows.*) Dust. Dust on everything. But not particularly thick. On the shelves—the shelves have the fragile warmth of mother-of-pearl—are specimens of implements and art work.

(*A click, like stone on stone. Chaney's breathing.*) I'm holding a statue about a foot-and-a-half high. It represents an Asadi male, full-maned and virile. But the statue depicts him with a kind of cape around his shoulders and a cruel pair of fangs such as the Asadi—those of today, at any rate—don't possess. (*Repetition of previous sound, followed by a metallic ping.*) Here's an iron knife, with a wooden handle carved so that the top resembles some animal's skull. Everything else in the cabinet looks like a weapon or a heavy tool, the statue's definitely an anomaly here.

I'm going across the chamber—to the wall without any cabinets on it. (*Footfalls. Echoes.*) The Flying Asadi Brothers are still up there, more rigid than the statue I just picked up. I'm passing directly beneath them now, directly beneath the dome, the iron ring, the energy globes, the weighted golden cord that falls from the dome. . . . Dizzy . . . the dimness and the distance up there make me dizzy.

Don't look at them, then, Chaney. Just keep moving—moving toward the opposite wall. Through an opening in the lower portion of the helical stairway. Toward the horn-colored wall on which there are no cabinets, gang, just rows upon rows of—damn this light, this hollowness . . . let me get closer—of what look like tiny plastic wafers . . . rows of wafers hung from a couple thousand silver rods protruding for about five or six inches at right angles from the wall. The wall's just one big elegant pegboard glowing like a fingernail with a match behind it. The rows of these wafers—cassettes, cigarette cases, match boxes—whatever you want to call them—begin at about waist-level and go up two or three feet higher than I can reach. Asadi height, I suppose.

(*Five or six minutes, during which only Chaney's breathing can be heard.*) Interesting. I think I've figured this out, Eisen, I want you to pay attention. I've just unfastened the carved wingnut from the end of one of these narrow silver rods and removed the first of several tiny cassettes hanging from it. Wafer was a serendipitous word choice, these little boxes are as thin as two or three transistor templates welded together. The faces of the things are about two inches square. I counted fifty of them hanging from this one six-inch rod and there are probably three thousand rods on this wall. That's about 150,000 cassettes altogether and this section of the pagoda, more than likely, is just a display area.

But I want to describe the one I've got in my hand. I want to tell you how it works and maybe—if I can restrain myself—let you draw your own conclusions. In the center of this wafer—which does seem to be made of some kind of plastic, by the way—there's an inset circle of glass with a diameter of less than half an inch. A bulb or an eye, call it. Beneath this eye is a rectangular tab, flush with the surface of the cassette. Above the bulb, directly under the hole through which the wall rod passes, is a band containing a series of different-colored dots, some of the dots touching each other, some not. The spacing of them probably has significance—or so I'd guess. (*A chuckle.*)

And here's how this little cracker box works . . . oh, Eisen, don't you wish you were here instead of me? I do, too. I really do. . . . It's purposely simple, I think. All you do is hold your thumb over the right half of the tab at the bottom of the cassette. Then the fireworks begin. (*A pleased laugh; subsequent echo.*)

Right now the eye in the center of the wafer is flashing through an indecipherable program of colors. Reds, violets, greens. Greens, sapphires, pinks. All premeditatedly interlaced with pauses—pregnant pauses, no doubt. . . . In this dimness my hands are alternately lit and shadowed by the changing colors. Beautiful, beautiful. That's just it, in fact. The entire system probably sacrifices a degree of practicality on the altar of beauty.

There—I've shut it off. All you do is cover the left half of the control rectangle with your thumb. It may be possible to reverse the program—replay it back to a desired point, so to speak—but I haven't stumbled on the method yet. At least I don't think I have. It's impossible for me to remember the sequences of colors—though it probably wasn't a bit difficult for the Asadi who composed, manufactured, and used these things, however long ago that may have been.

(*A thumping noise.*) I'm pocketing five of these cassettes, putting them in my backpack. For the greater glory of science. To set the shirttails of old Oliver Bow Aurm's ghost aflame with envy. So Eisen and Morrell will have something to put their screwdrivers to.

(*Musingly.*) Look at that wall. Can you imagine the information on hand here? The level of technology necessary to devise a storage and retrieval system for a "language" that consists of complicated spectra patterns? By the way, what do you suppose I was "reading"? I'd guess that the band of colored dots above the eye is the description of the contents. The title, so to speak. Maybe I was scanning *Fornications and Deflowerings* by the Marquis de Asadi. (*A chuckle.*) I noticed that my hands had begun to sweat while the program was running.

(*Sober again.*) No, the eyebook—let's call them eyebooks—was the first one on that particular rod. Maybe it's their *War and Peace,* their *Brothers Karamazov*, their *Origin of the Species*, their *Golden Bough*. And what the hell have they done with it? Stuck it in a crumbling godforsaken temple in the middle of the Synesthesia Wild and forgotten about it! What colossal waste—what colossal arrogance!

(*Shouting*) WHERE THE HELL DO YOU GET OFF DE-STROYING THE ACCUMULATED KNOWLEDGE OF MIL-LENNIA? LETTING IT SIT UNUSED AND ROTTING!

(*A cacophony of echoes, a painful ringing.*)

(*A whisper, scarcely audible.*) That's right, you two, you Bun-gling Brothers aerialists, pretend I don't exist. Pretend you can't hear me. Ignore the millennia. Ignore your ancestors whispering to you from their deaths. (*Venomously.*) And damn you both to hell!

3 CHANEY (*in a lifeless monotone*): I think I slept for a while. I went to sleep under the rows and rows of eyebooks. Maybe for an hour. Not any more than that. I can tell time with the bottoms of my feet —by the warmth of the depression in the backpack where I put my head.

A noise woke me, a ringing of iron. Now I'm on the helical stair-way high above the museum floor. I'm in a curve of the stairway a little below and opposite the glass platform where The Bachelor was standing. He isn't there anymore. A moment ago he chinned himself up to the cold ring of the chandelier, gained his feet and balanced on the ring, then reached out and grabbed the plumbline that drops down from the dome.

The huri? The huri squats on the globe, in the triangle of globes, pointing toward the front of the temple—he got off The Bachelor's shoulder a good while ago.

After grabbing the gold braid The Bachelor fashioned a noose and slipped his neck into it. Then he swung himself out over the floor so that his feet—right now, at this very moment—are hanging a little below the ring of the chandelier. I'm watching him hang there, his feet turning, inscribing an invisible circle inside the larger circle of the globe-set fixture.

But he isn't dead. No, he's not a bit dead. The noose is canted so that it catches him under the throat in the plush of his mane. In the two weeks since his designation his mane has thickened consid-erably, especially along his jaws and under his throat, and the new fur cushions the steadily constricting braid. So now he's just hanging there. The dangling man.

(*Listlessly.*) A pretty damn interesting development, I suppose. At least the huri acts like it's interesting. The huri's watching all this with either excitement or agitation, beating its wings sporadically and skittering to stay atop the globe it's perched on. (*A bump. Unintelligible mumbling.*) See if you can hear it. I'll hold the microphone out for you. (*Silence, vaguely static-filled.*) That's it, the huri's claws scrabbling on the globe—the sound of The Bachelor's feet turning north, northeast, east, southeast, south, southsouthwest. . . .

(*After almost ten minutes of near-silence.*) A while ago I saw that The Bachelor had begun to drool. A thin thread of something milky glistened on his bottom lip as he turned, his feet revolving first to the right and then back to the left. I saw his mouth working —almost like an insect's mouth. The strand of drool got longer, it didn't drop away into the abyss of the stairwell, it kept growing and growing, lengthening like a somehow milky extension of the gold plumbline.

Now the strand has fallen down the center of the helix so that it's a little below the place where I'm sitting. I can see that it's not a liquid at all, not any sort of spittle or vomit. It's a fiber, something spun from The Bachelor's gut and paid out through his mouth. (*Unawed.*) Beautiful and grotesque at once—and I'll bet you think I'm drunk or drugged. Making silk out of a souse's fears, so to speak. But I've imbibed no bourbon, laddies, played with no Placenol—and I wish you were sitting on this cramped iron stairway watching this disgusting show, this ritual unraveling of The Bachelor's innards. Gut-strands. Beautiful and grotesque gut-strands.

(*Unemotionally.*) God, but my patience has been tried. . . .

   (*Several more minutes pass. A faint flapping commences,*
  continues for a while, then ceases.)

The Bachelor's been paying out silk as if he were made of it. The single strand I told you about a while ago, well, it damn near reached the floor. Then he started working with his hands, reeling it back in and making his body turn faster in the canted noose. He's wrapping himself in the stuff, like an Egyptian king who's decided to be a mummy *before* he dies. Meanwhile he makes more and more cloudy thread.

Guess who's gotten into the act, gang? Right again. The huri flew off its globe when The Bachelor began reeling in his gut-strand and caught up a section of the strand in its claws. Then, with both its claws and hands, flapping in higgledy-ziggledy circles, it covered The Bachelor's feet, his ankles, and his shins. After that it settled on the old boy's wrapped feet. Now, its wings outspread, its claws probably hooked into The Bachelor's flesh, the huri's hanging up there like a bat and still wrapping its master in gut-extruded cable. And the damn thing's blind, mind you, blind as—a drunken xenologist. Good boy, Chaney.

I don't know how long it'll take, but in a while The Bachelor will be encased—completely encased, it seems—in a murky chrysalis. The huri looks as if it would like to finish and tie off the job as soon as it can. It's already binding in the Asadi's hands, pulling thread around his thighs, clawing up his long body inch by inch like a freakish circus performer. Then The Bachelor will be nothing but a lopsided pupa hanging from a gold cord inside the loft of his ancestors' rickety barn—I guess.

> (*Chaney grunts. Shuffling sounds; perhaps the shifting of a burden.*)

I guess. Don't ask me. I won't watch any more of this foolishness. I'm dizzy. I'm fed up with this nonsense. If I can make it down these steps in this hell-glow I'm going to lie down beside the wall of eyebooks and go to sleep. Directly to sleep.

> (*Footfalls on the iron steps. Unintelligible mumbling.*)

Interlude: early afternoon of Day 139*****

CHANEY (*speaking conversationally*): Hello. I'm talking to Benedict alone now. Ben? Ben, you're supposed to make a drop tomorrow. Your twentieth. Can you believe that? I can't either. It doesn't seem like more than ten or twelve years that I've been out here. Twenty drops. Well, I may not pick up this latest one. Not for a while, anyway. God knows when The Bachelor will want to lead me out of here and back to the clearing. At the moment he's occupied. Let me tell you how.

First, let me tell you what's going on. I'm standing here by one of the dusty display cases. All its shelves are folded up against the central axis, like the petals of a flower at night. But it's early afternoon, Ben—dull light is seeping through the dome. Even so, every cabinet in the place is shut up like a new rose. Every one of them. It

---

***** From the end of the previous section to the beginning of this one Chaney engaged in a great deal of "irrelevant blathering." I have deleted it. Altogether, about twelve or fourteen hours of real time passed, time during which Chaney also slept and ate. In this "Interlude" I have taken the liberty of borrowing small sections from the deleted passages in order to provide a continuity which would not otherwise exist. For simplicity's sake, these insertions are not marked.

happened, I guess, while I was sleeping. The globes overhead, the three globes in the chandelier up there—their fires have gone out of them, they're as dead and as mutely mottled as dinosaur eggs. I don't know exactly when that happened, either. One other thing—the eye-books don't work today. I've fiddled with twenty or thirty of them, holding my thumb over the rectangular tab beneath the eye—but nothing, not even two colors in a row, not so much as a glimmer.

Today the pagoda's dead. That's all there is to it: the pagoda's dead. And I have the feeling that it won't come alive again until Denebola has set and darkness sits on BoskVeld like the shadow, the crumpled shadow, of the huri's wings.

But The Bachelor—the cocoon—you want to know what happened to him. To it. Again, I don't know exactly. During the night the plumbline from which he fashioned the noose—the line from which he then hung out over the pagoda's floor while the huri wrapped him in the false silk of his own bowels—that golden line, I tell you, has lengthened and dropped through the ring of the chandelier so that it's now only a few feet from the floor. It descended, I suppose, of its own accord. (A *chuckle*.) I'd estimate that between the floor and the bottom of The Bachelor's chrysalis there's now only enough space to wedge a small stool. A very small footstool . . . and now the ungainly pupa hangs in the daylight gloom of this chamber and turns slowly, slowly, first to the right, then to the left, like the gone-awry pendulum in a grandfather clock. That's it, Ben, brawny Big Ben, this whole building's just an outsized timepiece. You can hear BoskVeld ticking in its orbit—Listen. . . .

As for the huri, it crouches on the uppermost node of the pupa—the point at which the braid breaks through—and rides The Bachelor's mummified head as it used to ride his shoulder. Each time the wrapped body turns this way I feel that the huri's staring at me, taking my measure. If I had a pistol, I'd shoot the damn thing—I swear I would. Even if it meant that the concussion would split the seams of this temple and send it crashing down on my ears—every fragile cabinet shattering, every eyebook bursting open. So help me, I would —which is probably why I didn't bring a pistol, a hand-laser, or a light-cannon out here in the first place. But now the little beastie is clawing nervously at the silken membrane, unhinging its wings and shaking their outstretched tips a little—I think, gang, we're going to get some action. Give me a few minutes, just a few. . . .

(*Later*.) Action, indeed. The huri's moving in its own catch-as-catch-can fashion down the swaying cocoon that houses The Bachelor. As it moves it peels back pieces of the membrane, snips them off with its feet, transfers the pieces to its greedy hands, and eats them. That's right, eats them. I had been wondering what the little bugger subsisted on and this apparently is the answer—it feeds on the husk of the Asadi chieftain's metamorphosis, it feeds on the rind of its master's involuntary change. That's phrasing it a little philosophically, I suppose, but I can't help thinking that the huri's eating The Bachelor's former self. It's crab-walking in a spiral down the cocoon —a spiral that mirrors the great corkscrew of the pagoda's staircase —and it furiously gobbles up the membrane that it has snipped away.

The beast is at the hollow of The Bachelor's chest and I can see my old friend's head. I mean that I can see the outline of his head— because even though the silken covering has been eaten away, a milk-blue film remains. It clings to his features like a thin hood. It's moist and trembly and through it I can see the death-mask of his face.

Ben, Ben, you can't expect me to stay here and watch this. Tell the others not to expect that of me. The bitch-goddess of xenology has worked me over too many times already and I'm nauseated with fatigue. With disgust. It's worse than last night. There's an odor in the temple, a smell like excrement and rot and the discharges of the glands—I don't know what. . . .

(*A retching sound. Then a rapid succession of footfalls, suggestive of running.*)

4 CHANEY (*his voice thin but genial*): We're in the Wild again. Out in the open. Out among the singing leaves, the dancing moons, the glittering winds, the humidity is horrible. It makes my nose run. But after spending one sore-necked night in the refrigerated vault of that Asadi warehouse—and one stomach-turning day in it when it changed from a warehouse into a charnel house—well, the humidity's a welcome relief. Yes, indeed. Let my nose run as it may, where it may— even though I don't know where the hell the face it's running on is running to. Actually, we're not running at all. We're moving quite leisurely, The Bachelor and me and the huri—in no hurry at all.

(*Clinically.*) I feel pretty well now. The horror of this afternoon has evaporated. I don't know why it made me ill. It wasn't that bad, really, I should have stayed and watched everything. That's what I came out here for. But when the smell in there got so bad—my system's been under a strain. I had to get out of there.

I bolted for the pagoda's entrance, pushed the heavy doors aside, ran down the tier of steps. The sunlight increased my nausea—but I couldn't go back inside, Ben, so I'm not entirely certain what the final circumstances of The Bachelor's removal from the cocoon were. Like a little boy waiting for the library to open, I sat on the bottom step of the pagoda and held my head in my hands. I was ill. Really ill. It wasn't just an emotional thing. But now I feel better and the night—the stars twinkling up there like chipped ice—seems like my friend.

(*Wistfully.*) I wish I could navigate by those stars—but I can't. Their patterns are still unfamiliar to me. Maybe we're going back to the clearing. Maybe I'll be able to pick up tomorrow's drop after all. I know I feel well enough now to try.

The Bachelor is striding ahead of me; the huri's on his shoulder. I know—

(*The sound of wind and leaves corroborates Chaney's testimony that they are out of doors, out of the temple.*)

—I know, you're wondering what he looks like, what his disposition is, what his metamorphosis accomplished for him. Well, gang, I'm not sure. You see, he looks about the same. As I said, I didn't go back into the museum. I waited outside until the sun had set, thinking all the while that I would go back up the steps when the darkness was complete. I knew that my two charming friends couldn't get out any other way, that I wouldn't be stranded there alone. At least I hadn't seen any other doors while I was inside. The ancient Asadi apparently didn't see any need to leave themselves a multitude of outs. The end they've come to supports that hypothesis. But before I could steel myself to reentering the pagoda—just as the twilight had begun to lose its gloss—The Bachelor appeared on the highest step.

And came down the steps.

And walked right by me. He didn't look at me. The huri, clinging to his mane, had the comatose appearance that I remember its possessing when Eisen Zwei came into the Asadi clearing for the second time. Now I know why it looked so bloated and incapable of movement—it had just ingested the old man's pupa, if Eisen Zwei could have so encased himself. So help me, I still haven't figured this out. I may never figure it out. Anyhow, I noticed only two small changes in The Bachelor as he stalked past me into the jungle. First, his mane is now a full-grown collar of fur—still a little damp from the filmy blue substance that lined the chrysalis. And second, a thin cloak of this film stretches between The Bachelor's naked shoulder blades and falls in folds to the small of his back. Probably, it just hasn't dropped away yet.

And that's it. His eyes are still as mute, as white, as uncommunicative as they had ever been.

We're in a tunnel, sort of. We've been walking, slipping beneath the vines, about thirty or forty minutes. A while ago we came upon a kind of footpath, a beaten trail that permits us to walk upright— just as if we were in a recreation park. The only such trail I've seen in the Synesthesia Wild, ever. The Bachelor's moving down it easily and once again I'm having no difficulty keeping up.

But I'm lost.

> (A *considerable pause during which the sounds of the Wild assert themselves: wind through the leaves, distant water, the soft shushing of feet in the dirt.*)

(*Pensively.*) All the time I've spent in the Asadi clearing, all that time watching them amble around and wear down their heels to no purpose—it seems like centuries ago. No kidding, Ben, Eisen. That time in the clearing just doesn't exist right now. Lost as I am, I feel like I could follow The Bachelor down this narrow trail forever.

But his metamorphosis—or lack of it—bothers me. I've been thinking about it. My considered, but not necessarily considerate, opinion is that the old chieftain is exactly what he used to be. Anatomically speaking, that is. Maybe the very brief time he spent hibernating in that homemade sleeping bag of his altered him psychologically rather than physically.

> (*Ten minutes of wind, water, and shush-shushing feet.*)

5 CHANEY (*whispering*): There's something in the trees ahead of us. A crouched, dark shape. The Bachelor just turned on me—he wouldn't let me approach with him. If I don't stay fairly close, I'll be lost out here. Damn you, you hulking boonie, I won't let you leave me. We're off the trail. We've been off it a good while and the trees, the vines, the twisted roots—everything looks the same; one spot is like another. I'm disobeying the bastard. I'm staying close enough to keep him in sight every second. He's out there in a ragged hallway of leaves moving toward the thing in the tree. I know that it's there because he knows that it's there. It's like a tumor in the branches, a lump to which the moonlight gives a suspicious fuzziness. You should see the way he's approaching that thing. He's spread his arms out wide and is taking one long step at a time, one long easy step. Like an adagio S.S. man. The membrane between his shoulder

blades has opened out, too, so that it makes a fan-shaped drapery across his back. Shadows shift across it, shadows and moonlight. . . . What a weird boonie. You should see him. He's a kind of moving, blown-up version of the drunken huri clinging to his mane. We're closer now. That thing up there, whatever it is, it's either dead or inanimate or hypnotized—hypnotized, I think. I'm sure that it's one of the Asadi. A gray shape. Ordinarily, you don't get this close at night, you just don't. The Bachelor's hypnotized it with his slow-motion goose step, the filmy rippling of the membrane across his back and arms—maybe even with his empty eyes . . . now we're just waiting, waiting. I'm as close as I can get without jeopardizing the purity of this confrontation. I can see eyes up there. Asadi eyes, stalled on a sickly pink. (*Aloud, over a sudden thrashing.*) The damn thing's just jumped out of the branches! It's one of the Asadi all right, a lithe gray female. The Bachelor's wrenching her backward to the ground, the huri's fallen sidelong away from him, fluttering, fluttering in the thicket under the tree!

(*A heavy bump; continued thrashing.*)

(*Chaney's voice skyrockets to an uncontrolled falsetto*) I KNEW IT, I KNEW WHAT YOU WERE! DEAR LORD, I WON'T PERMIT IT IN FRONT OF ME! I WON'T PERMIT YOUR EVIL TO FLOURISH! (*Scuffling. Then, weakly.*) Leave me alone, leave me.

(*Violent noises; then a hum of static and low breathing.*)

6 CHANEY (*panting*): My head aches—I've been ill again. But it's sweet here; I'm kneeling in grass under the trees by the edge of the pagoda's clearing. . . . I've been ill again, yes, but I've done heroic things. I'm doing a damn heroic thing right now. You can hear me, can't you? I'm talking out loud. . . . OUT LOUD, DAMN IT! And he's not about to stop me—he's just going to sit there opposite me with his long legs folded and take it. . . . Aren't you, boonie? Aren't you? That's right, that's a good boonie. . . . He can't believe the deed I've done, Ben. He can't believe I've freed him from that scabby little battlecock. There's blood on the grass. Dark sweet blood. Too sweet, Ben. I've got to get up. . . .

(*Chaney moans. A rustling of clothes—then his strained voice.*) OK. Fine. A little bark to lean against here, a tree with spiny shingles. (*A stumping sound.*) Good, good—I refused to let myself get disoriented, Ben. We came marching—slogging, more like—right through that opening there, that portal of ferns and violet blossoms

. . . oh, hell, you can't see where I'm pointing, can you? You wouldn't see, probably, even if you were here. But we slogged to this place from that direction I'm pointing and I kept my head about me all the way. My head, by the way, aches because he bashed me down —he elbowed me in the eye. They always elbow, the Asadi—they think elbows were given to them to jab in other people's ribs and faces, even The Bachelor. He knocked me down, bloodied me, damn him, when I tried to stop him from slaughtering this poor woman here, the one that lies here butchered in the grass. He knocked me down and I couldn't stop him. Then he whirled her up over his shoulder, grabbed the huri out of the bushes by its feet. Took off through the jungle, the Wild ringing like a thousand wind chimes because of my head, my aching eye. To keep from getting lost, I had to follow him. Dear God, I had to hobble along after that crazy crew. Then when we reached this little patch of grass among the trees—the pagoda's right over there—he threw the dead woman on the ground and disemboweled her. I saw him doing it as I came up through the jungle after him . . . you see, I got here three or four minutes after he did. I collapsed, I collapsed and watched. I held my bad eye and squinted through the other . . . in ten or twelve minutes I'd for-gotten what it all meant, and the woman didn't look like an Asadi anymore. Now the grass is littered with her—and The Bachelor didn't even have to strike me to keep me from interfering. But, Ben, I couldn't help that; it was all owing to my head and my fatigue—I wasn't thinking straight. I didn't realize he was butchering the crea-ture. As soon as I could I remedied the situation. And that's why I'm still a little sick. But my head's clear now; it aches but it's clear. And the boonie isn't about to strike me again. Are you, boonie? All he can do is sit and stare at me. I've intimidated the hell out of him. He thought I was some kind of maneless Asadi vermin and he can't reconcile himself to this new image of me. Poor mute bastard. My heroic deed kicked him right in his psychological solar plexus.

(*Almost pompously.*) As the moons are my witness, I killed the huri. I killed the huri! No, no, the boonie can't believe it either but I swear by holy heaven it's true.

Just look at him, look at him making slow figure eights with his chin. God, but I've boggled him! He thought me just another Asadi, a low Asadi dog—and when he had finished carving up that pitifully helpless woman, that sweet long-legged lady, he set the huri down atop her carcass—I had to do something then. I pulled myself up. But the huri was sitting there on her butchered body, staring at me blindly. Old boonie-boy had put it there to guard her corpse, just the way Eisen Zwei had done in the clearing the day he carried in three slaughtered kinsmen as a feast offering. The huri meant I wasn't supposed to move, I was supposed to be a good cannibal and wait until dinner had been properly served. I'm not an Asadi—I'll be damned if I'm an Asadi and I didn't—no, by God, I didn't—pay any heed to The Batchie-boy's stupid sentinel. I killed it. I ran up and kicked the huri with my boot. It fluttered backward and I was upon it with the heel of my boot, grinding its filthy little no-face into the grass. Its body split open. Pus spilled out like putty from a plastic tube, stinking to the skies—that's what made me sick, the sight and the stink of the huri's insides. I stumbled away, fell to my knees. . . .

The Bachelor couldn't move. Killing the huri had given me a hold over him, a power. He just sat, like he's sitting now, and watched me. The smell of the grass revived me, convinced me of my own heroism, my own crimson-blooded heroism—and that's when I knew I had to tell you about it, when I started talking through my sickness and the too-sweet smell of the grass.

(*Mockingly.*) Are you awed, boonie? Is that your trouble? Could I walk right over there and kick your face in if I tried? Yes, oh, yes, I could. Damn it, Ben, I'm in control, I'm on top!

(*Laughter, prolonged laughter; then virtual silence.*)

Power's an evanescent thing, Ben. (*Musingly.*) He just stood up, The Bachelor did, uncoiled and faced me like an enemy. I thought I was dead, I really did. I know that's a turnabout—you don't have to require consistency of me when I'm ill. But he only stared at me for a minute, then turned and walked across the open clearing toward the temple. He's climbing the steps right now, very slowly, a gray shape like the gray shape he killed. Every moon is up. The three of them ripple his shadow down the tier of steps behind him. I'm not going into that place again, gang, he needn't wait for me—and he isn't waiting. Fine. Excellent. I'll stay here in the grass, under the vines and fire blossoms, until it's morning. Let him go, let him go. . . . But, damn him, he can't leave me in this gut-strewn glade! It reeks; the grass is black with gore. And here—just look at this. What the hell is it? You've got to get down (*groaning*) to see it: a little pocket of globular tripe here on the edge of the grass, just where the moonlight falls. Three of them nestled in the grass, three palpitant little globes—I think they're ova, Ben, all of them about the size of my thumbnails. Much bigger than a human being's minute reproductive cells. But ova nevertheless. Ovaries. That's my guess. They glisten and seem alive, glowing as they do. . . . The Bachelor placed them here while he was butchering the poor lady. He was careful not to crush them—he laid them out so that they'd form an equilateral triangle here in this nest of grass. It's like—well, it's like the arrangement of the globes in the chandelier ring inside the pagoda. . . .

But I'm not going back in there, boonie—I'M NOT GOING BACK IN THERE! DO YOU UNDERSTAND THAT? I'M NOT GOING . . .

7 CHANEY (*bewildered*): Where is it? Eisen, you said we could see it from this hemisphere—you said it was visible. But I'm standing here, standing out here in front of the Asadi's hulking temple where there aren't any branches to block my view and, damn you, Eisen, I don't see it. I don't see it! Just those blinding moons dancing up and down and a sky full of sparkling cobwebs. Where's Sol? Where's our own sun? Eisen, you said we could see it with the unaided eye, I'm sure you said that—but I don't see it! It's lost out there in a cobwebbing of stars—lost!

(*Suddenly resolute.*) I'm going back into the temple. Yes, by God, I am. The Bachelor doesn't care if I stay out here and rot with the poor butchered lady he's abandoned. He's abandoned me, too. Twenty minutes I've been out here alone, twenty minutes staring at the dark grass, the dark sweet grass. He wants me to die from its cloying reek; that's what he's after. I killed his huri. A man who kills a huri isn't one to put up with a passive death, though. He forgot that. If I have to die, Ben, it'll be heroically, not the way he wants. I've taken too much to sit cross-legged under the trees and wait for either my own death or the corrupt hunger that would keep me alive. I won't eat his offering, that poor butchered lady, and I won't stay out here either!

There's a beautiful golden cord in the pagoda, a beautiful golden cord. That should do it. If the boonie's still too shaken up from his loss, his stinking bereavement, to lead me back to the clearing— the Asadi clearing—that plumbline ought to serve. I've worked with my hands; I can fashion a noose as well as any dumpling-hearted boonie. And then carry it through where he couldn't. Just come along, gang, and see if I can't.

> (*The shush-shushing of feet in the dirt, Chaney's short-windedness as he climbs the temple's steps, the inward-groaning utterance of a heavy door.*)
> (*From this point on, Chaney's each word has the brief after-echo,*

the telltale hollowness imparted by the empty volume of a large building's interior.)****** It's cold. You wouldn't believe how cold it is in here, Ben. Cold and dark. No light is filtering down through the dome and the chandelier—the chandelier's out! My eyes aren't accustomed. . . . (*A bump.*) Here's a cabinet. I've scraped my elbow. The shelves are down and I scraped my elbow on one of the shelves. I'm going to stand here a minute. The cabinets give off their own faint light, a very warm faint light, and I'll be able to see a good deal better if I just stand here and let my pupils adjust. It's the same cabinet I described for you last night! Or one just like it, I guess. The statue, the knife, the implements and weapons—nothing is different. (*A scraping sound, somewhat glassy.*) Well, wait a minute. Here's a difference. The bottom petals of this cabinet have been broken off, torn away. I'm standing in the shards. And I'm not the vandal, Ben—the shards were already here. I just stepped on them, that's all. The little bump I gave the cabinet couldn't have done this —someone had to work energetically at these shelves to break them away. The Bachelor, maybe? The Bachelor's the only one in here besides me. Did he want an ax to stalk me with? Did he need one of his ancestors' ornamental knives before he felt competent to take on the pink-fleshed Asadi outcast who killed his poor rubber rooster? Poor, poor rubber rooster—IS THAT IT, BOONIE? YOU AFRAID OF ME NOW? (*Crashing echoes. Chaney's voice becomes huskily confidential.*) I think that's it, Ben, I think that's why the globe lamps are out, why this place is so dark, why this cabinet is broken. The boonie wants to kill me—he's stalking me in the dark. Well, that's fine, too. That's more heroic than the cord, an excellent death —I'll even grapple with him a little. Beowulf and Grendel. It shouldn't take very long. The lady he killed felt almost nothing —I'm sure of that. OVER HERE, BOONIE! YOU KNOW WHERE I AM! COME ON, THEN! COME ON! I WON'T MOVE!

>   (*A confusion of echoes, dissonant and reverberating. Complete silence but for Chaney's chronic shortwindedness. This continues for four or five tense minutes. Then a forceful crack followed by a tremendously amplified shattering sound—like a box full of china breaking. Chaney gives a startled cry.*)

****** Just one of the many apparently unsimulable conditions that convinces me of the authenticity of the tapes. How much of what Chaney reports is hallucination rather than reality, however, I'm not prepared to conjecture.

(*Whispering.*) My dear God—the pagoda's flooded with light now —flooded with light from the three globes in the great iron fixture that yesterday hung just beneath the dome. It's different now—the iron ring is floating above five feet from the floor. The Bachelor is inside the ring, stabbing at one of the globes with a long-handled pick. He's already chipped away a big mottled piece of its covering. The piece shattered on the floor. You heard it shatter. (*Aloud.*) And all three globes are pulsing with energy, angry energy. They're filling the temple with electricity—a deadly chill—their own anger. I'm sure they've generated the field that keeps the iron ring afloat, the ring hovering like a circular prison around the Bachelor's shoulders. The plumbline whips back and forth as he jabs—it has damn near entangled him. And he's caught inside the ring—caught there and he keeps jabbing at the foremost globe with his pick.

(*The jabbing sounds punctuate Chaney's headlong narrative—apparently, another piece of the globe's covering falls to the floor and shatters.*)

Why the hell doesn't he duck out of there? Is he trapped in that field? I can see he's too damn busy to be worried about me, to want to kill me. All right. That's fine. I'll cheer him on, I'll give him moral support—HIT IT A LICK, BOONIE!

All the cabinets are open. All the shelves are down. I can see them now. The pagoda's alive again. All it took was the dark and a little violence.

The foremost globe has split wide open—he's knocked the crown off it. And listen, Ben, listen. Something is moving inside it, inside the intact bottom half. The ring is canting to one side and it's dimmer in here. Suddenly dimmer. If he keeps banging away at those globes this whole place will be drained of light—the shelves will fold back up and lock into position forever. Can you hear the scrabbling in the broken globe? Can you hear it, Ben? Do you already know what it is? I can see it and hear it both. In this dimness there's a flickering in that shell, a flickering like the hissing tatters of a black flame. . . . Sweet Jesus, Ben, it's a huri scrabbling about in there, a black-black, blind-blind huri! It's clawing at the shell and pulling itself upright even as the ring dips toward the floor.

(*A fluttering which is distinctly audible over both Chaney's voice and the tapping of The Bachelor's pick.*)

It's in the air—a clumsy beast a little larger than the one I killed. And there's a smell in here just like the smell when I ground out the guts of the other huri. Damn it! The Asadi are idiots! The Bachelor is stabbing at another globe—he wants to let another one out. He wants to let all three of them out so that we'll be plunged in darkness and flapping wings and maybe even the dome will fall in on us.

To himself he can do that—to me, no sir! I'm getting out of here, Ben, I'm going to go tumbling down the steps while there's still light to tumble by. What a madhouse, what a sacred madhouse. Old Oliver Bow Aurm should kiss the nearest maggot for saving him from this—figurative maggot, that is. BoskVeld crawls with figurative maggots—and I'm coming home. I'm coming home to you. To you, my kinsmen. . . .

> (*Footfalls, a heavy wooden groaning, and then the un-echoing silence of the night as Chaney emerges into the Wild.*)

8 CHANEY (*exhilarated*): God, look at them go off! I'm unloading my backpack. I'm lobbing them toward old Sol, wherever the debbil he at. Another Independence Day! My second one. (*Four or five successive whooshing sounds.*) I'm coming home, I'm coming home. To you, Ben. To Eisen, Morrell, and Jonathan. You won't be able to say I don't do things with a flare. Or flares. (*Laughter.*) God, look at them stain the sky! Look at them smoke! Look at them burn away the reek of Asadi self-delusion!

No, by God, we don't destroy every race we run across. Maybe the pygmies, maybe we did it to the pygmies—but the Asadi, bless 'em, they're doing it to themselves—they've been doing it to themselves for aeons. And, God, look at that clean phosphorescent sky! I only wish I knew which direction Sol was in—I'd like to see it. I'd like to see it like a shard of ice glittering in the center of those flaming cobwebs.

Thomas Benedict speaking: last things

We saw the flares and picked up Chaney. Moses Eisen was with me in the copter. We had come out extremely early on the morning of Day 140 in order to complete Chaney's customary supply drop and then to circle the Asadi clearing with the thought of making a naked-eye sighting of the cultural xenologist. Captain Eisen ordered this course of action when it became apparent that Chaney was not going to communicate with us of his own accord. The captain wished to appraise himself of Chaney's condition, perhaps by landing and talking with the man. He wanted him to return to base camp. If it had not been for these unusual circumstances, Chaney's flares might have gone off for no audience but the empty sky.

As it was, we saw only the last two or three flares that he set off

*and had to reverse the direction of our copter to make the rendez-
vous. By the time we reached him Chaney was no longer the exhilarated adventurer that the last section of his monologue paints him—
he was a tired and sick man who did not seem to recognize us when
we set down and who came aboard the copter bleary-eyed and un-
shaven, his arms draped across our shoulders. By removing his backpack we came into possession of the recorder he had used for the last
two days and the "eyebooks" he had supposedly picked up in the
Asadi temple. And that night I went back to the Asadi clearing alone
in order to retrieve the remainder of his personal effects.*

*Back at base camp, however, we committed Chaney at once to
the care of Doctors Williams and Tsyuki and saw to it that he had
a private room in the infirmary. During this time, as I mentioned
earlier, he wrote* The Ritual of Death and Designation. *He claimed,
in more than one of our conversations, that we had picked him up
not more than four or five hundred yards from the pagoda he describes. He made this claim even though we were unable on several
trips over this area to discover a clearing large enough to accommo-
date such a structure. Not once in all of our talks, however, did he
ever claim that he had been inside the pagoda. Only in the confiscated
tape does one encounter this bizarre notion; you have just read the
edited transcript of the tape and can decide for yourself how much
credence to give its various reports. One thing is certain—the "eyebooks" that Chaney brought out of the Synesthesia Wild with him
do exist. And they had to come from somewhere.*

*The eyebooks are a complete puzzle. They look exactly as Chaney
describes them in the tape, but none of them work. The cassettes
are seamless plastic, and the only really efficient way we've been
able to get inside one is to break the bulb, the glass eyelet, and
probe through the opening with old-fashioned watch tools. If the
"books" were indeed programmed as Chaney reports in his tape,
we've found nothing inside the cassettes on which these programs
could have been inscribed and no energy source to power such a
rapid presentation of spectra patterns. Morrell has suggested that
the programs exist in the molecular structure of the plastic casings
themselves, but there is no ready way to confirm this. The eyebooks
remain an enigma.*

*As for Chaney, he apparently recovered. He would not discuss
the tape that I once—only once—confronted him with, but he did
talk about putting together a book-length account of his findings.
"The Asadi have to be described," Chaney once told me. "They
have to be described in detail. It's essential that we get every culture*

we find out here down on paper, down on tape, down on holographic storage cubes. The pen is mightier than the sword and paper is more durable than flesh." But Chaney didn't do his book. Three months he stayed with us, copying his notes, working in the base-camp library, joining us only every sixth or seventh meal in the general mess. He kept to himself, as isolated among us as he had been in the Asadi clearing. And he did a lot of thinking, a lot of somber, melancholy, fatalistic thinking.

He did something else that few of us paid much attention to. He grew a beard and refused to have his hair cut. Later we understood why.

One morning we could not find Egan Chaney anywhere in base camp. By evening he still had not returned. Eisen sent me to Chaney's hut and told me to spend the night there. He told me to go through Chaney's belongings and to see if I could determine his whereabouts either from an explicit note or a random scrawl. "I don't think he'll be back," the captain said—and the captain was right. He was wrong about the note, though. I found nothing but battered notebooks in his book-littered cubicle. And though I read through all of these that night, I found no farewell note.

It was not until I checked my mailbox the next day that I found what Eisen had told me to look for. I checked the box merely out of habit—I knew there had been no probeship deliveries. Perhaps I was looking for a memo from one of the base-campers. And I found the note from Chaney. The only comfort it gave me was the comfort of knowing that my friend had not decided to commit suicide and that he had successfully fought off a subtle but steadily encroaching madness.

(Eisen read this last sentence in rough draft and took exception to it: "Now you're dead wrong, Ben. Chaney not only succumbed to his madness but he committed suicide as well—a slow suicide, but suicide nevertheless.") The note expressed a peculiar sort of optimism, I think, and if you don't see this slender affirmative thread when you first read through the note, go back and read the damn thing again. Because even if Chaney did commit suicide he died for something he believed in.

> I'm going back to the Asadi clearing, Ben. But don't come after me—I won't let you bring me back. I've reached a perfect accommodation with myself. Probably I'll die. Without the supply drops I'm sure I will. But I belong among the

Asadi, not as an outcast and not as a chieftain—but as one of the milling throng. I belong there even though that throng is stupid, even though it persists in its self-developed immunity to instruction. I'm one of them.

Like The Bachelor, I am a great slow moth. A tiger-moth. And the flame I choose to pursue and die in is the same flame that slowly consumes every one of the Asadi.

Good health to you,
Egan

A *note from Moses Eisen:* Because of Egan Chaney's defection to the Synesthesia Wild and Thomas Benedict's lucid compilation of Chaney's notes, the Academy of Cultural Xenologists bestowed upon Benedict rather than Chaney the Oliver Bow Aurm Frasier Memorial Fillet. Though we do not forget the dead, we bury them. It is for the living that honors were made.

CONSTRUCTION SHACK

CLIFFORD D. SIMAK

Simak short story production this year was surprisingly small—but as is to be expected of this fine and sensitive writer, he came up with a concept that combines the infinite with the simple curiosities of ordinary Earthlings.

In that same year when men first walked on Mars the probe was launched from the moon for Pluto. Five years later the first pictures were transmitted as the orbiting probe trained its cameras on the planet's surface. The transmission quality was poor; but even so, certain features of the photographs were productive of great anguish as old theories fell to shards and were replaced by puzzlement, questions with no hint of answers. The pictures seemed to say that the planet had a smooth, almost polished surface, without a single geographic feature to break the smoothness of it. Except that at certain places, equidistant from one another along the equator, were tiny dots that would have been taken for transmission noise if they had not appeared consistently. Too, the dots still persisted when some of the noise was eliminated. So it seemed they must be small geographic features or shadows cast by geographic features, although at Pluto's distance from the sun shadows would be suspect. The other data did nothing to lessen the anguish. The planet was smaller than supposed, less than a thousand miles in diameter, and its density worked out to 3.5 grams per cubic centimeter rather than the unrealistic figure of 60 grams, previously supposed.

This meant several things. It meant that somewhere out there, perhaps something more than seven billion miles from the sun, a tenth planet of the solar system swung in orbit, for no planet the size and mass of Pluto could explain the eccentricities in the orbits of Uranus and Neptune. The calculation of Pluto's mass, now proved inaccurate, had been based on the measurement of those eccentricities and it must be admitted now that something else must account for them.

Beyond that, Pluto was most strange—a smooth planet, featureless except for the evenly spaced dots. The smoothness certainly could not be explained by a nonturbulent atmosphere, for surely Pluto had to be too small and cold to hold an atmosphere. A surface of ice, men wondered, the frozen remnants of a one-time, momentary atmosphere? But for a number of reasons that didn't seem right, either. Metal, perhaps; but if the planet were of solid metal the density should be far greater.

The men on Earth consoled themselves. In five more years the probe would come back to Earth, carrying with it the films that it had taken and from them, the actual films and not the low-quality transmissions, perhaps much that was hazy now might become understandable. The probe swung in its measured orbits and sent back more pictures, although they were little help, for the quality still was poor. Then it fired the automatic sequence that would head it back to Earth, and its beeping signals from far out in space said it was headed home on a true and steady course.

Something happened. The beeping stopped and there was a silence. Moon Base waited. It might start up again. The silence might indicate only a momentary malfunction and the signals might start again. But they never did. Somewhere, some three billion miles from the sun, some mishap had befallen the homing probe. It was never heard again—it was lost forever.

There was no sense in sending out another probe until a day when technical advances could assure better pictures. The technical advances would have to be significant—small refinements would do little good.

The second and third manned expeditions went to Mars and came home again, bringing back, among many other things, evidence that primitive forms of life existed there, which settled once for all the old, dark suspicion that life might be an aberration to be found only on the Earth. For with life on two planets in the same solar system there could no longer be any doubt that life was a common factor in the universe. The fourth expedition went out, landed, and did not come back again and now there was on Mars a piece of ground that was forever Earth. The fifth expedition was sent out even while the Earth still paid tribute to those four men who had died so far from home.

Now that life had been found on another world, now that it was apparent that another planet at one time had held seas and rivers and an atmosphere that had been an approximation of Earth's own atmosphere, now that we knew we no longer were alone in the universe, the public interest and support of space travel revived. Scientists, remembering (never having, in fact, forgotten, for it had gnawed steadily at their minds) the puzzlement of the Pluto probe, began to plan a manned Pluto expedition, as there was still no sense in sending an instrumented probe.

When the day came to lift from the Moon Base, I was a member of the expedition. I went along as a geologist—the last thing a Pluto expedition needed.

There were three of us and any psychologist will tell you that three is a number that is most unfortunate. Two gang up on one or ignore one and there is always competition to be one of the gang of two. No one wants to stand alone with the other two against him. But it didn't work that way with us. We got along all right, although there were times when it was rough going. The five years that the probe took to arrive at Pluto was cut by more than half, not only because of improved rocket capability, but because a manned craft could pile on velocity that couldn't be programmed—or at least safely programmed—into a probe. But a bit more than two years is a long time to be cooped up in a tin can rocketing along in emptiness. Maybe it wouldn't be so bad if you had some sense of speed, of really getting somewhere—but you haven't. You just hang there in space.

The three of us? Well, I am Robert Hunt and the other two were Orson Gates, a chemist, and Tyler Hampton, an engineer.

As I say, we got along fine. We played chess tournaments—yeah, three men in a tournament and it was all right because none of us knew chess. If we had been any good I suppose we would have been at one another's throats. We dreamed up dirty ditties and were so pleased with our accomplishments that we'd spend hours singing them and none of us could sing. We did a lot of other futile things—by now you should be getting the idea. There were some rather serious scientific experiments and observations we were supposed to make, but all of us figured that our first and biggest job was to manage to stay sane.

When we neared Pluto we dropped the fooling around and spent much time peering through the scope, arguing and speculating about what we saw. Not that there was much to see. The planet resembled nothing quite as much as a billiard ball. It was smooth. There were no mountains, no valleys, no craters—nothing marred the smoothness of the surface. The dots were there, of course. We could make out seven groups of them, all positioned along the equatorial belt. And in close-up they were not simply dots. They were structures of some kind.

We landed finally, near a group of them. The landing was a little harder than we had figured it would be. The planetary surface was hard—there was no give to it. But we stayed right-side up and we didn't break a thing.

People at times ask me to describe Pluto and it's a hard thing to put into words. You can say that it is smooth and that it's dark—it's dark even in broad daylight. The sun, at that distance, is not much more than a slightly brighter star. You don't have daylight on Pluto—you have starlight and it doesn't make much difference whether you're facing the sun or not. The planet is airless, of course, and waterless and cold. But cold, as far as human sensation is concerned, is a relative thing. Once the temperature gets down to a hundred Kelvin it doesn't much matter how much colder it becomes. Especially when you're wearing life support. Without a suit containing life support you'd last only a few seconds, if that long, on a place like Pluto. I've never figured out which would kill you first—cold or internal pressure. Would you freeze—or explode before you froze?

So Pluto is dark, airless, cold, and smooth. Those are the externals only. You stand there and look at the sun and realize how far away you are. You know you are standing at the edge of the solar system, that just out there, a little way beyond, you'd be clear outside the system. Which doesn't really have to be true, of course. You know about the tenth planet. Even if it's theory, it's supposed to be out there. You know about the millions of circling comets that technically are a part of the solar system, although they're so far out no one ever thinks of them. You could say to yourself this really is not the edge—the hypothetical tenth planet and the comets still are out there. But this is intellectualization; you're telling yourself something that your mind says may be true, but your gut denies. For hundreds of years Pluto has been the last outpost and this, by God, is Pluto and you're farther away from home than man has ever been before and you feel it. You don't belong to anything anymore. You're in the back alley, and the bright and happy streets are so far away that you know you'll never find them.

It isn't homesickness that you feel. It's more like never having had a home. Of never having belonged anywhere. You get over it, of course—or come to live with it.

So we came down out of the ship after we had landed and stood upon the surface. The first thing that struck us—other than the sense of lostness that at once grabbed all of us—was that the horizon was too near, much nearer than on the moon. We felt at once that we stood on a small world. We noticed that horizon's nearness even before we noticed the buildings that the probe had photographed as dots and that we had dropped down to investigate. Perhaps buildings is not the right word—structures probably would be better. Buildings are enclosures and these were not enclosures. They were domes someone had set out to build and hadn't had time to finish. The basic underlying framework had been erected and then the work had stopped. Riblike arcs curved up from the surface and met overhead. Struts and braces held the frames solid, but that was as far as the construction had gone. There were three of them, one larger than the other two. The frames were not quite as simple as I may have made them seem. Tied into the ribs and struts and braces were a number of other structural units that seemed to have no purpose and made no sense at all.

We tried to make sense out of them and out of the scooped-out hollows that had been gouged out of the planetary surface within the confines of each construct—they had no floors and seemed fastened to the surface of the planet. The hollows were circular, some six feet across and three feet deep, and to me they looked like nothing quite as much as indentations made in a container of ice cream by a scoop.

About this time Tyler began to have some thoughts about the surface. Tyler is an engineer and should have had his thoughts immediately—and so should the rest of us—but the first hour or so outside the ship had been considerably confusing. We had worn our suits in training, of course, and had done some walking around in them, but Pluto seemed to have even less gravity than had been calculated and we had had to get used to it before we could be reasonably comfortable. Nor had anything else been exactly as we had anticipated.

"This surface," Tyler said to me. "There is something wrong with it."

"We knew it was smooth," said Orson. "The pictures showed that. Coming in, we could see it for ourselves."

"This smooth?" Tyler asked. "This even?" He turned to me. "It isn't geologically possible. Would you say it is?"

"I would think not," I said. "If there had been any upheaval at all this floor would be rugged. There can't have been any erosion—anything to level it down. Micrometeorite impacts, maybe, but not too many of them. We're too far out for meteorites of any size. And while micrometeorites might pit the surface there would be no leveling process."

Tyler let himself down on his knees rather awkwardly. He brushed a hand across the surface. The seeing was not too good, but you could see that there was dust, a thin layer of dust, a powdering.

"Shine a light down here," said Tyler.

Orson aimed his light at the spot. Some of the gray dust still clung where Tyler had wiped his hand, but there were streaks where the darker surface showed through.

"Space dust," said Tyler.

Orson said, "There should be damn little of it."

"True," said Tyler. "But over four billion years or more, it would accumulate. It couldn't be erosion dust, could it?"

"Nothing to cause erosion," I said. "This must be as close to a dead planet as you ever get. Not enough gravity to hold any of the gases—if there ever were gases. At one time there must have been, but they've all gone—they went early. No atmosphere, no water. I doubt there ever was any accumulation. A molecule wouldn't hang around for long."

"But space dust would?"

"Maybe. Some sort of electrostatic attraction, maybe."

Tyler scrubbed the little patch of surface again with his gloved hand, removing more of the dust, with more of the darker surface showing through.

"Have we got a drill?" he asked. "A specimen drill."

"I have one in my kit," said Orson. He took it out and handed it to Tyler. Tyler positioned the bit against the surface, pressed the button. In the light of the torch you could see the bit spinning. Tyler put more weight on the drill.

"It's harder than a bitch," he said.

The bit began to bite. A small pile of fragments built up around the hole. The surface was hard, no doubt of that. The bit didn't go too deep and the pile of fragments was small.

Tyler gave up. He lifted out the bit and snubbed off the motor.

"Enough for analysis?" he asked.

"Should be," said Orson. He took the bit from Tyler and handed him a small specimen bag. Tyler laid the open mouth of the bag on the surface and brushed the fragments into it.

"Now we'll know," he said. "Now we will know something."

A couple of hours later, back in the ship, we knew.

"I have it," Orson said, "but I don't believe it."

"Metal?" asked Tyler.

"Sure, metal. But not the kind you have in mind. It's steel."

"Steel?" I said, horrified. "It can't be. Steel's no natural metal. It's manufactured."

"Iron," said Orson. "Nickel. Molybdenum, vanadium, chromium. That works out to steel. I don't know as much about steel as I should. But it's steel—a good steel. Corrosion resistant, tough, strong."

"Maybe just the platform for the structures," I said. "Maybe a pad of steel to support them. We took the specimen close to one of them."

"Let's find out," said Tyler.

We opened up the garage and ran down the ramp and got out the buggy. Before we left we turned off the television camera. By this time Moon Base would have seen all they needed to see and if they wanted more they could ask for it. We had given them a report on everything we had found—all except the steel surface and the three of us agreed that until we knew more about that we would not say anything. It would be a while in any case until we got an answer from them. The time lag to Earth was about sixty hours each way.

We went out ten miles and took a boring sample and came back, following the thin tracks the buggy made in the dust, taking samples every mile. We got the answer that I think all of us expected we would get, but couldn't bring ourselves to talk about. The samples all were steel.

It didn't seem possible, of course, and it took us a while to digest the fact, but finally we admitted that on the basis of best evidence Pluto was no planet, but a fabricated metal ball, small-planet size. But godawful big for anyone to build.

Anyone?

That was the question that now haunted us. Who had built it? Perhaps more important—why had they built it? For some purpose, surely, but why, once that purpose had been fulfilled (if, in fact, it had been fulfilled) had Pluto been left out here at the solar system's rim?

"No one from the system," Tyler said. "There's no one but us. Mars has life, of course, but primitive life. It got a start there and hung on and that was all. Venus is too hot. Mercury is too close to the sun. The big gas planets? Maybe, but not the kind of life that would build a thing like this. It had to be something from outside."

"How about the fifth planet?" suggested Orson.

"There probably never was a fifth planet," I said. "The material for it may have been there, but the planet never formed. By all the rules of celestial mechanics there should have been a planet between Mars and Jupiter, but something went haywire."

"The tenth planet, then," said Orson.

"No one is really positive there is a tenth," said Tyler.

"Yeah, you're right," said Orson. "Even if there were it would be a poor bet for life, let alone intelligence."

"So that leaves us with outsiders," said Tyler.

"And a long time ago," said Orson.

"Why do you say that?"

"The dust. There isn't much dust in the universe."

"And no one knows what it is. There is the dirty ice theory."

"I see what you're getting at. But it needn't be ice. Nor graphite nor any of the other things that have been—"

"You mean it's that stuff out there."

"It could be. What do you think, Robert?"

"I can't be sure," I said. "The only thing I know is that it couldn't be erosive."

Before we went to sleep we tried to fix up a report to beam back to Moon Base, but anything we put together sounded too silly and unbelievable. So we gave up. We'd have to tell them some time, but we could wait.

When we awoke we had a bite to eat, then got into our suits and went out to look over the structures. They still didn't make much sense, especially all the crazy contraptions that were fastened on the ribs and struts and braces. Nor did the scooped-out hollows.

"If they were only up on legs," said Orson, "they could be used as chairs."

"But not very comfortable," said Tyler.

"If you tilted them a bit," said Orson. But that didn't figure either. They would still be uncomfortable. I wondered why he thought of them as chairs. They didn't look like any chairs to me.

We pottered around a lot, not getting anywhere. We looked the structures over inch by inch, wondering all the while if there was something we had missed. But there didn't seem to be.

Now comes the funny part of it. I don't know why we did it—out of sheer desperation, maybe. But failing to find any clues, we got down on our hands and knees, dusting at the surface with our hands. What we hoped to find, I don't know. It was slow going and it was a dirty business, with the dust tending to stick to us.

"If we'd only brought some brooms along," said Orson.

But we had no brooms. Who in his right mind would have thought we would want to sweep a planet?

So there we were. We had what appeared to be a manufactured planet and we had some stupid structures for which we could deduce not a single reason. We had come a long ways and we had been expected to make some tremendous discovery once we landed. We had made a discovery, all right, but it didn't mean a thing.

We finally gave up with the sweeping business and stood there, scuffing our feet and wondering what to do next when Tyler suddenly let out a yell and pointed at a place on the surface where his boots had kicked away the dust.

We all bent to look at what he had found. We saw three holes in the surface, each an inch or so across and some three inches deep, placed in a triangle and close together. Tyler got down on his hands and knees and shone his light down into the holes, each one of them in turn.

Finally he stood up. "I don't know," he said. "They could maybe be a lock of some sort. Like a combination. There are little notches on the sides, down at the bottom of them. If you moved those notches just right something might happen."

"Might blow ourselves up, maybe," said Orson. "Do it wrong and bang!"

"I don't think so," said Tyler. "I don't think it's anything like that. I don't say it's a lock, either. But I don't think it's a bomb. Why should they booby-trap a thing like this?"

"You can't tell what they might have done," I said. "We don't know what kind of things they were or why they were here."

Tyler didn't answer. He got down again and began carefully dusting the surface, shining his light on it while he dusted. We didn't have anything else to do, so helped him.

It was Orson who found it this time—a hairline crack you had to hold your face down close to the surface to see. Having found it, we did some more dusting and worried it out. The hairline described a circle and the three holes were set inside and to one edge of it. The circle was three feet or so in diameter.

"Either of you guys good at picking locks?" asked Tyler.

Neither of us were.

"It's got to be a hatch of some sort," Orson said. "This metal ball we're standing on has to be a hollow ball. If it weren't its mass would be greater than it is."

"And no one," I said, "would be insane enough to build a solid ball. It would take too much metal and too much energy to move."

"You're sure that it was moved?" asked Orson.

"It had to be," I told him. "It wasn't built in this system. No one here could have built it."

Tyler had pulled a screwdriver out of his tool kit and was poking into the hole with it.

"Wait a minute," said Orson. "I just thought of something."

He nudged Tyler to one side, reached down, and inserted three fingers into the holes and pulled. The circular section rose smoothly on its hinges.

Wedged into the area beneath the door were objects that looked like the rolls of paper you buy to wrap up Christmas presents. Bigger than rolls of paper, though. Six inches or so across.

I got hold of one of them and that first one was not easy to grip, for they were packed in tightly. But I managed with much puffing and grunting to pull it out. It was heavy and a good four feet in length.

Once we got one out, the other rolls were easier to lift. We pulled out three more and headed for the ship.

But before we left I held the remaining rolls over to one side, to keep them from tilting, while Orson shone his light down into the hole. We had half expected to find a screen or something under the rolls, with the hole extending on down into a cavity that might have been used as living quarters or a workroom. But the hole ended in machined metal. We could see the grooves left by the drill or die that had bored the hole. That hole had just one purpose, to store the rolls we had found inside it.

Back in the ship we had to wait a while for the rolls to pick up some heat before we could handle them. Even so we had to wear gloves when we began to unroll them. Now, seeing them in good light, we realized that they were made up of many sheets rolled up together. The sheets seemed to be made of some sort of extremely thin metal or tough plastic. They were stiff from the cold and we spread them out on our lone table and weighed them down to hold them flat.

On the first sheet were diagrams of some sort, drawings, and what might have been specifications written into the diagrams and along the margins. The specifications, of course, meant nothing to us (although later some were puzzled out and mathematicians and chemists were able to figure out some of the formulas and equations).

"Blueprints," said Tyler. "This whole business was an engineering job."

"If that's the case," said Orson, "those strange things fastened to the structural frames could be mounts to hold engineering instruments."

"Could be," said Tyler.

"Maybe the instruments are stored in some other holes like the one where we found the blueprints," I suggested.

"I don't think so," said Tyler. "They would have taken the instruments with them when they left."

"Why didn't they take the blueprints, too?"

"The instruments would have been worthwhile to take. They could be used on another job. But the blueprints couldn't. And there may have been many sets of prints and spec sheets. These we have may be only one of many sets of duplicates. There would have been a set of master prints and those they might have taken with them when they left."

"What I don't understand," I said, "is what they could have been building out here. What kind of construction? And why here? I suppose we could think of Pluto as a massive construction shack, but why exactly here? With all the galaxy to pick from, why this particular spot?"

"You ask too many questions all at once," Orson told me.

"Let's look," said Tyler. "Maybe we'll find out."

He peeled the first sheet off the top and let it drop to the floor. It snapped back to the rolled-up position.

The second sheet told us nothing, nor did the third or fourth. Then came the fifth sheet.

"Now, here is something," said Tyler.

We leaned closer to look.

"It's the solar system," Orson said.

I counted rapidly. "Nine planets."

"Where's the tenth?" asked Orson. "There should be a tenth."

"Something's wrong," said Tyler. "I don't know what it is."

I spotted it. "There's a planet between Mars and Jupiter."

"That means there is no Pluto shown," said Orson.

"Of course not," said Tyler. "Pluto never was a planet."

"Then this means there once actually was a planet between Mars and Jupiter," said Orson.

"Not necessarily," Tyler told him. "It may only mean there was supposed to be."

"What do you mean?"

"They bungled the job," said Tyler. "They did a sloppy piece of engineering."

"You're insane!" I shouted at him.

"Your blind spot is showing, Robert. According to what we think, perhaps it is insane. According to the theories our physicists have worked out. There is a cloud of dust and gas and the cloud contracts to form a protostar. Our scientists have invoked a pretty set of physical laws to calculate what happens. Physical laws that were automatic—since no one would be mad enough to postulate a gang of cosmic engineers who went about the universe building solar systems."

"But the tenth planet," persisted Orson. "There has to be a tenth planet. A big, massive—"

"They messed up the projected fifth planet," Tyler said. "God knows what else they messed up. Venus, maybe. Venus shouldn't be the kind of planet it is. It should be another Earth, perhaps a slightly warmer Earth, but not the hellhole it is. And Mars. They loused that up, too. Life started there, but it never had a chance. It hung on and that was all. And Jupiter, Jupiter is a monstrosity—"

"You think the only reason for a planet's existence is its capability of supporting life?"

"I don't know, of course. But it should be in the specs. Three planets that could have been life-bearing and of these only one was successful."

"Then," said Orson, "there could be a tenth planet. One that wasn't even planned."

Tyler rapped his fist against the sheet. "With a gang of clowns like this anything could happen."

He jerked away the sheet and tossed it to the floor.

"There!" he cried. "Look here."

We crowded in and looked.

It was a cross section, or appeared to be a cross section, of a planet.

"A central core," said Tyler. "An atmosphere—"

"Earth?"

"Could be. Could be Mars or Venus."

The sheet was covered with what could have been spec notations.

"It doesn't look quite right," I protested.

"It wouldn't if it were Mars or Venus. And how sure are you of Earth?"

"Not sure at all," I said.

He jerked away the sheet to reveal another one.

We puzzled over it.

"Atmospheric profile," I guessed halfheartedly.

"These are just general specs," said Tyler. "The details will be in some of the other rolls. We have a lot of them out there."

I tried to envision it. A construction shack set down in a cloud of dust and gas. Engineers who may have worked for millennia to put together star and planets, to key into them certain factors that still would be at work, billions of years later.

Tyler said they had bungled and perhaps they had. But maybe not with Venus. Maybe Venus had been built to different specifications. Maybe it had been designed to be the way it was. Perhaps, a billion years from now, when humanity might well be gone from Earth, a new life and a new intelligence would rise on Venus.

Maybe not with Venus, maybe with none of the others, either. We could not pretend to know.

Tyler was still going through the sheets.

"Look here," he was yelling. "Look here—the bunglers—"

DATE DUE

NOV 0 5 2009			